A CONTEST OF GODS

FATE OF WIZARDOMS: BOOK 6

JEFFREY L. KOHANEK

First Edition

Print Edition ISBN: 978-1-949382-28-0

PUBLISHED BY JEFFREY L. KOHANEK and FALLBRANDT PRESS

www.JeffreyLKohanek.com

ALSO BY JEFFREY L. KOHANEK

Fate of Wizardoms

Book One: Eye of Obscurance

Book Two: Balance of Magic

Book Three: Temple of the Oracle

Book Four: Objects of Power

Book Five: Rise of a Wizard Queen

Book Six: A Contest of Gods

* * *

Warriors, Wizards, & Rogues (Fate of Wizardoms 0)

Fate of Wizardoms Boxed Set: Books 1-3

Runes of Issalia

The Buried Symbol: Runes of Issalia 1

The Emblem Throne: Runes of Issalia 2

An Empire in Runes: Runes of Issalia 3

Rogue Legacy: Runes of Issalia Prequel

* * *

Runes of Issalia Bonus Box

Wardens of Issalia

A Warden's Purpose: Wardens of Issalia 1

The Arcane Ward: Wardens of Issalia 2

An Imperial Gambit: Wardens of Issalia 3

A Kingdom Under Siege: Wardens of Issalia 4

ICON: A Wardens of Issalia Companion Tale

* * *

Wardens of Issalia Boxed Set

JOURNAL ENTRY

W elcome to the final verse of the spectacle that altered the fate of a world. Unlike prior installments, I see no need to recount what has transpired thus far. To have reached this point, you are surely well-versed in the players and the stakes for which they play. Prepare for questions answered, truths revealed, and more than one twist along the way.

Our story picks up not where we last left off, but hours earlier as events unfold from another perspective. On the day the darkspawn arrive outside of Balmor, you will rejoin heroes as they prepare for the rising tide of darkness. Even they do not fully comprehend the gravity of the situation nor the destiny awaiting should they fail...or succeed.

Such is to be expected when mortals act as pawns in a contest of gods.

-Salvon the Great

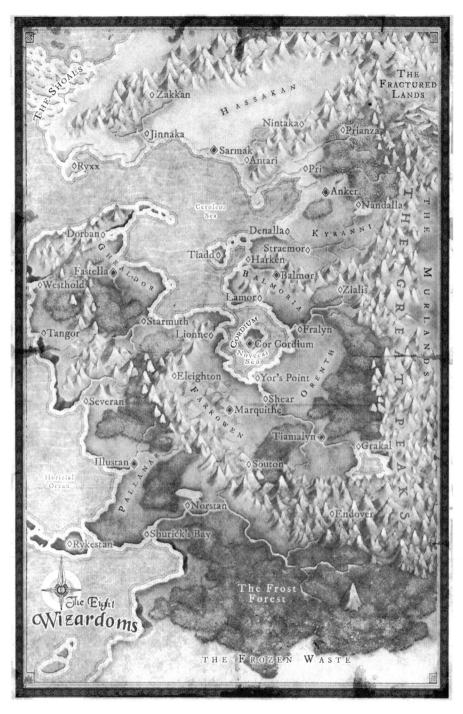

1

FORESIGHT

Pandemonium filled the streets of Balmor – people on foot, wagons, carts, horses, oxen, and other livestock all flowing into the city. With the sun draped over the western horizon, most of the city shrouded in shadow, only the taller buildings were still cast in light, the tallest of which was the Tower of Devotion. Atop the blocky, gray tower, a golden flame shimmered, informing the panicked citizens that their wizard lord remained alive and able to protect them.

Brogan Reisner led his companions through the crowded streets, his imposing presence forging a path for the others. He was used to being among the tallest in any crowd and often used his size to such advantage. The chainmail armor on his torso, plates on his shoulders, bracers on his wrists, and falchion at his hip added to the effect, people moving aside in fear of being trampled…or worse.

After crossing an intersection, he paused and glanced backward.

Blythe looked at him, her golden eyes filled with concern. "What's wrong?"

"Nothing," he said. "Just making sure we are still together."

His gaze shifted past her, checking on the other members of their party. Rhoa peered around Blythe, the short, coppery-skinned acrobat arching a brow. Behind her were the four dwarfs – Rawk, Algoron, Lythagon, and Filk.

Hood over his head, Tygalas brought up the rear, the elf slipping through the crowd, his golden-hued quarterstaff in hand. Emitting a satisfied grunt, Brogan turned and continued down the street.

They entered a sprawling square at the heart of the city, Balmor Palace coming into view. It was a massive, square building, six stories tall and over a thousand feet long on each side. Rectangular, glass-paned openings lined the upper three stories of the outer walls, the lower portions windowless and made of gray brick. A moat surrounded the structure, fed by fountains at all four corners, each bubbling down a series of tiered rocks into the moat itself. Wagons and tents occupied the square as refugees from the Great Bazaar gathered. Brogan knew it would only grow worse, the Bazaar not yet fully evacuated.

After meandering through the throng, he and his companions arrived at the drawbridge. Twenty soldiers in chainmail and yellow tabards blocked the way, armed with swords and halberds.

Brogan glared at the guards. "Let us through! We have returned."

The two guards in the middle lowered their halberds, pointing them at his chest. His hand slipped to the sword on his hip, a subconscious reaction.

During their capture and brief incarceration the night prior, he had been without the falchion, their weapons left behind with the menagerie. A sense of completeness filled him whenever he wore it. He had never forgotten the feeling, even during the fifteen years Despaldi had owned it. Since his recent reclamation, Brogan had become more attached to the blade than ever.

A shout came from beyond the cluster of guards. "Stop!"

The guards parted to provide a glimpse of an approaching figure wearing a helmet with metal wings on the sides. He stood six feet tall with broad shoulders, middle-aged, having the appearance of a lifelong soldier.

"Stand down. I have been informed that these people are allies."

Brogan gave the man a nod. "Odama."

Blythe slipped ahead of their group to address the man. "Thank you. We appreciate the assistance." She cast a glance back at Brogan, her eyes narrowing as she whispered, "Stop scowling." Turning back toward Odama, she patted the bow on her shoulder. "We have retrieved our things from the menagerie and are returning to the palace as instructed by Lord Jakarci."

Odama nodded. "Yes. I am to escort you inside." He beckoned. "Follow me."

They followed him across the drawbridge, their boots thudding on the sturdy wood. He led them into the shadowy interior and through the long receiving hall, their footsteps on the marble echoing off the high ceiling. Down a corridor they went, stopping outside the third door on the left. Odama opened it and led them inside, Brogan surveying the room as the others gathered.

It was a small chamber with a desk and bookshelves, a window facing the Arboretum in the middle of the palace, foliage outside obscuring the view of anything other than the Tower of Devotion jutting up toward the heavens. Seeing nobody else in the room, the occupants fell quiet as Odama closed the door.

"Are we to meet Jakarci or Vanda here?" Rhoa asked.

Odama put a finger to his lips. He crossed the room and sat on the chair behind the desk, fumbling beneath it. An audible click sounded. The man put his hands on the edge of the desk and shoved. It moved forward, the hum of rollers coming from beneath it. Brogan stepped to the side, peering around the desk to see a stairwell descending into darkness.

"Go on," Odama said in a hushed voice.

Brow furrowed, Brogan asked, "You aren't escorting us?"

The man looked down at the opening in the floor. "Of all the secret passages in this place, this would be the last I would choose to explore." He rubbed his neck, body quivering when a shiver ran down his spine. "In truth, I wish I didn't even know of its existence."

"Yet you wish us to go down there?"

"And you had better hurry. The sorcerer is waiting."

"Vanda." Brogan rolled his eyes at Blythe. "This guy sure enjoys drama."

She chuckled. "Yes. I believe it comes with his apparent adoration for keeping secrets." Pointing, she pushed him forward. "Go on. I'll follow."

Brogan circled the desk and began his slow descent into the murk. It soon grew dark, the stairs lost in the thickening gloom. He drew the sword at his hip, the enchanted weapon altering his vision, the blanket of black masking the stairs turning to gray, each stair edge outlined by shadow.

"Do you need that?" Blythe asked as she followed him into the gloom. "I realize you aren't very trusting, but Jakarci would have killed us already if that were his goal."

He spoke over his shoulder. "I am holding it for the enhanced vision. It's dark down here."

While thankful for the enchantment from his weapon, the others lacked such a tool. However, bonding to the Arc of Radiance had augmented Blythe's vision, so he suspected she could see well enough. As an elf, Tygalas had a similar advantage. The four dwarfs would have little issue, having lived most of their lives underground. However, Rhoa had no such ability, and it was likely pitch black for her.

A sound came from above, a hum followed by increasing darkness as the desk slid back into place. An ominous click, then silence.

"It's really dark down here." Rhoa's whisper filtered through the stairwell. "I can't see a thing."

"Hold my hand, Rhoa," Rawk said. "I'll help guide you."

Even with Brogan's augmented vision, the stairs were barely perceptible. After a two-story descent, they leveled off to a long corridor, the walls made of rocks and mortar, ceiling supported by periodic frames made of thick beams. They followed it for a while, rising anxiety twisting Brogan's stomach. After covering hundreds of feet, they came to a door. It was stained dark, the panels lined with rounded, metal bolt heads. Rather than open it, Brogan knocked.

A muffled, male voice echoed from within. "You may enter."

Opening the door, Brogan led the others into a spacious chamber lit by tiny points of amber light across the high ceiling. The room was rectangular, three walls covered in shelving, the longest filled with books. One of the shorter walls was divided into hundreds of small slots, each occupied by a rolled scroll. The other held odd trinkets and contraptions made of various materials in an array of sizes, shapes, and colors. A round table sat in the middle of the room, one side open to a circular gap in the center. There, in the middle of the table, sat Vanda, maps, drawings, and open books strewn around him. The man held a feathered pen in his hand, the quill moving rapidly as he jotted something down into a journal.

Silently, the group gathered just inside the door and gazed at the intriguing surroundings as they waited for the man to address them. After a full minute, he lifted his head.

Vanda had cropped, white hair and a beard to match, his skin tanned, lines on his face marking his age somewhere north of sixty. As the man's piercing, gray eyes surveyed them, Rawk and Algoron began to fidget.

Patience waning, Brogan said, "What is this about, sorcerer? Where are we?"

"All in due time." The man set the pen down. "I see you have reclaimed your weapons." He peered at the sword still in Brogan's hand. "Among them, I see the enchanted sword known as Augur." His attention turned toward the sheathed blades on Rhoa's thighs. "A pair of fulgur blades." Arching a bushy brow at Blythe, he asked, "I assume the Arc of Radiance hides beneath that sleeve?"

How does he know these things? Brogan wondered.

Blythe's hand went to the bowstring. "Yes."

The sorcerer grinned and rose to his feet. "Excellent." Turning, he walked from the middle of the table and toward a door, the fabric of his black robes swishing in the quiet room. "Come along."

They crossed the room and followed the man into a chamber twice as large as the first, also illuminated by points of light in the ceiling. A nasty stench lingered in the air, one triggering dark memories from Brogan's past. Blythe, Rhoa, and Tygalas all covered their noses at the pungent scent.

To one side of the room was a well, a table and shelving behind it. Knives and vials rested on the table, carafes of dark liquid on the shelves. To the other side of the room, the floor was covered in symbols made from sections of tile.

"What is that smell?" Rhoa asked, her nose covered.

"Blood," Brogan growled, recalling a room of torture and dark magic from long ago.

Vanda picked up a stoppered carafe from the table and looked back at Brogan. "An accurate statement. Much time has passed since I last had the room cleaned." He arched a brow. "How did you guess?"

Brogan grimaced. "I have seen it before." He gestured around the room. "All of it. This reeks of sorcery."

"Yes." Vanda nodded. "I suppose it does. However, do not allow prejudices to taint your impression of me or my abilities. I assure you, neither my methods nor intentions are nefarious. With my assistance, we may save the world from the approaching monster."

"Monster?" Blythe asked.

"Yes, for I believe Lord Thurvin comes tonight. I pray we have suffi-ciently prepared." The man turned and continued toward a door at the far end of the room.

When Blythe looked at Brogan, he saw trepidation in her gaze. After a lifetime of seeing the same look in the eyes of soldiers before a battle, particu-larly during his time in the Murguard, he understood fear. Facing creatures from nightmares often sent terror through the hearts of the bravest of soldiers. As he did back during those terrifying nights, he sought to instill courage in his companions by displaying it himself. With a firm, confident nod, he turned and strode across the room, the others silently following.

They passed through the doorway and climbed a dimly lit stairwell. After turning at a landing and rising a second flight, they entered an open room, square in shape, illuminated by shimmering, golden light.

No windows in the walls. No doors visible, save the one through which they had entered. He looked up and saw the flame of Bal flickering through windows in a ceiling many stories above. *We are inside the Tower of Devotion.* It felt odd for such a tall structure to be completely hollow. A hum arose from high above, and part of the ceiling began to lower. It took a moment to recog-nize the lift and the Wizard Lord of Balmor standing upon it. They stood in silence, watching as Lord Jakarci descended.

The wizard lord was an obese man, head bald, black goatee streaked with gray. Like most Bals, he had an olive complexion, eyes dark and slightly angular.

The lift reached the bottom and stopped, the man stepping off and waddling toward them. His voluminous robes – yellow with black symbols on the cuffs, hem, and collar – swished angrily with each step.

Jakarci spread his arms and smiled, jowls shaking as he spoke. "Welcome. I trust you are ready to face the might of a god."

Rhoa Sulikani had lived a lifetime on the edge, performing death-defying stunts in front of crowds long before her recent adventures. Still, Jakarci's statement sent a shiver down her back. She glanced toward her companions, seeing expressions ranging from determination to undisguised dismay. Her own feelings were a strange mixture of both.

The wizard lord asked, "Did the evacuation of the Bazaar slow your return?"

"A bit," Brogan said. "Before we entered the city walls, we saw the army approaching."

"Yes." Jakarci nodded. "My spies just reported the army's arrival. Priella's force is making camp along the southern wall of the basin." He turned toward Vanda. "We should proceed. The sun will soon set."

"Agreed." Vanda turned and waved for the others to follow.

In the middle of the room was a massive disk of glass, the surface milky and opaque. Eight positions surrounded the glass, each marked by a different symbol. An ornate, metal-framed structure, which included a ladder, stood over the disk.

Jakarci removed his robes, exposing his enormous body, symbols scrawled across the rolls of fat. Among them, a brand in the shape of a starburst graced the left side of his chest.

Vanda stood beside the wizard lord, removed the carafe stopper, and poured crimson liquid on the wizard's torso. The blood sparkled in the shimmering light. *Wizard's blood*, Rhoa thought. Jakarci spread it over the tattoos on his chest and bulging stomach. He then took a rag from Vanda and wiped his hands clean, staring up at the scaffold, jaw set as he appeared to focus.

The wizard floated off the floor, giving the appearance of standing upon an invisible lift. When even with the top of the scaffold, he stepped onto it, the metal frame creaking.

Similarly, Vanda removed his robes, revealing even more tattoos across his lean body than those on Jakarci's tremendous frame. He poured crimson liquid on his torso, rubbing it across the symbols, the blood glittering in the yellow light. Shockingly, the man then brought the carafe to his lips and drank, gulping as the blood slid down his throat. Rhoa covered her own mouth and gagged.

When finished, Vanda set the carafe down, wiped the crimson from his lips, and turned toward Rhoa and her companions. "Each of you needs to stand upon a symbol around the Lens of Foresight."

Brogan frowned. "Lens of Foresight?"

"Do not fret, warrior. You have nothing to fear. It is a tool, nothing more."

While Rhoa and the others dispersed, the sorcerer climbed up onto the scaffold.

9

She passed a symbol of a dog's head, another of a lightning bolt, a third in the shape of a diamond. Finally, she stood on a glyph in the shape of a bird of prey, her friends spaced around the ten-foot-diameter glass disk, each standing upon a symbol.

On the scaffold above, Jakarci and Vanda each strapped their waists and ankles to metal frames mounted to hinges. They then leaned forward, the frames rotating with a creak, the sorcerer's and wizard's arms outstretched until they gripped each other's wrists, both facing downward, their heads twelve feet above the center of the glass.

Vanda began to shake violently, eyes bulging, face growing red. Blood spurted from his mouth, splattering onto the glass. Rhoa flinched in shock, gaze going from the men above to the blood. The red splatter began to move, the crimson liquid swirling faster and faster, mixing with the white of the glass until all she saw was a pink haze. Within the haze, shapes began to materialize.

From an elevated view, a sea of white tents appeared, bordered by the tall walls of Balmor. *The Bazaar.* Remnants of daylight illuminated the western sky, the area blanketed in twilight. Across the grassy fields to the south, an army of thousands prepared for battle, the soldiers wearing armor from the wizardoms of Ghealdor, Farrowen, Pallanar, and even Orenth. Upon the hillside above the army, an azure flame arose, beams of light streaking across the southern sky. In the heart of the city, the golden flame upon the tower bloomed, initiating Devotion.

Screams arose from the Bazaar, a wave of monsters crashing in from the east, destroying everything in their path. People and horses stuck outside the city gates were slaughtered. Archers loosed on the attacking goblins, but there were too many.

The darkspawn extended across the eastern horizon, pouring across the grassy fields, straight toward the waiting army. The two forces met in a clash of blood, darkspawn falling in droves, the soldiers fighting with coordinated precision. However, the numbers they faced were too great, wave upon wave of goblins charging into the fray.

The flames of Devotion dimmed, the battlefield falling dark. Suddenly, lightning flashed along the ground, the blasts tearing through goblins, destroying them by the dozens. In the light of his magic, Rhoa recognized Lord Thurvin, eyes wild with the power he wielded. With flame, electricity, and other magical attacks, the wizard lord shredded the darkspawn army, his assault culminating in a furious storm, a towering twister destroying anything it touched.

The scene shifted, the fields littered with corpses, darkspawn and human soldiers alike. A flash of light appeared on the hillside, followed by an explosion. Lord Thurvin rose into the air and flew toward the city, sparks of electricity crackling around him as he approached the palace and descended into the Arboretum. The image blurred and faded.

Rhoa leaned forward and peered into the pink haze. "What happens next?"

From his position above, Vanda said, "The future is not yet assured." The two men released each other, their supports tilting backward. Vanda unbuckled the strap at his waist as he spoke. "As you can see, the wizard lord's might is immense, able to crush a darkspawn horde by himself."

Jakarci said, "Based on this vision, he will arrive within hours of sunset. We must prepare."

"What of the people still outside the city walls?" Blythe asked. "You cannot allow them to be slaughtered."

After disconnecting his second ankle, Jakarci stood on the scaffold and shook his head. "Regretfully, I can do nothing for them. I must focus on stopping Lord Thurvin."

The woman slipped her bow off her shoulder. "If you won't help them, I will." Jaw set, she strode across the room, tearing the cover off the weapon, the bow glowing with a golden hue.

Brogan rushed after her. "If you are going, I am going with you."

"Wait!" Rhoa called out as she set out after them.

"No!" Vanda said, drawing Rhoa to a stop. She turned toward him as he reached the bottom of the ladder. "Let them go. Free will shall determine the future." He approached Rhoa, gaze intense. "I only pray you find the determination to do what must be done."

Rawkobon Kragmor remained silent while the others took action. Blythe and Brogan sped out of the room, disappearing down the dark stairwell leading to the sorcerer's lair.

He looked back down at the glass disk, still streaked with swirls of sparkling blood, the images of the battlefield gone but not forgotten. Darkspawn had spread across the land, the Dark Lord seeking to expand his dominion. The teachings of High Priest Niko-Ono remained firmly entrenched in Rawk's mind.

"Urvadan the Usurper is the enemy of Vandasal, the Dark Lord having struck down his brother after augmenting his abilities with Netherplane magic."

Rawk had never understood that part of the story. *Why would a god seek magic from the Netherplane? What could he hope to gain? If the Dark Lord holds such power, why does he remain in Murvaran? If we still worship Vandasal, why does he not fight back against Urvadan?*

He had once voiced such questions. Never before had he seen Niko-Ono so angry, the priest's reaction causing Rawk to never again question his religion.

Jakarci put a hand on Rhoa's shoulder. "Are you ready to face Lord Thurvin?"

She glanced toward Rawk, their eyes meeting. "I will do my part."

Rawk blurted, "If Rhoa is to be placed in danger, I wish to fight at her side."

The wizard lord arched a brow. "While a valiant offer, I am afraid you cannot."

"But–"

Vanda held up his hand, stopping Rawk. "Thurvin's magic is thrice that of another wizard lord. Rhoa, alone, is immune to his might. If you were to fight at her side, you would only end up dead. What good will that do for your friend?"

Rawk frowned. "I cannot abide doing nothing."

Vanda's gaze swept across Rawk and the other three Makers. "You dwarfs cannot take a direct hand in this fight. Rather than dying for nothing, I suggest you find something else to do."

Filk looked at Lythagon. "Are you thinking what I am thinking?"

The other dwarf grinned. "There is a battle at the gate."

"So true." Filk patted his shield. "I suspect Brogan and Blythe could use some assistance."

Lythagon laughed, hefting his battle axe. "It's been a while since we cut up some darkspawn." He glanced toward Rawk and Algoron. "What say you two?"

Rawk looked at his uncle, the man shaking his head. "No. We will remain at the palace."

The two dwarfs from Kelmar rushed toward the stairwell, Lythagon shouting over his shoulder. "Suit yourself."

Tygalas started toward the stairs. "It might be best if I joined them. Left to themselves, those two are likely to find trouble."

When the elf disappeared from view, Rawk turned toward Jakarci. "Please, Your Majesty. There must be something we can do."

The wizard lord frowned. "Tonight's encounter has been a long time coming, a plan created specifically to twist Thurvin's arrogance in our favor." He shook his head. "I am afraid there is nothing you can do."

Vanda put his hand on Rawk's shoulder. "I suggest you get some food. Rest. If all goes well, Thurvin will be dead before midnight. If not, well... None of this will matter."

Reluctantly, Rawk crossed the room, Algoron at his side, while Jakarci and Vanda began explaining the plan to Rhoa. When Rawk overheard them mention waiting at the tower for Thurvin to arrive, he made up his mind.

They descended the stairs and entered the room of sorcery, both silent until they passed though the adjoining study and began down the long, dark tunnel leading back to the palace.

"You can go back to our room, Uncle," Rawk said.

Algoron gave him a sidelong glance. "What about you?"

"I am going to hide in the Arboretum."

"That is where the battle will take place."

"Yes. I will remain in wait until Rhoa needs me. After all we have been through, I cannot abandon her to whatever those two men have planned. Both Vanda and Jakarci seem to revel in secrets, their machinations extending far beyond what they have explained. I don't trust them. I could never live with myself if I didn't try to protect her."

"You feel strongly for her."

Rawk swallowed the lump in his throat. His reply came in a hushed tone. "I do."

They reached the stairs and began climbing, light coming from the room above, the secret doorway left open.

Algoron spoke from behind Rawk. "I once loved a female. I held the truth of my affection inside for many years. It wasn't until her betrothal to another that I realized I had waited too long."

Whenever Rawk thought about telling Rhoa how he felt, a part of him would lock up and threaten to choke him. Even considering it now, his palms began to sweat.

A tug on Rawk's coat had him stopping halfway up the stairs. He turned back toward his uncle.

Sorrow in his eyes, Algoron spoke, his voice little more than a whisper. "My life has been filled with failure and regret, Rawkobon. Even now, even surrounded by heroes seeking to save our world, I find myself held captive by my mistakes. I have lived for a hundred and ten years yet have done nothing of consequence. If I died today, would anyone notice or care?"

"I care, Uncle."

Algoron gave him a sad smile. "I am aware. It is the only reason I am here. Without that, I might still be a slave to the gemsongs, seeking and cutting jewels to suit the mad plot of a power-hungry wizard."

Rawk frowned. "I don't understand. Why are you saying this?"

"Don't turn out like me, Rawkobon. You must give purpose to your life. If you love this girl, show her you care. When she needs you, be there for her. If you do nothing, you may end up spending your years alone and lost in a fog of regret."

Falling silent, Algoron continued his ascent, while Rawk stared into the darkness below. He longed to tell Rhoa how he felt, but the fear of rejection made him hesitant. Worse, the thought of ruining their friendship terrified him to the core.

2

LUNATICS

Beneath the pale light of dusk, Blythe rushed down the crowded streets, Brogan in her wake. With all traffic flowing toward the heart of the city and her heading toward the outer wall, it was akin to swimming against a swift current.

As she neared the gate, she saw the portcullis still open, a line of wagons, carts, and people still outside. Nightfall was upon them, the attack imminent. Without pause, she headed toward the tower beside the gate.

Guards stood outside the tower base, watching the crowd with narrowed eyes. When Blythe made to dart past them to the tower door, two moved to block her path.

"You must let me through. We are under attack by darkspawn." She lifted her bow. "I can fight from the top of the wall."

One of the men laughed, the other responding, "What nonsense is this? There are no darkspawn beyond The Fractured Lands." The man's gaze fell on her bow, brows furrowed. "Is that thing glowing?"

Brogan stopped beside her. "My name is Brogan Reisner, former captain in the Murguard. What this woman says is true. A goblin army is about to strike."

The guard grimaced. He was tall and just as stoutly built as Brogan. "We are aware of the army, but it is an army of men – soldiers from the southern wizardoms led by the Queen of Pallanar."

Brogan glanced at Blythe. "We don't have time for this."

Screams arose from outside the gates, followed by cries of alarm. Someone called for the gate to close. The portcullis began to lower, and Blythe launched into motion, toward the gate.

Brogan called from behind. "Blythe, no!"

Ignoring him, she sped past an incoming wagon and ducked beneath the descending portcullis, already halfway lowered. Her bow ready, she turned and ran beside the wall, gaze sweeping the area.

Darkspawn appeared from between tents, the goblins going after a family near the rear of the line, children screaming in terror. Three armed men confronted the monsters, swords flashing, but they were overwhelmed in moments. The goblins chased the family toward the gate.

Lifting her bow, Blythe drew the string back. An arrow of light appeared, and she loosed. It struck a monster just strides from one of the children. The goblin froze, body shimmering with a golden light before it disappeared. Again and again, arrows flew from her bow, picking off monsters in rapid fashion, each evaporating when struck by a magic projectile.

Brogan rushed past the wagon, the gate no more than ten feet off the ground and dropping swiftly. He charged and dove, rolling beneath the spikes just before they slammed to the ground. Back on his feet, he surveyed the area beyond the torchlit entrance, people rushing toward him, screaming. Turning, he spotted Blythe along the wall, her bow glowing, arrows of light streaking into the darkness.

He pulled Augur from its sheath, the night brightening tenfold. Beyond where Blythe stood, a cluster of goblins circled, the monsters rushing toward her flank.

Releasing a roar, Brogan dashed past Blythe and toward the charging monsters. With a broad, roundhouse stroke, he met the vanguard, his blade tearing through the flesh of three goblins. A fourth came at him with a rusty sword. He turned, a backhand parry knocking the blade aside. With his other hand, he gripped the monster by the throat and lifted it off the ground, the goblin's wiry legs kicking frantically as Brogan smashed it into another attacker.

A call came from the top of the wall, arrows arcing through the air, raining death down upon the attacking horde a hundred feet out. Standing below the wall, Brogan focused on the frantic mob trying to kill him.

Blythe loosed again and again, drawing the bow back as quickly as she could. Her enchanted arrows ate through the rushing goblin horde, killing dozens every minute. All the while, arrows from the guards on the wall arced down in waves, taking down monsters farther out.

The citizens trapped outside the wall had abandoned their wagons and carts to cluster against the closed gate. She glanced toward them, fifty men, women, and children screaming for it to open.

To her other side, Brogan fought off goblins, corpses surrounding him while more rushed in. She raised her bow and picked off three, but Brogan shifted into the way, preventing her from loosing upon any others.

Farther out, a line of monsters rushed toward her and the city. She rotated and resumed loosing upon them, but the darkspawn army seemed endless, three live ones replacing each taken out by arrows. She suddenly worried that the well of magic feeding the bow might run dry. Worse, she feared she would tire before the enemy ceased attacking.

A creaking arose from the gate, the portcullis reopening, frightened people rushing inside. She considered running in after them, but by then, Brogan was surrounded.

Cuts along Brogan's bicep and thigh trickled blood, his breath coming in ragged gasps. He spun with his sword extended, slicing through any goblin within reach. Darkspawn bodies and appendages lay strewn around him, but he was surrounded, the monsters closing in. Exhaustion made his muscles heavy, but he refused to give in.

Every monster I kill is a strike against the Dark Lord.

Goblin screams and shrieks arose behind him. He spun, ready to fight, when Tygalas appeared from beyond the mob, the elf using his staff to vault into the air, twisting to bring the weapon around and striking three monsters across the top of their heads, bodies folding beneath them. He landed in front of Brogan, staff spinning too fast to see, goblins shying away.

The elf shot Brogan a grin. "Did you think we would let you have all the fun?"

"We?"

More shrieks came from the direction of the gate, Lythagon and Filk felling goblins in rapid fashion, one with a bloody battle axe, the other with a sword and shield.

"What are you doing out here?" Brogan shouted.

Lythagon lopped off the head of a monster and grinned. "We love a good party."

Brogan laughed and spun around, his back to Tygalas. With a new sense of vigor, he met his attackers.

As had occurred during the darkspawn battle in the elven forest, the arrows of light from Blythe's bow caused the monsters visible concern. Rather than rushing toward her, they sought to circle around.

She saw Tygalas, Lythagon, and Filk dart out of the open gate and rush past her to engage the darkspawn surrounding Brogan. Once the last refugees ducked beneath the partially opened portcullis, she shifted toward her companions, continuing to loose arrows to keep the enemies at a distance.

When she neared the two dwarfs, she called out, "Lythagon! Cut a path to Brogan! We need to get back inside the city!"

The dwarf cleaved an arm off one goblin, kicking another away, the monster stumbling over a corpse. "But we just got out here!"

Blythe rolled her eyes and muttered, "I am surrounded by lunatics." Raising her voice, she yelled, "Just do it!"

The two dwarfs attacked furiously, releasing grunts and growls as they cut down the monsters. In moments, Tygalas and Brogan were visible.

"Brogan!" Lythagon bellowed. "Back to the city!"

The big man swung a mighty swipe, cutting through two goblins and forcing five others to back away. He then spun and bolted past Tygalas.

"Run!"

The dwarfs turned and ran toward the gate. Blythe followed while loosing arrows toward the mob. A wave of goblins burst forth and filled the gap between the retreating warriors and Tygalas. Blythe turned and began to carefully target enemies between her and Tygalas when the elf suddenly leapt high, his body parallel to the ground, feet taking a few steps along the wall. He thrust his staff into the chest of a goblin, the monster falling to its back, the butt of the staff pinning it down. The elf then vaulted forward. He landed just strides from Blythe and flashed her a grin.

"Let's get out of here."

They both raced toward the gate, ducked inside, and stopped beside Brogan and the two dwarfs as the portcullis slammed down, locking the monsters outside. Soldiers rushed in, swords and spears thrusting through the bars to impale any that came close.

Blythe backed away from the gate while watching the soldiers fend off the frenetic goblins. Suddenly, something seemed to change.

The darkspawn looked confused. Shrieking, they tried to climb over each other, some goblins even attacking their brethren. The fracas ended in an instant, the monsters scattering and fading into the night. Soon, the only darkspawn remaining were the corpses outside the gate.

Cheers arose from the soldiers and citizens, joined by whoops of victory from those upon the wall.

Blythe turned and followed Brogan away from the gate, citizens they passed patting them on the back and thanking them profusely. One woman embraced Blythe, tears in her eyes as she thanked her for saving her children, a warmth filling Blythe's chest. The interaction lasted until they cleared the crowd and found a quiet corner in the square to catch their breath.

Blythe ran a hand across her sweaty brow and looked at Lythagon. "Why are you three out here?"

"After you left, Vanda told us we could add no value in the fight against the wizard lord." He glanced toward Filk. "If we couldn't join *that* fight, we thought to join yours."

Filk grinned broadly, his face streaked with blood and sweat. "How could we turn down the chance to kill a few darkspawn?"

Brogan laughed and clapped both dwarfs on the shoulder. "Well said!"

Blythe rolled her eyes, chuckling. "Lunatics. I am surrounded by lunatics."

A cry came from the top of the wall, all eyes turning toward the night sky.

3

TRAGEDY

M agic roiled through Thurvin Arnolle's veins as he flew across the night sky, the Balmor Tower of Devotion his guide. A shield against physical attacks surrounded him, appearing like a bubble to anyone with the Gift. When he passed over the wall, a few brazen archers loosed toward him, the arrows shattering when striking the shield.

Thurvin laughed and bellowed, "Nothing can harm me! I am invincible!"

He now knew it to be true, his brain no longer clouded by the influence of the witch, Priella. Any lingering doubts had been obliterated when he, single-handedly, defeated an army of ten thousand darkspawn. Even shaman magic could not stop him. Not any longer. Now it was Jakarci's turn to grasp the depths of Thurvin's power, fed by the prayers of three wizardoms.

When Jakarci falls at my hand, Balmoria will become mine, and I will rule half the world.

As he reached the palace, Thurvin descended toward the square, wooded area in the middle of the structure. Trees, shrubs, statues, a hedge maze, and paved patios filled the Arboretum, all surrounding the Tower of Devotion, the shimmering golden flame of Bal creating a halo of light around the tower.

Thurvin touched down in the plaza outside the base, eyes searching the area. Paved with square, stone blocks, the plaza extended a hundred feet beyond the tower on all four sides, each outer corner occupied by a pillar three foot in diameter and made of fluted, white stone. Shrubs, trees, and pathways led into the darkness beyond the plaza. There was nobody in sight.

He dismissed the shield, his voice booming, augmented by the magic he held. "Jakarci! Come out, you fat bastard! Come out and face me!"

Silence.

Thurvin clenched his fists and grit his teeth. He had come for a fight and did not wish to waste time or energy searching for the rival wizard lord.

"I know you spend your time out here, Jakarci!" Thurvin bellowed. "My informants are thorough and detailed. I know you can hear me!" With his boosted voice, half the city might hear his words.

Motion drew Thurvin's attention. An obese man in yellow and black robes stepped out from behind one of the pillars.

Jakarci waddled toward Thurvin. "I long suspected we might face each other in person one day, even before you rose to claim the throne." His hands remained hidden in opposing sleeves of his robes. "Tell me, do you ever feel guilt or regret for killing Malvorian?"

Thurvin frowned. *How could he know? Nobody knows Malvorian died at my hands. He is guessing.* "Nice try, Jakarci, but you'll not goad me. I have come to depose you and claim the prayers of Balmor for myself."

Jakarci stopped twenty strides away, hands still hidden in the sleeves of his robes. "I don't doubt that is your intent. You have shown little concern for others – killing anyone in your way and converting cities to Farrow without regard for the citizens. How many have died in your quest for power?"

"The end justifies the means."

"To what end, exactly?"

"I will unite the world, Jakarci. Under combined rule, there will be neither wars nor trade disputes."

The Wizard Lord of Balmor laughed. "Even you cannot believe such rhetoric." He shook his head. "No. You seek power. You wish to prove something to all those who ridiculed you – the wizards who called you names and the wizardesses who spurned your advances. At least that was how you began this conquest."

Thurvin frowned. "What does that mean?"

"Such logical thought is now lost to you. The power you hold is too much for your feeble mind. Madness now drives you. If this continues much longer, your mind will break."

Shaking, fists clenched, Thurvin roared, "You know nothing!"

He formed a construct and thrust his hands forward, lightning arcing toward the other wizard lord. Jakarci formed a shield of grounding, the lightning bending to strike the stone tiles, chunks blasting in all directions.

Thurvin altered his construct to one of heat, a roaring cone of flames enveloping Jakarci, obscuring him from view. Driven by the heat of his anger, Thurvin maintained the flames, making them hotter and hotter until they turned white. Even a wizard lord could not forever heal such burns.

Rhoa stood at the tower's edge, giving her a bird's-eye view of the battle on the plaza hundreds of feet below. When Thurvin's flames died down, Jakarci was once again visible, the man curled up in a ball, clothing turned to ash. He rose to his feet, naked but otherwise intact. Thurvin roared and attacked again and again, bolts of lightning, blasts of fire, blankets of ice, and buffeting wind destroying the surrounding plaza. Yet Jakarci survived.

"How long will this go on?" Rhoa asked, her gaze lifting to the man standing beside her.

Jakarci, the real Jakarci, remained focused on the battle, executing spells in response to those of his attacker. "His well of magic runs impossibly deep. We can only succeed if he drains so much, he cannot heal himself faster than the wounds inflicted."

A dead weight sat in Rhoa's stomach when she considered what she was to do. Killing Taladain had been driven by an unrelenting desire for revenge, a need fermented by years of hate. Even then, she had found killing him less than satisfying. She did not regret his death, only that she had been the one holding the blade. In this case, she had no such personal drive to kill Thurvin. Instead, it felt like cold-blooded murder.

The battle continued, if one could call it that. Battle usually meant both sides taking an offensive, not one side launching attack after attack as the other struggled to survive. The wizard lord beside her continued to wave his hands, eyes narrowed as he released spell after spell, all from a distance.

Jakarci grit his teeth, focused on the battle below. "Although I have trained in illusion for decades to prepare for this night, it remains a skill more suitable for women." Beads of sweat covered his bald head and ran down his temples. "I can't keep this up much longer. You had better get into position."

Rhoa nodded and took a deep breath of resolve.

A forceful wind blasted from Thurvin, strong enough to launch the over-weight Wizard Lord of Balmoria across the plaza. Jakarci struck the white pillar and fell in a heap. Thurvin strode toward him, moving carefully through the blackened rubble. Incredibly, the fat wizard rose to his feet, naked and stumbling, but apparently healed.

"Time to end this," Thurvin growled.

He gathered his magic, altered the construct, and blasted foulfire at the other wizard lord. A beam of light, three feet in diameter and tinted with the azure of Farrow, burned right through the man and blasted a massive section from the pillar. The marble column toppled down upon the wizard in a mighty crash, sending a cloud of dust in all directions.

When the dust cleared, Jakarci was still standing, his torso jutting up from the broken pillar.

Brow furrowed, Thurvin muttered, "What in the blazes?"

His eyes widened as he realized the truth. He had been fighting an illusion the entire time.

Thurvin spun around, eyes searching. "Where are you?!" he screamed.

The man had to be within eyesight to maintain the illusion and cast the spells. Distance made it difficult and complex, but Jakarci was a wizard lord. Even so, it must have drained much of his power.

The tower, Thurvin thought as he looked up, seeing Jakarci standing in the shimmering yellow light. Grinning, Thurvin wrapped a shield around himself and launched into the sky, slowing at the top of the tower. Jakarci backed away, hands up, fear in his eyes.

Thurvin laughed. "You cannot avoid your fate, Jakarci!"

He sent himself forward, the other wizard lord now beyond the ring of yellow flames. When Thurvin landed on the tower's edge, Jakarci stumbled backward and fell into the crystal throne in the center.

"Careful, Thurvin," Jakarci yelled. "If you destroy the throne, how will you claim the prayers of my city?"

A frown drew on Thurvin's face when he realized the gravity of the statement. "Maybe so, but I can kill you without destroying the throne."

He leapt over the flames and approached the dais, energy construct ready. The man on the throne cringed in fear, not even attempting to fight back. When Jakarci formed a shield against energy spells, Thurvin altered his construct, forming six swords of solidified air. The blades launched forward, piercing Jakarci's stomach, shoulders, and thighs, pinning him to the throne. Twisting his wrist, Thurvin wrapped bands of magic around the other wizard's hands, binding them to tight fists and preventing him from executing complex spells. Jakarci's eyes bulged, mouth gaping as blood oozed from his wounds.

Thurvin laughed

~

Rhoa lay still, masked within the shimmering yellow flames of Bal. Anyone else, save for Jakarci himself, would have been burned alive.

Blades ready, she listened to the wizard lords exchange words. When Thurvin's voice came from inside the circle of flames, she sat upright, her view clearing.

The man's back faced her, his attention toward Jakarci, who appeared to be dying on his own crystal throne. Rising to her feet, Rhoa stepped out of the flames and charged, one blade swinging around to strike Thurvin in the chest, the other plunging into his back, both targeting the man's heart.

Thurvin staggered, his attention turning toward her, eyes bulging with a blend of madness and shock. Rhoa lost her grip on the blade in the man's back and doubled her efforts to hold the other in his chest. White-hot flames enveloped him, blinding Rhoa but otherwise ineffective. He pushed at her, but she pushed back, driving her blade deeper into his heart, forcing him backward. The flames faded, electricity crackling around him, the noise deafening. Like the flames, the magic had no effect on her.

Still backing away, Thurvin stepped into the recess where the yellow flames burned. He lost his balance and fell backward, hand grappling for Rhoa. Gripping her coat in his fist, he fell over the edge and pulled her with him.

Their bodies twisted in mid-air, his weight pulling her away from the wall, her tightly gripping the hilt sticking from his chest as he rotated around her, the pair of them racing toward the ground. Desperate, Rhoa pulled the blade free and pushed off, sending the wizard lord away from the tower, her drifting toward it. She gripped the hilt and swung an overhead strike. The tip of the fulgur blade struck the wall in a trail of sparks, then skidded off when her momentum pulled her from the tower.

The ground raced toward her, and Rhoa knew she would die.

With Algoron at his side, Rawk watched the fight across the plaza. The magic Lord Thurvin wielded was terrifying, filling him with worry for Rhoa. When the wizard lord realized he had been duped by an illusion, he sailed into the sky and faded from view in the top reaches of the tower. There, the final confrontation was to take place. Despite Rhoa's immunity to magic, a gnawing anxiety filled Rawk to the core. Unable to contain his concern, he waded out from his hiding spot among the shrubs and strode across the plaza.

"What are you doing?" Algoron whispered.

"I am worried for Rhoa," Rawk said over his shoulder. "If something happens, I will be ready."

"He is a wizard lord," Algoron hissed.

"And she is my friend."

He stared up at the tower as he approached the base. Noise came from above, two people appearing at the edge. Suddenly, they both fell off, bodies grappling and rotating as they plummeted. Rhoa tried to slow her descent, but her blade skidded off the wall. Rawk's heart leapt into his throat as he helplessly watched his friend, the woman he loved, fall to her death.

Thurvin suddenly slowed, the man using his magic to catch himself fifteen feet above the ground. Rhoa smashed into him, the pair of them crashing to the plaza with frightening force.

"Rhoa!" Rawk blurted as he ran toward her.

The wizard lord lay face down, arms spread, a hilt jutting from his back, the area around him covered in sparkling blood. Rhoa lay on her back beside him, eyes closed, unmoving.

Rawk knelt beside her and gently caressed her forehead. "Rhoa, please wake."

He put a hand under her back and legs and lifted her from the ground. Her hair was matted with wet, sticky blood at the back, head drooping lifelessly. He held her close, feeling weak breath tickle his cheek.

She is still alive.

Rawk tilted his head up, peered toward the top of the tower, and screamed, "Help!" He took a ragged breath, his heart tearing apart. "I need help! Jakarci! She is going to die!" Tears blurred his vision.

The clatter of metal striking stone came from behind. He spun to find Lord Thurvin standing, Rhoa's fulgur blade on the plaza floor behind him. The man's eyes were wild, a terrifying grin on his face.

"You thought to kill me?" He laughed. "I am invincible!"

Rawk backed away, shaking his head. "Leave her alone."

Thurvin strode toward him. "My magic did not affect her. She must possess the amulet. I will have it!"

The man lifted his hands, ready to strike, seemingly unaware of Algoron creeping up behind him holding a spear crafted from rock. Thurvin suddenly spun around and released a blast of fire, the flames engulfing Algoron as Rawk watched in helpless horror. Algoron screamed as his body and clothing burned. Hurriedly, Rawk set Rhoa down and prepared to protect her.

The burning dwarf fell to his knees, stone spear falling from his grip. Thurvin turned away, his gaze going to Rhoa.

"Stay away from her," Rawk warned.

"Or what? You cannot stop me!"

The wizard lifted his arms again when Algoron, still burning, smashed into him, tackling the wizard, both falling to the ground as the wizard's robes caught fire. Thurvin screamed and pounded fists against Algoron, but the burning dwarf held tight. Rawk darted over to the stone spear and picked up the heavy weapon. Filled with horror for his uncle and fear for his friend, he lifted it over his head and drove it down through Algoron's back, plunging it through Thurvin's body and burrowing the tip into the stone plaza. He then willed the rock spear to meld with the stone tiles. The two joined into one with the three-inch-thick shaft sticking up at an angle, now a permanent part of the plaza itself.

Algoron fell still, flames still burning his destroyed, blackened body. Thurvin lay trapped beneath the dwarf, convulsing as he burned and trying to break free from the thick rod of stone through his chest. Sparkling blood seeped across the plaza, the stone turning to red, shimmering crystal. Similarly, the stone spear began to crystallize, a crackling sound emitting from it as the crystal worked its way up the shaft. Finally, Thurvin lay still and a song arose, the call of the crystal whispering to Rawk, as if it were a precious jewel.

Rawk backed away, wringing his hands, numb from shock. "I had to do it," he muttered, staring at his uncle's charred corpse. "Algoron was in pain. I had to kill him." Logic told him it was the right thing to do. His heart screamed otherwise.

His gaze turned back toward Rhoa, who lay still, blood on the pavement beside her tilted head. He knelt and carefully lifted her again, turning in search of someone who could help, ignoring the beckoning from the crystal.

Jakarci slowly lowered toward the ground, his torn, yellow robes flapping in the breeze. The wizard's feet touched down, gaze fixed on Thurvin and Algoron. "The prophecy comes to fruition. *'Two Makers shall accompany them, both cast out for their forbidden obsessions. One will die to save the world.'*"

Xionne's ominous foretelling replayed in Rawk's head. *"One will die to save the world, the other will unleash his magic to destroy it."* His gut suddenly ached, his gemsong-tainted soul silently crying out. *How can my magic destroy the world?*

The wizard lord looked at Rhoa, her bloody head drooping lifelessly. "I am sorry."

"No!" Rawk cried. "She is still alive. Use your magic. Save her!"

Jakarci shook his head. "I cannot. She is blind to my Gift. It will have no effect."

Tears ran down Rawk's cheeks. "There must be a way. Somehow you can save her!"

The wizard lord stepped closer and put his fingers against her neck.

"It is too late. She is dead."

The world tilted and spun, Rawk falling to his knees, chin dropping to his chest as he cried.

4

SORCERY

Brogan burst through the door and rushed out into the Arboretum, Blythe, Tygalas, Lythagon, and Filk following him down the dark, tree-lined path.

The foliage opened, revealing the tower, the top still shimmering with the yellow flame of Bal, the soft light illuminating the square below. Patches were scorched, the stone tiles shattered. Near the side of the tower, he saw silhouettes – one standing, others on the ground around him.

He raced across the plaza and slowed as he drew near, attempting to comprehend the scene before him.

A twisted, burnt body of a dwarf lay over another man, equally burned, robes still smoldering. A thick shaft of glowing, red crystal stuck through both bodies, the stones surrounding them also sparkling crimson. Jakarci stood a few feet away, his expression resolute. At the wizard's feet, Rawk knelt, bent over a small form held against his chest.

"Rhoa," Brogan breathed, his voice cracking.

"No!" Blythe darted past him and knelt beside Rawk. "What happened?"

Rawk lifted his face, cheeks wet, eyes red and puffy. "She fell. She... She is dead."

"What?" Brogan snarled. He stepped closer to Jakarci and prodded the wizard in the chest, forcing him back a step. "*Thurvin* was to die, not Rhoa!"

The wizard lord shook his head as he knelt beside Thurvin and withdrew a glass vial from his robes. "The wizard lord had to die, but I never promised others would not join him."

"You need to do something."

Jakarci looked up and shook his head. "I cannot. My magic will not touch her. Besides, it is too late."

Brogan clenched his fists and grit his teeth. "There must be a way." Then an idea struck, a memory of something once said long ago. "What about sorcery?"

"I…" The wizard lord frowned. "I do not know."

"Where is Vanda?"

Jakarci pointed toward the tower. "Down in his lair." He then twisted his hand, a gash opening in Thurvin's throat. Another twist, and glittering blood spurted from the wound, filling the vial in his hand.

Kneeling, Brogan put a hand on Rawk's back. "Give her to me."

Rawk frowned at him. "Why?"

Brogan scooped Rhoa from the dwarf's arms. "You must open a doorway into the tower. We are taking her to Vanda."

The dwarf blinked. "What?"

Standing upright, Brogan growled, "Now, Rawk. Hurry!"

Rawk scrambled up and approached the tower, fingers flexing, lips moving as he ran his hands along the bricks, tracing an outline six feet high and three feet across. He then pushed, the section of bricks toppling inward. Before the dust settled, Brogan ducked through the opening, careful not to trip over the rubble.

He circled the glass disk in the middle of the room and headed for the doorway. Since he couldn't pull his blade from its sheath, the stairwell was pitch black. But he had no choice. Rhoa in his arms, he descended hastily, recalling it to be straight and roughly forty stairs. At the bottom, he came to a closed door, fumbled with the knob, and kicked it open so hard, it slammed against the brick wall inside.

He stepped into the room with the blood and symbols, the ceiling still glowing with amber dots of light.

Vanda ran in from the other door. "What's happening?"

Brogan stomped toward the man. "You must use your blood magic to save her."

The sorcerer grimaced, eyes on Rhoa. "Is she dead?"

"She passed moments ago."

The others rushed into the room, including Jakarci.

When the wizard lord's gaze met Vanda's, Jakarci nodded gravely. "The monster is dead."

"His blood?"

Jakarci extended his hand. The vial in his palm glowed with a crimson brilliance from the liquid within.

Vanda took the vial. "It is enough, but I must hurry." He gestured toward the star-shaped symbol on the floor. "Place her on the diagram."

Brogan walked over, knelt, and carefully set Rhoa down. He stood and backed away as Vanda approached.

The man tore Rhoa's tunic open, exposing her chest.

"No!" Rawk blurted and tried to go after Vanda, but Lythagon and Filk each grabbed an arm, holding him back.

Vanda frowned. "She cannot be marked with magic, and we have no time to apply ink." He looked up at Jakarci. "Grab the brand from my table and heat it."

The wizard lord crossed the room and picked up a long rod with a metal pattern at one end. Using his magic, white-hot fire billowed from his hand, burning the end of the rod until it glowed orange, the smell of burnt metal filling the room and mixing with the stench of blood.

He returned to Vanda's side, the sorcerer pointing above Rhoa's left breast. "Here."

Jakarci pressed the hot metal against Rhoa's flesh. It sizzled, smoke rising. When he pulled it away, a mark of a sunburst remained, the skin dark and raw.

Vanda poured sparkling blood from the vial and rubbed it into her burn. He then stepped back, removed his own robes, and poured some onto his chest. He set the vial down. "Stand around the symbol, holding hands."

Everyone did as he asked, including Jakarci, leaving only Vanda and Rhoa in the center. The man closed his eyes, lips moving as he muttered an incantation. He then knelt and placed one hand against the brand on Rhoa's chest, his other hand on a similar tattoo on his own. The sorcerer began to shake, a glow rising from him. The glow emanated from where his hand met Rhoa's skin and slowly spread across her body, the air humming.

Then Brogan felt a pull. Not against his body, but of his energy. As he watched, eyes wide, bits of light bubbled from his chest and floated toward Rhoa and the sorcerer, the same happening to everyone else in the room. He felt himself growing weak, tiring rapidly.

Am I dying?

Just when he thought he might faint, Rhoa's back arched and she gasped, taking in a long, deep breath.

Vanda released his magic, the glow around him and Rhoa fading, the draw on Brogan ceasing.

Brogan wobbled and fell to one knee, panting like he had run for miles. In fact, everyone, save Jakarci, appeared exhausted.

Vanda stood, stumbling before righting himself. He staggered past Brogan and reclaimed his black robes. "She needs time to recover. In fact, we all must eat to replace the energy we just expended. Afterward, I suggest a good night of sleep."

He turned and waved them off. "Now, leave me." He grasped the vial containing the remaining blood. "I have things to which I must attend."

5

VISIONS

The round moon shone down upon the Valley of Sol, casting it in pale light. It was quiet, the city across the lake a myriad of towers, arches, and buildings of all shapes and designs. A giant pyramid was the most notable structure in the valley, five hundred feet tall and capped by a crystal peak. It was undoubtedly among the greatest wonders in the world.

Jerrell "Jace" Landish climbed a rocky outcropping to the north of the pyramid, bare feet stepping carefully as he approached the edge. Although completely naked, the night air was comfortable, the heat of the day having faded. Beside him, water rushed down the cliffside and over the edge, the falls stirring white foam on the lake's surface fifty feet below.

In the moonlight, he spotted three people in the water, pale limbs and shadows visible above the surface.

"Are you sure this is a good idea?" Narine called from below. She stood in neck-deep water, twenty feet from the edge.

"You don't want to injure any important parts!" Hadnoddon laughed.

The dwarf and Narine's bodyguard were closer to shore. Hadnoddon because he stood less than five feet tall, Adyn because her metal body was too heavy for swimming.

Chuckling, Adyn added, "Or it will be a while before you and Narine get to–" Her sentence was cut off as Narine splashed her in the face.

Cupping his hands over his crotch, Jace leapt, body straightening as he fell feet first, plunging deep into the pool. The water felt refreshingly cold, especially when over a dozen feet down. He swam up, broke the surface, and shook his head, spraying droplets through the night air. With easy strokes, he swam toward Narine.

"You are crazy," she said as he drew near.

"I'd jump from higher if there was a spot to do it. However, I might not do so while naked." His feet touching the rocky lakebed, he stopped in front of her, his hands slipping to her smooth hips.

"Is everything still in working order?" She arched a brow.

"Would you like to test it out?"

Adyn splashed water toward them. "Oh, stop."

They all laughed.

Jace pointed up the shore, away from the pyramid. "I see a flat rock over there, just above the surface. Care to swim with me?"

Narine smiled, her teeth white in the moonlight. "Let's do it."

Turning on his back, Jace swam with his face above water, the lake surface smoothing as they grew farther from the falls. When he drew near, he flipped back onto his stomach, easing toward the rock sticking a foot above the water. The side facing him was vertical and sharp. He shifted toward shore, finding a slope. The stone was slippery below the water, but once he was on top, he found a good grip.

Narine held his hand as he helped her onto the dry, rocky surface. With her at his side, they both sat and caught their breath, his gaze going to the sea of stars above before inevitably being drawn toward the moon. *It is so close.* While it was still east of them, their position was parallel to it, which felt strange. In all his travels, he had never been so far north.

Salvon said the moon shines directly down on Murvaran. The legendary city was said to be the home of the Dark Lord. *I wonder if the city is real. If so, how far would the journey be from here?*

When she squeezed his hand, he looked at her. Even in the moonlight, she was a vision to behold.

He grinned as his gaze drifted to her torso. "I can see that the water is cold."

She arched a brow and looked down at him. "As can I."

He laughed. "Fair enough."

"Are you sure nothing is injured? I'd normally see more of a reaction from you by now."

Jace shook his head. "Nothing injured. I'm just... My mind is elsewhere, I guess."

"Is it about today?"

"Yes." He put his arm around her, and she snuggled against him.

"What was it like for you?" she asked. "Do you remember?"

The ritual in the pyramid had been unforgettable, as had the vision he experienced. *Was it a vision, or something more?* It had felt so real.

Softly, he said, "I saw Salvon."

She lifted her head, gazing into his eyes. "What happened?"

"I met him in a tower...somewhere. We just sat and talked for a while, me asking questions, him answering...until I asked one he obviously wished to avoid."

She rested her head against his chest again. "Tell me."

"There is so much." Jace sifted through his memory, unsure of where to begin, knowing there were some things he could not reveal. Not yet. Finally, he told her the crux of the conversation. "Salvon admitted to being behind it all."

"All what?"

"Key events in my life, and Rhoa's, dating back more than two decades. Some of it I can only tell Rhoa. It wouldn't be right to say it to anyone else. At least not until she knows the truth."

"What can you tell me?"

"Well..." He paused for a moment. "The Eye of Obscurance. It's return to the world began years ago when I retrieved it from Shadowmar Castle, escaping the minotaur. That happened because of him. In fact, Rhoa and I coming together with the amulet, then working together to kill your father..." Jace hesitated. He always felt odd talking about Taladain with Narine.

"It's all right, Jace," she said, her hand on his chest. "I am aware of what my father had become. My brother, as well."

"Anyway, it was all his doing. He also influenced the events that occurred afterward, all toward one end."

"Which was?"

"Crystal thrones falling vacant."

She sat up and looked at him. "Malvorian?"

"He claims he planted the seed in Thurvin's head."

"Raskor?"

"He poisoned the man the night after the dragon attack."

She grimaced. "Lord Horus?"

"Thurvin received a secret book of magic, which encouraged the assassination."

Narine nodded. "Augmentation."

Jace arched a brow. "You knew?"

"I knew those men had been gifted with augmentations. They worked for Thurvin, so the dots were easily connected."

He put a hand on her cheek and smiled. "I am so glad you are more than just beautiful. Stupid people drive me insane."

She laughed. "I have noticed."

"Anyway, after Horus, Lord Belzacanth died at the hands of Master Enchanter Ghenten."

"Yes. I remember it well."

"Salvon admitted he played a hand in Ghenten turning to sorcery. He suspected our visit to Cor Cordium to retrieve the amulet might spur Ghenten into action. If not, he had another plan in motion to encourage the man to topple his wizard lord."

Narine frowned. "But both Horus and Belzacanth died after Salvon disappeared."

"Yes. Yet he was aware of each."

"So, he wants the wizard lords dead. Did he say why?"

Jace shook his head. "No." *I hate lying to you, Narine.* "That was basically when our conversation ended."

"Hmm. That's too bad. However, his intentions seem to align with those of the Order."

"My thoughts exactly. He mentioned that he knows something of the Order, but I get the feeling it was an understatement."

"Perhaps we should ask Chandan if he knows Salvon."

"We can try, but this group hasn't exactly been forthcoming beyond what they choose to share."

They fell quiet, and Jace glanced toward Adyn and Hadnoddon. Both were on shore, getting dressed. Seeing them made him curious about their part in the ritual.

"Did Adyn tell you what she experienced in the temple?"

Narine snorted. "I asked her. She said it was a private matter and refused to speak of it."

"That's strange."

"When she asked me about my experience, I told her being naked in front of those people was among the hardest things I have had to do."

Jace chuckled. "It made parts of me hard, as well."

She poked his chest, laughing. "You are incorrigible."

"I am who I am." He shrugged. "Some hate me for it, but most appreciate my humor."

"I certainly don't hate you. In fact, I have been thinking about our future–"

He interrupted her, afraid of where the conversation was heading. "Did you tell her anything about your...vision?"

"No. I told her if she wouldn't share, I wouldn't, either."

His voice softened. "Will you share with me?"

She gave him a broad grin. "I have been dying to share it with someone."

Her excitement was infectious, a smile forming on his own face. "All right."

"I met Barsequa!"

His smile fell, brows furrowing. "Who?"

She sat up and stared at him. "Barsequa the Magnificent?" When he shook his head, she rolled her eyes and huffed. "I forget the ungifted don't learn what we do at the University."

"You know, I don't exactly enjoy the term *ungifted*. I can introduce you to a long list of people who would admit I have *some* gifts."

She gave him a naughty grin. "I can attest to that."

Jace laughed.

"For you, I'll try not to use the term." Narine continued. "Anyway, Barsequa is the most famous wizard in history. He founded the University and discovered many of the constructs we wizards use today."

He frowned. "Wasn't the University founded a long time ago?"

"Two millennia."

"You met a man who is two *thousand* years old?"

"Yes, well… He *was* old, but I met him back in his own time." She ran a hand through her hair and began wringing water from it. "We were in a hidden lair on the island of Tiadd. While there, he taught me the secret of the eighth construct."

"Eighth construct?" Jace had heard the term before. "Chandan mentioned it while we were on the ship."

"Yes. While I believe he knows of it, he must not know what it is or how to use it."

"But you do?"

She smiled broadly. "I do. Barsequa taught me two applications, and I wish to try the first in the morning."

"Which is?"

"With it, I can communicate with someone I know, regardless of distance."

Jace arched a brow. "Sounds like a useful trick."

"I think so. We can reach out to Rhoa and the others to discover where they are and if they were successful in retrieving the Arc of Radiance."

He shrugged. While he liked his companions well enough, he had grown used to the smaller group of just him, Narine, Adyn, and Hadnoddon. "What was the second application?"

Narine's eyes lit with excitement as she knelt before him, her hands on his knees. In that position, her nudity became a distraction, drawing his eyes from her face and sending his blood racing. Her touching him at the same time was almost more than he could handle.

She continued. "The other application is called spatial transference. With it, I should be able to create a gateway that would allow us to travel great distances as effortlessly as stepping through a doorway."

His brow furrowed, having a hard time comprehending her words as his body reacted.

Narine noticed and arched a brow. "I assume your…excitement is not due to the revelation I just shared."

He grinned sheepishly. "Sorry. You just look so beautiful in the moonlight…"

"Well, put that thing away. Now is not the time."

She climbed over him and slipped into the water. "Come on. Adyn and Hadnoddon are waiting." Pushing off, she began the swim toward shore.

With a sigh and a belly full of disappointment, Jace followed, hoping the cold water would quench his heated blood before the others noticed.

6

PRECIPICE

Priella Ueordlin balanced upon a precipice, her magic keeping a sea of monsters at bay, the plains below her thick with darkspawn. The rocks beneath her feet began to crumble. She stumbled and slid down the steep hillside, toward the waiting horde. Scrambling, she tried to grab hold of an exposed root, but it broke free, sending her backward.

My magic..., she thought, weaving a spell to catch her, but it faltered. *I have lost the power of Pallan.* The realization struck her to the core. There was no saving her now.

She jerked awake with a gasp, morning light filtering through the white canvas of her tent. On her stomach, she lay on the edge of her pallet, arm extended toward the one a few feet away where Kollin slept. His wounds were healed, but he remained unconscious.

When Priella tried to move, she realized her arm had fallen asleep, her fist resting on the thick carpets between the two pallets. The arm looked familiar but foreign, like an old enemy returned to haunt her. It was thick and soft, skin a pale pink with freckles. Nothing like the fit arms she had grown used to since rising to the throne.

My magic has waned. I can no longer maintain the illusion without effort.

Despite her lifelong disdain toward the vanity of others, she loathed the sight of her old self – another form of the curse that had plagued her.

She sat up and swung her legs off the pallet, leaning forward to look at Kollin. Her hand went to his handsome face, caressing his cheek. Eyes closed, she used a construct of repair and delved into him, searching for any lingering trauma from the wounds inflicted the night prior. Nothing remained that she could heal. He simply needed time to recover. Opening her eyes, she stared at him, wondering if he would toss her aside with the illusion of her beauty now shattered.

Her gaze went down to the plunging neckline of her dress. Gone was the tawny, smooth skin, the cleavage and curves, replaced by a far less idealized complexion, her chest modest at best, her hips too wide, thighs too thick. She sighed.

"My Queen," Garvin's voice came from outside the tent. "May I enter to report?"

Gasping, Priella ducked beneath her covers, pulling them up and over her head like a hood, face shrouded.

The tent flap opened, a handsome, athletic soldier entering, followed by a tall, thin man with dark hair and a mustache.

"Priella?" Garvin asked. "Is everything all right?"

"Yes. I am just... I am not wearing anything."

The soldier glanced toward the man at his side. "Rindle and I have updates regarding our troops."

Her gaze shifted to the thief, appearing nothing like the shadow he was the night prior. "When did the augmentation wear off, thief?"

"I'm not sure. When I woke, it was gone."

She frowned. *Did it expire because the magic infused wore out, or does it have something to do with the reduced supply of my Gift?*

"My ability is gone, as well," Garvin said. "Can we move on to the report?"

She nodded once. "Go on."

"The casualties from last night number just north of twelve hundred, twice as many injured. Hardest hit was the Farrowen infantry, since Quiam and Henton were positioned along our northern face."

Wrapping the blanket around herself, careful to keep her face hidden in shadow, she sat up. "Twelve hundred? We are lucky to have lost so few. What of the wounded? Are the wizards from Tiamalyn and Yor's Point attending to them?"

41

Rindle guffawed.

Garvin elbowed him and flashed a scowl. "The wizards never arrived."

Priella pressed her lips together. "What?"

"When asked, Lieutenant Jardine told me he doubts they will come, despite your threats and demands. He believes they have decided to wait to see what happens. Should your conquest fail, they have nothing to fear. If successful, they will attempt to gain your forgiveness. Clearly, they expect you to fail."

"What of the Farrowen wizards?"

The commander shook his head. "Forca and the others remain in Marquithe, defying the orders you and Thurvin gave them. In truth, that bunch is of little use, especially after most of the talented ones died during our campaign in Ghealdor."

Who will heal all the wounded?

Priella knew she could not do it. Without the magic from her throne, healing a dozen would tax her for hours. There were two hundred times that number in need of attention.

Bosinger is dead, my throne destroyed, and Thurvin has gone mad. Without my magic, he will seize the army and take the world. I can do nothing to stop him.

Everything she had worked for...the planning, the sacrifices she had made...would all amount to nothing. She could not defeat the Dark Lord's army. Thurvin was far too consumed with his own greed to understand what must be done. Humanity, and the world, were now destined to fall.

Her head drooped in defeat.

Garvin cleared his throat. "Perhaps we could focus on the positive."

She lifted her head, which seemed impossibly heavy. "What could be positive about any of this?"

Rindle stepped forward, arm extended toward her. He held an ice-blue stone in his hand. "I found this among the wreckage of your destroyed throne."

Priella stared at the fist-sized gem. "What good will it do me now?"

He shrugged. "We have converted thrones and obelisks to Farrow using similar stones." Grimacing, he asked, "What happened to your face? You look dreadful."

Priella pulled the covers back up. "Perhaps you two should leave."

"There is more," Garvin said. "While our count is preliminary, we estimate in excess of ten thousand darkspawn were defeated last night."

"At least something went right."

"Also, a yellow flame still burns upon the Balmor Tower of Devotion."

Forgetting her vanity, Priella sat forward and pulled her blanket down behind her head. "Lord Jakarci still lives?" The last she had seen of Lord Thurvin, the wizard lord darted across the sky, determined to destroy the Wizard Lord of Balmor.

"It appears so." Garvin withdrew a folded note from his pocket and handed it to her. "A messenger arrived minutes ago and awaits your response."

She accepted it, noting the yellow seal, an insignia of a bee pressed into the wax. The seal had been broken, likely by Garvin. She unfolded it and read the smooth script.

Queen Priella of Pallanar,

We stand upon a precipice, surrounded by the Dark Lord's minions. Should we fall, the world is doomed.

Priella paused, struck by the similarities between the sentence and her dream. Shaking her head, she continued.

I applaud the army you have raised and the effective manner in which you have handled things thus far, despite losing grip of your weapon. Do not fret. It is impossible to place a leash upon madness. To have done so as long as you have demonstrates your capabilities and mental fortitude. Therefore, I wish to extend a gift to you. Meet me an hour prior to sunset, and we will dine together to discuss. If you are reluctant after your recent sting at Fralyn Fortress, I understand. You have my assurance, betrayal is the furthest thing from my mind. Unlike the former Wizard Lord of Farrowen, I am aware of the approaching darkness and am unwilling to place my own desires above the fate of our wizardoms.

My condolences for the loss of Bosinger Aedaunt. He was a fierce and talented protector. In his absence, I suggest Commander Garvin and the thief accompany you. If he is able, bring Chancellor Mor's son, as well. I would like to meet him.

Wizard Lord of Balmoria,

Jakarci Ortazal

She closed the missive, frowning at the imagery from the man's language and how well it connected with her nightmare. The rest of the message pointed toward information few could know. "You have read this?"

"I have."

"We have a traitor among us." She wondered if the traitor might be standing in her tent.

"I agree," Garvin said. "Or at least someone who is sharing information. Someone close. Beyond that, the missive mentions Lord Thurvin more than once."

"Yes, with the word *former* attached."

"If Thurvin is dead, Jakarci has solved a problem."

She looked back down at the message, a sense of relief creeping in, temporarily pushing aside her worries. "True. But what are the man's designs? Can he be trusted, or will he betray me?"

"The way I see it, Jakarci wields enough magic to do to us what Thurvin did to the darkspawn last night. If you have something to fear of him, you had best get far away quickly. However, since he invited you to meet with him, he must have something to offer…or gain."

"All true," Priella sighed. She had forced herself and her army into this position all to stop the Dark Lord. Fleeing would do nothing to stop the darkspawn. Jakarci left her no choice. "I cannot…*will not* run. Not now. Not with the darkspawn at our door."

"So you will meet with him?" Garvin asked.

"I will. Draft a message informing Jakarci that I accept his request." Her gaze fell on Kollin resting peacefully. "You two had best do what needs doing and get yourself prepared. We have a dinner to attend."

"Oh no," Rindle muttered.

"Yes." She lifted her eyes, jaw set. "You are joining me for a ride into the city to meet with the Wizard Lord of Balmoria. I only pray this meeting is nothing like what happened in Fralyn."

Garvin ducked outside, Rindle following, the tent flap falling closed, the tent silent.

Priella turned her attention back to Kollin. She knelt next to him and smoothed his hair from his forehead. *I need to wake him.* She bit her lip, concerned about how he would react to her appearance. *He has seen you before, Priella. His hands have been on your body. Better than anyone else, he is aware of the illusion.*

She crafted a construct of mental manipulation and applied it, gently at first. When he did not react, she twisted the construct. His eyes shot open as he gasped.

"There you are," she whispered while caressing his cheek.

His brow furrowed. "Priella?" he croaked.

"Yes, my love." She scooped up the waterskin beside her bed, uncapping it and tipping it to his lips.

Kollin drank, water trickling down his chin. After a brief bout of coughing, he asked, "What… What happened?"

"Thurvin's madness happened." Her hand went to his forehead. "I feared you were dead. It…was a near thing."

His eyes narrowed. "You were controlling him."

"Yes."

"I suspected as much." He looked away. "Have you…used your influence on me?"

"No!" She shook her head, gripping his chin, turning him toward her. "Never. I could have. It would have been easy…before. Now, I cannot even maintain my illusion without a focused effort. My throne… It was destroyed last night. I never even took Devotion."

He stared at her for a long moment. "Is that why you appear as your true self? The girl I knew from the University?"

Lump in her throat, Priella turned away. "Yes. I am sorry if you are disappointed."

He gripped her hand, drawing her gaze back toward him. "In truth, I feared you were manipulating me, although I never sensed it. The fact I still care…"

Tears blurred her vision. "You do?"

"I recall Thurvin attacking me, followed by overwhelming pain. You healed me." It was not a question.

"I did."

"After using your magic to contain Thurvin and never getting the chance to hold Devotion, you used the last of your reserves to save me."

"Yes." Her response was barely a whisper.

Kollin smiled and pulled her hand to his lips, kissing it. "*That* is the kind of person I wish to be with."

A bubble of laughter escaped as tears poured down her cheeks. She leaned forward and kissed him, her lips lingering until he coughed. Pulling back, she brought the waterskin to his mouth. He pushed himself up, resting on his elbow while taking a deep drink.

With Bosinger dead, Kollin was the only one she trusted, the only one she could share anything with. "I need to tell you the rest, Kollin."

He capped the waterskin, brought his legs around and slowly sat upright, his bare torso exposed. He looked down and lifted his covers. "I am naked."

She shrugged. "Your robes were torn, bloody, and beyond repair."

Looking up, he arched a brow. "And my smallclothes?"

A guilty smile formed. "I prefer them off."

He chuckled. "I assume that is not what you meant about telling me the rest."

Her smile faltered. "This campaign into Balmoria, the army, Thurvin, all of it... It has nothing to do with conquest. The darkspawn army we fought last night was just the beginning. I was to rise in power and create a force to stop them." Her gaze dropped to the ground as she shook her head, tears forming again. "We were too late. I was too weak."

Kollin took her hands in his. "We are still alive. We will find a way."

She looked back up at him. "You don't understand. This is not about goblins and their ilk. This is about the being driving them."

"Urvadan? Surely you don't believe in the legends of the old gods."

"Worse. I speak of the demon Lord Urvadan enslaved thousands of years ago. This demon will break free, and when he does, nothing can stop him."

Kollin's eyes narrowed. "What you say sounds like nonsense. Even if it were true, how could you know of such a thing?"

"I am going to tell you a story, one that began years ago. Perhaps you might better understand me because of it. Regardless, it is time you comprehend what we face."

7

PURPOSE

Nine years ago

Priella stood upon Sea Lord's bow, waiting as the ship eased into Tiadd City's port. From the bluff high above, the stone buildings of the University watched over the city and the bay like a mother monitoring her young.

The journey from Illustan had taken the better part of two weeks. As Priella's first voyage longer than three nights, the thrill of exploration had dulled with each successive day. Bosinger's company hardly made things better. While his presence made her feel safer, nobody would accuse him of being an accomplished conversationalist. Him being a generation older did not help, their perspectives misaligned and interests rarely intersecting.

The ship slowed as it neared the pier, the sailors quickly and efficiently securing it to the mooring posts. Captain Helgrued met Priella at the rail, said his goodbyes, and promised to send her trunks up to the University within the hour.

Bosinger led her down the plank and along the docks, toward the waiting wagon, Priella eyeing the small town with disdain. *How can they call this a city?* It consisted of no more than fifty buildings, a far cry from the grandeur of Illustan. *It does not matter. I am here to train, to become a master wizard. Nothing else matters.*

The bodyguard reached the carriage first, opened the door, and peered inside. He then stepped back and waved for Priella to enter.

She stopped and looked up at the driver. "How long is the ride to the University?"

He glanced at her and tipped his hat. "While the distance is not great, the drive has many turns and is uphill. I should have you there in half an hour."

Priella nodded and climbed into the carriage. As the bodyguard started to join her, a scuffle ensued at the foot of the pier. He spun toward it, and the carriage lurched into motion, the open door swinging wildly as the coach sped toward the road. Priella leaned out the door and saw Bosinger running after the wagon, but the distance steadily increased. She pulled the door closed and sat back, brow furrowed as she considered calling for the driver to stop.

She jumped when the seat across from her lifted, a man emerging. Dressed in black robes, his skin was tanned, hair and beard both white and cropped short.

He climbed out, groaning, pressing his hand against his lower back. "That was uncomfortable, especially for these aging bones."

Priella recoiled from the old man and prepared her magic. She only knew two spells – one that might cause someone to wet themselves, the other likely make them fall asleep. The latter was her slim hope. "Who are you, and what do you want with me?"

The man closed the bench, sat, and ran his hand through his hair while stretching his neck. "My name is Solomon Vanda. As for what I want with you… That is a long story." He leaned forward, his gray eyes peering into hers. "Know this, though. I wish you no harm. More importantly, the next twenty minutes may be the most important of your entire life."

Priella relaxed but did not release her grip on her magic. "I am listening."

The man sat back. "I am aware of your suffering, of how a madman placed a curse upon you as a young child. Despite the guilt you feel, you are not at fault. Do not believe the hushed accusations of the ignorant. The fault lies with Serranan, the man who misused his Gift in retaliation against your father. You were an innocent toddler, and your innocence remains true. One cannot wrong another by simply existing, but your family and the people of Pallanar would have you believe otherwise."

She shook her head. "My family never–"

"Your family never tried to protect you!" he roared, then leaned forward, eyes bulging with anger. "Did they once attempt to douse the rumors? Did they deflect the accusations when Luthor died? Why should they? They did nothing to stop similar rumors after the deaths of Rictor, Galdor, Arlan, and Yeldin, yet you weren't even present for any of those."

Tears blurred Priella's vision, buried pain resurfacing.

The man shook his head. "I realize you were with Luthor when he fell, but you were both children, simply playing as children do. The cord catching around his neck was not your fault. It was the curse, for I know something of sorcery.

"Curses are quite distinct in nature, creating small shifts in chance for the targeted individual. You could not have prevented Luthor's death any more than you could have stopped the others from dying. Even if you had, the next close call would have ended him, for the curse ensured the outcome." He took her hand. "Your brothers are gone, and the curse is ended. You must leave the past behind you and look toward the future."

Turning toward the window, she wiped the tears from her eyes. "That is why I am here. I seek a fresh start. Perhaps I can make something from the disaster my life has been."

He spoke softly, his voice taking on a compelling quality. "You can save us all, Priella."

She looked at him. "What do you mean?"

"There are things of which mankind is unaware. Beings of power beyond comprehension."

"You speak of the gods."

Vanda shook his head. "Not of the gods you know, but of Vandasal and Urvadan."

"I have heard stories of the old gods. One defeated the other and cast him down. Eventually, both succumbed to the gods people worship today."

"What else do you know of Urvadan?"

"Some call him the Dark Lord…if you believe in such things."

The man laughed. "Oh, I believe. However, there are details undocumented in the histories of mankind."

"Such as?"

"Urvadan rose in power after capturing the moon, seizing it from its journey across the night sky and locking it in place so it forever shone down upon the city of Murvaran – home to the Dark Lord. The act of doing so caused the great Cataclysm, tearing the world apart, drowning lands and forming new mountains in the process."

Priella waved him away. "Yes. I have heard the fairy tale before."

"Oh, but it is not a fairy tale. Not in the least." He tilted his head. "If I could convince you to accept the tale as fact, consider this. How could this god ever acquire enough power to capture the moon? Does it not seem odd for two equal beings to suddenly become so unequal?"

She frowned in thought. "I suppose. I would think their very nature should prevent one from vastly outstripping the power of the other."

"Exactly. Therefore, it was not Urvadan's power alone that captured the moon."

"Did he somehow acquire an object of power?"

"Not an object, but a being."

"What?"

He gazed out the window. "Our world is one of many, each with its own gods, nature, and limitations. Beyond that, some worlds exist not out there..." He pointed toward the sky, "but right here, beside us, on another plane of existence. One example is the Netherplane, a place where evil and troubled souls go after departing our world. As with any plane, there are also beings that naturally exist there. You would call them demons."

Most had heard dark tales of demons, the superstitious often blaming such beings for their troubles or for odd occurrences. Priella had been taught such beliefs were nonsense.

Vanda smiled. "I sense your doubt, but I ask you to listen with an open mind. Similar to our own wizard lords, the Netherplane has rulers called demon lords – beings of immense power. Urvadan found a means to open a portal to the Netherplane and captured a demon lord, imprisoning it in our world. With the combined might of gods from two planes, Urvadan captured the moon and changed the nature of our world forever." He leaned forward and squeezed her hands. "This demon lord is going to escape its prison, and when it does, this world is doomed."

Priella blinked. "What does this have to do with me?"

"The event I speak of is years away. You will know the time has come when wizard lords begin dying at an unprecedented rate. The balance of magic will shift, the bonds holding the demon lord weakening. Only a supreme wizard lord, a being who wields the magic of many wizard lords, can face and defeat this monster.

"You are this person, Priella. You are the only one who can save our world."

~

Priella sat back and stared into space, recalling the conversation as if it had occurred yesterday. During her telling, Kollin had remained silent, listening intently

"The man, this sorcerer, told me to focus on my studies, to keep myself isolated, and to harden my emotions. My training at the University was to prepare me for a dark future. One day, I would claim the throne of Pallanar, raise an army of nations, and march north to confront the darkspawn horde.

"He gave me a journal filled with prophecy and instructions, which I was to follow. Within the journal, I found constructs never taught at the University. I trained in secret, perfecting each and testing the application. Among those were various constructs of mental manipulation, including the forbidden construct of compulsion. It took me five years before I had the nerve to test it on someone. You recall the incident involving Ydith Gurgan?"

Kollin arched a brow. "The pretty girl from Eleighton? The one who ran naked across the University Commons to bathe in the fountain?"

"Yes." Priella looked away, ashamed about the spectacle. "The girl was cruel and often made me the butt of jokes. One afternoon, she cornered me and asked about the curse. She accused me of secretly killing my brothers and blaming their deaths on a rogue wizard who was long dead. I applied the construct, told her to strip, and twisted her mind to believe she was covered in bees. Shrieking, she raced outside, ran to the fountain, and proceeded to douse herself again and again, scrubbing and swatting at her body, trying to rid herself of something nobody else could see."

Kollin chuckled. "Serves her right. More than once, she publicly humiliated me by making jokes about my...incident."

"That sounds like her." Priella sighed. "While it was obvious to the

University Masters that someone had manipulated Ydith's mind to cause such behavior, I was never found out. It was years before I tried the construct again.

"However, there was another important construct Vanda shared. It enabled me to communicate with him regardless of distance. With it, he and I would talk numerous times a year. The discussions were focused on my progress, determination, and discipline...until late autumn, when Vanda informed me my father had died, his death proceeded by two other wizard lords over a period of a few weeks. It was time.

"So I took my Trial, passed, and set sail back to Illustan to claim my father's dormant throne. All went as planned until we arrived here, outside of Balmor. I planned to defeat Jakarci and claim the prayers of his people before the darkspawn army appeared, but I was too late."

Her gaze lowered, crestfallen, tears running down her cheeks. "I lost control of Thurvin. Bosinger is dead. My throne is destroyed. All those years of preparation and planning... All for nothing. When the demon lord comes, nobody will be able to stop him."

Kollin wrapped his arms around Priella, her face pressed against his warm, bare shoulder. "It's all right. We are alone. With me, you can set your emotions free."

Just hearing him say the words gave her relief. She pulled away and wiped her eyes.

A male voice called from outside the tent. "My Queen!"

Priella drew her blanket around herself again, Kollin doing the same. "Yes?"

Outside the tent, the man spoke in a loud voice. "I have full plates for you and Wizard Mor. Commander Garvin said you two would wish breakfast."

"Very good. Bring them in."

A guard ducked inside, set two plates on the table, and disappeared.

Kollin took her hand and stood. "We must meet with Jakarci tonight. Come. Let us eat and consider how to deal with the man."

She arched a brow and smiled. "Shouldn't you put some clothes on first?"

He looked down at his nakedness. "Yes. I believe that is a good idea."

8

IMMUNITY

Narine Killarius concentrated, ensuring the construct appeared just as it did in her mind's eye. The memory of it had been imprinted on her by the old wizard, Barsequa – impossible to forget. *Why is it not working?*

Morning light shone through the window in the third-story room she shared with Jace in Chandan's tower. The wizard was likely waiting for them to join him for breakfast, but she was determined to test the construct first.

"Are you sure you have this right?" Jace sat on the edge of the bed, slipping his feet into his boots.

From the only chair in the room, she replied, "Yes. It is *exact*."

The gold band on her ankle and the array of golden chains on her hand added to the scope of her magic, effectively tripling her abilities. Strength in the Gift was not the issue, nor was the construct itself. Determined, she set her jaw and tried again, her magic flowing through the construct, a ghostly image of Rhoa appearing before her, floating in the air. Like the last time, Rhoa lay still, eyes closed, face placid.

"Rhoa?" Narine said. "Can you hear me?"

Nothing.

Jace shook his head, frowning. "I still can't see anything. Are you sure it's not just your imagination?"

Narine flashed him a threatening glare, cutting off any additional comments. Frustrated, she tried again. "Rhoa! It's Narine!"

Toying with the amulet on his chest, he jerked with a start and clapped his hands together. "I know! It isn't working because of her immunity to magic."

She turned toward him and dismissed the spell. "By the gods, I should have thought of that."

The realization saddened her. Of her companions, Narine missed Rhoa the most. Both were young women, Narine only a few years older. The two shared a connection, despite vastly different upbringings. Besides, Rhoa's fierce sense of justice and unwavering loyalty were qualities Narine found endearing.

I pray she is well.

"Maybe try contacting someone else," Jace suggested.

A knock sounded at the door.

"Come in," Jace said before Narine could stop him.

The door opened, Adyn peering in. "Good. You two are actually dressed."

Narine glared at her bodyguard. "You think you are funny, don't you?"

Adyn smiled, her metallic face flexing, sunlight glittering off her silvery eyes. "Yes, I do." She waved for them to follow. "Come along. Chandan and breakfast are waiting."

Crestfallen, yet determined to try the spell again after eating, Narine joined Jace, the pair following Adyn across the sitting room and down the stairs. The scent of spices and breads filled the air, stirring her hunger, the idea of eating suddenly appealing enough to dismiss her disappointment.

They arrived on the second level to find Chandan, Hadnoddon, and Harlequin at the table. Narine paused and glared at the female ship captain, an ember of anger glowing.

"Good morning," Chandan said as he spread something on a piece of flatbread. "I trust you slept well after your late-night swim."

Narine's cheeks flushed. "You know about that?"

The wizard chuckled. "Very little occurs in this valley without my knowledge." Still grinning, he added, "Besides, sound travels incredibly well across water and the lake is quite small. Everyone in the village heard you.

Those with enhanced night vision, such as the dwarfs and drow, likely caught an eyeful, as well."

Somehow, Narine's cheeks grew hotter.

Adyn laughed and put her hand on her shoulder. "It is good to see we can still make you blush."

Flashing a sheepish grin, Narine shrugged. "I haven't changed *that* much."

Adyn, Jace, and Narine sat, joining the other three.

"I am disappointed you didn't ask me to join you last night," Harlequin said. "Swimming by the falls is my favorite part of staying in the valley."

Narine pressed her lips together, biting off a retort. The heat of her distaste for Harlequin's previous attempts to seduce Jace had cooled to a simmer, yet it still remained.

Obviously sensing Narine's stirred emotions, Harlequin shook her head. "You needn't worry. My pursuit of Mister Landish has come to an end. He is obviously smitten with you." She grinned. "We all saw his reaction when you removed your robes yesterday."

And just like that, Narine's cheeks flushed again.

Everyone laughed, even Chandan.

While they ate, the conversation turned to small talk – the coming heat of mid-day, the deliciousness of the food, favorite dishes each of them missed from their youth. Harlequin then went on to tell a tale from her past, a quest she had once led deep into the shoals north of the wizardoms. The adventure sounded harrowing and included elements Narine would have dismissed as outlandish embellishments just two seasons earlier. Now she knew there was much more to the world than what she had been taught at the University.

Stomach filled, Jace sat back and downed his water, wishing it were something more interesting. It was a bit early to start drinking, but he worried the day would be long, dull, and uneventful. Chandan had already mentioned they were all scheduled for a mid-day meeting with Master Astra. Why? He would not say. Jace was not surprised. Information from the Order seemed to come in a slow and steady drip, sharing only the minimal required amount, each piece seemingly too valuable to give up without just cause.

The meal ended, the group dispersed, Hadnoddon and Adyn heading outside in search of a shady spot to spar, Chandan and Harlequin off to attend to some Order business, leaving Jace and Narine alone. They headed back up to the third level, and Jace stopped to stare at the stairwell rising to Chandan's apartment.

"What is it?" Narine asked.

His curiosity ached for more information about the wizard and the Order. "With Chandan out, we could do some snooping."

Narine furrowed her brow, appearing doubtful. "I don't know…"

"I know you want to try the construct again. We can do it in a bit. Come on." He took her hand, pulling her up the stairs with him. "This might be our only chance."

The stairwell brought them to the fourth level, an open space broken up by pillars. The area near the stairwell was filled with furniture of Hassakani design – dark leathers, black lacquered wood, red and brown fabrics.

He crossed the room and entered a study. A desk and chair sat in the center, bookshelves lining the walls wherever windows were not present. The books drew Narine's attention, her gaze scanning the spines, while Jace turned his attention to the desk.

The papers on the surface seemed to be messages, each written by a different hand. The first mentioned the death of Belzacanth and the rise of Ghenten. The person knew of the man's sorcery and claimed he had secured a position of strength while waiting on the next Darkening. Another paper was a missive from Anker. Jace scanned it, discovering the other Kyranni cities had all fallen to darkspawn, leaving Anker as the last resistance against an invasion. Four times, Kelluon had fought the monsters and chased them off. There was fear it might not last. He looked at the date on the message and realized a week had passed since it had been written.

He turned to Narine. "Anything interesting over there?"

"No." She shook her head, obviously disappointed. "Most are books on the history of various wizardoms, and others are even more mundane. I see ones about cooking, construction, and even sailing, but nothing about magic."

Jace waved her over, holding the last missive toward her. "Come here and read this."

As she read it over, he searched though the others, finding nothing of interest.

Finished, she looked up at him. "This sounds bad. The Murguard has already fallen. If Kelluon and the rest of Kyranni are defeated, the horde will surely press south."

"My thoughts, as well." He moved away from the desk and headed across the room. "Let's try upstairs."

Jace led her up the curved stairwell where a closed, wooden door waited at the top.

Narine grabbed his hand, stopping him mid-flight. "What if the upper floors are warded with enchantments?"

His hand went to his chest, feeling the amulet beneath his tunic. "The Eye will protect me."

"What about me?"

Brow furrowed, he said, "If I go first, I'll trigger any traps, but they won't affect me. Just keep your distance and you should be fine."

He resumed his ascent, Narine pausing until there were a handful of stairs between them. When Jace reached the door, he carefully placed his hand on the wood. Nothing happened. He tested the knob. It turned, the door swinging open. Waving for her to follow, he stepped inside.

The entire floor consisted of the wizard's private bedroom, bathing area, and wardrobe, three walls dividing the latter into two pie-shaped spaces. To his side, another door waited. This one was completely black, five unfamiliar symbols on the wood. *Something hides behind this door.* He eased toward it, hand extended, focused on his sensitivity to magic.

Narine still stood in the entrance, not far to his side. "Are you sure this is a good idea?"

He gave her a smile. "Relax. Magic cannot harm me."

His hand neared the door, and still, he felt nothing. Slowly, he reached for the handle. When he touched it, red sparks struck, his entire body seizing up. He collapsed to the floor, paralyzed, unable to move or even breathe.

Narine appeared above him, her long hair hanging toward his face as her mouth moved. Yet he heard nothing. Although she shook him, he could not respond, could not even blink. She dug beneath his shirt, pulled out the amulet, and lifted his head up while slipping it off. His head slammed back down on the stone floor with a crack, pain searing through his brain. Still, he was frozen. Panic arose, but he could do nothing about it.

Her hand on his forehead, Narine narrowed her eyes and wielded her magic. An ice-cold wave ran though his body. Jace gasped, taking his first breath since he had fallen. The pain in his head was gone. He gripped her wrist.

Still panting for air, he said, "Thank you."

"What happened?" she asked, worry on her face.

Pushing himself into a sitting position, he shook his head. "Something… paralyzed me. I couldn't even breathe. I… I am so glad you were here."

Narine handed him the amulet. He gripped it in his hand and stood, staring at it before looking at the door, his mind turning, gears clicking into place.

"The amulet stops wizard magic. We know that without a doubt." He turned to Narine. "Apparently it does not stop sorcery. Whatever it is… It's different."

She nodded. "I believe you are correct. What an interesting revelation." Taking his other hand, she pulled him toward the stairwell. "Come on. We are done here."

He followed her downstairs, unable to shake the sense of panic he had felt moments earlier.

9

_____

COMMUNICATIONS

Adyn Darro climbed the stairs of Chandan's tower, Hadnoddon following while grumbling beneath his breath. She had donned the robes Chandan had given her, while he remained in only his smallclothes, his robes draped over one shoulder. They passed the second floor, the kitchen and dining area empty, and came to the third level to find Jace and Narine in the sitting area, the latter speaking while staring off into space.

"–will press them for more information," Narine said. "I pray Rhoa is all right."

When Narine fell silent and continued to stare toward the wall, Adyn's brow furrowed. Jace, lounging on the sofa beside her, put a finger to his lips.

Quiet, he mouthed.

After a silent moment, Narine nodded to the wall. "Tell the others we miss them. Take care of yourself...and Brogan. We will see you soon."

Hadnoddon snorted. "I thought the Seers were strange, but I never saw one talk to a wall."

Startled, Narine turned sharply. "Oh. I didn't hear you two come in." She frowned. "What happened?"

Adyn glanced toward Hadnoddon, his hand pressed against his upper arm. "We were sparring and had a little...accident."

The dwarf scowled at her. "Yes. We were *sparring*, not trying to kill each other."

She smiled at him. "You are lucky it was a wooden weapon. If it had been my blades, you'd no longer have a right arm."

Narine walked over. "Let me look at it."

Hadnoddon removed his hand to reveal a purple, swollen welt.

"It looks like it might be broken," Narine noted.

"Yeah. *Somebody* hit it hard enough to do that..." He shot a glare toward Adyn.

Narine put her hand on his arm, eyes narrowed in concentration. After a moment, she pulled her hand away, the color normal, swelling gone. "I was right. The bone was fractured, but nothing was displaced, so it was simple to heal."

"Thanks." Hadnoddon smiled and crossed the sitting area, walked into the bathing room, and began washing himself.

Adyn arched a brow at Narine. "So, want to tell me why you were talking to the wall?"

Narine glanced at Jace, who shrugged. "If you must know, I used my magic to reach out to Blythe."

"Blythe?" Adyn looked around. "Where is she?"

Jace snorted. "She and the others are in Balmor."

"Balmor?" Adyn blinked at Narine. "The city is hundreds of miles south of here."

Narine smiled. "So you have learned something of geography."

"Very funny." Adyn sat on a chair, looking up at Narine. "Since when can you use your magic like that?"

She shrugged. "Perhaps you don't know all my secrets."

Scowling, Adyn said, "I told you, Narine. I will not talk about what I saw. It was a private thing. I know what I must do, and it does not include telling you."

The princess put her hands on her hips, lips pressed together as she glared down at Adyn. "If that's the way you're–"

Jace stood and took Narine by the shoulders, turning her toward him. "Let it go. Some secrets are best kept that way. You need to trust her judgment."

Narine glanced toward Adyn, her anger melting. "I suppose you are right. It's just… I am not used to her hiding things from me."

"Me, either," Adyn muttered.

Hadnoddon walked back into the room, brow furrowed when he saw the expressions on their faces. "What did I miss?"

"Nothing," Adyn said. "Narine was just about to–"

Footsteps from the stairwell caught her attention, Chandan appearing in the doorway. "Ah. You are all here. Master Astra is ready to meet with you." He turned, waving for them to follow. "Come along. Time is short, and your quest continues."

Adyn rose to her feet and followed the others down the stairs.

During the descent, Jace looked back at Hadnoddon. "You mentioned wooden sparring weapons. Where did you find them?"

"The sparring yard behind the city has a rack filled with weighted, wooden weapons." The dwarf rubbed his shoulder. "Even in the morning shade and wearing only smallclothes, it was hot. I can't imagine training there in the middle of the day when the sun is beating down on you, especially if wearing armor."

They arrived at the lowest level and stepped outside.

The sun had passed the tall cliffside east of the village, intense desert heat bearing down upon them. Despite her metallic flesh, Adyn felt hot, even under the loose robes of the Order.

She glanced at Hadnoddon. "We could try a rematch with you properly dressed. Had you been wearing your armor, the blow would have done little damage."

He wiped his brow. "In this heat, I would have rather fought naked. Besides, I wouldn't want my armor dented by a crazy woman."

Adyn chuckled as Chandan led them over a small bridge and turned toward the entrance to Astra's underground quarters. Through the door and down the stairs they went, the air cooling. They passed through the next doorway and into the underground greenhouse, sunlight streaming through the crystal pyramid above.

The trickle of water and green palms gave the sprawling chamber a peaceful air that, somehow, made her feel tired. They followed the tiled path through the greenery, across bridges over running rivulets, and came to the dais.

61

As before, Astra sat cross-legged in the center of the starburst marking the top of the dais. The sunlight shone upon the small man's bald head, his eyes closed, expression tranquil. He wore loose, white robes with a golden sunburst on his chest, palms pressed together before him. After a moment, he opened his eyes.

"It is well you have come." Astra stood. "We must talk, for you will soon depart." He stepped off the dais and headed deeper into the room.

Narine and Jace exchanged a worried glance. Adyn felt the same concern after the small man's ominous statement. Chandan gestured for them to follow, so they headed down the path, Chandan at the rear.

Astra led them down a different corridor than the day prior, this one long and dark save for torches spaced every twenty strides. The walls had been carved from solid rock, the surface smooth and seamless.

Hadnoddon ran his hand along the wall. "This tunnel was made by a stone-shaper."

Astra paused to glance over his shoulder. "Indeed, Maker Hadnoddon."

After rounding a long bend, they came to a stairwell, Astra beginning the climb while the others paused at the bottom. As far as Adyn could see, the stairs, lit by dozens of torches, faded into the distance.

"There must be a thousand stairs," Jace muttered.

"In truth, there are closer to two thousand." Chandan waved them forward. "Go on. They will not climb themselves."

With a sigh, Adyn followed Jace and Narine upward. Toward what, she had no idea.

Adyn's metal legs felt heavy, each step requiring focused effort. When Narine paused at a landing, Adyn stopped, as well, both panting from the exertion, Narine much harder than herself.

A few steps above, Jace glanced over his shoulder and stopped, brow furrowed. "Are you two all right?"

"Yes," Narine breathed. "I just need some air."

He nodded and glanced upward as Astra reached the next landing. "I don't understand how the old man does it. I don't think he's even winded."

Adyn placed a hand on Narine's back. "You are doing well. Far better than any of our climbs in Tiadd."

She recalled those jaunts from Tiadd City up to the University. None had been easy, Narine needing to rest often. This climb was twice as long. Clearly, their recent adventures had done more than shave extra weight off Narine's hips.

With a deep breath of resolve, Adyn resumed the climb, legs growing heavier as she ascended. The next landing turned into a sloping tunnel, the floor rising into darkness. Jace and Narine stood just ahead, but Astra was nowhere to be seen.

A rumble came from the far end of the tunnel, light seeping in as a hundred feet ahead, a round stone rolled aside. Adyn was reminded of the doorways to the tunnels connected to Oren'Tahal. Following Jace, they walked the length of the tunnel, passed the rounded stone door, and entered a natural cavern with daylight visible at the far end, Astra's small frame standing just outside. A table and chairs occupied the cavern, along with a firepit closer to the entrance. Oddly, a clay jug and six cups sat on the table.

Chandan walked past, the others following him toward the entrance. Adyn stepped out and squinted in the sunlight. Shielding her eyes with her hand, she gazed at their surroundings.

They stood upon a mountainside, the peak a few thousand feet above. Mountains stood to the north and south, but a gap between two offered a clear view of the land to the east. Unlike the desert to their west, the mountains were green, as was the low land beyond them. Beneath dark clouds in the distance, Adyn saw the haze of rain. Hot from the climb, the thought of rain seemed appealing.

Astra pointed. "There, through the mountains, lies the jungle of Kyranni." He moved his arm to the northeast. "Past the jungle are The Fractured Lands, the gateway to the Murlands."

"Wonderful," Jace said, pointing south. "And in that direction is the sea, a place where ships sail and mermaids perform belly flops for drunken sailors."

Adyn and Hadnoddon chuckled, Narine covering her mouth while nudging Jace in the midriff.

Astra turned toward him. "Ah, our illustrious thief. Always ready with a witty quip and making light of serious matters." He waggled a finger in

Jace's face. "Beware. Your future is tenuous, and you had best focus; otherwise, you might lose more than you wish."

Jace frowned. "Are you threatening me?"

Astra smirked. "I believe you have discovered your talisman cannot protect you from sorcery."

Jace gave Narine a sidelong glance, eyes meeting in a silent exchange.

Adyn leaned toward Narine and whispered, "What is he talking about?"

The princess whispered back, "After breakfast, Jace and I snuck into the upper levels of Chandan's tower. Something...happened. Somehow, he knows..."

Astra walked back into the cavern. "Come. Let us sit and talk while we wait for your things."

"Our things?" Adyn asked.

"Yes. The supplies you need for your journey, along with your personal belongings."

He led them back inside and sat at the table. Chandan stood at Astra's side, picked up the jug, and began filling the cups while the others took seats.

Astra lifted his cup. "Drink. I suspect you are thirsty after the climb."

Jace lifted his cup and sniffed cautiously before dipping a finger inside.

Chandan smiled. "It is simply water. Nothing to fear. If we wanted you dead, we could have killed you eight times over by now."

They drank, Adyn downing two cups to quench her thirst. Since her flesh had turned to metal, she no longer perspired, but the need for water remained. Rather than dwell on it, she accepted it as fact.

"Why did you bring us up here?" Jace asked.

"I thought it was clear," Astra remarked. "To send you on your way."

"On our way to where?"

"Ah. *That* is the question. Perhaps you and Narine would like to share what you discovered today."

Narine gave Jace a worried glance. "Regarding?"

"Regarding your companions."

Adyn frowned. "Which companions?"

"He means the ones who went after the Arc of Radiance." Narine shook her head. "How did you know about that?"

Astra grinned. "Many years ago, prophecy foretold of someone discovering the secret of the eighth construct. We just had to follow the signs of recent events to determine who it was.

"Upon your arrival in the valley, I was able to read your unique essence. With it, prophecy becomes far more exact. Today, I captured a vision of you reaching across a far distance to speak with a companion whom you have not seen in weeks." Astra leaned forward. "You will use a version of the very same magic to leave here today."

Adyn frowned. "What is he talking about, Narine?"

The princess sighed. "During the ritual in the temple, I visited Barsequa the Magnificent. Or at least some specter of him, for he has been dead for two thousand years. In the vision, he shared the secret of the eighth construct. Using this new ability, I reached out to Blythe to discover where she and the others have gone and what has transpired since we departed Kelmar."

"That is the secret you are keeping from me?" Adyn exclaimed.

Narine shot her a glare. "You won't tell me yours, so..." She frowned. "Perhaps I was acting a bit childish."

"No disagreement from me," Adyn replied. "What did Blythe say? Where are they?"

"She and the others are at the palace in Balmor. An army made of soldiers from Pallanar, Farrowen, Ghealdor, and even Orenth waits outside the city."

"Just how big is this army?"

"They lost a number of soldiers in prior battles, but close to fifteen thousand remain."

Hadnoddon whistled. "Who could amass an army of that size?"

"I am told Pallanar has a new queen, a woman who wields the power of a wizard lord."

"What?" Jace scowled. "You didn't mention that earlier."

"I didn't get the chance. We were interrupted when Adyn and Hadnoddon came back, then we headed here soon afterward."

Jace rubbed his stubble-covered jaw. "I thought a woman taking the throne was forbidden after what happened to Pheromone."

Narine rolled her eyes. "*Pherelyn.*"

He waved her off. "Whatever."

Gesturing between Adyn and Jace, Narine said, "Are you two going to let me tell the story, or do you intend to keep interrupting?"

Jace sighed. "Fine. Let's hear the rest."

Narine nodded and turned to Astra. "Apparently, there was a darkspawn attack last night. The army outside the city faced the monsters, but most of the damage was caused by Lord Thurvin. The monsters eventually fled. Thurvin then came into the city and attacked Lord Jakarci." Narine closed her eyes and shook her head. "It seems Jakarci and some sorcerer who works for him prepared for the attack and convinced Rhoa to ambush Thurvin, intending to kill him. However, the man had amassed the magic of three wizard lords after claiming the Tower of Devotion in Tiamalyn and obelisks across Orenth, adding to those he already controlled in Ghealdor and Farrowen. During the skirmish, Rhoa and Thurvin fell off the tower. When the wizard lord landed, Algoron attacked him but was consumed by fire in the process. Rawk ended up killing his own uncle to spare him the agony of burning to death, also ending Thurvin."

"Algoron is dead?" Hadnoddon asked.

"I am afraid so." Narine sighed. "In addition, Rhoa was badly injured in the fall...her injuries terminal."

"What?" Adyn leapt to her feet. "No."

Narine held up a hand. "Blythe told me Jakarci's sorcerer somehow brought her back to life by using his blood magic. She remains unconscious, but very much alive."

Adyn sat back down, confused. "But Rhoa is immune to magic."

"Apparently she is not immune to sorcery."

Jace nodded. "That confirms my suspicion from this morning."

"Serves you right for trying to snoop in my quarters," Chandan chuckled.

Jace shot a scowl toward the wizard. "I could have died, you know."

"The princess was with you. We were confident she would prevent your demise."

The two men stared at each other, Jace's frown an inverse of Chandan's smirk.

Adyn turned back to Narine. "What else did Blythe say?"

"She and Brogan have been invited to dine with Jakarci and this new wizard queen tonight. Since the queen brought a foreign army to Jakarci's doorstep, the situation is tense. She fears what will come of this meeting."

Narine fell silent. Beside her, Jace sat with his arms crossed, eyes narrowed in thought. Adyn rubbed her smooth head, considering all she had heard while trying to decide what to do about it.

Footsteps on the stairs drew everyone's attention. Harlequin appeared, carrying two packs. Members of the Order followed, packs and waterskins over their shoulders, some carrying armloads of clothing, armor, and weapons.

"Ah," Astra said. "Your things have arrived. It is time to prepare for your journey."

10

GATEWAYS

Narine slid her arms into her dress. It smelled clean, as did her shift, which was refreshing.

She turned to Adyn, who was already dressed in a leather vest, shorts, and knee-high boots. "Will you lace me up?"

"Sure. Spin around."

Turning, Narine watched Jace insert knives into his sleeves and boots while Adyn did her laces. Brow furrowed, she asked, "Where did you get the blades for your boots? I thought you lost them back on Ryxx."

"Chandan gave them to me. There is an armory somewhere in the village. They differ slightly from the ones I lost, but they are close enough." He stood and sniffed his lapel. "They even washed my coat."

Narine snorted. "Thank the gods. After our ride across the desert, you smelled awfully ripe."

"We all did," Adyn said, finishing and stepping away. "Narine worst of all."

"Hush now."

Narine turned as Hadnoddon secured bracers to his forearms. Dressed in full armor, hammer in hand, he looked fierce. "You appear ready to bash in some skulls."

The dwarf grinned. "The last was a wizard lord. It will be tough to top that, but if we come across darkspawn, I'll do my best."

"Rogues." Narine shook her head. "I am in the company of a bunch of rogues."

"Clearly." Jace took her by the arm and led her toward the cavern exit. "You have excellent taste in companions, Narine."

They stepped out into the sunlight, Astra and Chandan in conversation with Harlequin and the others. When Chandan's gaze met Narine's, he approached them.

"You appear ready for your journey." He pointed toward the pile of packs in the shade of the cliffside. "Your packs are stocked with rations, waterskins filled. Once Astra is finished, you will depart."

Narine's brow furrowed. "You still haven't told us where we are headed."

The wizard arched a brow. "Isn't it obvious? You must rejoin your companions."

"Balmor?" Jace asked.

"Precisely."

Recalling her conversation with Barsequa, a complication came to Narine's mind. "I cannot get us there using my magic."

Chandan arched a brow. "Truly?"

"Yes. Much like illusion, it requires me to picture the destination perfectly. I have never been to Balmor."

Chandan winked and tapped the side of his nose. "Fear not, Princess. The answer will come to you shortly."

Astra finished speaking to the members of the Order. They turned and entered the cavern, save Harlequin, who approached, her gaze fixed on Narine.

"I hope you hold no ill will against me," Harlequin said. "If you will allow the past to be forgotten, I will, as well." She ran her hand over the stubble on her head. "I just hope my eyebrows grow back soon."

While Narine was not eager to trust Harlequin, she did trust Jace. He had earned that much. Thus, she had nothing to fear of the conniving pirate being in their midst. She nodded. "Very well. I am willing to look forward rather than dwell on past indiscretions."

Harlequin chuckled. "Well said. My past involves far too many indiscretions to count. Besides, we fight for the same cause."

"Which is?"

"Saving the world, Narine. While I fear the burden of responsibility lies with you and your companions, the world does need saving. I worry about what we face should you fail."

The woman turned and entered the cavern, fading into the darkness, her ominous statement echoing in Narine's head.

She turned to find Astra approaching, a metal tube in his hand. It was a foot in length, the diameter easily gripped. While made of brass, the body was blackened, silvery script running the length. In the middle of the tube on one side was a glass, concave disk.

"Are you ready for your final briefing?" Astra asked.

"What is that?" Jace asked, gesturing toward the tube.

"This is a special tool." Astra lifted it and tapped the metal body. "It is called a solar lens."

"What does it do?"

The small man grinned. "With the collector pointed in the direction of the sun..." He tapped on the glass piece, "you peer through it, enabling you to accurately see for a great distance."

Hadnoddon grunted. "While neat, it is hardly a special tool for the likes of us."

"No, but it is the perfect tool for your journey."

Adyn tilted her head. "How so?"

Astra turned toward Narine. "You have never been to Balmor, but that is where you must travel. With this, your journey will go much faster."

Narine's eyes widened as realization struck. "If I can perfectly recreate a spot many miles away, I can craft a gateway to it, allowing us to reach it in a few strides rather than taking half a day."

"Very good, Princess," Chandan said, grinning. "I knew you were clever."

The old man handed the tube to Narine. The metal felt cool in her grip but soon warmed.

"This will be interesting," Jace muttered.

"Yes." Astra nodded. "I agree." Apparently, he had not grasped the note of sarcasm in Jace's tone. "As for the future... There is little I can tell you for fear of causing more trouble than what I might resolve. I *can* tell you that few wizard lords remain. With the deaths of the others, an unforeseen complication has arisen. One we never anticipated.

"Imprisoned beneath the city of Murvaran was a demon lord, a being from another plane. It turns out the connection between the wizard lords and the new gods was an integral aspect of the prison. When enough wizard lords died, the demon lord escaped.

"Last night, the demon killed Kelluon, Wizard Lord of Kyranni. Next, he will set his sights on Balmoria. Should he defeat the wizard lords, he will claim their magic for himself and enslave the world."

"What?" Jace exclaimed. "You have been trying to get rid of wizard lords all this time, but *now* you tell us the entire world is doomed because of it?"

Astra looked at Chandan, who shrugged. The old man turned back to Jace. "There is a way, but you must hurry. Only with the might of a supreme wizard lord, a single being powered by the prayers of all Eight Wizardoms, can you defeat this demon."

Jace grit his teeth, appearing frustrated. "Where do we find this person?"

"In Balmor, of course."

The information was coming too quickly, Narine attempting to wrap her head around it.

"How do we know if any of this is true?" she asked.

Astra tilted his head, expression one of sadness. "Visit the cities of Kyranni on your way south. When you discover what has become of Prianza, you might believe. If you choose to stop at Anker and witness what has occurred there, you cannot deny this truth. Beware, though. You will wish to be far from the city when night falls."

He clapped his hands. "Time is fleeting. You must go. Chandan and I will watch until you are gone."

The pair moved to the cave entrance and stopped, both standing with hands clasped at their waists, robes fluttering in the breeze.

Jace put his hand on Narine's hip. "It looks like you get to test out the final construct. I just hope this works. I'd hate to be vaporized or something because you did it wrong."

Narine glared at him. "You are not being helpful."

He grinned. "Do it correctly then."

She turned, peering east. "Where to?"

Jace pointed toward a distant peak. "How about the side of that mountain? Just find a nice, safe spot to land."

She arched a brow. "Land?"

He shrugged. "Whatever."

Lifting the tube, she rotated it until the glass disk on the side pointed toward the sun, then peered into it. To her surprise, the hillside appeared as if it were twenty feet away rather than twenty miles. Slowly, she moved the tube until she found a clearing among the trees, three large boulders in the middle, the arrangement, size, and shape of each distinct. Concentrating, she memorized everything.

Narine lowered the tube, gathered her magic, and formed the construct of spatial transference. Through it, her magic formed an image, much like when she created an illusion, but this one was framed by a circular gateway roughly fifteen feet in diameter. Unfortunately, it hovered five feet off the ground.

"Incredible," Chandan said from behind her.

"Is there any way you can lower it?" Jace asked. "Even for Brogan, it's impossible to get up that high."

Concentrating, Narine recast the gateway. It materialized about a foot above the ground, near the edge of the cliff they stood upon.

"Go ahead," she said. "I'll hold it open and come through last."

Jace gave her a doubtful look. "What if it does something to me?"

Adyn rolled her eyes. "I'll go first." She put her hand on Narine's shoulder. "I trust you." Then she strode toward the gateway and stepped through, a shimmer passing over her as she slid to the other side. Turning back, she waved. "Come on. Nothing to fear."

Hadnoddon stomped toward the portal, pushed his hammer through, and stepped over the edge. In moments, he was at Adyn's side, staring back at Narine and Jace.

Jace put his hand on Narine's back. "It's not that I don't trust you. I just don't trust magic." He took a step toward the gateway.

"Stop!" Astra cried. When Jace turned back toward the man, he said, "Remove the Eye or you will not be able to pass."

The thief nodded. "Good idea." He pulled the amulet from beneath his tunic and over his head, the talisman dangling from its chain as he stepped through the gateway and to the distant mountain.

Still feeding it with her magic, Narine walked to the gateway, then cast one last glance back toward Astra and Chandan.

"Be well, Princess," Chandan said.

Astra added, "Be warned. Should you defeat the demon lord, your quest does not end there. If you do not journey to Murvaran and face the Dark Lord, we will all perish."

The statement left Narine cold. Murvaran was a name only used in stories meant to cause nightmares, the Dark Lord the primary subject of such nightmares. She turned back toward the gateway, stepped through, and was greeted by a noticeable increase in humidity. Releasing her magic, the gateway flashed closed with a *pop*, disappearing in an instant.

11

ANKER

The broad fronds of ferns and palms defined the edge of the jungle, making it nearly impossible to see anything beyond the wall of green. Fine, white sand covered the beach between the jungle and the sea, waves crashing in and running up the shore, stopping just inches from Adyn's boots before receding. With Hadnoddon at her side, she followed Jace and Narine along the beach.

They climbed over rocks that led out to the point where the waters merged in a swirl of brown amid a sea of blue. At the top of the rocks, the view expanded to reveal a river, the north shore miles away.

"I was right," Jace said. "The last gateway put us on the south side of the river."

Narine shrugged. She appeared worn, eyes drooping as she leaned against him. "Without points of elevation, the shoreline is the only place we can get a far enough view for a decent jump. I told you before. I have never been to this region and can only plant a gateway in spots I can view through the lens."

He put his arm around her. "You look exhausted. Perhaps we should stop for today."

She shook her head. "No. Anker should be just a few jumps upriver. We are too close not to investigate. If it's safe, we have a place to eat and sleep for the night."

"And if Kelluon is dead and the city is destroyed, like what we found when visiting Pri and Prianza?" Adyn asked.

Jace said, "Then we will have verified that Astra told us the truth."

"I pray to the gods he was wrong," Narine mumbled.

Hadnoddon's brow furrowed. "I was raised to believe the Seers were infallible, destined to steer us away from trouble. However, their guidance conflicts with what we heard from Astra." He shook his head. "It's difficult to determine whom to believe when the story continues to change."

Jace snorted. "That's what I have been saying since you and Xionne showed up in Illustan. The entire thing rubs me the wrong way. Somehow, Salvon is wrapped up in this, as are Astra and the Order. A trip to Anker will help clear up some of it, but it still feels like we are being manipulated."

"Given what we might face," Narine said, "what choice do we have?"

"Apparently none." He pulled the solar lens from his pack and handed it to Narine. "Here you go. When you are ready, let's make the next jump. Just remember, the sun will set in little more than an hour. Darkspawn hide during the day. If they occupy the city, I would hate to be there at night."

Narine took the device and held it to her eye, peering through in search of a safe spot along the riverbank.

The dwarf wiped his brow. "It's humid here. How do these people stand it?"

Adyn chuckled. "I suspect it will grow far worse inland."

"My point exactly."

She smiled. "Luckily, I no longer sweat, so humidity has little effect on me."

He grunted. "In the meantime, I'm being boiled alive beneath this armor."

Narine extended her hand while still peering through the tube. A portal opened before them, this time no more than six feet in diameter. As the afternoon had worn on, the size of the gateways she crafted decreased, each smaller than the one prior. Adyn worried they might have to crawl through if Narine continued much longer without proper rest.

Adyn took the lead and leapt through the opening, landing on a dirt hillside surrounded by jungle. She scrambled up the hill and looked around before waving for the others to follow.

Anker stood beside a river of the same name, the city surrounded by tall, amber-hued walls. A half-mile of jungle had been cleared, leaving a broad field any attacker would have to cross. Thousands of twisted, gray corpses lay on the ground, rotting in the failing sunlight. The smell was horrendous, even to Adyn's dulled senses. Narine covered her face and gagged. Jace pinched his nose closed. Hadnoddon scowled, like he had a bee in his armor.

"Well…," Jace said in a nasally tone, still pinching his nose. "There was definitely a battle here."

Adyn nodded. "Yes. But do humans still hold the city?"

"The tower flame has been doused," Narine said. "I fear Astra was correct."

"We must be sure," Jace added. "Let's check the city."

With a nod, Narine stared toward the gate facing the river, the portcullis down. The docks stood empty, not a single vessel in port, no river traffic in sight. In fact, there had been no signs of people all day. Adyn feared the entire wizardom had fallen to darkspawn.

The doorway opened to just outside the city gate. Through the bars, Adyn saw no people or monsters, dead or alive. She ducked through the doorway and waved for them to follow.

Jace grasped the bars, face between them as he stared across the city square. It was eerily silent, the shadow-covered streets empty.

"It's like a mausoleum," he said.

"Do you visit the dead often?" Adyn asked.

"No. However, I have had the displeasure of recovering a few items that were buried with their owners."

"That's horrible," Narine said, aghast.

He furrowed his brow. "It's not like the dead need possessions, Narine. Why would they care if I claimed a weapon or piece of jewelry some idiot chose to bury away?"

She set her jaw. "Those *idiots* cared for the person they lost. Burying items their loved ones adored while alive is a common practice. It shows respect and honor for those who passed."

He rolled his eyes. "How long do the dead need these items?"

Frowning, she shrugged. "I'm not sure. Forever, I suppose."

"So hundreds of years from now, when their bodies have rotted to a pile of bones, these items should just remain with them rather than doing some good, like saving lives or putting food on some family's table?"

Narine pressed her lips together but did not respond.

Adyn put her hand on Narine's shoulder. "Can you get me inside?"

The princess turned to her, concern in her eyes. "You don't know what is in there. What if something attacks?"

"Based on what happened in Ryxx and Sarmak, I am all but invulnerable. As long as I don't run into a magic user, I should be fine. Even then, shaman magic takes time to manifest. If I see one, I will run like the wind."

Narine nodded, stepped back, and created a gateway, the other end appearing in the square beyond the gate. "Go on."

Adyn stepped through and turned toward the gate. "Dismiss it. Wait for me. I'll be back soon."

She drew her swords and headed deeper into the sleeping city, unsure of what she might find. It wasn't long before she realized the situation was dire.

Shop doors stood open, windows broken, the interiors looted. Some buildings were blackened by fire, others crumbled to rubble. However, she saw no corpses.

Continuing, she passed numerous intersections, debris filling the streets and alleys. The next square was empty, save for a broken wagon, a couple of broken carts, and the destroyed fountain at the center. She lifted her gaze to the Tower of Devotion, the structure rising above the buildings along the square. The top was capped by a pyramid with a flat roof, no flame burning.

Deciding she was halfway to the palace, the most likely place to find survivors, she turned to gaze west. The sun had dipped below the city wall, darkness fast approaching. Despite the rising sense of dread filling her, she pressed onward and entered the next street at a jog.

After passing three more intersections, she arrived at the square outside the palace. Again, it was devoid of life. The palace gate was destroyed, half the wall caved in. Darkspawn corpses littered the area, but she saw no humans.

She cupped her hands to her mouth. "Hello! Is anyone here?"

Her own echo was the only response.

This is crazy. Everyone is dead or gone.

She turned and headed back toward the gate, entering a narrow, shadowy street when she heard a scraping sound ahead of her, followed by a low rumble. Swords ready, she crept toward the dark alley from which the noise had come.

At first, she saw nothing but shadows and a dark recess in the ground. A goblin popped up from the opening and into the alley. It had a sword in its hand, squawking and waving its arms.

"One goblin?" She grinned. "This will be quick."

She entered the alley, the goblin's voice turning to a shriek. More monsters began pouring from the hole. Adyn stopped, counting eight armed goblins before deciding to rethink her plan. The monsters made the decision for her.

The goblins released a simultaneous cry and sped toward her, weapons brandished as more monsters poured out from below. Roaring in response, she burst forward with a broad sweep, blades slicing across torsos in a spray of blood, monsters squealing in pain. Others attacked, but she used her swords and metal forearms to block their blades before jumping backward. When the monsters made to attack again, she dropped to her knee and swung low. Her sword sheared through ankles and cut across shins, five monsters falling in a heap to block the alley. She then stood, turned, and ran.

She raced down the streets, the shadows thickening, goblins pouring out of alleys by the dozens, all gathering in her wake. Hoots and cries came from behind her as the monsters gave chase.

Finally sighting the portcullis ahead, she called out, "Narine! Gateway!"

Outside the gate, Narine stood back, arms extended before her. A portal appeared. Adyn charged for it as monsters rushed in from another street connected to the square. She dove headfirst, landing beside Narine outside the gate.

"Close it!" Jace shouted.

The first goblins reached the gateway and rushed through. The portal snapped shut, shearing two monsters in half, bloody, squealing bodies landing beside Adyn, lost appendages falling to the ground inside the city, but three goblins had made it through safely. Jace launched a blade, taking one in the throat. It stumbled forward as Jace jerked Narine from its path. Hadnoddon smashed his hammer into the chest of another, driving the goblin backward and crushing its sternum in the process. It fell to its back, flailing as it died. The third met its end when Adyn plunged her blade through its stomach, the creature falling to its knees, eyes bulging. She put a boot against its chest and shoved the creature to free her weapon.

Panting, she stood over the dead goblins and raised her gaze to the portcullis. Just inside, thousands of hooting monsters swarmed, arms reaching through the bars, ready to grasp anyone dumb enough to stray too close.

"Just a guess," Jace said as he retrieved his knife. "Anker has been taken over by darkspawn."

Adyn nodded. "Good guess."

"You saw nobody?" Narine asked.

"Not alive or dead. It's as if they were...consumed by something." The statement felt right, despite the context.

Narine gasped. "That sounds dreadful."

A cranking sounded, the portcullis slowly rising.

"Narine...," Jace said with trepidation. "Make a gateway. Now!"

Frantically turning, Narine glanced around. "Where?"

Jace pointed to a small beach across the river. "There. Hurry!"

She wove her hands as goblins crawled under the rising gate. The portal appeared, no more than three feet tall this time.

Jace dove through, rolled, and waved hurriedly. "Jump!"

When Narine looked her way, Adyn said, "Go. I'll come last."

She turned as the goblins scrambled beneath the rising portcullis and rushed forward. With a leap, Adyn spun, blades extended, lopping three goblin heads off in the process. She kicked, driving another into ones coming from the gate.

Hadnoddon's hammer struck, driving another goblin backward before he turned and followed Narine. Adyn sliced with her blades again and again, turned, and dove through the gateway. She landed in the dirt, twisted to her back, and rolled. The portal snapped closed, shearing off the arms of two goblins, swords still in their grips as the severed arms pelted her before falling to the sand.

Stained blades still in hand, she stood and frowned at the dark blood splattered on her leather vest. "I just got this outfit, too."

Hadnoddon chortled and Jace laughed, Adyn chuckling with them.

Narine sat with a grunt, appearing exhausted as she shook her head. "Rogues."

12

INDULGENCE

The door to the Arboretum opened, Izedon, the head of the Balmor palace staff, leading Brogan and Blythe out into the light of sunset.

Brogan stopped. "You are sure I don't look like a fool?"

Turning toward him, Blythe straightened the ornately stitched collar on his black coat. "You look fine. Why all the concern?"

The yellow doublet beneath the coat was too tight in the shoulders, chest, and stomach. He feared he might burst a seam if he took too deep a breath.

"I am about to meet my new queen."

Blythe arched a brow. "You have met her before."

He recalled the three-year-old girl with red hair and striking, green eyes. "Yes, but she was a toddler and is hardly likely to recall an old soldier she met twenty years ago."

"Do not worry. You will do fine." She pushed him into motion.

Izedon faded from view as the path rounded a hedgerow. Brogan hurried, his long strides catching up to the man before the path came to the open square surrounding the tower. While Izedon continued along the edge of the square, heading toward the hedge maze, Brogan slowed to stare at the sight of the recent wizard battle.

The stone pavement was scorched, shattered, and destroyed. Around the corner, a corpse remained, a sparkling rod of red crystal poking up from Thurvin's charred body. Even at a distance, the burned, broken remains appeared grotesque. Although Rawk was not present, Brogan was thankful Algoron's body had been removed. The incident had been traumatic for Rawk. *He was quiet and moody before this happened. How much worse can it become?* Brogan feared the answer. As it was, the dwarf refused to leave Rhoa's side until she was fully recovered.

Another party appeared across the square, a soldier in gray and yellow leading four others toward the maze. Among them was a striking woman with bright red hair, wearing a revealing dress of purple and pale blue. Upon her head sat a silver crown with an aquamarine at the front. *Priella.* Her party faded from view when Izedon led Brogan and the others into the maze.

The turns seemed random – first left, second right, first right, third left, and so on. When the hedges opened to reveal the courtyard at the center, two guards walked past carrying an unconscious man in black.

"What happened to him?" Brogan muttered.

Jakarci appeared from the shadows and waddled over. "Do not worry. He was nothing more than an unapproved spy. It occurs more often than you might think."

"What will happen to him?" Blythe asked.

"Once he wakes, he will undergo interrogation."

Brogan grunted. "What makes you think a spy will be truthful?"

Jakarci grinned. "My interrogator is a skilled wizardess. She can be incredibly…persuasive."

He turned toward Blythe. "How is our young acrobat?"

"She remains unconscious, but I suppose that is expected. One of our companions remains with her, in case she wakes or is in distress."

The wizard lord nodded. "Yes. The other stone-shaper. I am not surprised. He appears to care for her greatly. Still, I am relieved she survived."

"Are you?" Brogan asked, not bothering to mask his doubt.

"Of course. You see, the performance now nears its conclusion, and Rhoa plays a critical role in the final act." The wizard lord spoke softly with Izedon, who then turned and left.

Brogan leaned toward Blythe and whispered, "Jakarci is the worst of the bunch, pulling strings and manipulating others into acting on his behalf."

Rather than the elbowing he expected, she whispered back, "But to what ends?"

Brogan frowned. It was the question he most wished answered.

Footsteps approached from the maze. Everyone turned as the guard led the other party into the courtyard.

Three men, all tall, accompanied Queen Priella. One was a young, handsome wizard with dark hair, dark eyes, and a square jaw. Dressed in green and black robes, Brogan assumed him an Orenthian. Another man looked to be in his mid-thirties with short, brown hair and an athletic build. He wore a Farrowen military uniform but no armor. A sword rested at one hip, a dagger at the other. His alert, intense eyes watched every move. The signs were obvious, informing Brogan the man was experienced in battle and likely skilled to have survived to his age.

The last man was the most curious of all. *Rindle? Why are you here?* Brogan recalled him from his days working for Cordelia in Fastella. The thief appeared much the same as he remembered – a head of dark hair, thin mustache, long, lean build. Wearing a brown tunic, black breeches, and a black coat, he still dressed like a thief. His noticeable twitchiness remained, as did the rapier at his hip. Rindle's eyes flickered with recognition when he looked in Brogan's direction.

Squashing his curiosity, Brogan's gaze returned to Priella as Jakarci introduced himself. The wizard lord gave her a shallow bow and flashed a smile, which she returned.

Jakarci then turned and made introductions. "Queen Priella, please meet two of your own subjects, Blythe Duggart and Captain Brogan Reisner."

Priella stared at him, and he tried to connect the tall woman with the child from his memories. All that remained were the same green eyes. Her dress was scandalous by Pallanese standards, but she wore it with confidence, displaying her body like a weapon intended to disarm others. She was beautiful, her presence commanding, despite her youth.

Brogan bowed. "My Queen."

"You were my brother's bodyguard," she said.

"I...was."

"After Rictor died, you captured Serranan. The sorcerer cursed you before his execution."

The memory was one he had relived often yet longed to forget. "He did," Brogan croaked.

She reached out and touched his cheek, soft words coming from her lips. "You understand."

Unused to such empathy toward his twisted past, Brogan's throat constricted. He turned and coughed, masking his sudden urge to cry.

Jakarci said, "Perhaps you could introduce the men who accompany you, Priella. Not all here are familiar with your entourage."

Brogan was relieved for Jakarci's intervention, allowing him time to recover.

The wizard queen smoothed her dress and turned toward her companions. "The man in uniform is Trey Garvin, formerly of the Midnight Guard. He is commander of the combined armies of Farrowen, Pallanar, Ghealdor, and Orenth.

"The man beside him is called Rindle. He is a specialist who–"

"He is a thief," Brogan said before he realized he was interrupting his queen.

Priella nodded. "Quite true. However, he now utilizes those skills for my cause."

She gestured toward the young wizard at her side. "And this is Kollin Mor, son of Chancellor Mor, who now rules Tiamalyn."

Jakarci arched a brow, a smirk on his face. "Well met, young Wizard Mor. I trust you have the queen's best interests at heart?"

Kollin's gaze flicked toward Priella. "I, um…"

Clapping his hands together, the noise causing Kollin to jump with a start, Jakarci said, "Since everyone is present, let us sit and eat. We have much to discuss. Besides, I am hungry, and it is bad form to keep a fat man from his meal."

He laughed and waddled to the table beneath the shade of the awning, claiming the oversized chair at one end. Six other chairs surrounded the table, each with a plate and silverware set in front of it, the middle of the table occupied by platters of fruit, breads, three whole chickens, and more. Like the others, Brogan sat and began to eat. It struck him that two wizard lords sat at the same table. He wondered how many others remained alive. His thoughts then turned to Jace, Narine, Adyn, and Salvon. Much had occurred since they had departed with Hadnoddon's crew and the Frostborn.

What are you up to, Jace? Brogan mused to himself. Of anyone he had ever known, whether as Jace or Jerrell, the thief had a knack for stirring up trouble.

Jakarci, a drumstick in each hand, turned toward Priella. "So, my young Queen, I would like to hear the tale, in your own words, explaining how you delivered an army to my doorstep and wrangled another wizard lord to join you."

~

Priella conveyed the series of events, from her father's demise to her arrival in Balmor, careful to leave out any details regarding compulsion or any forms of mental manipulation. She also shared little of Kollin in her story, keeping their relationship separate from matters of state. While she ate sparingly, she experienced an odd mixture of marvel and revulsion at the amount of food Jakarci consumed – breads, meats, cheeses, jams. She lost track but suspected the man had eaten two entire chickens by himself.

Her tale finished with the darkspawn battle and Thurvin heading off toward the city, ignoring her command to remain in camp.

Jakarci slurped chicken grease off his chubby fingers, then wiped them on his robes, leaving dark streaks on the yellow. Priella frowned, thinking the man's behavior odd, even for a wizard lord.

Raising his voice, Jakarci called out, "Dessert!"

Priella looked around. Not seeing any servants, she wondered to whom the man was speaking.

"Thank you for sharing your story," Jakarci said. "Despite your avoidance of the truth."

She bristled. "I spoke no lies."

The man waggled his finger at her. "Intentionally omitting the truth equates to telling lies, for it produces the same result. Deceit."

Pressing her lips together, she glared at him. "To which omissions do you refer?"

He grinned. "So you admit it."

She chose not to reply.

The wizard lord turned his scrutinizing gaze toward Kollin. "You said nothing of your relationship with young Wizard Mor."

"My personal affairs are none of your business."

Jakarci gave her a knowing smile. "What of your use of compulsion to control others?"

Gasping inwardly, Priella fought to keep her expression stoic. *How does he know?*

The obese wizard continued while buttering a bun. "As you discovered, controlling those with the Gift is complex. Controlling a man with the power of three wizard lords... I am aware of what happened last night." He gestured toward Kollin again. "Your lover would have died if not for your abilities. Unfortunately, Bosinger was not so lucky." Stuffing the bun into his mouth, he used a napkin to dab his lips as he chewed. Once he swallowed, he added, "Nor was your throne."

He knows I cannot conduct Devotion, likely that I was unable to do so last night.

Priella realized her disadvantage, both with her magic and in under-standing what was transpiring. "What do you want of me?"

"Fear not, my Queen. If I wanted to kill you, we would not be dining together."

Ten servants appeared from the maze, half with trays in hand. They dispersed, two gathering empty plates, another placing a fresh one before them, two more refilling their drinks. The others placed pies, cakes, pastries, and cups of pudding upon the table. Although Priella had eaten little, the thought of indulging in dessert turned her stomach. She was unsure whether it was a result of watching Jakarci gorge himself or due to her tenuous predicament. The obese wizard lord had no such reservations, claiming an entire pie for himself and eating it like he had consumed nothing for days.

Priella glanced around the table. Garvin's intense eyes were narrowed at Jakarci. Rindle prodded at a piece of cake, as if unsure it were safe to eat. Kollin stared back at her, waiting for a signal. Brogan and the woman at his side looked at each other, neither choosing a dessert.

Jakarci finished his pie and moved on to a cup of pudding, closing his eyes and savoring the first bite, a dreamy expression on his face. He then began to scoop as if ravenous, swiftly finishing it and setting it aside. Lifting his napkin, he wiped his lips and sighed.

"At last, I have reached my limit." Resting back in his chair, Jakarci's hands rubbed his paunch. "If my stomach were to explode... I wonder if it would be a good way to die." He laughed. "While I might enjoy it, the servants would surely wish I chose another route."

Priella glanced toward the others, confusion and shock on their faces. Thus far, the dinner had been an exercise in patience, hers wearing thin. "Excuse me, Lord Jakarci. I must ask again. Why did you invite me here?"

He glanced toward the darkening sky. "Devotion nears."

Anger rose and captured her tongue, threatening to lash out. Rather than bend to it, she took another approach, one she had avoided thus far. "Would you like to hear the truth behind my campaign into Balmoria?"

Jakarci turned toward her. "My, my. Finally, this conversation grows interesting."

She decided on boldness. "As I told you, I did not come north with an army to conquer your wizardom. What I did not say was I came north to stop the darkspawn and the creature that rules them."

"Creature?"

"Yes."

"Do you speak of Urvadan?" he asked with exaggerated sarcasm.

Priella frowned at his tone. "I believe you know of whom I speak."

"So you believe you can defeat H'Deesengar?"

She frowned, never having heard the name. "Who?"

"The demon lord that created the darkspawn."

He does know. "If he is not stopped, mankind will perish."

Jakarci shook his head. "Not just mankind, but all beings. Given time beneath a demon lord's rule, every being of light will be consumed – humans, elves, dwarfs, animals, birds...everything."

"Where did you learn all of this?"

The man grinned. "Your guide, Vanda. You see, he works for me."

Priella's jaw dropped.

Everything she had done for the past nine years, each step of the way, had been under the guidance of the old sorcerer. He had told her she would save the world. That she was the only one capable of doing so. *If he worked for Jakarci all that time...* She could not even finish the thought.

Jakarci laughed. "Finally, I have sufficiently shocked the young queen."

Her anger resurfaced. "If you are aware of the demon lord and his army, why do we sit here indulging in food and sweets? Why are you not doing something to stop it?"

The wizard lord touched the side of his nose. "Oh, but I am. You see, after tonight, there will be only one wizard lord."

Priella blinked. "One?"

"Yes. Last night, Lord Thurvin of Farrowen and Lord Kelluon of Kyranni both died. With four other thrones already empty, only you and I remain." The man grinned, a chill running down Priella's spine.

Panic suddenly arose. She looked at the food on the table, then at the wine.

"Yes," Jakarci crooned. "Poison."

With the magic derived from Devotion expended, she could not cure herself. She turned toward Brogan, who stared at her in alarm. "How could you sit there and allow this fat bastard to murder your queen?"

Brogan opened his mouth. "I–"

"No!" Jakarci rose to his feet, his flippant demeanor banished. "This is between two wizard lords. I will have no interference until this is finished."

Brogan stood, face twisted in fury. "You cannot do this."

The big warrior jerked backward, arms bound as he was lifted off the ground by Jakarci's magic.

"I rule here, Reisner. I will do as I please." The wizard lord turned to Priella. "Did you bring the gem?"

"Gem?"

"Yes. The one the thief retrieved from your destroyed throne."

"I..." She swallowed, debating whether she should tell him. *If I am poisoned, I am dead anyway. Perhaps he can use it to stop the demon lord.* "Yes." She reached into her cleavage and pulled out the aquamarine jewel, which covered her open palm. "Here."

Grinning, Jakarci took it from her hand and turned from the table. "Come, my Queen. We have business to discuss before an untimely death."

The man waddled toward the maze, pausing as Priella hesitated. When she followed, Garvin and Kollin both moved to join her. A dozen armed guards in black leather rushed in, weapons drawn. Each had a yellow arrow on both shoulders.

Black Wasps...

Jakarci nodded. "Yes. You are all aware of the Wasps' reputation." He stepped up to Priella. "We go alone. Do not attempt to follow. Start a fight, and you will die. Even you, Wizard Mor. Three times this many Wasps lie in hiding, ready should anyone try anything. Once Devotion begins, you may leave. Until then, anyone who moves dies." Jakarci gripped her upper arm and led her into the shadowy hedges.

13

ONLY ONE

The hedge maze ended, Priella and Jakarci returning to the plaza surrounding the Tower of Devotion. The square, gray monolith loomed over them, the flame of Bal shimmering at the top, bright against the darkening sky. Turning from the area of charred, broken stone tiles, the pair circled the tower.

Jakarci still held her arm in a tight grip, but she refused to react to the pain. She was stronger than that. *Soon, my pain will end.* After all she had endured, the thought brought a sense of peace. Still, she wondered why Vanda had led her to ruin. *Was the sorcerer using me all along? Was I merely a pawn intended to fuel Jakarci's rise? Is there truly a demon lord, or were the visions he shared nothing but lies?* It was all happening too quickly, doubt, concern, and confusion overwhelming her usual determination.

They turned the corner, and she stopped cold.

A charred corpse lay at the foot of the tower, the stone tiles around it emitting a red, sparkling light.

"Come along. You will wish to see this." Jakarci pulled her toward the body.

As she drew close, it became clear. It was Thurvin. The man's eyes and mouth gaped, as if locked in a permanent state of shock, his hair singed, face burned, the remnants of his robes blackened and charred. A rod of crystal ran through his chest at an angle.

Jakarci stared down at the dead man. "His power was vast. Even after the darkspawn battle, destroying your throne, and another confrontation here, he was a force of nature. Two enchanted blades through the heart and a fall off the tower did not kill him."

Despite her hate for Thurvin, the sight of his corpse turned her stomach. "This occurred last night. Why is he still lying here?"

The wizard lord arched a brow. "With his ability to heal himself again and again, would *you* risk removing the rod piercing his heart?"

She recalled how handily he healed himself on the battlefield. "No, I suppose not... At least not for a day or two."

"Exactly." He pointed toward an opening in the tower wall. "Let us go inside."

They passed through the doorway and into the hollow innards of the tower, the yellow flame at the top providing shimmering light to the interior. A fifteen-foot-tall metal scaffold covered half the space. Beneath it, a sunburst marked the floor, encircling a massive glass disk. He led her past the structure and to the lift at the far end of the room. They stepped on, him placing a palm against the control panel before it began to rise.

Two stories up, Jakarci winced, his face twisting as he held his stomach.

"Is something amiss?" she asked. The man had eaten enough for an army. *Perhaps his stomach is about to burst.*

"Nothing I have not anticipated." He gave her an appraising look. "The illusion you cast is quite fetching."

Suddenly, she feared he wished more than just to kill her. She peered down, the lift nearing the midpoint. *Jumping now would bring a swift end.*

Jakarci chuckled. "Do not worry. Many decades have passed since I gave up pursuits of the flesh. I simply admire your strength. Even now, you believe you are going to die yet appear resolute."

She frowned. "Thank you?"

"You may have wondered why your life has led you to this moment. All the trials you have endured, the training, the sacrifice, the hardening of your heart... It has been in preparation for this moment and what lies ahead."

Priella's eyes narrowed. "What do you know of my pain?"

The lift reached the top and stopped, Jakarci stepping off to stare out over the city. They were behind the crystal throne, the shimmering ring of yellow flames surrounding the lift, the throne, and themselves.

With his back to her, he said, "In truth, I know nothing of the pain you feel. What I do know, what Vanda and I have long suspected, is that the minds of men are too weak to contain the power of many wizard lords. Thurvin's madness would have only grown worse if he had been allowed to claim this tower in addition to the power he already held." Jakarci turned toward her. "I doubt there is a man alive who can contain even five wizardoms' worth of magic."

Brow furrowed, she said, "You said one wizard must control them all in order to defeat the demon lord."

"More accurately, one *wizardess*." He winced again, doubling over while holding his stomach.

She blinked in realization. "You poisoned yourself," she breathed.

His voice was strained. "Yes. Did you expect me to jump?" A chuckle emerged, although he was still doubled over. "Think of the mess I would make. Oh, the servants would hate me for decades after that." Again, he laughed.

The situation had turned in an unexpected direction, leaving Priella more confused than ever. "Why did you bring me up here then?"

"The lift is the only easy way up." The big man stumbled back to the lift and fell upon it. With obvious effort, he pushed himself upright until he sat with his back to the control panel. His breath came in gasps, beads of sweat coating his forehead. "There can be...only one."

By the gods, he means it. "You intend for me to face the demon lord."

He held out his hand, the jewel she had given him resting in his palm. His breathing calmed. "Take it. When the flame is doused, swap the gem and claim the tower."

She picked up the jewel, gripping it tightly.

"How could I possibly claim all the other towers? If the demon is free, there is not enough time."

"Vanda," he said through gritted teeth. "He will...guide you." He coughed, red spittle spraying on his robes. "You should have...little trouble replacing me. I left strict instructions. Everyone is to obey you without..." The man winced in pain, "question."

It was difficult to watch, but Priella steeled herself. She knelt beside him and took his hand. "I could heal you."

He chuckled. "I could heal myself." A gasp followed, his eyes squeezing closed. He then exhaled, opening them. "Do not worry. I have lived a long life. If not for the magic of Bal, I would have eaten myself to death many decades ago."

A tear tracked down her face. "I pray I am strong enough to do what must be done when my time comes."

He coughed, more blood spraying from his mouth. After a few panting breaths, he nodded. "You...will. You...must."

A spasm shook his body, eyes bulging, sweat pouring down his face. Another spasm hit him, blood running from his lips. He stiffened, then went limp, head lolling to one side. The ring of yellow flames went out like a snuffed candle, the tower falling dark as with one last, shuddering breath, the Wizard Lord of Balmoria died.

Priella allowed herself to cry. It felt good to feel, to allow her walls to fall away, for emotion to flow freely. After a few minutes, she kissed the back of his limp hand and set it down. She wiped her face and stood, pushing grief aside in favor of determination. Gripping the gem in her hand, she circled the throne to stand before it.

In the crystal sat a topaz, dull and dormant. She drew on her magic and used it to loosen the gem, prying it from the setting until it popped into her hand. In its place, she inserted the aquamarine. It snapped into place, the throne blooming to life, the ring around the tower flaring with ice-blue flames.

She ran her hand over the chair arm, caressing it lovingly, her desire to harness prayers rising like an inferno inside her. Turning, she sat, embraced her magic, and initiated Devotion. Pale blue flames engulfed everything, blotting out the world as the prayers of Balmor and the entire wizardom of Pallanar fed her magic.

14

PLANS

Priella marched down the palace corridor, Commander Garvin at her side. Nearing mid-day and still not having answers, she had grown impatient. The anxiety she felt about the approaching army, while she remained unprepared, left her fuming. Izedon turned the corner, his eyes bulging when he saw the look on her face. As head of the palace staff, he might possess the answers she sought.

Before he could turn away, she called out, "Stop!"

He turned back toward her and straightened his coat, bowing as she drew near. "My Queen."

"Don't *my Queen* me. I am looking for Vanda."

"Yes. I ran into Odama. He told me the same."

"Where is the old sorcerer? As far as I can tell, nobody has seen him since yesterday morning."

Again, the man fiddled with his coat, as if it could be any straighter. "Master Vanda often disappears for stretches. Sometimes for weeks."

"*Weeks*?" she shrieked. "We don't *have* weeks. There is an army of monsters on our doorstep. I need the sorcerer, and I need him now."

"You have found him."

At the familiar voice behind her, she spun around to discover Vanda standing a few strides away. "Where have you been?"

"Seeking answers."

"Good." She glanced at Garvin. "Because we have need of them."

"The flame burns ice blue," Vanda said. "Jakarci is dead, and you have taken his throne."

She paused at the sadness in his tone, her anger cooling. *I did not even consider his feelings.* "I am sorry. It wasn't my idea. He–"

The old man held up a hand, stopping her. "Killed himself. I know. He had been resigned to taking his own life for quite some time, assuming he survived the confrontation with Thurvin. While the wizard lord from Marquithe died, it did not occur as we had envisioned." Vanda shook his head. "There are always variables to prophecy, and it is difficult to discern which are true and which are false, the phrases scribbled from the visions often resulting in improper interpretation."

Priella frowned. "I...cannot say I understand your meaning, but I am sorry for your loss."

Vanda smiled. "Jakarci was a better wizard lord than most. Yes, he overindulged in food and enjoyed the game a bit too much, but he, alone, has had the interest of the world in mind, while most other wizard lords focused on their own greed. Thurvin worst of all." He put his hand on her shoulder. "You are the other exception, Priella. Even when you had to make hard decisions, you have done them with one goal in mind. Now, you must save us all."

Her voice a whisper, she asked, "How? I don't know what to do. The prayers of Pallanar and this city are insufficient. There is not enough time to travel to the other wizardoms to claim the Towers of Devotion."

"Ah, but there is. You simply need the right tool."

"Which is?"

Vanda waved for her to follow as he turned down a side corridor, heading toward the Arboretum. He spoke softly as they walked outside. "Every obelisk you claim will add to your strength, but the towers are the key. For now, you have the ability to travel short distances and return the same day. With your magic, you could travel to Harken, Straemor, and even Lamar in just a few hours, convert their obelisks to Pallan, and fly back."

Priella considered it. She had the augmentation spell to alter the gems and the ability to make the trip as the man described. However, the prayers of those three cities would not equal those from one great city. "You said it yourself. I must take the capitals of the other wizardoms."

He stopped outside the hedge maze. "Someone is coming to help. Someone from your past."

"Who?"

"Narine Killarius."

Priella frowned. "Taladain's daughter? How can she help?"

Vanda smiled. "She has discovered the secret of the eighth construct. With her at your side, you can claim the remaining six towers in a single day."

She considered his statement. "Even if that were true, she isn't here now. What if the demon lord and his army appear before I am ready?"

The man's grin fell away. "Then we are doomed."

Her heart sank, dread resting heavy in her stomach. "How long do we have?"

"H'Deesengar killed Kelluon and captured Anker the same night as the darkspawn attack outside of Balmor. The bridge between Kyranni and Balmoria is destroyed, so it will take extra time for the darkspawn to circumvent the river…unless the demon lord finds another means to cross. Regardless, we have at least two days before the army reaches us. If we can slow his advance in any way, it will buy us time."

Priella set her jaw and turned toward Garvin. "You heard him, Commander. You are responsible for preparing our defenses. More importantly, you now know where the demon lord is located. The creature surely has its sights set on Balmor, but they cannot arrive before I am ready. You must do everything in your power to slow the advance of the darkspawn army." She put a hand on his shoulder. "Use the gift I have bestowed upon you. I pray it makes a difference."

Garvin dipped his head. "Yes, my Queen."

She turned back toward Vanda. "In the meantime, I had best claim the remaining cities in Balmoria."

Vanda bowed. "Well said, my Queen." He extended a hand, an aquamarine stone filling his palm. "Here is the first gem. Follow Bal's Sound west to the sea, then turn north. You should be able to reach Harken, swap the gem, and return here before nightfall. Denalla, Straemor, and Lamor may follow in the coming days, but the great cities are far more critical. Once Narine arrives, you must claim them rapidly."

Priella took the gem, gave him a nod, and wrapped a shield around herself. She sailed into the air and over the city, flying along the waterway, toward the distant ocean.

≈

Trey Garvin, commander of the combined armies of Pallanar, Farrowen, Ghealdor, Orenth, and Balmoria, leaned over the table in his tent. Upon it were maps of the regions surrounding Balmor, including where his armies currently camped and lands to the north and east, ranging all the way up to Northern Kyranni. Assuming the intel provided by Vanda was true, Anker had fallen, as had the other Kyranni cities. The darkspawn army was expected to press south, toward their position. It was up to him to protect the people and find a way to stop the horde's advance.

The thumping of his own pulse sounded like a drum, adrenaline rushing through him, as if he were in the heat of battle. It was a distracting side-effect of the augmentation Priella had bestowed upon him. Already, he had accidentally leveled one tent, startling the three men inside. He hoped such inconveniences were worth the abilities he had gained.

Henton ducked into the tent, his helmet beneath his arm. He was as tall as Garvin with slightly more bulk. With a shaved scalp and brown goatee, his age was difficult to discern, but Garvin suspected Henton was a few years his senior. Donned in full armor, a star on his chest, the Farrowen captain appeared every inch a soldier.

"Commander." Henton gave a quick nod.

No fist to the chest, Garvin noted. *He does not respect my rank. Still, I need to know I can trust him.* "I am glad you are here, Captain," Garvin said in earnest.

The other man frowned. "Are you? Since my forces have joined this venture, you have not said a word to me."

Garvin stepped away from the table, his gaze meeting Henton's. "The way we parted after taking Dorban... I wish it had gone otherwise. I said some things I wish I had not. At the time, I only wanted out. However, military life is akin to a flame, me the moth drawn to it, regardless of my wishes. So, I currently find myself at the head of an army unlike any other." He stepped closer and clapped a hand on Henton's shoulder. "Unlike the

97

campaign in Ghealdor, this one is not fueled by a lust for power nor political gain. This fight is about survival. Not just ours, but the entire human race. I believe in this cause, and I could use good men I can trust to see it through."

Henton's expression softened. "Well said, Commander. How can I help?"

Turning back to the table, Garvin pulled out a map of Southern Kyranni and laid it on top. "I have just received word that the creature in command of the darkspawn recently defeated Kelluon and took the city of Anker."

The captain arched a brow. "What can defeat a wizard lord?"

"A demon lord."

"You cannot be serious," Henton scoffed.

"I wish I were not. This...*thing* has abilities we cannot fathom."

"How can we hope to defeat something able to kill a wizard lord?"

"We cannot. However, we can slow its army's advance. Priella is preparing something to face this demon lord, but she requests time."

"So we don't need to clash directly with the enemy. You wish only to harry this army and slow the progress?"

"I do."

Garvin ran his finger along the map, beginning at Anker and moving south to the Balmorian border. "Darkspawn hide during the day and only travel or attack at night. I estimate the monsters can cover roughly twenty miles per evening, but we will assume twenty-five, just to be safe. That puts them at the river along the border three days after the fall of Anker, which occurred two nights past. Thus, they should reach the river tomorrow evening. The bridge to Straemor has been destroyed, forcing them to head upriver to the next bridge, located here..." He tapped a mark on the map east of the destroyed bridge, "costing them another night. If they choose to attack Straemor, that puts them outside the city walls five days from now. If they decide to ignore the city and march straight toward Balmor, they could arrive in four days."

"I am with you thus far."

"I am going to take our cavalry, every mounted soldier, and meet this force. I don't intend to attack the vanguard, but instead to use any means possible to slow their advance. If successful, I might buy us a day or two."

"But you are the commander. Aren't you supposed to remain here to prepare the defenses?"

"Under normal circumstances, yes. However, this war is not about defeating the darkspawn army. It is about killing the one *driving* the army. That's Queen Priella's job. Ours is to buy time, saving as many lives as possible in the process."

Henton nodded. "All right. What do you need from me?"

Garvin pulled out the map of Balmor and the surrounding region. "I want you to prepare our forces to face the darkspawn when they arrive. Set up a perimeter northeast of the Bazaar. Should the darkspawn breach the outer defenses, the Bazaar becomes the battlefield. Should they claim that, they must lay siege to the gate. Odama will hold the city walls at all costs, but you must make the creatures pay to reach them." He pointed toward the bay. "The Farrowen, Pallanese, and Balmorian ships are in the harbor. Have them moor close to shore from outside the harbor gate all the way to here." He tapped on a point northeast of the Bazaar. "Load siege engines and archers on those ships and place them close to shore. We will fire upon any darkspawn within range."

The captain grinned. "Unless they steer clear of the waterfront, it will be a killing zone."

Garvin clapped the man's shoulder again. "Then you must find a means to keep them near the waterfront. These monsters vastly outnumber us, but they are not infinite. The more we kill, the less we have to face should Priella fail."

15

PROMOTION

Tugging on the reins, Garvin slowed his mount on the downside slope of a hill, a thousand riders gathering on the road behind him. The sun was low in the sky, casting long shadows over the river valley below. The elevated position gave Garvin a clear view of Straemor, nestled on the south bank of the Trifork River. The name came from the three tributaries flowing from the mountains south of the river, feeding the main channel. The nearest of the tributaries was visible just east of Garvin's position – a brown strip of water surrounded by brush.

A wall, two stories tall, encircled Straemor, short docks along the riverbank beside it. Near the docks was a roadway that ended at the stub of the destroyed bridge, mirroring what remained on the opposite bank three hundred feet away. It was not a massive span, but it was enough to prevent any crossing, other than by watercraft or walking to the next bridge twenty-five miles upstream.

Most importantly, the city appeared intact. With fishermen visible along the river, wagons entering and exiting the city, guards standing outside the open gate, all appeared normal. It was a welcome sight.

Thank the gods Straemor has not already fallen.

He turned toward Valgo, the Balmorian lieutenant assigned to his command. The man appeared competent and respectful. Those were qualities Garvin needed at the moment.

"Would you call High Wizard Victrin a respected leader?"

The lieutenant pulled his winged helmet off and ran a hand through his shoulder-length, dark hair. "Reports say he is hard but fair. Rarely laughs, but also does not indulge in frivolous activities."

Garvin nodded. "I can work with that. I want you to take twenty of your soldiers and ride into the city. Inform Victrin that Jakarci is dead and Priella stands to unify all wizardoms against the darkspawn threat. Tell him to lock down the city and prepare his defenses, for the enemy could arrive as soon as tonight. Even if the darkspawn cannot cross the water, they could wreak havoc on anyone within reach of their bows or magic."

"What about you and the others?"

"I am going to have a look at the bridge while the others set up camp outside the city walls."

Valgo thumped his fist against his chest, turned, and began selecting riders in yellow tabards. Once he had fifteen chosen, he added five dressed in black leather, faces covered.

Smart, Garvin thought. *Victrin will not ignore Black Wasps.*

When Valgo's contingency rode off, Garvin turned toward Quiam. "Have the men set up camp outside the city walls. They are to eat and prepare for battle."

"Yes, sir!" Quiam thumped his chest, turned, and began shouting orders as he rode down the line.

Garvin turned toward Rindle, the last of the four riders in the vanguard. "Ready to take a look at the bridge?"

The thief shrugged. "Can't say I know much about bridges, but if it allows me to get off this horse for a while, I am ready."

"Let's go." Garvin kicked his horse into a run and raced down the hill.

Trees sped past, a trail of dust rising behind them. Rindle leaned low over the neck of his mare, expression one of intense focus. His skill had grown noticeably over recent weeks, knees absorbing the rise and fall of the horse beneath him. The thief had grown in more ways than one, his gradual transformation a source of pride for Garvin.

As the ground leveled, the road turned, a fork appearing ahead. One route led to the city, the other to the docks. Taking the latter, Garvin slowed as the road approached the river, the dirt rising to a ramp with a wooden frame blackened by fire. Charred logs jutted out a few feet, partially burned pilings visible above the water, which flowed toward the sea.

Rindle stopped beside him, his horse puffing and releasing a sneeze. "Crossing here appears doubtful."

Garvin pointed toward a rope a couple hundred feet upstream from the destroyed bridge. It ran across the river, secured to a thick tree on each bank. On the far shore, a flat vessel waited at a dock, the rope running through pulleys on poles at the front and back of the craft. "Someone has added a ferry. Likely because of how much they can charge for a crossing."

The thief nodded. "But it appears too small to carry a wagon."

On the other shore, a path ran up the riverbank to a wooden building. "I bet that's where they store wagons. Whoever is running this must be making good money."

A few boats floated down the river near the city, but nothing was visible upstream. Garvin considered what he saw, deciding he needed a man on the Kyranni shore. "You have just been promoted to scout."

"Promoted?" Rindle blinked. "How is that a promotion?"

Garvin grinned. "Did you have a title before?"

Frowning, he shrugged. "I guess not."

"There you go. From no title to scout, just like that. At this rate, you'll be commander within decades."

"Very funny," said the thief. "All right. What do you need me to do?"

"Find a fisherman who can get you to the other side, one with a big enough craft to take your horse. Ride north and search for the enemy, but do not get caught. When you have their position and heading, get back here and take the ferry across. Report to me immediately. I want to know what they are doing. Specifically, I need to determine if they are heading here or toward the bridge upstream."

"And if I find a fisherman and he says no?"

Garvin dug out a few silvers and plopped them into Rindle's palm. "There you go. Now, off with you. It will be dark soon."

Rindle rode toward the city while Garvin considered his options. *I wish I knew the limits of demon magic.* He wondered if anyone knew the answer. *I do not even comprehend the extent of my own abilities.* With that in mind, he decided to train one last time before nightfall, urging his horse into a trot along the river, away from the city.

Since obtaining his new magic, his heart had been thumping like a drum from the adrenaline flowing through him, making it nigh impossible to sleep. The lone night on the road from Balmor had been sleepless, Garvin rising and leaving camp on three separate occasions, telling the men on watch he could not sleep and needed to walk it off. Each time, he had snuck off to a field a mile away to train with his new magic. In truth, the sheer power he wielded frightened him to the core.

His prior augmentation was nothing compared to what he now controlled. However, Priella's magic was greater than before, and she had gifted Garvin twice this time, effectively quadrupling the power he commanded.

When his horse stopped, he climbed off and led it to a patch of long grass along the river, tying the reins to a fallen tree. He then proceeded toward a glade beyond the trees, determined to be out of view rather than have anyone aware of the magic coursing through his veins.

Terrin "Rindle" Delmont rode along the Kyranni road at a walk, the sky above purple, save for the lingering light to the west. The shadows in the trees along the road had thickened, along with the nervous tension he felt. His lone encounter with darkspawn had happened so swiftly, he didn't have time to consider what he faced. At the time, he had also been nothing more than shadow, the monsters' weapons unable to kill him. Now he had no such protection.

I wish Priella had gifted me with magic before this mission. Perhaps she is too consumed with doing...whatever it is she does. Regardless, it was too late. He was many miles north of Balmor and alone...in the woods...in the dark.

A noise came from ahead. He stopped his horse and listened, his own heart behaving as if it were attempting to break from his ribcage.

A distant rumble came from the forest, growing louder, but he could not define the noise. He waited, his heart beating faster as he stared toward the dark bend a few hundred feet in front of him. Shapes came around the corner, a wall of spindly shadows with red eyes. When the creatures spotted him, they burst into a run, hooting. Faced with hundreds of goblins rushing toward him, Rindle turned his horse and kicked it into a gallop. Twangs came from behind, the whistle of arrows sailing past. He ducked low, hugging the mare's neck as it raced down the dark road.

Only ten minutes had passed since the fishermen dropped him off at the north bank. *Maybe they are still there.* Doubting it, he decided to make straight for the ferry.

His horse sped out from the forest, the river appearing ahead, amber lights from the city visible downstream. He angled the horse toward the stable near the riverbank, sped past it, and headed down the bank. The drop was too steep, a foreleg buckling, Rindle crying out as he flew over the horse's head and splashed into the shallow water. His shoulder struck the bottom, a jolt of pain joining the sudden cold enveloping him.

He scrambled to his feet and trudged through the water to climb on shore. His horse tried to rise, but the foreleg gave again, a high-pitched whinny shrieking in the night. Hoots and cries came from the forest, the monsters emerging at a run.

Dismissing the horse, he rushed over to the ferry and heaved. It moved slowly, the beached keels dragging across the sandy shore while the hoots grew closer. When it broke free from land, he pushed the platform out and climbed on. Picking up one of the long poles from the deck, he propelled the craft farther from shore, the pulleys mounted to the front and back squeaking noisily. The pain in his shoulder seemed to scream in time with them.

He looked back just as the monsters reached the top of the riverbank. Some raced toward the water, other raised bows.

"Oh no," he groaned.

Dropping the poles, he drew his dagger, climbed onto a bench, and began sawing at the rope between the two pulleys. An arrow flew past, just missing him. Another struck the bench at his feet. He furiously cut at the thick rope. It broke, and he hastily grabbed the end tied to the south shore.

The current pulled the rear of the ferry downstream, Rindle holding the rope, bracing himself against the railings secured to the deck. Arrows flew over him, some landing on deck as the ferry floated toward the middle of the river. All the while, more and more goblins appeared along the riverbank, hooting and barking while their brethren loosed arrows toward the ferry.

When the craft was three quarters of the way across the river, the tension against the rope became too great and it tore from Rindle's hands. The current caught the craft and it sped toward the city, Rindle without a means to control it. The ferry crashed into the pilings from the destroyed bridge with a mighty crack, sending him tumbling across the deck and into the river with a splash.

He went under, rolling in the current, before righting himself and resurfacing with a gasp. Kicking and swinging his arms wildly, he turned until he found the south shore. With the effort of a man afraid to die, he swam, his progress across the river far slower than his pace floating downstream.

Spotting silhouettes along the shore, he screamed, "Help!"

Shouts echoed in response, but they were unintelligible over the rush of water and his splashing.

Nearing the docks, he headed toward them, but they slipped past too quickly. Again and again, he passed docks, until his injured shoulder smacked into a boat. With his other hand, he reached up and caught hold of the boat rail, hanging there for a moment to try and catch his breath before pulling himself, hand over hand, around the front. Once past the bow, the current caught him and started to yank him downstream again. Hands reached down and grasped his wrists, pulling him from the river and onto the dock.

Exhausted and panting, he rolled to his back and stared up at the two soldiers standing over him.

"What were you doing in the river?" one asked.

"I...was scouting...the other bank," he said between pants.

The man looked across the water. "There is an army of monsters over there."

Rindle pushed himself to a sitting position. "I know." *They almost killed me.* Forcing himself to move, he rose to his feet. "Where is Commander Garvin?"

"With the camp, outside the city walls."

A cry echoed in the night, the eerie pitch sending chills down Rindle's spine. He turned as a shape sped past the moon. It was huge, far too big to be a bird.

"What in the blazes is that?" one soldier muttered.

"Wyvern," Rindle breathed.

Raw fear chased away his exhaustion, replaced by an urgency to escape. He darted off the dock and circled the city wall, his eyes never leaving the monster descending from the sky.

16

THE BATTLE OF STRAEMOR

G arvin rode along the perimeter of camp to ensure everyone remained awake and alert. He called out numerous times, stating that an attack could come at any moment. Yes, sleeping during the day was difficult, as was remaining awake all night after a day in the saddle. Yet both were better than dying.

Fires had been lit, but bedrolls remained in piles, unused. The men had no tents, lacking both the time to wait on a wagon and the willingness to burden the horses with the extra weight. Thus far, the weather had remained dry. He prayed it remained so. War was hard enough without enduring rain.

He came to the lone tent in camp, a small version of the command pavilion he had used outside of Balmor. This one lacked furniture, the interior occupied only by rolled maps and a single enchanted lantern. Valgo waited inside, the man thumping a fist to his chest when Garvin entered.

"Well done, Lieutenant," Garvin said. "The men in camp appear alert, as do the soldiers posted around the perimeter."

"Thank you, sir."

An inhuman, unfamiliar cry echoed in the night. Both men rushed outside and turned toward the river as a massive, winged beast descended from the sky. Shouts arose, soldiers along the riverbank rushing to engage.

"Is that a dragon?" Valgo asked.

"Wyvern. Like a dragon, but smaller. Also, they cannot breathe fire."

"Smaller?" Valgo sounded doubtful.

"Tell the men to mount up."

While Valgo rushed across the camp, shouting orders, Garvin ran to his horse and hurriedly climbed into the saddle he had vacated moments earlier. He rode toward the nearest fire and caught the attention of a soldier.

"Get me a torch!"

"A torch, Commander?"

"Just do it!"

The man ran to a bucket beside a pile of bedrolls, pulled out a torch with cloth wrapped around one end, and ran to the fire. It lit, the man rushing the burning torch over to Garvin, who took it, turned his horse, and rode toward the river.

He slowed at the first pole, lit the top, and continued to the next, each creating an island of light.

The men fighting the wyvern were dying, bodies strewn around the flailing monster, its neck, chest, tail, and wings littered with cuts. The hoots from thousands of goblins carried across the water, Garvin thankful to have the river as a barrier and for the darkspawn's inability to swim.

I wonder if Rindle made it back safely. Even as the thought crossed his mind, Garvin spotted the tall thief speeding along the city wall.

Another wyvern flew past the moon, banked, and lowered toward the river. When it slowed to hover, Garvin spotted a shape on its back. A dark purple glow appeared around the figure, a beam of dark light shooting toward the river. The light spread out, spanning the water and solidifying. Goblins rushed out onto the arcane bridge, weapons brandished as they raced toward the south bank.

Realizing he could hold back no longer, Garvin called upon his magic.

Swirling winds lifted him off his horse and into the air. He gathered more pressure, then slammed his hands together. A massive gust blasted toward the bridge, striking the goblins and launching them into the river. The monsters on the far bank hesitated.

The wyvern over the water flew toward Garvin, closing the distance rapidly, giving him a better view of the creature upon the monster's back. Frighteningly tall with a muscular build, the human-like being was all black, save for glowing, yellow eyes. The creature thrust its fist forward, a beam of purple light bursting out. Garvin released the air keeping him aloft and fell, the malevolent magic narrowly missing him and striking a man on horseback, vaporizing both him and his mount.

Just before he hit the ground, Garvin crafted a cushion of air, lowering himself the last three feet. He landed in a crouch and watched the wyvern and its rider speed past.

That must be the demon lord. Based on what Vanda had told him, the demon lord could not be vanquished by any normal means. *I don't need to kill him or the army. I just need to slow them.*

The mounted wyvern banked, a cry echoing in the night. Other wyverns appeared, joining the first, as they circled and came back toward Garvin and his men. He spread his arms and drew upon the magic gifted by Priella. With it flowing through him, he twisted his hands in the air, forming a tunnel of swirling wind directed at the attacking wyverns. The wind struck, the lead creature flipping upside down and crashing to the ground with a thunderous boom. The two wyverns closest to the beast wobbled, lost control, and tumbled through the air in opposite directions. One landed in the river, the other smashing into trees beside the road.

Garvin spun as the fore of the darkspawn horde crossing the magical bridge reached the south bank. Mounted soldiers armed with swords, lances, and spears met the monsters in a clash of blood and severed limbs.

He looked back up toward the sky, searching for more wyverns but saw nothing. His gaze lowered to the dead wyvern in front of him, neck twisted and body broken. The demon was nowhere to be seen. The wyvern corpse shifted, lifted, and flopped over, the demon crawling out from beneath it and standing.

Turning toward him, the demon laughed. "Puny human. You dare defy H'Deesengar?" The creature extended a fist toward him, prepared to unleash its magic.

Desperate, Garvin shot compressed air beneath him, launching himself fifty feet into the air. The beam of purple light missed him and struck his horse, disintegrating it. The demon roared and released another attack, Garvin narrowly dodging it.

With the monster's attention on him, Garvin called upon the wind and launched across the sky, the trees racing past, stars a blur. The speed too great, he lost control, flailing as he fell toward the forest. He conjured an upward draft just ahead, sending him spinning head over heels toward the heavens. Clearing the draft, his momentum slowed, allowing him to right himself upon a platform of air. He turned and saw additional wyverns diving toward the battlefield.

I must stay away from the demon. I cannot help them if I am dead. His abilities were too valuable to waste.

He sent himself toward the river, dipped low, and rode a draft while hovering twenty feet above the water. The glowing, purple bridge came into view, thousands of goblins clustered on the north bank, funneling across toward the southern side.

Garvin drew on his magic, increasing the wind a hundred-fold, his speed growing at a frightening rate. As he sailed over the heads of the goblins crossing, the destructive gust struck the bridge and launched the monsters over the edge, sending a thousand into the water. His momentum took him past the city, the wind lifting fishing boats and even a few docks, flipping them in a spray of water and splinters.

He rose higher, releasing the powerful breeze as he sailed up into the sky. Turning, he gazed upon the moonlit battlefield where soldiers on horseback engaged the goblins. Wyverns dove through the sky, smashing into horses and soldiers alike. One lifted a horse into the air with its claws, dropping it to crush a pair of unlucky soldiers. City soldiers upon the walls loosed arrows at darkspawn below, but he saw no sign of wizard magic. *Does Victrin believe he can avoid this battle?* It was obvious the city would fall, the battle his soldiers waged merely delaying the inevitable. Flashes of purple lit the night, the demon striding through the throng killing soldiers with ease while discarding any attack that came its way.

I must do something. He just did not know what.

Garvin then recalled the battle outside of Balmor and the damage Lord Thurvin caused with his magic. It was his only hope. But first, he had to issue the order.

He dove down and created a long, curved slide of hardened air. When his body hit the invisible structure, the momentum sent him along it, across the river, and toward the battle. Dismissing the slide, he cushioned his fall, slowing his momentum and stumbling to the ground, tripping and rolling to a sliding stance that stirred a cloud of dust.

Bursting into a run, he raced toward a rider with wings on his helmet.

"Retreat! Retreat!" When he neared Valgo, he shouted again. "Retreat to the pass! Now!"

The man grabbed the horn on his saddle, lifted it, and blew, a low hum echoing over the din of battle. Garvin turned away from the soldiers, seeking an open space. He spotted Rindle on a horse, bent low as he sped toward the road.

At least the thief is alive.

He drew on his magic and launched himself upward, steeling himself to his duty, to the destruction he would cause. Slowing upon a platform of air five hundred feet above the battlefield, he watched the riders turn away from the fight and ride toward the road. Some lingered, a few fighting the monsters, others blocked by goblins and wyverns on the ground. There was nothing he could do to save them, so he said a brief prayer and extended his arms, calling upon the wind.

Air rushed in from the north, the south, the east, and the west, spinning him. He gave himself over to it, drawing in air from all four directions, combining into a swirling vortex, lifting him higher and higher. The cyclone extended from the sky to the ground like a finger of a god, creating a tornado of massive proportions. It tore up the earth, lifting goblins, soldiers, horses, and anything else in its path, leaving a trail of churned earth and bodies in its wake.

He tightened his arms to his body, creating a calm about himself, slowing his own momentum in the eye of the storm while feeding the magic of the four winds, increasing the tornado's energy. He looked down and saw wyverns taking flight. Increasing the north wind while reducing that from the south, the twister shifted toward the wyverns, the wind catching one, drawing it into the maelstrom. Like the humans and other creatures, it spun around Garvin, helplessly caught in the sheer power of the storm until it reached the top and was launched into the night. Altering the whirlwind's path, he chased the other two wyverns, but they split apart, both evading the storm.

His gaze returned to the battlefield. Mounted soldiers raced south, ahead of the tornado, no monsters in sight. He altered the winds, the storm shifting to head back toward the bridge where darkspawn continued to cross the river.

A thousand feet above the ground, he rode the storm, laying waste to anything below. The cyclone raged toward the magic bridge and the monsters on the opposing bank. He saw a fire glowing among the creatures, wiry forms dancing around it. *Shaman magic.* Lord Thurvin had been struck by such magic while riding a storm, sending the wizard lord crashing to the ground. Unlike Thurvin, Garvin had no ability to heal himself. Such a fall would be beyond fatal.

With a final push from the south, he sent the storm toward the bridge and lifted himself higher. The storm's momentum slowed over the river, the winds lifting water into the air, the fury of the spray buffeting the monsters, hundreds falling off the bridge. A ball of red magic flew up from the fire and arced through the sky, straight toward him. Upon a platform of air, he raced away. The magic missile sailed past and fell toward the battlefield below.

As he sped south, Garvin spotted a single, dark shape standing on the torn earth, its yellow eyes watching him fly off into the night.

17

REUNION

Narine peered through the solar lens across Balmor Sound, sighting an army of thousands camped outside the city, soldiers constructing something large. Some used shovels to dig a long pit, the churned earth built up into a mound where other soldiers drove tall posts into the ground. Another group secured crossbeams to the posts, still others carried stripped logs and stood them along the outside of the structure. Narine assumed it had something to do with the approaching darkspawn army.

She turned, the view through the lens shifting to the docks beside the city, dockworkers busily unloading ships, people lined up, waiting to board. At the end of one pier, she located a quiet spot, distinctive by the post at the end marked with the number twelve. She concentrated on the location, capturing the image in her mind, fixing it precisely as she formed the construct.

Lowering the lens, Narine channeled her magic and opened a gateway that perfectly matched the image in her mind. Before she was even finished, Adyn leapt through and landed on the pier, blades ready. She looked around and waved. Hadnoddon climbed through, hammer in hand. Jace followed, the breeze off the sound causing his cloak to billow. Narine came last, taking Jace's hand as she stepped onto the pier, immediately noticing the wind blowing harder than it had on the north shore. She withdrew her magic, the portal snapping closed. Down the pier, sailors and dockworkers stood in a cluster, staring in their direction, eyes wide, jaws dropped.

Adyn snorted. "I was wondering how people would react. It must be shocking to witness us appearing from nowhere."

Narine realized the gateway had opened perpendicular to the pier. From the side, it would have appeared like they had materialized from thin air.

Adyn in the lead, they headed toward the city, the dockworkers and sailors scrambling aside, gaping at the metallic-skinned bodyguard.

She needs a cloak, Narine thought. *Or she will attract attention everywhere we go.*

Until now, the journey had been one of solitude, having seen nothing of people as they hopped from mountain peak to mountain peak, from beach to beach, always seeking a distant point for the next gateway. The lone exception had been their stop in Anker, the memory sending a chill down Narine's spine. *An entire great city lost to monsters.* Tens of thousands had died in Anker, yet no human corpses had been found. It left her wondering what had become of the bodies.

They reached the end of the dock where a crowd waited – men, women, and children with fear in their eyes. The young huddled beside their parents, wide-eyed stares following Adyn as she walked past. Each family had heavy packs with them, ready for travel.

They flee the city, Narine thought. *I do not blame them.*

They neared the city where three guards in chainmail and yellow tabards stood outside the harbor gate, another cluster of six lingering just beyond it. Two soldiers with halberds stepped in front of them, blades crossed to block their progress, the third man approaching to stand behind the weapons, arms crossed over his chest. A black, triangle-shaped patch had been sewn to one shoulder of his tabard.

"What are you?" the man said to Adyn.

She lifted a fist. "Come here. I'll show you."

Jace put his hand on Adyn's arm and stepped past her. "No need for that." He stopped a stride from the guards, hands raised. "Listen. We have come far and have little time. An army of monsters approaches from the north, and we are here to help stop them."

The two guards holding the halberds looked back at the third. "What do we do?"

"I wish Valgo or Odama were here," the man muttered.

"Well, they aren't, and you are our squad leader."

"I'll make it easy for you," Jace continued. "Arrest us and take us to the palace. Let someone there decide."

The squad leader thought for a moment. "Will you surrender your weapons?"

"Touch my blades and see what happens," Adyn growled.

Hadnoddon lifted his hammer. "This is made of dwarven metal from the forge of Vis Fornax. You are not worthy of touching it."

The guards shifted their feet, glancing toward one another, the leader frowning, his brow furrowed.

Jace rolled his eyes and turned to Narine. "Can you do something?"

"I'd rather not. I am tired and need to save what energy remains."

He sighed and turned back to the guards. "Gather as many men as you wish and escort us to the palace. We will be armed but promise not to cause trouble."

The man's scowl deepened before he nodded. "I guess we have bigger problems than to worry about you four." He turned and barked, "Gezkar, Blandon!"

Two guards, one tall and thin with a young face, the other thickly built and twice the other man's age, walked over.

"Yes, Matashi?" the older one said.

"Escort these four to the palace. Ask for Odama. He will decide what to do with them."

The halberds were raised, Narine and her companions following the two guards into the city. As they cleared the gate, her gaze rose to the tower ahead. The flame burned ice blue.

Priella has claimed Balmor.

Priella sped across the sky, the city of Balmor appearing in the distance. The day prior, she had converted the Obelisk of Devotion in Harken, today igniting the one in Lamor to the pale blue flame of Pallan. Both cities would add to her magic, but they were insignificant, the combined population just over twenty thousand.

Time is fleeting. I must claim the towers in the great cities before it is too late.

She floated over the city wall and toward the palace. It was already mid-afternoon, and she feared the darkspawn army arriving when night fell. *Please, Garvin. Please hold them back one more night.* She prayed it would be enough.

Slowing her speed, she descended into the Arboretum, her feet touching down on the stone tiles mere strides from the ones cracked and burned from the battle between Jakarci and Thurvin. She stared at the damaged area, ten strides across and twenty deep. It bore the marks of lightning and tremendous heat,, leaving her curious about the battle and how Jakarci had survived it.

"My Queen!"

She turned as a guard ran toward her, the man slowing to bow. "I apologize for the disturbance, but Odama asked for you to join him as soon as possible."

"Odama?"

The soldier nodded. "Vanda is on his way, as well. There are visitors."

Finally. "Take me to him."

The man turned and strode down the shaded walkway leading to the palace. He opened the door and held it for her before leading her down a corridor and to a closed door. The guard knocked, Odama's muffled voice coming from inside.

"Come in."

Rather than wait, Priella opened it and entered Odama's office.

"Ah. Queen Priella," the man said from beside his desk. "I am glad you have returned."

Across from him stood a woman with blonde hair and obvious curves. She turned to reveal a face Priella had not seen since late summer.

"Narine. You are here."

Narine appeared thinner than Priella recalled. More mature, as well. The combination made her more beautiful than ever, the girl she had known now appearing every inch a woman. A pang of jealousy stirred inside her, something Priella thought she had overcome. It, along with her single-minded goal of hardening herself, had created a distance between her and Narine at the University, despite living in adjacent apartments for over seven years.

At Narine's side was a handsome man with unkempt, brown hair and a stubble-covered jaw, dressed in dark clothing. His gaze climbed Priella's body, lingering at the deep neckline of her dress before rising to her face.

He arched a brow and leaned into Narine, muttering, "Your description of the queen was more than a bit understated."

Narine elbowed him and whispered, "Behave yourself." She stepped closer to Priella, staring into her eyes. "Is it really you?"

"Yes." Priella looked away. "It is an illusion, enabling me to present myself as I wish others to see me."

"You are beautiful," Narine said. "However, I always thought you were prettier than you saw yourself."

Priella looked at her. "That is...kind of you to say."

"Hi, Priella," a voice came from the side of the room.

She turned to find a woman made of metal, eyes shimmering like mercury. Beside her was a short, stout warrior with a thick, black beard, a massive hammer in his hand.

"In case you don't recognize her..." Narine smiled, "you may recall my bodyguard, Adyn."

Priella blinked. "Adyn?" She looked at the woman's arms, charcoal in color and made of banded metal. "What happened to you?"

"If you have not noticed, the world has gone mad." Adyn grinned. "So, I decided to join the madness."

"I...see."

Narine continued. "The warrior beside Adyn is named Hadnoddon. He is a dwarven protector from Kelmar." She put a hand on the shoulder of the man beside her. "And this is Jace, better known as Jerrell Landish. He might be a thief and a scoundrel..." Removing her hand, she slipped it beneath his arm and pulled him against her, "but he is special to me and among the best men I have ever known."

Priella arched a brow. *The princess cares for this thief.* The realization brought thoughts of Kollin to mind. Narine and Kollin had a brief relationship years earlier, and a piece of Priella had dreaded Narine coming to Balmor for fear of losing him to her. *If she is with the thief, perhaps I have nothing to worry about.*

The door opened, Brogan and Blythe entering, Tygalas, Filk, and Lythagon steps behind them.

"Narine!" Blythe said as she rushed across the room and hugged the princess.

Brogan grunted. "The conniving thief has returned."

"Yes," Jace said. "It turns out I have a soft spot for surly old warriors."

The two men grinned and met each other with an embrace, both beating the other on the back, Jace grunting from the force of Brogan's blows.

Blythe turned to Adyn, eyes filled with concern. "Narine told me what happened, but I... Are you all right?"

"I am fine. In fact, I am better than ever. I chose my path and have decided to embrace it."

Filk and Lythagon each gripped one of Hadnoddon's forearms, the three dwarfs grinning broadly. Tygalas was introduced to the newcomers, stories and hugs continuing while Priella's patience waned. The door opened again, Kollin walking into the room.

His steps faltered as he blinked. "Narine?"

"Hello again, Kollin," Narine said. "I'm glad to see you are well."

Priella took Kollin by the arm and pulled him close. "He is better than ever, the malady you gave him now fully healed."

Narine arched a brow. "Truly?"

Kollin fidgeted. "Yes. I... Let us forget the past, Narine."

"I would like that. Besides, I fear the near future leaves little room for grudges or personal agendas."

The desk suddenly slid aside, forcing Odama to scramble out of the way, the newcomers taking a step back, brows furrowed. An old man in black robes appeared from the hidden, dark stairwell.

"Well said, Princess," Vanda said. His gaze swept the room. "I see all are present, save for the acrobat and the stone-shaper."

Blythe responded, "Rhoa woke this morning, but she is weak. She ate well and drank a lot of water but is resting."

Narine put a hand to her chest. "Thank the gods she is all right."

"What of the dwarf?" Vanda asked.

Brogan shook his head. "The little runt is stubborn. He refuses to leave Rhoa's side until she is fully recovered."

The old man nodded. "Very well. We will proceed without them. The roles they play do not resume quite yet anyway."

"Who are you?" Jace asked.

"My name is Solomon Vanda. I had acted as Jakarci's advisor for over three decades before his death. More importantly, I am here to guide you toward the final battle."

The thief snorted. "Are you some sort of Seer or something?"

"Or something." Vanda smiled. "I have gone by many titles. Of most import right now, I am a sorcerer. Some might say the most accomplished sorcerer in the world."

Jace looked at Narine, his eyes narrowed as he turned back toward Vanda. "Have you heard of the Order of Sol?"

"Heard of it?" Vanda laughed. "My ancestor founded the Order two thousand years ago."

18

THE GAUNTLET

The scent of spiced meat filled the air, Jace digging into his meal with gusto. He and his companions sat at a long table, Queen Priella at one end, the mysterious sorcerer at the other. Once the servants left the room, Vanda rose to his feet. The man withdrew a stick of charcoal from his pocket, squatted, and began drawing a line on the tiles while shuffling around the table, everyone watching with furrowed brows. Once he returned to where he started, he crafted a symbol, connecting both ends of the line to it. He then produced a vial and tipped it over his open hand, red liquid dripping into his palm.

Blood, Jace thought as Vanda rubbed his hands together. *He means to cast some sort of spell.*

The man closed his eyes and muttered beneath his breath while holding his blood-covered hands just above the symbol. Light flashed from his palms. He stood and wiped them clean, setting the blood-stained cloth onto the table.

"That should do it." Vanda's voice sounded oddly deadened, the room lacking any sense of echo. "It will surely drive the spies on duty crazy." He grinned. "For that reason alone, it is worth the effort."

Priella sighed. "What is this about, Vanda? We have little time."

"Yes. Of course." The man stroked his short beard. "By now, you have a sense of why you are here. To ensure you have a full grasp of what we face, I will explain it once again."

While Jace ate, he watched the man closely. Since the moment the sorcerer had appeared from the secret passage in Odama's office, Jace felt as if he had met him somewhere before. His appearance, voice, mannerisms all tickled at memories just beyond his recollection. The man droned on while Jace watched, his mind elsewhere. All the while, he stuffed food into his mouth – spiced meats, blended beans, steamed vegetables, triangles of flat bread – then washed it down with water, wishing it were wine or ale.

When he could eat no more, he took another drink and leaned toward Narine, whispering, "This is the best meal I have had in weeks."

"Hush." Narine shooed him away, focused on the man standing at the head of the table.

Jace sat back, his hand on his stomach as he refocused on Vanda, the old man repeating the same dire warnings issued by Chandan and Astra. Jace needed no further information to understand they faced a terrifying force. After seeing Anker overrun by darkspawn, the cities of Prianza, Pri, and Denalla deserted, he had a tangible sense of the enemy, reminding him of a locust infestation five years earlier. The swarm of insects had run across Farrowen, destroying crop after crop, leaving empty, shredded fields in its wake...until Malvorian rode out one morning to meet the advancing swarm. The wizard lord incinerated the locusts in moments. An entire vineyard had been lost in the process, but nobody ever spoke of it, instead focusing on how Farrowen's vaunted leader had saved the nation. This time, the swarm consisted of darkspawn led by a creature of Netherplane magic, the fate of the entire world at risk.

Jace shook his head. *I am just a thief. How did I ever get caught up in this craziness? I am no hero. Someone else should be doing this.* His gaze shifted to Narine. While her beauty had drawn him in, her spirit, inner strength, and kind nature had captured his heart. *She will not abandon this fight, and I cannot abandon her.* Sighing inwardly, he resigned himself to staying until the end... whatever end that might be.

He was not alone, for Adyn, Hadnoddon, Filk, Lythagon, Brogan, Blythe, and the elf, Tygalas, were to join the fight, along with Priella and Kollin Mor. Jace was still curious as to why the younger Mor had left Tiamalyn and was at Priella's side.

Dismissing his musings, he returned his attention to Vanda.

"–and while our armies frantically prepare to meet this horde of monsters, a smaller force attempts to slow their advance." The man leaned forward, fists resting on the table, gaze intense. "If this demon lord reaches Balmor before we are ready, none of it will matter."

Priella spoke from her seat at the head of the table, opposite from where the sorcerer stood. "I hold two wizardoms, but how can I claim the others in time? You said I needed to wait for Narine to arrive." She looked toward Narine. "Well, she is here. Now what do I do?"

"You must run the gauntlet."

Brogan frowned. "The gauntlet?"

"Yes. You must travel to the capital of each wizardom, claim the tower located there, and return here in time for Devotion tomorrow evening." Vanda shook his head. "If you do not, Balmor will fall. Each life captured feeds the demon lord, the lives of wizards fueling him most of all. Should you face him and fail, he will become unstoppable."

"How can we travel to six different wizardoms in a single day?" Priella asked, aghast.

Rather than reply, Vanda arched a brow at Narine.

Taking the hint, she turned to Priella. "The eighth construct."

She frowned. "Eighth? They only teach six."

Narine smiled. "It sounds like you've already discovered the seventh – augmentation."

The queen nodded. "Yes. And the eighth?"

"It involves the bending of space. It can be used to contact someone a great distance away."

Priella looked at Vanda.

The old man nodded. "Yes. The construct I shared with you is spatial transmission."

"Another application," Narine continued, "is spatial transference. With it, I can open a gateway to any location I have previously visited, provided I can accurately picture it in my mind. Since I have spent so much of my life perfecting illusion, my brain is well-trained to capture and retain such images."

Priella shook her head. "If true, such an ability opens the door to many things."

"Yes, which is why Barsequa kept the knowledge of it hidden from the world," Narine explained. "The power wizard lords possess helps maintain a balance only because they are also bound to the capital of their wizardom. If one were able to open a portal and transport themselves anywhere in the world, the ambitious might seek to expand his or her reign."

Jace snorted. "Isn't that what we face today? It began with Malvorian, then Thurvin."

"Regardless..." Narine gave him a telling glare, "we have this ability. With it, we can expeditiously take the other towers."

"You have been to each of these capitals?" Priella asked.

Narine nodded. "Yes."

Vanda stood upright, his gaze on Narine. "I pray you now feel rested. Tonight may be our last before the darkspawn arrive. Once Priella has taken Devotion, you are to depart." His gaze swept the table. "All of you. I will also send a contingency of Black Wasps to assist should you run into any resistance. Speed is of the utmost importance, stealth preferred over force. Take each tower, and when you are finished, return here.

"The demon lord, and your destiny, await."

Rindle woke to the afternoon sun shining upon his face, warming him. He sat up and blinked, long strands of dead grass clinging to his coat, a leaf stuck in his hair. The tree he lay beneath had given him shade earlier in the day, but as the sun traveled across the sky, his shade had abandoned him. *I hope I'm not sunburned.* It was a rare thing for a city thief to sleep in the wilderness. Even more rare to do so during the day.

He stood and dusted himself off, turning toward the voices in the distance and spotting Garvin, fifty soldiers circled around him. Walking down the hillside, Rindle headed toward them, Garvin's voice turning from a muted mutter to something intelligible.

"–and when you light them, get on your horses and ride. You need to clear the pass before the horde reaches it, or you will be trapped on this side with them." Garvin's intense gaze scanned their weary faces.

The soldiers turned and headed downhill, toward the grazing horses occupying a meadow along the road.

Rindle walked toward Garvin, smacking his dry mouth. *I bet my breath is horrendous. I need water.*

The man turned toward him. "Do you feel rested?"

"Why didn't you wake me?"

Garvin shrugged. "It might be another long night, yours longest of all. I figured you could use the sleep."

Rindle looked down the road below, where the barricade they had started building in the morning now stood ten feet high and spanned the road.

"How long will this slow the darkspawn?"

"Depends on how well the fire spreads. The barricade was doused with naphtha, so I'm confident it will burn well. The surrounding trees, well… We'll see. We are out of accelerant, but my men will do their best to make it ignite."

"Then what?"

Garvin turned toward him. "Then they race up to the pass."

"What about me?"

"You race there even faster." He turned toward the horses. "Walk with me."

Rindle followed Garvin down the hillside. When they reached the meadow, he spotted a series of mounds covered by freshly churned earth. *Graves.* He wondered how many had died during the skirmish with the darkspawn. Never before had Rindle been so frightened, and that was before he saw the demon lord. A shiver ran down his spine. *I hope to never see that thing again.*

Garvin noticed him staring at the graves. "We lost five more during the day today." The man walked up to a black stallion and began rifling through the saddlebag, withdrawing a rolled map. "At least I have a mount of my own now." He climbed into the saddle.

"Where are you going?" Rindle asked.

"I need to check on the progress Valgo and his men have made. If the darkspawn make it past the fire tonight, we must stop them in the pass in order to buy one more day." Garvin looked north. The darkspawn army was in that direction, somewhere between them and Straemor. "Nightfall is approaching. I suggest you ride back to the bridge we took out this morning and wait."

Rindle climbed into the saddle and turned his mare toward Garvin, considering the plan the man had hatched. "How many of us are left?"

"Just over two hundred," Garvin said somberly.

"That's all who remain after what happened at Straemor?"

"Yes."

Rindle recalled the wild nature of the battle – swarming goblins, diving wyverns, the terrifying black creature of darkness…and Garvin riding the wind.

He looked at the man. "What's it like?"

Garvin arched a brow. "It?"

"Yeah. Flying and controlling the wind. What's it like?"

The man sighed. "It is both thrilling and frightening. One moment, I feel like I can do anything; the next, I lose control and am on the brink of disaster."

"And that…tornado?"

"Inspired by Thurvin's display a few nights back. In truth, I had only a mild grasp on how to make it work." He sighed. "When it did, it was far more powerful than I had imagined."

Rindle shook his head. "I can't be sure, because I had just crawled out of the river, but I may have wet myself when the storm appeared. I thought the demon had created it and we were doomed."

The commander grunted. "I killed many of our own men in the process."

He gave Garvin a sidelong glance and saw him staring straight ahead, eyes haunted. "Had you not done something drastic, we *all* would have died. You may have killed some of our own, but you destroyed a few wyverns and hundreds, if not thousands, of darkspawn." After a moment of silence, he added softly, "It was the right thing to do."

Garvin sighed. "I keep trying to convince myself of that, but I can't stop wondering if there had been a better way." He lifted his hand, clenching it, staring at his fist. "If I had more time to train with these abilities, perhaps I could have done better."

"Aren't you the one who says *'The most noble thing a soldier can do is die to save the lives of others'*?"

No response.

Rindle frowned. "Regardless, we cannot change the past. We can only strive toward a better future. If that thing…that demon wins, what will become of us?"

Garvin looked at him. "You have a point. Vanda was correct about Thurvin, and he was spot-on about this demon. If he is right about Priella's ability to stop the creature, we must give her the time she needs to prepare."

Inwardly, Rindle sighed, relieved to have his friend once again focused on the mission.

Garvin turned his horse toward the road. "I pray I will see you later. May the gods be with you, Rindle."

"And with you, Commander."

Kicking his horse into a trot, the man turned to follow the road into the mountains. In moments, he was gone. Rindle sighed and nudged his horse into motion.

Guiding the mare to the gravel, he rode down the gentle slope until he reached the barricade. It was taller than his head and ran into the woods a few feet on either side, forcing him to ride through the trees to circumvent it. A dozen soldiers stood on the other side of the wall, watching as he rode past. Others were visible in the woods on either side of the road. Some nodded at him, many just watching him pass by. He continued down the road, his horse moving at an easy walk.

The tops of the trees were still lit by sun, the trunks and road covered in shadow. Other than the clopping of hooves and the rustling of the wind-stirred branches, it was quiet.

A few minutes later, the ravine came into view. He continued toward it, recalling the morning efforts to dismantle the structure that had spanned the gap.

The bridge had been made of thick beams covered by flat boards, the beams having been burned after Garvin's crew had finished stripping the boards off of them. Those same boards had then been used to build a barricade half a mile beyond the ravine. Rindle stopped his horse a stride from the edge and peered past what remained of the charred beams.

The ravine was small, no more than twenty feet across and of a similar depth. Amid twisting lines of gravel, rocks and boulders lay at the bottom, the steep hillsides covered in weeds and scrub. Without a doubt, it was the least of the hurdles placed before the army of monsters. Yet it served a purpose – slow the darkspawn advance, even if for just a few moments. If any died in the process, all the better.

Turning his mount, Rindle rode fifty feet from the ravine and stopped to wait. His gaze went to the sky, the sun nearing the horizon. *I pray you know what you are doing, Garvin. Today is not the day I wish to die.*

The sun had touched the horizon by the time the ground leveled, and Garvin entered the narrowest point of the mountain road leading to Balmor. A high cliff stood on one side, a tree-covered slope rising to a mountain peak on the other. The road ran along the cliff before turning and descending the south side of the pass. In a distant clearing ahead, clusters of horses grazed lazily.

Garvin surveyed the area as he drew closer, a valley waiting below the peak to his right, the road following a bend around the cliffside. A rivulet ran down the cliff and across the road, a small, wooden bridge spanning the gap. Just beyond the bridge, he guided his horse into the meadow to join the others.

Garvin dismounted as Sergeant Valgo appeared from the other side of the road.

"Ho! Commander!" Valgo blared as he approached. "It's good to see you. Is all well at the foot of the mountain?"

"Well enough, all things considered. How are your efforts progressing here?"

"As you said, there were a number of boulders above that appeared likely candidates. We found some stout trees and created two dozen levers. The last of them is being carried up the hillside now."

Garvin peered up and saw men climbing the steep slope adjacent to the cliff while carrying a fifteen-foot-long pole.

"What about the other peak?"

The man shook his head. "No boulders. Even if there were, the trees are too big and too numerous. They would only get in the way."

Garvin stared toward the tree-covered mountainside and nodded. "All right. We will work with what we have." He turned to Valgo. "Do the men understand that this might be our last fight?"

The man peered up the hillside. "They saw what we faced last night.

There is no running from that. At least not for long." He looked at Garvin. "These soldiers realize they would already be dead if not for you, Commander. If Queen Priella can truly stop this…creature, we must give her time to prepare."

As a life-long soldier, Garvin had always known a time might come where he must sacrifice himself to save innocents. These men understood that. They would do what they must and wish for the best. However, Garvin feared the worst.

19

ROADBLOCKS

Following Adyn down the palace corridor, Jace stopped Narine just inside the door leading to the Arboretum. The bodyguard stepped outside, pausing to look back while holding the door open.

Jace said, "You two go on. I want just a moment alone with Narine."

Hadnoddon slipped past, the door closing to leave the couple alone in the palace corridor.

Narine peered into his eyes. "What's wrong?"

"What's wrong?" His tone was incredulous. "*Everything* is wrong. The world has gone mad and little makes sense."

Her voice softened. "Jace–"

He put his finger to her lips. "Despite what I fear lies ahead, I am happy you came into my life. I would rather face the end of the world with you at my side than continue as I was – no one to care about, nobody who loved me, nothing to believe in except myself. I pretended I was happy...and maybe I was at times. Since I met you, I discovered another side of life and found a part of myself I had denied for too long."

A tear tracked down her face. "Why are you telling me this?"

He took her hand and held it to his chest. "If something happens to one of us...I just want you to know I love you."

She smiled and leaned in, her hand cupping his cheek as they kissed, her soft, warm lips lingering before she pulled away. "I already know that, silly."

"Well... I needed to say it."

"I love you, too, Jerrell Landish." She squeezed his hand. "Now, let's capture some towers."

"I am with you." Still holding her hand, he pushed the door open.

They followed a shadow-covered path, the ice-blue flame from the tower visible through the branches overhead. As the path opened to the plaza surrounding the tower, the flames dulled, the beams of light in the sky fading.

Clustered below the tower, people waited, dressed for battle – Brogan, Hadnoddon, Lythagon, and Filk in full armor, Blythe with a glowing, golden bow, Tygalas with a staff of golden wood, Kollin Mor in black robes, Adyn and a dozen Black Wasps in leathers, the Wasps' faces shrouded, thin, short swords at their hips. Other than the blades themselves, yellow triangles on their shoulders were the only elements not black.

Priella floated down from the tower, her dress fluttering in the breeze as she landed. "My power is recharged. I am ready."

Vanda approached from across the plaza, trailing guards carrying a palanquin of sorts. Rather than a framed chamber covered by curtains, a throne made of clear crystal rested upon a platform, six men to each side carrying it by a thick pole resting on their shoulders.

"What is this?" Priella asked.

Vanda turned and held up a hand, the soldiers stopping. "This is Thurvin's throne. Without it, you cannot claim the tower in Marquithe. Only with the throne back in place can you reignite the flame."

The man withdrew a gem from his robes, Jace ogling it while releasing a whistle. The sapphire was as big as his fist. "That must be worth a fortune."

Vanda arched a brow. "In truth, it is worth a wizardom." He extended his hand toward Priella. "Here is your first gem, taken directly from Thurvin's throne."

As she took the sapphire, Jace kept his gaze on Vanda, brow furrowed. Then he clapped his hands together in recognition. "I've got it! You called yourself Brenshaw!"

Brogan frowned. "Brenshaw? The man who tried to double-cross you back in Fastella seven years ago?"

Jace nodded. "Yes. I am sure of it."

Vanda chuckled. "Very good, my young thief."

"You had me search for the amulet."

"I did, all the while knowing you would one day reclaim it from the Enchanters." Vanda arched a brow. "Has it not been useful?"

Jace ignored the question. "You are working for the Order, aren't you?"

"I told you, my ancestor founded the Order. Regardless of my involvement, their agenda aligns with mine. Assuming we survive the challenge before us, we can approach this conversation at another time." He gestured toward Narine. "I pray you are well-rested, Princess. Please, craft a gateway to the palace in Marquithe. It must be large enough for the soldiers and the throne to pass through."

Jaw set in determination, Narine nodded and extended her hand toward the open plaza beside them. The hair on Jace's arms stood on end as she embraced her magic. He pulled the amulet over his head and slipped it into his coat pocket.

A gateway opened to reveal a familiar throne room. It was dark, nobody visible. The gateway started at six feet in diameter and slowly widened. Adyn leapt through, followed by the Black Wasps, all searching their surroundings as they spread out in the room.

The guards carrying the throne approached the gateway, slowing before they stepped through, the top of the shimmering doorway mere inches above the throne. The soldiers and palanquin continued toward the dais at the fore. Weapons ready, Brogan, Blythe, Tygalas, and the dwarfs followed. Priella nodded to Narine and stepped through, Kollin at her side. Apparently satisfied, Vanda spun and walked away, leaving Jace and Narine alone.

Jace shook his head. "It's ironic to return to Marquithe like this." He looked at Narine. "Is there any chance we can swing by my apartment while we are there? I had often dreamt of bringing a woman of your beauty home with me."

She tilted her head and gave him a flat look. "I have *been* to your apartment."

He grinned. "Yes, but you were clothed, so it doesn't count."

She laughed. "Just go, so I can close this doorway."

Stepping through, he glanced around the quiet throne room. With Thurvin dead, he wondered who, if anyone, ruled in Marquithe. He turned back toward the gateway and extended a hand. Narine took it and stepped to his side. The eight guards, having set down the palanquin, returned through the gateway, back to Balmor Palace. Narine lowered her hands, and the portal winked out of existence.

~

The night was silent, the full moon casting long shadows across the road. Darkness lurked in the surrounding trees, rustling leaves whispering softly, conjuring thoughts of evil spirits.

Rindle remained in his saddle, his horse sleeping beneath him. His own legs had fallen asleep, as well. Numerous times, he had considered climbing down and walking to get his blood flowing, but fear held him still. *I am a city thief,* he told himself. *Why am I out here in the forest? I know nothing of woodcraft or the creatures that lurk in the wilderness.* Oddly, conversations within his head helped keep him grounded, preventing him from turning his horse and riding off as fast and as far as he could.

A distant cry arose, a chill racing down his back. *Was that a wyvern?* He imagined a wraith appearing from the shadows, come to claim his heart. Such creatures were once the subjects of stories that made Rindle scoff. Now, after everything he'd seen, he feared the truth was more frightening than the myth.

A distant rumble carried through the forest, joined by the hoots of goblins, the noise growing louder, Rindle's heart beating faster. He had prayed the monsters would not appear. Not tonight, not ever. *No such luck,* he thought as he nudged his horse. It stirred, Rindle patting the steed's neck as it woke.

He leaned forward and said, "Get ready. You must run fast."

When he pulled on the reins, the horse turned its neck and whinnied, hooves shuffling as it spun away from the ravine. Rindle watched over his shoulder as the noise grew louder, his heart racing, the horse shuffling nervously.

Shadowy, lanky forms came around the bend a few hundred feet from the ravine. When the goblins spotted him, their hoots became frantic, arms flailing, weapons flashing as they rushed forward. In a blink, hundreds of monsters sprinted toward him. He knew far more followed.

Noticing the ravine, the goblins in front slowed, but those behind crashed into them, the momentum of the steady stream of monsters forcing those in the vanguard forward. Shrieks arose as they tumbled out of sight, the sound of bones snapping rising above the din.

Rindle kicked and whooped, swatting his horse on the rump as the mare burst into a gallop.

Trees sped past on both sides, the gravel road a pale ribbon in the moonlit night. He rounded a bend, raced down a straight section, and rounded another bend, the barricade coming into view.

"Attack!" he blared as he slowed his horse. "Light the fires! The darkspawn are here!"

He reached the barricade, hopped off his horse, and grasped the reins. Moving as quickly as he dared, he slipped between two trees and emerged at the back of the barricade. In the dark forest, the sparks of flints arose again and again, small fires starting in the kindling beneath dead trees.

"*Dead trees burn fastest,*" Garvin had instructed. "*Once the dry wood catches fire, it will spread.*"

Rindle knew nothing of such things, but he trusted the man.

Ten archers stood on a platform at the back of the barricade, bows ready, arrows nocked. Two soldiers with lit torches stood a few feet behind the structure, waiting.

Rindle continued two hundred feet beyond the barricade, then climbed back onto his horse. From the saddle, he waited as the rumble of the approaching darkspawn grew louder and louder. The horde rounded the bend as the fires in the woods took hold, the soldiers furiously stoking the flames. The archers behind the barricade loosed, arrows striking monsters, which then fell in flailing heaps to be trampled by their brethren. Again and again, the archers loosed, killing monsters at the fore of the army, but others soon replaced them, the goblins rushing forward with wild abandon.

"Run!" Rindle screamed.

At the same time, Sergeant Ferring cried out, "Retreat!"

The archers jumped down and ran, the two men with torches rushing in and lighting the barricade. Doused with the last of their naphtha, the boards ignited with a roar, the flames spreading quickly. From the woods, soldiers emerged at a run, joining the fleeing archers.

Rindle turned his horse and kicked it into motion, racing past the meadow of waiting horses as the first soldiers reached them and began to mount up. Once clear of the area, he slowed his horse and looked back. The barricade burned mightily, fires flickering through the trees. Goblin shrieks came from the road beyond the barricade.

A cry echoed in the night, a dark shape emerging in the sky over the forest. The wyvern dove toward the barricade, a silhouette on its back. *The demon lord.* Rindle's fear resurfaced as he froze, even as other soldiers rode past him in flight.

The wyvern fluttered its wings to land between Rindle and the barricade. The demon lord's back to Rindle, it lifted its hands and extended them toward the fire, a purple glow appearing and reaching toward the barricade. A vortex of magic coalesced, sucking the flames into it, a swirling inferno that raged toward the demon. Rather than burning the creature, the flames appeared to feed it. When the barricade no longer burned, the demon turned toward the forest and began absorbing those flames, as well. All the while, a low, gravely laughter came from the creature. Sure of it this time, Rindle wet himself.

A hand gripped his wrist, startling him.

"You need to ride, soldier!" Ferring shouted, the man quickly riding off.

Rindle nodded. He turned his horse and kicked it into a gallop, racing away from the nightmare.

Garvin stood on an outcrop of rock at the north edge of the pass. The full moon illuminated the land below, the forest in shadow, the fires his men had lit already snuffed out. He had hoped the flames would slow the darkspawn advance, but they had burned only a few minutes before fading to black. Anxiety twisted his gut as he battled doubts and fear. *We don't know anything about the magic the demon wields.* The creature had already proven it was near impossible to kill. All he could do was try to slow the horde's advance.

Minutes passed, distant noises coming from the night. Horses soon appeared on the road below, dust stirring as they raced up the hillside. As the last horse drew near, Garvin recognized the rider. He scrambled down the rocks and ran through the brush to intercept him.

He burst out onto the road, waving his arms to catch Rindle's attention, but the thief was looking over his shoulder.

"Stop!" Garvin bellowed.

Rindle turned and pulled on the reins, his horse slowing as he passed by.

Garvin ran up to Rindle's horse and grasped the reins, drawing it to the side of the road. "What happened?"

The thief looked over his shoulder again, eyes frantic. "The darkspawn showed. We lit the fires just as you planned, but the demon... I-I think it consumed the flames."

Garvin scowled. "Consumed?"

"Yeah. It seemed to absorb the flames into itself. I fear we made it even stronger."

As the noise of the other riders drifted away, Garvin asked, "What about the darkspawn?"

"They will be here soon." Rindle shook his head. "The demon is riding one of those wyverns again. I think we made it angry last night and it now wants to crush us."

Garvin nodded. "I don't doubt it. Go on. Don't stop until you reach the meadow where the other horses are waiting." He gave Rindle an intense glare. "Remember, you are now a scout. Not a thief. Not a soldier. When all is lost, you must ride. Stop for nothing. Your personal battle is against your own exhaustion. Regardless of the cost, you must reach Balmor and inform Priella of what has occurred here. The fate of the world may rest in your hands."

"What about you?"

"I intend to use the gift Priella gave me and will do so until I have nothing left to give."

Garvin swatted the backside of Rindle's mare, the animal jumping into a gallop, and backed from the road as the horse faded into the night. He walked through the brush and climbed back up the rocks to wait for the enemy. The wait was not long.

Just a few minutes after Rindle and his horse faded into the pass, a giant, winged beast appeared in the sky. He spotted another, then a dozen more, the monsters flying in slow, twisting loops, gradually advancing toward his position.

They hover over the front of the horde, protecting it. At least it gives me a sense of their location.

Hoots and cries arose in the night, the fore of the goblin army appearing on the road below. It was like watching a swarm of angry roaches racing toward the trap he had laid.

Garvin drew upon his magic, crafting a platform of solidified air beneath his feet and lifting himself upon a zephyr. He fed the magic, rising higher and higher as the winged beasts drew nearer. One spotted him and released a high-pitched cry, the others shrieking in response. Five wyverns angled toward him, the dark silhouette of the demon upon the middle creature.

Calling upon the west wind, it struck and launched Garvin eastward just as a beam of purple magic blasted from the demon. The magic struck a copse of trees upon the hillside. They glowed briefly and disappeared. By then, Garvin was a mile away and dropping as he lost momentum. He lifted both hands, and a mighty gust launched him upward. From the elevated view, he watched as the flying creatures altered direction to give chase.

Rindle stopped in the meadow just beyond the pass, his horse huffing and snorting from the exertion of the climb. He hopped off and led the mare to the creek where other soldiers waited with their own mounts. Nobody said a word, the whites of their eyes visible in the moonlight. The ten remaining archers gathered near the bridge and waited.

A few minutes later, the darkspawn army appeared, the archers drawing arrows. The goblins spotted them, hoots and cries rising as the horde rushed down the road. In moments, a thousand monsters filled the pass. The archers loosed, arrows taking the monsters in the lead, but the horde did not slow.

Rindle's gaze went toward the top of the cliff high above the pass, seeing men working frantically. One boulder twice the size of a horse broke loose and tumbled down, smashing into smaller rocks. Another, even more massive boulder tipped and fell to a lower ledge with a tremendous crack. The shelf slid off, the landslide crashing upon the horde, burying hundreds of goblins in seconds.

Some monsters made it past before the rocks struck, the archers firing again and again, but there were too many. Even as additional boulders fell and buried more goblins in the heart of the pass, Rindle realized they would have to fight.

"To arms!" the soldier beside him cried as he drew his sword and raced toward the road.

Rindle drew his rapier and joined his fellow soldiers as they rushed to the bridge. The humans and darkspawn clashed, blades flashing, metal clanging, monsters and men dying in a furious fight for their lives.

A blast of demon magic shot toward Garvin, who called upon a gust of wind, altering his course. The purple beam struck a mountainside in a shimmer, leaving a massive crater, rock and debris from above tumbling down in a landslide.

He was tiring, the constant use of magic like fighting a battle and driven by adrenaline…until muscles felt thick and weapons grew heavy. Through force of will, he lifted himself higher, the pursuing wyverns following. He then flew southwest, toward the gap between peaks where his soldiers were positioned.

The darkspawn must be inside the pass by now, the trap sprung.

As the peaks drew nearer, he scanned the forest below in search of the road. It appeared through a gap in the trees, thousands upon thousands of goblins flowing southward. He banked, flying lower, speeding toward the narrow point in the pass.

A massive landslide covered the road, goblins climbing over it, more scrambling around on the tree-covered hillside of the opposing peak. Just beyond the debris, his soldiers fought goblins, holding the bridge over the creek – the last chokepoint. Bodies lay on both sides of the bridge, men and darkspawn alike. It was merely a matter of time before the monsters over-whelmed them.

Garvin banked west, turning toward the peak opposite the cliff. He slowed over the trees and gathered his magic, drawing as much of the west wind as he could until his head felt dizzy from the pressure. He then released it in a gush, driving the wind down the mountainside. When it struck the nearest trees, they toppled with a staccato of mighty cracks, many uprooted. The devastating blast continued down the hillside, felling every tree in its path. In seconds, hundreds of trees lay flat, the momentum driving the pile into the landslide, smashing into the rocks and forming a dam thirty feet high.

Panting from the exertion, Garvin suddenly lost hold of his magic and plummeted toward the mountainside. He tried to call upon a breeze or craft something from air to save himself, but it was like trying to grip a fistful of fine sand, the grains slipping through his fingers. Just before he struck, an upstream of air swooped in, altering his course and sending him tumbling down the hillside. He got a foot down and tripped, rolling and coming to a sudden stop when he landed in a crater left by an uprooted tree. The collision was violent, abrupt, excruciating pain radiating from his shoulder and back. Gasping for air, each breath feeling like knives through his chest, he lay still, body broken and unable to move.

A dark shadow descended from the sky, a wyvern landing twenty feet away. A creature as black as night leapt off and landed with a thud. It walked toward him slowly, soil crunching beneath clawed feet, yellow eyes glowing beneath a head of spikes, fangs jutting up and over its upper lip. The creature grinned.

"Puny human. You thought to test your pathetic magic against H'Deesengar?" The creature leaned down and reached for Garvin, talons tearing through his chainmail cuirass and into his skin. With ease, the demon lord lifted him off the ground and held him over his head. "This world belongs to me, human. As does your magic."

A purple glow arose from the demon, dark and malevolent. It surrounded Garvin, blotting out his surroundings. His pain increased a hundred-fold as his life force was ripped from his body. His own screams were the last thing he heard.

The fight at the bridge was intense, men dying by the dozens, darkspawn by the hundreds. Rindle took care to remain away from the fore, instead lunging between gaps of soldiers to plunge his rapier into darkspawn whenever possible. Even after the soldiers stationed on the cliffs had come down to join the fray, it became clear there was only one ending to this fight. When only fifteen soldiers remained, Rindle ran back to the mounts, took one set of reins in his hand, then climbed upon another horse.

He then spotted a wyvern on the hillside above, the demon standing before it. The monster lifted something above its head, a man hanging limply. A purple glow appeared, growing brighter and brighter, a horrific scream rising above the din. When the light faded, the man was gone. *Garvin...* Rindle knew for certain his friend was dead. A sadness washed over him, and he sobbed, briefly forgetting where he was.

The demon raised its arms high and released a roar that reverberated throughout the pass. Terror rose. Forgetting the pain of his loss, Rindle turned his mount, tugging on the reins of the other, and kicked his horse into motion.

Rindle and the trailing horse galloped onto the gravel and headed deeper into the mountains. As Garvin had instructed, he would ride one horse for an hour, then switch mounts, the man's final command echoing in his head.

"When all is lost, you must ride. Stop for nothing. Your personal battle is against your own exhaustion. Regardless of the cost, you must reach Balmor and inform Priella of what has occurred here. The fate of the world may rest in your hands."

20

TWO TOWERS

The throne room was eerily quiet, giving the impression that someone or some*thing* could burst from a shadowy corner at any moment.

Brogan stood beside Blythe, his gaze sweeping their surroundings, while Priella used her magic to alter the nature of the gem in her hand, the dark blue shifting to aquamarine. She then climbed onto the makeshift palanquin and sat in the crystal throne. Priella narrowed her eyes and twisted her wrist. The throne rose into the air, floated across the room, and disappeared up the shaft above the lift. With her gone, the Black Wasps spread out, stalking the perimeter of the room, while the others stood before a dais occupied by an ornate wooden throne with blue fabric on the seat and back.

The room fell quiet again, the silence making Brogan uncomfortable. He fidgeted, trying his best to endure it.

"Now what?" he muttered. "Is this all we do? Step through a doorway and wait while she flies around and changes gems from one color to another?"

"It *does* seem slightly anticlimactic," Blythe admitted.

Jace snorted. "After what we have been through, something going according to plan would be a novelty." He looked at Brogan. "I realize you want to break some heads, but our quest involves your queen claiming these towers. Isn't that the goal?"

Tygalas nodded. "The thief has a point."

Jace's face took on a hurt expression. "Thief? You don't even know me."

The elf glanced toward Brogan. "You told me he was a thief and not to be trusted."

Brogan rolled his eyes. "You can't say that kind of thing right in front of him, Tygalas."

"Why not?"

Jace tilted his head, arms crossed, and narrowed his eyes at Brogan. "Yes. Tell him why you would rather say bad things about me to others and not to my face."

"I…" Brogan looked at Blythe.

She shook her head. "Oh no. This is your doing. You need to make it right."

Jace gestured toward Brogan's feet. "Do you know I almost died right where you are standing?"

Brogan arched a dubious brow.

"He's telling the truth," Adyn said. "A guard ran him through from behind moments after he saved our arses from Thurvin and Malvorian. Without his heroics, we wouldn't be here today."

Brogan rolled his eyes. "Look. I never said he wasn't brave or useful–"

"Just not worth trusting?" Narine asked.

His companions glaring at him, Brogan scowled. "Fine. He has earned our trust…with most things. He has certainly proven he will do the right thing when it matters most."

Narine arched a brow. "Is that the extent of your apology?"

Brogan growled. "Listen–"

Jace put a hand against Brogan's chest. "It's all right. Forget about it, big guy. In truth, such things don't really bother me. I was just giving you a hard time."

"A hard time?"

Jace shrugged. "Well, I couldn't really let you get away with such under-handedness, could I? Normally, I would underhand you right back, but we are pressed for time and there may never be another opportunity." He looked toward the lift shaft as Priella floated down to land lightly on the dais. "Something tells me we will run into trouble before the night is through."

The queen walked toward them, Kollin meeting her. She nodded to him. "It is done."

He glanced toward the lift. "The tower burns with the flame of Pallan?"

"It does."

"So the prayers of Marquithe now feed your magic?" Brogan asked.

"They will when I next hold Devotion."

His brow furrowed. "Yes. Of course." He bit his tongue, upset with himself for asking his queen something so stupid. *You are a warrior. Keep your blade ready and tongue sheathed.*

With silent footsteps, the Black Wasps converged from all directions to settle around their new queen.

Priella turned to Narine. "Where to next?"

Narine frowned and looked at Jace. "I'm not sure…"

"I'd rather not visit Anker at night," Adyn said. "Not with darkspawn holding the city."

Jace tapped his chin in thought. "That leaves Tiamalyn, Fastella, Sarmak, and Cor Cordium." He shrugged, turning toward Narine. "Why not Fastella? You know it well enough since you grew up in the palace."

She frowned. "Those are not the fondest of memories. But I know we must return there eventually. Best to face it."

She wove her hands together and the air before her shimmered, another gateway appearing to reveal a private chamber. It was dark and empty, a moonbeam shining through the window.

As before, the Black Wasps darted through the portal and fanned out, Adyn a step behind them. Brogan climbed through with Blythe, a part of him marveling at how easy it was to travel hundreds of miles in a few steps.

He turned and saw a copper tub beside the gateway, the shimmering rim of light at the edge cutting through the lip of the tub. Beyond it was a sitting area and, finally, a bed – all empty.

Tygalas, Lythagon, Filk, Hadnoddon, Jace, and Narine came through before the portal closed, the area rapidly crowding. Brogan walked away to get some space, while Priella strode to the balcony door.

A female Wasp blocked the queen's path. "Let us open it and ensure it is safe, Your Majesty."

She arched a brow. "You are aware I hold the power of multiple wizard lords."

"Yes. Of course." The masked woman in black dipped her head. "However, our orders are to keep you safe while you save your magic for other purposes."

Priella sighed. "Very well."

A pair of Black Wasps threw open the doors while four others darted outside. In moments, one of the Wasps gestured Priella forward, Kollin at her side as they stepped into the moonlight. Once upon the balcony, she floated into the air and toward the dark, flameless tower above.

The door behind Brogan suddenly opened. He spun around, sword in hand, his view brightening dramatically from the enchantment of his blade. Guards rushed inside, purple capes swirling, four with swords, two with loaded crossbows. Everyone froze as a hulking man in armor entered, a lethal looking metal mace in hand.

Brogan's brow furrowed. He had met few men larger than himself and only two in Fastella. "Herrod?"

The big man grunted and stepped aside to reveal a petite blonde woman of middle age. She wore an elegant purple and silver gown, a smirk on her face and crown upon her head. "Brogan Reisner. Of all the people I thought might attempt to kill me, you were among the last."

"Cordelia...," Jace said before Brogan could form the word.

The woman arched a brow. "Jerrell Landish. I thought you might be gone forever after what happened with Taladain. I suppose I should not be shocked that you have survived. You always were a slippery one and had a way of twisting luck in your favor."

She looked at Narine, her smile slipping away. "You are the Killarius girl."

"*Princess*," Narine corrected firmly, her arm still locked with Jace's.

"You are with your father's assassin? Or did the man die at your hand as Eldalain proclaimed?"

Narine glanced at Jace. "I–"

The thief held his hand up, stopping her before turning to Cordelia. "You have the wrong of it, Cordelia."

"Truly? Which part?"

"All of it. I thought you were smarter than that."

Herrod lifted his mace and stepped toward Jace menacingly.

"Stop!" Cordelia's smile had melted, her face drawn in anger. "Speak, Landish. Explain why you are here."

"First, why are you in the palace? What is with the crown and the soldiers?"

"Since your last visit, I have moved up in the world." Cordelia toyed with a golden ring on her finger. "When certain people in power passed, it left vacancies longing to be filled. I now run both sides of the city."

Jace arched his brow. "You are high wizard?"

"I am…until the Darkening. The tower Farrowen stole from us now lies dormant, ready for a new wizard to claim it. In just a few weeks, I will stand before Gheald, and he will anoint me wizard lord." She lifted a fist, knuckles whitening. "We will no longer kneel to Farrowen. Eldalain failed to protect us, but he lacked the power I will soon wield."

Jace laughed, loud and hard, while Narine's face was etched with worry. Brogan shot Blythe a warning glance. She nodded and eased her bow off her shoulder.

"What is so funny?" Cordelia demanded, appearing ready to snap.

As his laughter calmed, Jace dug into his coat and pulled out the amulet. He held it up, the gold disk spinning in the moonlit room. "Do you know what this is?"

She frowned. "Should I?"

He slipped the chain over his head and tucked the amulet under his shirt. "The Eye of Obscurance is special. With it, I am protected from magic. It is what allowed me to attack Taladain and come out unscathed, although I was not the one to kill him. And no, Narine had nothing to do with his death, despite the rumors and lies."

"Why is that funny?"

"Oh, it's not. I just wanted to put the amulet back on before I told you the rest."

The woman clenched her fists, lips pressed together. "Which is?"

"You will not become wizard lord, for we have come to claim the tower in the name of Pallan."

Her eyes widened. "What?"

"Even now, Queen Priella, a *true* wizard lord, is up in the tower."

Cordelia nudged the guard at her side before gesturing toward the open balcony doors. "Go out there and check if you see someone."

The man crossed the room, warily avoiding the warriors in black. When he reached the balcony, he looked up and gasped. "The tower! It burns with an ice-blue flame!"

"*No!*" Cordelia shrieked.

Her arm lashed out, a thread of magic bursting forth. Jace leapt in front of it, the magic fizzling with a hiss. Everyone hesitated, some held by shock, others by fear, save for Herrod, who swung his mace. Jace dove aside, the weapon shattering a table in a spray of splinters. The thief rolled toward Cordelia, popped up, and twisted behind her, his arm snaking around her torso, pressing his dagger against her neck.

"Nobody move!" Jace stared at Herrod. "Fight and she dies."

Kollin came in from the balcony, a globe of light appearing above him so bright that Brogan had to look away. "Multiple wizards and skilled warriors stand before you. I suggest you back away before you all die. As you witnessed, magic cannot harm Landish, and should anyone make a wrong move, he will kill her."

Just then, Priella floated to the balcony, red hair waving in the breeze. "What is this?" she demanded as she strode into the room.

Brogan had no ill feelings for Cordelia, or Herrod. For their sake, he intercepted Priella. "My Queen, it is nothing but a misunderstanding." He nodded toward Cordelia. "Jace and I are past acquaintances of High Wizard Cordelia–"

"Dalia," Cordelia interrupted. "It is High Wizard Dalia."

"Decided to use your real name?" Jace asked.

"I thought it...more appropriate."

Turning back to Priella, Brogan continued. "The high wizard believed she might be raised to wizard lord upon the next Darkening. Of course, she did not understand that we face the end of the world, nor does she understand our mission."

"What mission?" Cordelia asked, Jace's blade still against her neck.

"Our mission..." Priella strode toward her, "is to claim the tower of every great city."

Cordelia's jaw dropped. "You intend to hold the power of all eight gods?"

"I do, and I must. It is the only way to save the world." Priella frowned at Jace. "Let her go. She and her guards can do nothing I cannot stop with a single thought."

Jace released the wizardess and sheathed his blade. "Sorry, Cordelia. I didn't want anyone hurt, and it was the only way to stop you or anyone else from doing something stupid." He walked over to Narine's side and turned back toward the high wizard. "I hope there are no hard feelings between us. I always thought we had a...special connection, and I'd hate to lose a friend, assuming we ever see each other again."

Cordelia glared at Jace a moment longer before turning to Priella. "You have what you came for, so leave, but do not expect me to bow to you."

Priella smiled. "Oh, I could make you bow if I wished, but I prefer allies over enemies. Be well, Dalia. If I survive this ordeal, we *will* meet again."

She turned toward Narine. "We need another gateway."

"Perhaps we should visit Cor Cordium next," Jace suggested. "If you can place us in the upper portion of the city, Priella can take it before the Enchanters are aware."

"I recall the chamber where Belzacanth died."

Jace nodded. "Good enough."

Narine turned and walked to the balcony, her back to the room. A line of light stretched out, the edges shimmering, a dark room appearing beyond the widening oval. It was odd to see the moonlit balcony and the city beyond the gateway. Almost akin to staring into a window built in the middle of a tapestry.

Cordelia gasped. "How did you do that?"

Narine looked over her shoulder and smirked. "Not all constructs are taught at the University."

"You turned away to hide it from me," the wizardess said.

"I did. The world cannot learn of this ability. Not yet. Perhaps not ever."

"All right." Priella clapped her hands. "The night is passing. Time to take another tower."

The Black Wasps rushed through the gateway and spread out, followed by Adyn. Brogan turned to Blythe, who shrugged and advanced, her bow ready. He followed, pausing to glance back.

"Goodbye, Cordelia. Sorry I never said it when I left last time."

"That was seven years ago, Brogan. Sure, I was upset for a while, but time softened the anger and simply left me wondering why."

Tygalas darted past him and through the gateway, followed by the three dwarfs.

Brogan shook his head. "It was simple. I hated myself and my life. I needed a change."

"I hope you found some happiness."

He smiled. "I have…and if I survive this, I intend to make the most of it."

Turning away, he climbed through the gateway.

21

GREED

Much like taking the tower in Cor Cordium, claiming the tower in Sarmak was uneventful and allowed everyone except Priella a chance to rest in the quiet throne room. It was past midnight when the flames awoke, and she stepped to the tower's edge to peer over the sleeping city.

The breeze from the nearby sea blew her hair into her face. She drew it back with a finger and stared into the night for a moment of reflection, her first opportunity to do so since departing Balmor. Besides, she had never been to the desert wizardom before and did not know if she would ever return. Pausing a moment to look upon its capital city would have little effect on her quest.

The prayers of two wizardoms already fed her magic and left her feeling invincible. The day prior, she had accidentally cut herself while swapping the gem in the obelisk overlooking Lamor. The cut had healed instantly without her having to apply a construct. When she next took Devotion, prayers from across the known world would flow into her, raising her magic beyond imagination. The thought made her stomach flutter, partly from eager anticipation, mostly from dread as to what it might do to her. She had witnessed Thurvin unravel as his power increased. Hers would nearly triple his.

Her gaze drifted to the streets below, enchanted lanterns creating islands of light. She spotted a cluster of guards pointing up at the tower. *They wonder at the flame and why it burns something other than the red of their god.* Her actions would bring similar confusion to every city she visited, leaving each disconnected from the god worshipped by its citizens for thousands of years. *What becomes of the young gods as we disconnect them from the prayers of their people?* She wondered if even Vanda knew the answer.

Discarding her musings, she embraced her magic and leapt, arms spread as she plummeted toward the palace roof. She formed a pocket of air under her, slowing her descent. Gently, she lowered herself to a courtyard and stepped off the platform of air, striding along a shadowy walkway to the guard stationed beside the door.

"My Queen!" The man in red and black thumped his chest and opened the door. "I trust all went well."

"As expected."

He bent to one knee as she walked past. With a wave of her hand, she dismissed the spell she had placed in his mind, simultaneously erasing the memory of her passing.

She followed the dark corridor back to the receiving hall. The Black Wasps stood in an arc around the throne room door, each bowing as Priella approached.

"The tower is ours," she said. "Let us go."

They parted as she walked into the throne room, the Wasps then following. She marched toward the dais where the others waited and nodded to Narine. The wizardess turned and began to gather her magic, brow furrowed, teeth clenched, a bright glow surrounding her. Priella frowned. *She is tiring and struggles to cast the spell.* It had become more obvious with each jump, Narine's eyes drooping, shoulders slumping. She had said little since leaving Balmor.

A gateway materialized, expanding until it was no more than six feet tall and half the width, a stairwell visible through the opening.

Brogan grunted. "Is that it?"

Adyn replied, "She is too worn to make anything larger."

The bodyguard jumped through first, the Black Wasps following. Priella and the others climbed through the opening and up the short rise of stairs. She looked back as Jace stepped through and took Narine's hand. The wizardess misplaced her foot on the edge of a stair and stumbled into his arms. Just inches behind her, the portal snapped shut. Priella wondered what would happen if it closed with someone halfway through.

It would likely be a nasty way to die.

"What is this place?" Tygalas asked from the railing at the top of the stairs as he peered beyond it.

His arm around Narine, Jace led her up the stairs. "The Bowl of Oren."

Since Priella's last visit had only allowed a glimpse of the stadium exterior, she took a moment to gaze at her surroundings. After all, the building and the events held within were legendary across the Eight Wizardoms.

They stood beside a section of benches with two wooden thrones at the front, a railing between the thrones and the stadium floor. The sparring area was circular in shape and hundreds of feet in diameter, the surrounding seats covered in shadow, except for the western side, lit by the full moon, a portion of the light shining down upon the dirt field below. All was quiet, the complex empty.

Priella turned to Narine. "Why did you bring us here?"

Narine stumbled as her legs gave out, Jace lowering her into a seat.

"Are you all right?" he asked.

"Yes. I just need to rest," Narine muttered. "Sorry, Priella, but this was the place I recalled best from our visit a few weeks ago. It was a stressful time, so I remember little of the palace itself."

The queen frowned at Narine. "Are you truly so exhausted?"

She nodded weakly. "The spell is taxing, and we spent much of the day traveling to Balmor with only a few hours rest before we set off on this quest."

Priella frowned. "You should have allowed me to try crafting a gateway. I recently visited Tiamalyn Palace and likely could have transported us there."

"It's a little late for that," Jace said.

Brogan snorted. "Can't change the past. I should know. I've tried."

Priella sighed. "There is nothing for it now. Our only remaining destination is Anker, which I have never visited. I saw the power you used to open the gateway. As you said, it is taxing." She glanced toward Kollin. "I don't suppose you have been there."

He shook his head. "Sorry."

"Well, you should all rest, Narine most of all." She glanced at her surroundings. "While not comfortable, this place appears safe at night." Her gaze returned to Narine. "Get some sleep if you can. We will leave in a few hours."

Priella started down the stairs, Kollin grasping her arm. She turned toward him, brow arched.

"I would like to come with you," he said.

"I can do this alone."

"It's not that. I... I would like to see my father." His dark eyes met hers. "With what we face, I may never see him again."

Frowning, she considered the request and the risk involved. Kylar Mor was a talented wizard, but his magic was nothing compared to hers. If they ran into any trouble, she was more than capable of dealing with it.

Priella glanced toward Narine, who was nestled against the thief's shoulder, her eyes closed. She nodded. "We have time, so I suppose it will be all right."

The pair headed down the stairs and out into the quiet plaza, the Black Wasps trailing.

Stopping, she turned toward them. "You needn't escort us. I am more than capable–"

A female Wasp held up a hand, stopping her in mid-sentence. "Rather than you waste your magic unnecessarily, we will protect you so you may focus on what is important."

Priella sighed. "Fine."

Kollin took her hand, the couple walking down the street and toward the palace, the Wasps surrounding them.

"I am his son. He will see me," Kollin demanded.

The sergeant on duty, a man Kollin did not know, shook his head. "I don't care who you are. I'm not about to wake the high wizard in the middle of the night." He pointed toward the Wasps. "And your guards remain at a distance, or the archers I have stationed on the wall will fill their hides with arrows."

Kollin glared at him. "How about I use a bit of magic to wedge your own foot up your arse?"

The man blinked. "I...am not that flexible."

He grinned. "Not yet."

When the man blanched, Priella decided to intervene. "What about Fertello?"

Kollin turned toward her. "What about him?"

"He would recognize you and could then wake your father."

"Good idea." Kollin turned toward the guards. "Will you wake the head of the palace staff? Tell him Kollin Mor is waiting at the gate."

The sergeant flicked his hand toward a guard. "Go get him."

The man ran off, and Kollin turned to Priella. "It's a good thing we aren't in a rush this time."

"If we were, these men could not stop us."

He chuckled. "True. Still, I would rather not do anything unnecessary to my own people."

Priella smiled. "You are a good man."

"I wish my father were, as well." Kollin frowned. "Deep down, he means well, I think... I hope."

She cupped his cheek. It felt of stubble, his jaw square enough she sometimes wondered how it did not cut her. "Are you sure you wish to see him? I get the feeling you don't exactly like him."

"I don't, but I do love him."

"And?"

"And if I can explain to him what we are doing, if he understands what is at stake, perhaps he will see beyond his personal goals."

She considered his statement, feeling something was missing. "There is more, isn't there?"

He turned away. "The man has rarely been supportive of me, unless it was to feed his own agenda. Never has he shown an ounce of pride for anything I have accomplished." He looked back at her. "If he knew of my role in the darkspawn attack, maybe..."

Priella hugged him, her head on his shoulder. "Even if he does not see it, I know the man you have become."

He buried his face in her hair and squeezed her tightly. Footsteps racing in their direction drew her attention. She pulled back and turned to find the guard jogging toward them, a gray-haired man in a robe and pajamas trailing behind.

The guard slowed. "Master Fertello is here, Sergeant."

The old man slowed to a stop and stared at Kollin, blinking. "Young Wizard Mor? Why are you out here? Is that Queen Priella?"

The sergeant's face paled again. "I see."

Fertello smoothed his hair and secured the sash on his robe. "How about I escort Wizard Mor to his father's room?"

The sergeant nodded. "Very well. However, their guards remain outside palace grounds."

"Hold on...," the female Wasp said, stepping forward.

Priella held up a hand, stopping her. "Do as he says. I wield the magic of two wizard lords. If necessary, I could defeat the entire palace guard by myself. We will be safe."

"Very well." The female nodded, stepping back.

"Go back and rest with the others." She gave Kollin a smile. "We will remain at the palace until daybreak and depart at sunrise."

Priella turned away, her arm in Kollin's as they followed Fertello inside the gate.

~

The old man knocked again. "High Wizard? Are you awake?"

A muffled male voice came from inside. "Go away."

"Sir, your son is here. He says it is urgent."

Priella arched a brow at Kollin, who stared at the door while biting his lip. Rustling came from inside, followed by footsteps. The door opened to reveal a tall woman with dark hair, a male wizard robe cinched at her waist, an obscene amount of her chest exposed.

"Queen Grenda." Fertello bowed. "I didn't realize..."

She put a hand on her hip and gave him a level stare. "Oh, stop, Fertello. Don't pretend you were not aware that I have been sleeping in the high wizard's chamber."

"Um... Yes. Of course, my Queen." Fertello glanced back at Kollin. "Is the high wizard available?"

Grenda smirked at Priella, ignoring his question. "Have you claimed our broken little wizard, Priella? Do you wish he were more of a man?"

Kollin's face turned red, but Priella squeezed his arm with hers and spoke before he could reply. "He is all the man I need."

"Truly?" Grenda arched a brow. "How sad."

"Oh, he told me of the troubles he had with you. However, I have discovered his sword is hardened and ready for battle whenever I come calling. In fact, he is *spectacular* and brings me to heights of passion I have never before known." She arched a brow back at Grenda. "Perhaps *you* were the problem all along."

The woman's smile melted, her expression darkening.

Kylar Mor entered from an adjoining room. He wore golden robes with green trim and a green sash, his dark hair disheveled, jaw unshaven. Kollin had much of his father in his appearance, both men tall and handsome with broad shoulders. However, whereas Kollin had soft, kind eyes, his father's were hard, like steel.

"Queen Priella," Kylar said. "What brings you to the palace at such a late hour?"

Before she could reply, Kollin pushed his way past Grenda. "It was my request that brought us here, Father."

Priella entered the room, leaving Fertello alone in the corridor, the man fading from view when Grenda closed the door. The chamber had a sitting area to one side, a long table surrounded by ten chairs to the other, the chandelier above glowing with tiny enchanted lanterns. Through the window on the far wall, moonlight shown upon the lower portion of the city hundreds of feet below and stretching into the distance.

Kylar arched a brow at his son. "Well?"

Kollin glanced at Priella before replying. "I wanted you to know that the army Priella led into Balmoria was not to conquer but was assembled to fight the darkspawn."

Kylar turned toward Priella. "You intend to enter The Fractured Lands and drive into the Murlands?"

"No." She shook her head. "It is the darkspawn that drive into the wizardoms. Kyranni has already fallen. A horde numbering in the tens of thousands marches on Balmor as we speak."

The wizard stared at Priella in silence, his gaze shifting to Kollin. "You must be joking. Surely you don't expect me to believe such nonsense."

Kollin held his hands out in supplication. "You must believe us, Father, for the entire world is at risk. At the head of this army is a demon lord, a creature of dark magic and unknown power. Priella is the only one who can stop this monster from destroying everything."

Grenda snickered. "Demons are nothing but myth, no different than dragons and other creatures from stories."

Priella turned away from Grenda, focusing on the high wizard. "When I was here last, I healed your wounds, both physical and mental. You owe me, Kylar. All I ask is that you listen."

The man set his jaw. "All right. I am listening, but what does this have to do with me or Orenth?"

"If we cannot stop this monster and the army it leads, Orenth will fall next."

"Listen, tomorrow is the Darkening." Kylar pointed toward the moon through the window. "When Oren appears and grants me the power of a god, I will be equipped to protect Tiamalyn from anything…even if this darkspawn army is real."

Priella looked at Kollin, the two sharing a silent exchange. *He is not going to like this.*

She turned back to the high wizard. "I am sorry, Kylar, but you will not be raised to wizard lord."

His face darkened. "What do you mean? I have already paid off the wizards who might pose a challenge. The remaining two applicants are jokes – one so old he cannot walk, the other among the stupidest wizards I have ever met. I am assured to gain the throne."

Anger stirred in Priella's gut. "The wizards remain in Tiamalyn? The same wizards who were supposed to ride north to join my army?"

The man appeared flustered for a moment, his hand running through his hair. "Yes. Um… I gave them the instructions you left, but they voted and decided to remain here."

"And you permitted this?"

He grew angry. "Even though they allow me to hold the title of high wizard, I lack the power of a wizard lord. Without it, they will not obey."

Her eyes narrowed. "And if they supported your rise to the throne, you promised you would protect them from me?"

The wizard fell silent, his lack of denial all the confirmation she needed.

Priella forced a smile. "Too bad you won't have the chance to claim the throne."

"It will be mine," the wizard snarled.

"It will not!" Priella clenched her hand into a fist and stepped close to the man, no longer willing to play nice. "I am here to convert the tower to Pallan. Come tomorrow, I will hold every tower in the world, the prayers of all Eight Wizardoms feeding my magic. Only then will I be able to face the demon and–"

From behind Priella, Grenda roared. A crack sounded, pain exploding in Priella's head. Her face struck the floor, Kollin's cry echoing in the distance. Blackness crept in, like a tunnel. It receded, her vision returning as she rolled over with a groan.

Grenda stood over her with a statue in hand, a scowl on her face. Across the room, Kollin hovered in the air, coils of magic around him, hands bound at his sides, his father standing before him with an arm extended.

"Her head is healing," Grenda exclaimed.

"Hit her again," Kylar insisted.

Grenda lifted the statue. Priella grasped for her magic, but her thoughts were fuzzy, unable to form a construct. The statue came down, smashing into her face, pain exploding, the world going black. Again and again, Grenda struck, until Priella felt nothing.

22

INFILTRATION

Jace walked away from the guards posted outside the Tiamalyn Palace gate, crossing the plaza to where his companions waited. The area was busy, filled with citizens heading toward the side entrance where the Temple of Oren stood. He glanced up and squinted at the morning sun. The moon would eclipse it within the hour.

He came to a stop between Brogan and Narine, his gaze sweeping the group. "Priella and Kollin are surely inside. It is obvious with how the guards evade my questions when I ask about either of them." Glancing over his shoulder, he counted the guards again, stopping when he reached forty, which included the archers atop the wall. "They claim the extra men are to ensure citizens don't attempt to enter the palace grounds during the Darkening ceremony." He shook his head. "What a complete crock of–"

"Jace," Narine chided. "Focus. We don't have much time."

"Right." Brogan gripped his hilt and began drawing his sword. "Let's go break some heads."

Jace put his hand on Brogan's wrist, stopping his blade when it was half-exposed. "There is a good chance we will need violence, but not yet."

Brogan furrowed a brow. "What makes you think you are in charge? I was a captain in both the Gleam Guard and the Murguard."

"True, but this is not a battle. This is a sneak and rescue." Jace thumbed his chest. "I am the best sneak. It is what I do."

The big warrior scowled, about to retort, when Blythe elbowed him. He turned toward her, falling silent at her glare.

"Good." Jace turned to Narine. "Are you rested enough to use a gateway to get us in, take the tower, and still get us out of the city?"

She nodded. "Much better than I was last night. If we can take the tower, we only have one more to capture."

"All right." Jace rubbed his palms together. "Here is the plan. Yes, it starts with me, but that's because guards like this don't take me seriously, whereas they might see some of you as a threat."

He laid out his plan to get in, followed by what he knew of the palace. There would be fighting, but he warned Narine against using any magic unless there was dire need. Before long, Adyn and the three dwarfs were grinning. When asked if everybody understood, Brogan grunted in agreement, while Blythe and Tygalas both appeared resigned. The Black Wasps, who never seemed to speak unless addressing the queen, would do as commanded, which was all Jace needed.

When finished, he drew the Eye of Obscurance up and over his head, pocketing it in his coat. A chill of vulnerability ran down his spine, feeling like his back was to someone who held a poisoned blade in their hand. It was the same feeling he experienced every time he removed the amulet.

He took a breath and crossed the square, heading directly toward the gate. A dozen of the guards drew blades and blocked his path. Another cluster stood just inside the gate, watching intently. Jace stopped ten strides from the line of guards and put his fists on his hips, feet shoulder width apart.

"I know you hold my friends captive!" he yelled. "If you don't allow me inside to see them, I will use my powers to render you helpless."

The sergeant on duty, a man named Paello, took a step forward and laughed. "You are no wizard. What could a simple little man such as yourself possibly do to us?"

Jace waggled his finger. "Oh, I am no simple little man. As you may or may not recall, I visited Tiamalyn a few weeks ago and appeared in the Bowl of Oren. Wizard Kylar Mor sought to make it an unfair contest, pitting me against eight gladiators." He inspected his fingernails before allowing a smile. "Those eight men discovered it was, indeed, an unfair contest. The remaining pieces of their bodies were carried out in carts, while I strode victoriously around the stadium." Truthfully, when the augmentation had faded, Jace fainted. He wished he had it now, but Narine's magic was too precious to waste.

The soldiers looked at each other, suddenly doubtful, some appearing nervous. Many whispered to one another. Even if they had not seen the battle themselves, everyone in the city knew of it by now.

Sergeant Paello was not so easily swayed. He waved toward the men behind him. They made another wall just inside the gate, standing shoulder to shoulder. The man then turned back toward Jace. "You claim to have amazing abilities. Prove it."

Jace shook his head. "You asked for it."

He turned, undid his belt, and pulled his breeches and smallclothes to his knees. Bending forward, he aimed his bare arse at the guards and passed gas. Loudly.

The guards burst out laughing, the laughter growing louder as Jace waved his bare rear from side to side. Looking over his shoulder, he noted the sergeant's face growing red, the man appearing like he might explode. All the guards gathered to watch, those at the gate stepping outside of it, the ones on the wall lowering their bows as they guffawed at the scene.

Jace pulled his breeches up and secured his belt as he spun back toward the guards.

Paello spoke through clenched teeth. "Is that the extent of your abilities? Stupid, childish pranks?"

A gateway opened beside Jace, perpendicular to the guards and invisible from their position. Jace smiled and sidestepped through it, disappearing from sight. An audible gasp followed.

~

Jace stepped onto the palace wall and glanced down, the guards below all staring toward the spot he had vacated. He drew his dagger and burst into a run as the gateway snapped closed behind him.

Charging, he shoved the first archer before the man even turned his attention to him. His screams trailed as he fell between two merlons and tumbled out of sight. The next one turned, and Jace thrust low, his dagger taking the man in the groin. When the archer fell to his knees, Jace rose up and rammed a knee into his face, breaking his nose. He rushed toward the third as the man pulled an arrow from his quiver and took aim. With a flick of his wrist, Jace released his dagger. It plunged into the man's throat, the arrow sailing off to the side as the archer stumbled backward, blood gushing from his gaping mouth. He reached the man, pulled the blade free, and ran through the open tower doorway, slamming the door closed and throwing the bolt before turning around, panting.

Two men stood over the portcullis winch, one drawing a sword and holding his shield ready. In one fluid motion, Jace threw his dagger and drew the blades hidden up his sleeves. The guard blocked the dagger with his shield, the second blade taking him in the thigh, causing him to cry out. Jace released the third blade. By the time it buried in his eye, Jace had already rushed toward the man on the winch.

The soldier backed away, palms up. "Don't kill me."

Jace glared at him. "Close the portcullis and you live."

Eyes widening, the man considered it for a second, then shoved the lever forward. The chain rattled noisily as the portcullis crashed down.

Narine released the gateway that brought Jace to the top of the wall and started across the square to join the others. The guards outside the gate looked around in search of Jace, none turning backward until a scream drew their attention. An archer smashed into the plaza tiles at the foot of the wall, another crying out from above.

"Attack at the top of the wall!" the sergeant shouted.

Arrows of light shot from Blythe's bow and flew across the plaza, the first taking the sergeant in the leg. The man fell to the ground, other arrows striking guards as they cried out. The portcullis slammed closed, trapping them all outside. It was pandemonium, the palace guards unable to properly respond.

Narine opened another gateway, the palace grounds visible through it. Beginning with the Black Wasps, her companions all darted through the opening. Adyn took Narine by one arm as Hadnoddon grasped her other, running her through the portal. The moment they reached the other side, she released her magic, the gateway disappearing.

They stood a hundred strides inside the gate, the guards stationed there all trapped outside, except for the six archers remaining on top of the wall. Blythe drew her bow and began loosing, arrows of light striking the archers. Three fell on the wall, two toppled over the outer lip, and one tumbled inside the palace grounds.

Brogan turned to Tygalas. "You say the arrows kill only darkspawn and stun anyone else?"

"That's right."

"How long does the effect last?"

"I have no idea."

The door at the bottom of the portcullis tower burst open, Jace emerging at a run. He slowed as he drew close. "All right. We are inside."

"You mentioned you would distract those men. Did you really have no better idea than that?" Narine asked.

Jace grinned. "It worked, right?"

She frowned. "Yes, but it was not your proudest moment...nor mine."

Hadnoddon thumped Jace on the back. "I can't believe you bared your arse again! I think you have a problem."

"Well, we have more important issues to worry about right now. Let's go find Priella and Kollin before those guards get the gate open."

Jace jumped a gap in the hedgerow, ducking beneath trees and weaving around shrubs to emerge on a shadow-covered path. After a brief pause to allow the others to catch up, he ran down the path and to a side door. It was unguarded, as he expected. With the Darkening soon upon them, most of the palace guards were at the temple and outside the gate they had just entered.

The others gathered, Brogan panting heavily.

Jace faced them. "This is the entrance to the guard quarters. While most of them are on duty elsewhere, some are likely inside resting before a late shift. Remain quiet. When we reach the stairwell, Brogan, Blythe, Tygalas, and Hadnoddon will go down. Follow the torches to the dungeon cells. They should not be heavily guarded. Do whatever it takes to get the keys and inspect each cell, because one or both of them might be down there. Once you are finished, meet back out here. Hopefully, the guards at the gate will start searching elsewhere, unlikely expecting us to take this entrance."

"What about you?" Brogan asked.

"The rest of us are going up to the royal chambers, the other place Priella or Kollin might be held."

"Why you?"

Jace pulled the amulet from his coat and slipped it over his head. "Because Kylar is a wizard."

Brogan grunted. "Fair enough."

Jace turned to Narine. "Save your magic unless you have no choice."

She nodded. "I will do my best."

He opened the door and slipped in, casting one last backward glance, his finger to his lips.

Creeping down the dark corridor, he put his back to the wall beside an open doorway. Quickly, he peered around the corner and jerked back out of sight, thankful for his ability to recall something with only a brief glance. Eight guards were inside the bunkroom, six lying on beds, two playing cards at a table. A lantern shone from just inside the doorway. It would be bright to anyone who looked at it, so he took a chance and darted past the doorway, hoping the one guard facing his direction might not notice. He waved for the others to follow while he drew the blades at his wrists, ready to throw should an alarm be raised.

The Black Wasps crept ahead first, followed by Blythe, her bow covered by her cloak, and Brogan, who held his sword ready. Filk, Lythaon, and Tygalas came next, stepping carefully. When Hadnoddon tried to sneak past, his armor clanked noisily.

"What was... Intruders!" a guard exclaimed.

Jace spun around the corner and threw in rapid succession, the first knife striking a seated guard in the base of his neck, the second hitting the standing guard in the cheek. He screamed and stumbled backward as Adyn rushed in, sword slashing. Blythe loosed arrows of light, striking the men scrambling from the bunks, each collapsing in a heap – three on the floor, the others back on their beds.

Rushing in, Jace reclaimed his two blades, quickly wiping them on a fallen guard's tunic before racing into the corridor. They came to a stairwell, and he pointed toward the descending stairs.

"The dungeon is down there."

Brogan nodded and began his descent, sword in hand, jaw set, as Blythe, Hadnoddon, and Tygalas followed.

Jace waved for the others to follow him as he began his ascent.

Brogan paused at the bottom of the stairs, the walls made of dark, stone blocks, the floor dirt. He peered around the corner and into a long, dark corridor, amber light seeping through an open doorway twenty strides away. Nobody was in sight. Moving with care, he headed down the hallway, Hadnoddon and Tygalas a few steps behind, Blythe at the rear. When he reached the open doorway, he put his back to the wall and slowly peered inside.

It was a long, rectangular room, the floor made of stone blocks. Doors, some open, some closed, lined the walls to each side of the room. At the far end was a desk, a tall, stoutly built man seated behind it, arms crossed over his chest. His eyes were closed, chest slowly rising and falling.

Brogan eased his sword into its sheath, waved for the others to follow, and entered the room, moving as quietly as possible. Just before he reached the desk, the sleeping guard's eyes snapped open.

"What—"

Brogan leapt forward as the guard rose to his feet, knuckles connecting with the man's jaw. The guard fell backward over his chair, his head striking the wall with a crack. He collapsed in a heap, legs tangled in the overturned chair, chin slumped against his chest, a smear of blood along the wall behind his head.

Hadnoddon grunted. "Nice."

Brogan inspected his knuckles with a frown, flexing his hand. "That was one hard jaw."

"Apparently not hard enough," Blythe said. "He is out cold."

Kneeling beside the man, Brogan unhooked the ring of keys from the guard's belt. He then rose and turned to the nearest closed cell. The first two keys produced no result. With the third key, it opened, the door creaking as light bled into the small chamber. A man on the pallet inside held up his hand to block the light, blinking. He was unshaven, his unwashed body reeking of sweat and urine.

"Is it time already?" the man asked.

"Time?"

"For the Immolation of Darkening."

Brogan realized what the man meant. "Oh, no. Guards will be coming down here for prisoners." He turned toward Blythe. "They will use them as sacrifices for the Darkening. We had best hurry."

Jace reached the top of the stairwell and peered around the corner. A full contingency of twelve guards stood outside the royal chambers. He pulled back and sighed.

"This will be a real fight. There are twelve guards ahead and two wizards inside." He considered the situation and came to a quick conclusion. "Adyn leads the way. They cannot harm her body and she is largely unaffected by wizard spells." He turned to the leader of the Wasps. "Your squad will follow. Kill them as quickly as possible. However, do not enter the chambers. If the doors open, give Adyn space to go after the wizards." He then turned to the two dwarfs. "You will trail them and clean up. Don't worry about being gentle. We have little time."

Lythagon grinned, rubbing his axe handle. "Music to my ears."

"What about you two?" Adyn asked.

Jace thumbed toward himself. "As soon as I see an opening, I will go after the wizards. The Eye will protect me. Narine will linger behind, ready in case things go sideways."

When the others nodded in acknowledgment, he waved hurriedly to Adyn. "Go."

She darted around the corner, swords in hand, the Wasps following. The guards turned toward them, weapons drawn, shields ready, as they called out in surprise. The guards nearest Adyn prepared to block an attack, but she didn't swing her swords as they expected, instead barreling into the men and driving them into the ones behind. All four went down in a heap, the guards behind scrambling to get clear. A trio of Wasps leapt over the pile, blades flashing as they attacked. The other three sped past to engage with the next row of guards, shouts and cries echoing in the corridor. Filk and Lythagon came in last, roaring as they dove into the fray.

The doors flew open, two guards barreling out. Filk's blade slid into the first, while the other thrust a sword at Adyn as she regained her feet. The blade clanged off her neck, knocking her aside, before the tip struck the stone wall and broke off. She drove her blade through his gut and pushed him aside.

Flames blasted through the door and into the corridor, engulfing Adyn and anyone around her. Two Wasps, Filk, and some palace guards were caught in the flames, screams erupting. Jace burst into a run, dodging the burning men as he raced into the fire, the amulet against his chest turning ice cold.

The fire faded to reveal Kylar Mor, the wizard's clenched teeth loosening when his jaw dropped.

"Landish? How?"

Jace lunged toward the wizard and drove his dagger into his abdomen. Lightning crackled from Kylar's hands but fizzled as it struck Jace, who pushed harder and lifted, the wizard's eyes bulging as he stumbled backward until he was pinned against the wall.

"No!" a female screamed.

Jace looked over his shoulder to find Grenda standing in the doorway to the adjoining room. She was dressed in an elegant but revealing gown, a gold and emerald crown in her hair.

She extended her hand toward him, gaze intense. "You *will* back away, Jerrell!"

The amulet against his chest turned frigid cold, whatever magic she attempted failing.

"Sorry, Grenda. Your spells cannot affect me. Kylar will not become wizard lord. Not today. Not ever." Jace turned back to the wizard, who shook in pain, breath coming in shallow gasps. "Where are Kollin and Priella?"

"She…is…dead," the man choked out.

The statement was like a blow to his stomach, twisting it into a knot. "Dead?"

Sensing movement behind him, Jace turned as Grenda swung a three-foot-tall statue toward his head. He ducked, the object narrowly missing him before it smashed into Kylar's chin. The man's head snapped back, hitting the wall with a crack. He crumpled to the floor.

"No!" Grenda shrieked. She knelt beside Kylar while Jace backed away.

Adyn stumbled into the room, the edges of her leather vest blackened, cuts in the material visible here and there. Narine followed, along with Lythagon and three of the Black Wasps. Bodies filled the corridor outside the room, most of the guards dead, a couple moaning in pain. Filk lay among them, his skin badly burned, vacant eyes staring into space. Corpses of three Black Wasps lay with him.

Jace gestured toward the fighters in black, a woman and two men. "You three, check the other room. Shout if you find Kollin or Priella. Kill anyone who tries to stop you."

They ran off and disappeared into the adjoining room.

Jace turned toward Grenda and the dead wizard. Her back was to him, tanned skin of her shoulders exposed, black hair draping over them, body shaking as she sobbed. He frowned, thinking it unlike Grenda to care for anyone save herself.

She cries because of lost opportunity, he thought.

With a sigh, he turned toward Narine and Adyn, the latter rubbing at the scorches on her metal skin, one blade in hand, the other sheathed.

"I hope he was lying about Pri–"

With a backhand swing, Adyn shoved Jace aside. Grenda's thrust missed his neck, his own knife burying into his shoulder. He cried out in pain and spun away as Adyn plunged her blade into Grenda's chest. Eyes bulging, the wizardess stumbled backward, sliding off the blade and falling to the floor beside Kylar's corpse.

Jace went to one knee, jaw clenched in pain as he watched sparkling crimson emerge from Grenda's rounded chest, staining her green gown. The woman's face reflected shock, her hand over the wound as she tried to stop the flow. He glanced toward the corridor where Lythagon stood, the dwarf's eyes closed as he stood over Filk's charred corpse.

Grenda looked at Narine. "Please..." She grimaced in pain. "Heal me, and you can have anything."

The three Wasps appeared from the bedchamber, one saying, "We found nobody."

Narine frowned at the woman. "Where are Kollin and Priella?"

She nodded toward the corridor. "Kollin is in the room...across the hallway."

"Go get him," Jace said to the Wasps, the trio rushing out of the room.

Adyn pointed her bloody sword at Grenda. "And Priella?"

"She...would not die." The wizardess gasped. "But she *must* be...dead by now."

"Where?"

"Dun...geon."

Jace looked up at Narine. "We need to get down there. If she is alive, you can heal her."

Grenda whimpered. "Please, Narine." She gasped, tears running down her face. "I told you...what you wanted."

"I don't think so." Narine crossed her arms. "You see, we have a world to save, and I must take care to use my abilities wisely. Saving a greedy, self-centered whore like yourself will do the world little good."

Grenda's hand dropped from her chest, the dress soaked with glittering blood. Her mouth moved, but only strangled croaks emerged. Her head fell to the side, body leaning against Kylar's and falling still.

Adyn moved to Jace and squatted, gripping the hilt of his dagger. "This is going to hurt."

"Just do it," he said tightly, preparing himself.

She yanked the blade free, Jace moaning loudly, pain shooting down his arm and across his chest. The wound bled heavily.

"Take the amulet off him," Narine said to Adyn.

Panting, Jace said, "But we need your magic–"

"Just do it." Her tone left no room for argument.

Sword sheathed, Adyn gripped the chain and pulled the amulet from his tunic. She lifted it over his head, and Narine put her hand on his brow. A wave of cold washed over him, his pain fading instantly, blood stopping. He lifted his arm, working it. With his other hand, he felt the area. There was a hole in his coat and tunic, the edges slick with blood, but his wound was gone.

He stood and cast one last glance at the dead wizard and wizardess before turning to the room across the corridor as the Wasps broke down the door. With him in the lead, the three of them left the room, stepped over the bodies on the floor, and entered the other chamber.

Kollin sat on the bed, wrists tied to bedposts, hands wrapped in cloth, blindfolded, mouth gagged. When the Wasps cut his wrists free, he yanked the blindfold away and tugged the gag below his chin.

Seeing who stood before him, his eyes widened. "Priella," he blurted. "We must help her!"

~

Brogan unlocked the cell door and swung it open. Someone lay curled up on the pallet, facing away from the door. All he could see was long, red hair.

"Priella!"

Blythe pushed past him and knelt beside the pallet. She put her hand on the sleeping woman's shoulder and rolled her over, the light from the room outside shining upon a face unknown to Brogan.

"Who are you?" the woman asked sleepily, blinking in the sudden brightness.

"You are not Priella," Brogan said.

"Who is Priella?"

Frustrated, he turned away from the cell. It was the last one, and they were running out of time. He saw another door along the wall beside the desk and the unconscious guard.

"Let's try in there."

He crossed the room and fumbled with the keys, inserting the only silver one into the lock. It clicked, and the door swung open.

The torchlit room was filled with devices of torture. Upon the far wall, attached to chains with shackles around her wrists and ankles, hung Priella, her head drooping, hair covering her face, hands bound in cloth. Her dress was stained with sparkling blood, a dagger buried in the middle of her chest. The floor below her had turned to red crystal.

Blythe gasped and rushed past Brogan. She reached Priella and lifted her head, seeing she was blindfolded and gagged. In haste, Blythe pulled the blindfold away and lowered the gag.

"That's not Priella," Brogan exclaimed.

The plain, homely face was unfamiliar to him. He took in the woman's heavy arms, modest chest, and wide hips, but the dress was Priella's.

"I don't understand," he muttered.

The woman gasped, eyes blinking open. When she looked at him, he recognized the eyes.

"It *is* you," Brogan said, his voice no more than a whisper.

"Help me get her down!" Blythe ordered.

He shook his head to discard his confusion and rushed over. He found the key for the shackles and unlocked one wrist, Tygalas and Hadnoddon holding her up. Hurrying, he unlocked the other three shackles. They then carefully lowered her to the floor, laying Priella on her back.

"Should we remove the blade?" Brogan asked.

Blythe shook her head. "I don't know."

The sound of approaching footsteps came from the corridor.

Brogan growled, "It's the guards, come to take the prisoners for the ceremony."

Twelve guards entered the outer chamber, quickly reacting when they saw the unconscious jailor and the open cells. The ring of swords being drawn echoed in the dungeon. Brogan tossed the keys aside and drew his falchion, rushing to meet the charging guards at the open door. He lunged and swung, forcing the enemies back.

"Move aside!" Blythe demanded.

As he spun away, she loosed, arrows of light flying through the doorway in rapid succession. Seven guards crumpled to the floor, stunned and paralyzed. The others shouted at each other but remained out of sight. Brogan hesitated, unsure of what do to.

Adyn and three Black Wasps stormed into the room and struck the five guards from behind, dispatching them swiftly. Jace, Narine, Lythagon, and Kollin followed, all rushing into the cell where Brogan and his companions waited.

Kollin knelt beside Priella, caressing her face, a tear running down his cheek. Her eyes blinked open, then fluttered shut again. He looked up at Narine. "You must save her. *Please.*"

She rushed to kneel beside him. "When I say, pull the blade free."

He nodded.

"Now."

Kollin yanked out the blade, Narine's hand pressing against the wound as blood gushed from it. Eyes closed, she wove her magic, her form glowing in Brogan's enhanced vision, thanks to Augur's enchantment. Priella's back arched and she inhaled deeply, eyes bulging. She fell back to the floor and exhaled, her breathing returning to normal.

"Are you all right?" Kollin asked softly, his hand on her cheek.

Priella's heavy-lidded eyes gazed up at him. "I...will live. My magic is expended from trying to heal myself, but I will live."

He placed his hand behind her back and pulled her to a sitting position. "You will regain your magic at Devotion tonight."

Priella's head hung as she muttered, "But I must yet take two towers."

"No." Kollin shook his head. "*We* must take those towers...together."

She shook her head. "You don't understand. Without the magic of Pallan flowing through me, I cannot alter another gem to aquamarine."

"Then you must return to Balmor and hold Devotion," Narine said.

Priella shook her head again. "It cannot occur during the day. I do not know why, but the throne will only ignite after the sun has set. I tried it during our march to Balmor, and nothing happened."

"In that case, we had better return and rest until sunset. If the darkspawn army reaches Balmor tonight, we will have little time to take those last two towers."

Jace nodded. "Narine is right. However, there is something we must do first, and quickly. Brogan and Kollin can help Priella outside. The rest of you, come with me." He took Narine by the hand and rushed into the corridor, turning the opposite way they had come.

Brogan sheathed his blade and sighed. "I get the feeling I am about to miss out on the fun."

Jace pulled Narine out into the garden, his gaze sweeping the area. There were no guards in sight. As they rushed down a path lined with trees and shrubs, their surroundings darkened. He looked up, the moon partially blocking the sun. The Darkening was almost upon them.

"What is this about?" Narine asked as he dragged her behind him.

He turned and climbed upon a dais with a gazebo in the center, benches around it. Pointing toward the structure above the palace, he said, "You need to open a gateway and get me up there...now. If I cannot get the jewel out of the throne, another wizard might become wizard lord."

Narine's eyes widened. "You're right."

She reached for the bag at her side and withdrew the solar lens. Peering through it, she aimed the lens toward the top of the tower. Moments later, the hair on Jace's arms stood on end as she worked her magic. A gateway opened to reveal the top of the tower, a recessed ring in the floor surrounding a dais with a throne of crystal in the center. Thick, white pillars surrounded the tower, holding up the domed roof.

Jace leapt through, landing beyond the recessed ring. The wind struck, his hair fluttering. He climbed onto the dais and drew his dagger – the same blade that had almost killed him just minutes prior, still red with his own blood.

Carefully, he wedged the tip between the crystal and the dormant sapphire. Seeing the dark blue stone caused him to pause, until he recalled what had occurred. *That's right. Thurvin was the last to harvest the prayers of Tiamalyn.* He wondered if the Darkening ritual would have changed the gem back to an emerald. He glanced toward the sun as the moon neared its full eclipse, his pulse racing.

"Come on…," he grunted as he pried at the jewel, realization suddenly hitting him.

Adyn still holds the amulet. There was nothing to protect him should the tower turn to flames.

Fearful of what might happen should it wake, he reached into his boot and pulled out another knife, using it to work the other side of the gem. The sunlight dimmed, the sky turning a dull red as the moon fully eclipsed the sun.

The sapphire popped free and fell. He dropped his dagger and snatched the gem just before it struck the throne. Pulse hammering in his ears, he stepped back. *That was close.*

Bending, he picked up his blade, sheathed it, and leapt back through the gateway.

23

HARBINGER

Driven by fear and the nightmarish scene of Garvin's death, Rindle rode through the night. He stopped to change horses three times, yet by the time he reached the basin beyond the mountains, both appeared exhausted. As the sky grew lighter, he spotted a quiet farm and turned off the road, riding at an easy walk until he reached the barn. Inside, he found an old horse sleeping. It took him a while to saddle it, but he could not afford to wait for the other horses to recover. Once it was ready, he left his two mounts inside and walked the old horse out.

The farmhouse was quiet, the occupants yet to wake. A rooster crow erupted from a pen beyond the barn, startling him. *I had better be off before anyone sees me.* Looking at the house once more, he realized he needed to do something, thanks to Garvin's recent influence.

He jogged over to a window and peered inside, unable to see beyond the closed curtains. Drawing his rapier, he reversed his grip and struck the window, the pommel cracking the glass. A cry of surprise came from inside. He wound up and did it again, the glass pane shattering.

Through the opening, he hollered, "Get out! You must run. War comes tonight, and you will die if you don't leave!"

The front door burst open, a middle-aged man holding a crossbow emerging. "Horse thief!" The man pulled the trigger.

The bolt struck Rindle in the arm, the force twisting his upper body as he cried out in pain. "I am trying to save you!"

The farmer began cranking the release back to prepare another shot. "Then why are you stealing Dottie?"

Rindle looked at the horse. "I need to warn Balmor. An army of dark-spawn comes through the pass. They aren't far behind me, but they only travel at night."

The man produced another bolt, and Rindle realized he was in trouble. He charged, reversing his grip on the hilt, the tip of the rapier striking the crossbow and almost cutting off the man's finger. The weapon fell to the ground as he cried out, blood gushing from the wound. The man backed up a step when Rindle placed the tip of his sword against his chest.

"Listen," he said firmly. "I just watched a demon consume my friend… my *only* friend. I rode through the night and am exhausted and hungry. Then, when I try to save your life, you bury a crossbow bolt in my shoulder." The wound throbbed, forcing him to grit his teeth. "I need your horse to take me to Balmor as quickly as possible. I must warn Queen Priella of the approaching army. I left you two mounts in exchange. Do with them what you will, but if you are here when the sun sets, you will die."

He turned from the man, sheathed his blade, and walked to the horse. Taking a deep breath, he pulled himself into the saddle with one arm, the other dangling limply, the bolt still lodged in his flesh. As he rode off, he cast one last glance at the farmer, the man still holding his nearly severed finger while staring at Rindle.

I did what I could, he told himself, not used to having a conscience. *Damn you, Garvin.* He urged the horse into a trot.

It was mid-morning when Rindle reached the eastern end of Balmor Sound. Ships sat moored near the shore, each positioned parallel to land. Weapons of war sat upon every deck, half with small catapults, half with ballistae. Soldiers and sailors stood upon those vessels, many holding bows. Here and there, Rindle even spotted wizards in silken robes.

On the inland side of the road was a massive bulwark, a five-foot-tall mound of dirt with a trough along the north side, sharpened stakes jutting up the face of the mound. At the top was a wall made of logs, heads visible above it. The structure ran for half a mile across the grassland, ending at the forest's edge. The near end of the bulwark turned east, toward the city, and ran for another hundred feet. As he rode past it, he was able to spot a scaffold on the backside, archers standing upon it.

Southwest of the bulwark, along the tree line, Priella's army camped. Tents ran across the far edge of the grassland and up the hillside. While he knew there were thousands of soldiers stationed there, few were visible. Most were likely resting, dreaming that the attack would never come. Rindle knew better. The next time those men closed their eyes might be the last. A shiver ran down his spine.

Similar to the bulwark, sharpened stakes stuck up at angles from the gravel field of the Bazaar. He rode through it, curious as to why the tents remained. *Perhaps it was too much work to take them down.*

When he finally reached the city gate, armed soldiers in chainmail and yellow tabards stepped out to block his way.

"Hello, traveler."

Rindle reined his horse and scowled. "I am tired and have no time for this."

Another guard pointed nonchalantly. "You have a crossbow bolt in your arm."

"Really? I hadn't noticed."

"You wouldn't be a bandit who came across a feisty farmer, would you?"

Rindle guffawed at the near accuracy of the question. "I am...*was* a scout for Commander Garvin. I was given the task of reporting what happened."

"Where is the commander?"

"Dead. They all are dead. Every soldier in his command." Rindle shook his head. "Only I remain. Now, I am exhausted, starving, and have lost a fair amount of blood. Can someone escort me to the palace before I pass out?"

The guards in the palace corridor blocked the way. The older of the two, a man whose bearing and hard eyes reminded Rindle of Garvin, shook his head. "She must rest and commanded us to see she is not disturbed."

Rindle clenched his fist in frustration. He had been challenged each step of the way. Now, standing so close to his destination, he was caught by another roadblock. "I don't care what she said. Commander Garvin insisted I report to her immediately."

His stomach growled, the bolt still in his shoulder. The arm had long since gone numb, and he wondered if he might lose it. Worse, he feared the demon would soon kill everyone in the city.

Who needs an arm if you are dead?

His patience expired, he took a deep breath and belted at the top of his lungs, "Priella! My Queen! Your thief is here!"

The guards rushed him and slammed him to the floor. One wrapped an arm around his neck and squeezed. He gasped, unable to breathe. The man was too heavy, too strong, the arm impossible to pry away. Spots danced before his eyes, his vision narrowing.

The door opened and Kollin stepped out. "What is this?"

"We are sorry, Master Wizard. We know the queen–"

"Release him. *Now!*" Kollin demanded.

The arm around Rindle's neck relaxed, and he wheezed. He lay on his side, gasping, as the guard stood over him.

Kollin walked over and squatted. "Why are you here, Rindle? Where is Commander Garvin?"

"Dead," Rindle croaked. "They are all dead."

"What happened?"

The image replayed in his mind – the demon lifting Garvin off the ground, pieces of the man breaking off and flowing into the creature. "The demon…consumed him. Afterward, it glowed brighter. I think… I fear it feeds off magic and Garvin made it stronger."

"How long do we have?"

"They were no more than an hour behind me when the sun rose. Tonight, they will arrive."

Kollin sighed and stood. "Help him up."

The two guards helped Rindle to his feet, him wincing from the pain in his arm.

"Go request a healer. Get some food and rest. We will need you on the walls tonight."

"What about your quest?" Rindle asked, hopeful.

Kollin scrubbed a hand down his face, appearing weary. "Incomplete. We ran into…complications. We will try again once she has rested. Hopefully she will be ready by the time the demon reaches the city." He turned to the guards. "Allow nobody except me inside. She must rest."

"Yes, sir."

"Where are you going?" Rindle asked.

"I must relay your news to Odama and Henton. We have a city to defend."

24

BEST LAID PLANS

Stomach filled and feeling rested, Narine walked along the palace corridors with Jace and Adyn. The rhythmic chant of Devotion hummed throughout the building, drowning out their footsteps. Adyn opened the door to the Arboretum and held it for Narine, who peered up toward the tower in the heart of Balmor Palace. It burned with the flame of Pallan, beams of light streaking across the evening sky, the western horizon still lit with the soft glow of dusk. When she counted the beams of light, she was unsure if there were sixteen or more. It was difficult to tell from the tightly fanned connections to the distant south.

They followed the shadowy path to the plaza below the tower and found the others already gathered. She scanned the faces. Brogan, Blythe, Hadnoddon, Lythagon, and Tygalas all appeared resolute in the glow of the flame. The group had been through a lot together, but it felt incomplete without Rhoa, Rawk, Algoron, and Filk.

Two small figures appeared from across the plaza – one petite and fit, the other short and stout.

"Rhoa! Rawk!" Narine exclaimed.

Rhoa rushed over and hugged her.

Jace grinned and patted Rawk on the shoulder. "It is good to see you, Rawk. We sure could use your help. We still have two thrones to claim."

Rawk furrowed his brow and looked at Rhoa. "I don't think so, Jace. Rhoa only just regained her feet. She is still weak."

Narine held Rhoa's hand and looked her in the eye. "How do you feel?"

The acrobat shrugged. "Mostly tired. However, since I have eaten, I feel better."

Jace shook his head. "Rhoa couldn't join us even if she wanted to. Just as I cannot travel through a gateway while wearing the amulet, she is immune to magic and can never use one."

Rhoa's gaze dropped to her feet, visibly crestfallen.

However, Rawk seemed relieved. "If Rhoa cannot go, I will remain here, as well." He nodded, a decision made. "If the rest of you are away, someone must remain behind to protect her."

Rhoa lifted her gaze to his, eyes narrowed as she drew a fulgur blade, the spiked tip sizzling with blue sparks. "I can take care of myself, Rawk."

"Um… Yes. Of course. I mean… I just mean until you are fully recovered."

"I would be safe here."

He set his jaw. "I am not leaving you, Rhoa."

The light of the tower dimmed, Devotion ending. Priella appeared atop the tower and stepped off. Pale blue magic flared, a platform of air appearing beneath her feet and slowing her descent. Narine marveled at the ease with which Priella could both create the platform and manipulate it. Skilled male wizards might perform a similar act, but it would be taxing. Much less so for a male wizard lord. For a woman to do it, even one blessed with the magic of a god… It was impressive.

Priella touched down, glowing like the sun itself with the magic she held. Once again, her illusion was intact – face striking, form appearing fit, lean, and positively female…the type of body most women longed to possess and most men longed to conquer.

Kollin met her, placing his hand on her upper arm. "How do you feel?"

"In truth, the magic I hold… It nearly overwhelmed me. It is as if I have swallowed the sun." She shook her head. "I cannot comprehend how I can possibly hold the power of two more thrones."

"You must find a way," he said softly.

She nodded. "I know."

Jace produced the sapphire he had taken from Tiamalyn and held it out to

Priella. She accepted it, an augmentation construct appearing around her other hand, bending and turning inward until the points of the eight ovals met to form a sphere. The magic of Pallan flowed through the sphere and into the gem. Pale blue light flared quickly, then dimmed, revealing a sparkling aquamarine. The entire process took mere seconds, Priella executing it as easily as breathing.

"It is ready." Priella turned to Narine. "Hurry now. Let us take Tiamalyn and move on to Anker. The demon lord and his horde could arrive at any moment."

Shouts came from the palace and guards rushed in, Odama at the lead. "Your Majesty! We are under attack!"

A dark, winged shape flew overhead, a cry echoing in the night, a chill running down Narine's spine.

"Wyverns!" Brogan said aloud what Narine had feared.

"Quickly, Narine," Priella said. "We must take Tiamalyn and make for Anker."

She embraced her magic and crafted a gateway. The gazebo in the palace grounds of Tiamalyn appeared through the opening. Her companions rushed through, Narine and Jace coming last. She cast one final glance toward Rhoa and Rawk before closing it, wondering if they would ever see each other again.

Kneeling on the top of the city wall, Rindle chanted Devotion, his prayers, along with those of everyone in Balmor and the surrounding area, feeding Queen Priella's power. Actively taking part in Devotion was a rarity for him, yet he had never done so with such conviction, pouring his heart and soul into each and every word.

The end of the world looms.

His past came into perspective, and he laughed upon realizing the meaninglessness of his actions, the shallow nature of his motives. Stealing, jealousy, murder for profit... Such petty behavior had defined him for much of his life. Only recently had he found a cause beyond his own concerns, somehow giving significance to his existence.

Devotion ended, he rose to his feet. The cuirass he wore was heavy and too big for his thin torso, but it was the one thing of Garvin that remained. It would either protect him or he would die while wearing it.

He walked through the tower beside the harbor gate and headed east, knowing the enemy would approach from that direction. After passing a few dozen archers, he spotted Odama speaking to a pair of squad leaders. When finished, the two soldiers headed in opposite directions, and the newly raised captain turned toward Rindle.

"Ah, thief. You are here."

He had considered remaining in his room and praying for survival, but Garvin never would have stood for it. In memory of his lost friend, he would fight the darkness.

Rindle shrugged. "I have nowhere else to be."

"Walk with me." Odama waved for him to follow. "Perhaps your eyes and recent experience will be of help."

"Yes, sir."

The two headed toward the eastern gate, following the gradual curve of the wall, passing hundreds of soldiers. Odama patted the shoulder of every single one. Rindle noticed most were archers, but there were swordsmen among them. Every couple hundred feet was a brazier, small buckets below the merlons filled with arrows dipped in naphtha. When they reached the eastern ramparts, they came across something he had never seen before.

"What is this?" he asked, pointing toward the second one they passed.

"An idea one of my engineers had." He slowed and pointed. "These logs are twenty feet long and doused in naphtha. Each end is secured to a heavy-duty bolt loaded into a ballista anchored to the wall." Rindle examined one of the bolts, four feet long and as thick as a spear. Tugging on a rope secured to one, Odama continued. "A rope runs from every bolt, the other end secured to a merlon. When the darkspawn reach us, we intend to light the logs on fire and loose." He grinned. "We tested one. The log shot out a hundred feet from the wall, reached the end of the rope and quickly dropped to strike the wall about two feet off the ground. Anything down there at the time would be crushed and subsequently lit on fire. It will keep them clear of the walls for a good while."

They reached the tower beside the eastern gate as the last bit of light faded from the sky. Moments later, shouts emerged in the distance, followed by a rising hum. Flames lit up the night beyond the bulwark, a mile from the city. Within the firelight, a swarm of darkspawn flowed toward them.

"And so it begins," Odama said.

From the ships along the shore came the thuds of siege engines loosing, their missiles arcing through the sky with an orange glow. When the objects landed, fires erupted, the grass igniting. Hoots, shrieks, and screams came from the goblins as they burned.

In the glow of the firelight, wyverns appeared, far more than Rindle had ever seen. The monsters dove toward the ships, attacking the men on board, some dropping objects from their claws. Flames erupted on a few ships, distant shouts echoing over the water. Wizards attacked from one of the ships, bolts of lightning arcing through the sky, striking a wyvern, the creature spiraling toward the water. Another dove toward that ship, a cone of purple magic bursting forth. The blast completely engulfed the ship, the vessel shimmering and disappearing.

"The demon lord." Rindle pointed. "It rides upon that wyvern."

Odama looked at him, blinking. "What did you say?"

Rindle pointed. "That magic... It is the demon lord."

"Did it just vaporize an entire ship?"

He nodded, gaze focused on the battle. "It used the same magic to kill Commander Garvin."

From a distant bonfire, beyond the darkspawn army, a ball of flames shot up into the sky, arcing and dropping to the soldiers behind the bulwark. The fire struck, flames splattering and igniting dozens of soldiers. From another bonfire, a flaming missile launched into the air, landing to set the bulwark ablaze. More shaman fires dotted the field far beyond the bulwark, each releasing flaming missiles toward the human army, some launching far enough to land in the city.

"I pray Priella comes back soon," Odama said.

A wyvern dove toward the wall midway between the two gates. Archers took aim and loosed, arrows pelting it, most bouncing off harmlessly. The creature landed on top of the wall, crushing three soldiers. It spun, tail whipping. Two soldiers were knocked from the battlements, another slamming against the merlons, bones shattering. A soldier lunged in with a sword, piercing a wing. The creature roared and chomped down on the man, lifting him by his head, legs kicking as he was thrown off the wall. With two mighty flaps, the beast lifted into the air and swooped forward to grab a soldier in its rear claws, then flew off into the night.

"How do we stop such creatures?" Odama asked.

Rindle swallowed. "Magic."

"Right!" He leaned over the inner edge of the wall and shouted, "Where are those wizards? We need them up here. Now!"

Rhoa stared out the fifth-floor window of Balmor Palace while standing in the room Blythe and Brogan shared, both away with the others to claim the last two thrones. The attack had come moments after their departure.

The square surrounding the building was filled with people huddled in clumps, worried cries rising from the crowd. Beyond, fires burned in the night, both within and outside the walls, the amber glow framing silhouettes of the soldiers on the wall. The skies were thick with giant, flying beasts circling and diving toward the defenders. Often, a wyvern would rise back into the sky with a soldier in its claws, releasing them to fall from a height impossible to survive. It was a horrible sight to witness, made worse by her inability to act.

Footsteps arose in the corridor and paused outside the open door, resuming when the person entered the room. She glanced over her shoulder and saw Rawk's face in the flickering amber light coming through the window.

"I was worried when you weren't in your room," he said.

She turned away, gaze returning to the chaos in the city. "I cannot rest any longer. Not with people dying and the world on the edge of disaster."

"Hmm... Is there anything I can do?"

"Yes."

He put his hand on her shoulder. "Name it."

"Help me save these people."

Rawk jerked with a start. "How? There are thousands of darkspawn out there. And then there are the wyverns..." He shivered.

She looked back toward the sky. "I recall how difficult it was to kill one of them. Now, dozens swarm the sky." A wistful memory resurfaced. "Still, they are pale imitations of a true dragon…" Her voice trailed off. She gasped, spun, and ran from the room.

"Rhoa?" Rawk called after her. "What's wrong?"

Opening the door across the corridor, she raced into her room. She lifted her pack off the floor and dug inside, pulling out a foot-long talon, hollow in the center.

"The dragon claw," Rawk said in wonder from the doorway. "I'd forgotten you had it."

"As did I." She flashed him a grin and ran to her window overlooking the Arboretum, Zyordican's words echoing in her head.

"If you ever find yourself in dire need, blow upon this horn. I will hear it and will come."

She opened the window and lifted the small end of the talon to her mouth. Taking a deep breath, she put her lips on it and blew. Nothing happened. No sound, no magic. Nothing.

Again, she tried it but with the same result. Her arm dropped to her side, shoulders slumped in disappointment.

"Maybe I should try," Rawk offered. "If it is a thing of magic, perhaps you cannot make it work."

She handed it to him, doubting it would make a difference. It did not, for when Rawk attempted, no sound came from the talon.

"Why?" she asked. "Why was I pulled into this ordeal if there is nothing I can do?"

He put a hand on her back. "Without you, Thurvin would have killed Jakarci and we would have a whole other problem on our hands. You cannot solve them all but must play the role you were given."

Frowning, Rhoa's gaze returned to the orange-tinted skies.

When the tower above Tiamalyn Palace bloomed with the flame of Pallan, Brogan turned to the others. He drew his sword, the night brightening to his eyes, a fire filling his veins. "Weapons ready. Darkspawn will be waiting for us in Anker."

Jace frowned. "Who put you in charge?"

Brogan lifted his falchion and grinned. "This is no rescue mission or heist, thief. This a battle, and none here have survived as many as I."

Jace shrugged. "True. Just remember our goal is to get Priella to the tower, not to kill every darkspawn in the city."

"If we happen to kill them all?"

Jace rolled his eyes and looked at Blythe. "Can't you do something about him?"

She gripped her glowing bow and shook her head. "Brogan is right. We will kill every monster we can while taking the tower. There is no reason to hold back."

Lythagon chuckled and elbowed Tygalas. "Time to crack some heads."

The elf smirked. "So be it."

Jace shook his head. "I am surrounded by maniacs."

"Now you know how I feel," Narine mumbled.

Priella landed a few feet away and nodded to Narine. "Ready."

Aglow with magic, Narine prepared herself. "The best I can do is place us just inside the city gate. From there, we will have to make for the heart of the city."

A beam of light appeared in the air, splitting into a gateway, a dark, empty city square visible through the opening. Brogan rushed forward, over the shimmering edge, and into the humid city of Anker. In moments, beads of sweat rose on his brow, thick, hot air filling his lungs.

"I forgot about the blasted jungle weather," he muttered. It was among the things he missed least about his stint in The Fractured Lands.

The others came through the gateway and gathered around him. Narine dismissed it, the glow fading, eyes searching the darkness. Brogan spotted a tower jutting into the night sky near the heart of the city.

That must be it.

"Maybe the darkspawn all left?" Jace suggested. "Priella could just fly up and do her thing."

Brogan spotted several massive, winged creatures in the sky.

"I see multiple wyverns circling the tower." He looked at Priella. "Could you fight them off if they attack while you are floating in the air?"

Her brow furrowed. "It would be dangerous. If something happened, the fall *might* kill me. If not, it would cost a fair amount of my magic to heal."

"Magic you need to face the demon," Kollin added.

A blood-curdling shriek came from down the street.

Eyes wide, Jace whispered, "What was that?"

"Wraith," Brogan growled, gripping his sword, gaze searching the area.

"What is a wraith?"

"Twisted spirits that suck the life from your body. Don't let one touch you."

"Are you serious?"

"Deadly serious."

"What do wraiths look like?" Priella asked.

"Nothing more than shadow. However, they cannot abide metal. Poke one and they die. Legend says it frees the trapped soul." Brogan shrugged. "Either way, it gets rid of the creatures.

"Form a phalanx, each person a stride back and to the side of their nearest companion," Brogan commanded. "I'll take the lead. To my left, Blythe, Jace, Priella, and Adyn. To my right, Kollin, Tygalas, Lythagon, and Hadnoddon. Narine, remain in the center and try not to waste your magic. The rest of you, watch for rear attacks. Those with ranged weapons, retreat to the inside of the phalanx if we are pressed."

With everyone in position, he began toward the street.

Debris, refuse, and blackened streaks of blood were everywhere. Doors were destroyed, windows shattered, some walls crumbling. Nothing moved, no evidence of life. It was the eeriest thing Brogan had seen outside of The Fractured Lands.

As they neared an intersection, a shadow flitted out of a broken window, shrieking, eyes glowing as it reached for him. Twisting away, he thrust his sword, the metal piercing the shadow. A high-pitched wail came from the thing and it dissolved.

"That was a wraith," he said.

"It didn't seem so bad," Adyn noted.

"Just don't let them touch you."

He began walking again, light flaring from the far end of the street when a fire burst into existence. Wiry forms danced around it, waving their arms.

"Shaman magic," Jace said.

"Yes." Brogan continued his advance. "If they are here, you know what's coming."

A mass of bodies rushed past the fire, filling the street ahead. The goblins hooted and howled as the mob raced toward them.

"Blythe!"

Her bow was already lifted, arrows of light flying from it in rapid succession. Each goblin she targeted froze and vanished.

"Adyn, Narine," Jace said as he pulled the Eye of Obscurance out of his pocket and slipped it over his head, tucking it under his tunic. "Let's sneak around to approach the shaman fire from the side."

"No," Brogan said. "We remain together."

Ignoring him, Jace raced off toward a side street, the two women running after him.

Brogan growled, "That thief never listens."

He turned toward the charging goblins with a sneer and burst forward, his sword carving a wide arc and taking out three at once. Tygalas ran up the wall beside Brogan, placed the end of his staff on the ground, and flipped over a group of monsters, landing in a gap just ahead, his staff whirling and striking goblins faster than Brogan's eye could see.

To his other side, Hadnoddon swung his hammer, crushing the chest of a rushing goblin and driving it backward into its brethren, a twist of limbs going down in a heap. Lythagon stood at Hadnoddon's side, his axe cleaving a darkspawn in two. Kollin released lightning bolts, the blasts arcing through the rushing monsters, while Blythe's arrows vaporized one after another.

With a smile and a roar, Brogan attacked again.

Jace peered around the corner, the street dark and empty. He took Narine's hand, a throwing knife still gripped in the other, and pulled her around the corner. Adyn followed, a sword in each hand, the trio jogging down a street parallel to the one they had just vacated. Goblin hoots and shrieks mixed with the sounds of fighting. In his opinion, Brogan was reckless, but the man was strong and knew how to use a sword.

The walls at the end of the street flickered with the amber glow of the fire in the square. He slowed as they neared those buildings, all three stepping with care to remain quiet. When he reached the corner, he peeked around and jerked backward, blinking away the afterimage of the flames.

Six shaman wearing bone necklaces danced around the fire, goblins still emerging from the nearby palace. *There could be thousands in there*, he thought. The only way to stop them was to kill every shaman.

He turned and whispered, "There are six. I'll rush them to draw their attention. Their magic cannot harm me." He pulled another throwing blade out. "I'll take two out right away. Adyn, you must take three of the others. Narine, just be ready in case we need you."

Her gaze intense, she nodded. "You couldn't stop me."

Jace grinned. "Let's go."

He rounded the corner and raced across the square. The goblins dancing around the fire noticed, a fireball bursting forth, striking Jace. Briefly blinded, he slowed, eyes clenched as he recalled the last image of the monsters and released both blades. The light faded, the fireball dissipating. One shaman lay on the ground, another holding its shoulder.

Adyn charged past him with a roar, leaping and kicking out with both legs, the impact launching a shaman backward and into the fire. Burning, it screamed and flailed. She spun and attacked, taking three more down in rapid succession. The goblin with Jace's blade embedded in its shoulder scurried off, others passing it as they rushed Adyn, surrounding her in an instant.

Racing along the side of a building, Jace remained focused on the wounded, retreating shaman. The other goblins seemed to ignore him, focused on Adyn. He reached into his boot and drew another blade, waiting for a clear shot. Just before the goblin turned the corner, Jace threw. His blade buried in the nape of the monster's neck. The shaman spun and fell to the ground, twitching.

Jace ducked into a recessed doorway as the other monsters screamed and scattered in all directions, hundreds racing past him and fading into the night. He stepped out to find Adyn standing in a ring of corpses. His gaze went to the end of the street where he had left Narine. Empty.

He rushed over and turned the corner, but only saw the backs of fleeing goblins.

"Narine!" he bellowed.

From the other direction, Brogan, Blythe, Hadnoddon, Lythagon, Tygalas, Priella, and Kollin ran into the square. She was not with them.

He shouted again. "Narine!"

Adyn ran over. "Where is she?"

His heart in his throat, he shook his head. "I don't know."

25

THE FINAL THRONE

G ripping her swords, Adyn rushed inside the palace gate, the others following closely behind. The palace itself consisted of a series of flat-topped pyramids, the tallest in the center. A tower stood above the area, a small pyramid with a flat roof at the top.

They gathered in a long, rectangular plaza, pools of water running down the center, thick, green foliage standing to either side, towering, dark statues among the trees. It gave Adyn the impression they had returned to the jungle outside the city. Other than palm fronds waving in the breeze, nothing moved in the plaza. High above, dark shapes circled in the sky.

"Where are the darkspawn?" she asked.

Brogan grunted. "I don't see any, but they could be hiding in those trees."

"You are familiar with these monsters, Brogan." Jace looked around. "Where would they take Narine?"

He shook his head. "I don't know exactly, but I'm certain we will find a shaman behind it. The creatures need fire to perform much of their magic. Follow any sign of fire, and we'll likely find her."

Priella looked up at the sky. "We must take the tower, regardless of what happens to Narine."

Adyn turned toward the wizardess and snarled, "After all she has sacrificed, you would discard her so thoughtlessly?"

Scowling, Priella said, "This is about saving the world. I don't wish anything bad for Narine, but I cannot sacrifice everyone else to save her. She would understand."

"What about returning to Balmor?" Kollin asked.

"I have been watching Narine closely. I believe I can duplicate the gateway spell. If not, I could fly there myself."

Jace shook his head. "I'll not leave without her. Besides, she is our best chance to get you back safely and quickly." He pointed toward the tower. "If you think you can reach the top without being attacked by those wyverns, go for it. However, I believe you will have better luck if you start at the base and use the tower itself to block their view."

Priella nodded. "Fine. Get me as close as possible. If we find Narine, all the better."

Temple throbbing, thoughts fuzzy, Narine's head drooped against her shoulder. Jostled, she blinked, lids heavy, the pain in the side of her head causing her to clench her eyes shut. Somewhere in the back of her mind, a voice spoke to her. *Wake up, Narine. You are in trouble.* She swam through the muddiness in her mind and surfaced, her eyes opening to a nightmare.

She sat upon a throne inside a spacious chamber, wrists tied to the wooden arms, torso bound to the padded back. The rope was so tight she could not take a deep breath, hands numb from the lack of circulation. Below the dais, hundreds of goblins stared into a fire burning in the heart of the room. Beside the fire, a goblin shaman chanted while waving its arms wildly. On the other side of the flames, another shaman held a curved knife, the creature squatting while warming the knife in the flames.

When the chanting ceased, the flames turned purple, dark, and malevolent. The monsters crooned in response, hands in the air, as a hulking form materialized within the flames.

It stood eight feet tall with yellow eyes, slits for pupils, muscular and obviously male. Black scales and spikes covered its body. When the thing turned its gaze toward Narine, an overwhelming terror held her still, her breath catching. Never before had she wanted to run away so badly.

The creature waved its hand, those around it falling to their knees. In a deep voice, it spoke in the guttural language of the goblins. Then the monster vanished, the flames returning to normal, the goblins rising to their feet. The shaman with the knife walked toward Narine, the others clearing a path. Led by the other shaman, they all began to chant, eyes bulging as they stared toward Narine, who was still held captive by raw terror.

The shaman stepped onto the dais, blade blackened from the fire, smoke rising from it. She tried to pull away, but her bonds held fast. Her breath came in panicked gasps, heart pounding, nails biting into the wood.

It leaned toward her, eyes bulging as it grinned, knife turned in a flat angle. The shaman pressed the hot blade against her skin, and she screamed in pain. It pulled the knife along her forearm, peeling a layer away and leaving a bloody, steaming streak behind. She shrieked.

At the top of the stairs, Adyn, Brogan at her side, led the others past thick, rectangular columns and into the open doorway of the central pyramid. They entered a long, open receiving hall. From high windows above, moonbeams angled in between pillars made of massive stone blocks, casting long shadows. Their advancing footsteps echoed. Another open doorway waited ahead. They walked through it and came to an outdoor area, another set of stairs leading to the next level of the pyramid.

Brogan pointed toward the top of the pyramid. "I see black smoke coming from that section of the building. It could be from a shaman fire."

Jace added, "It could be Narine."

"It leads us closer to the tower base anyway," Blythe said.

With Adyn and Brogan in the lead, they climbed the stairs. Jace, Hadnoddon, Lythagon, and Tygalas followed closely, with Blythe and the two wizards in the rear.

A scream came from inside.

"That was Narine!" Jace said.

They ran up the stairs. When Adyn reached the top, she charged toward the closed door. Her metal body slammed into it with a heavy boom, but the door held fast. She tried the handle. Locked.

Another, far more horrified scream came from inside the room.

∼

Somewhere deep in the vaults of her mind, Narine's will gathered, pushing beyond the pain and terror holding her hostage. A shout echoed in her head. *Your hands are not bound. Use your magic!*

She embraced her Gift. Raw power flooded in, boosted by the rush coming from both the anklet and the jewelry on her hand. A construct formed around her hand, and she channeled the magic through it, a wall of air striking the shaman with the knife. It launched backward and smashed into a cluster of goblins, the entire pile tumbling, some falling into the fire. Shrieks and squeals came from the group, the others in the room responding with hoots and calls.

Narine cast another spell, recreating the terrifying image affixed in her mind. The illusion appeared before her, a replica of the nightmarish demon she had seen moments earlier. It turned toward the goblins and lifted its arms.

The goblins cringed and backed away as the demon advanced. Narine had bought herself some time. Ignoring the agonizing pain from her partially skinned arm, she tried to think of how to get free.

∼

Squeals and inhuman cries came from inside the room. Adyn put her shoulder to the door and struck it again and again, but it held steady.

"Back away." Hadnoddon advanced, his massive hammer in hand.

Adyn stepped away from the door, and the dwarf swung. The hammer struck with a mighty boom, the doorframe cracking. He struck again, the frame breaking away from the surrounding stone. Brogan charged and slammed into the door. It fell back in a swirl of dust.

Adyn rushed past and into a chamber filled with chaos.

It was an open throne room, all the seats missing. Benches had been piled in the middle and were burning, the flames eight feet tall, black smoke rising toward an opening in a lift shaft at the rear of the room. Beyond the fire was a massive creature with black, leathery skin and yellow, slitted eyes. The creature advanced toward the goblins, the monsters backing away.

Priella gasped. "It is the demon lord."

The words carried a sense of dread that fell over the group. Priella had not yet captured the eighth tower or taken Devotion.

"Help!" A cry came from across the room.

The demon moved, advancing a step, allowing Adyn to see beyond it. There, upon a dais, sat Narine, tied to a throne, head and arm covered in blood.

Jace said, "I'll free her if you can cut a path for me."

"What about that thing?" Adyn asked.

"What thing?" He frowned and followed her gaze, shaking his head.

"You cannot face the demon," Priella said. "It would be suicide."

"I don't understand what you two see..." Jace smiled slowly. "It's an illusion. That's why the monsters are backing away from Narine and ignoring us."

Adyn grinned. "In that case, let's kill some darkspawn."

She charged into the mob, swords slashing, goblins screaming as they died. Hadnoddon appeared on one side of her, Tygalas on the other, swords, hammer, and staff felling beasts in rapid succession. Arrows of light flew past, vaporizing any monster they struck. Brogan waded into the mess, roaring as he cut through the monsters with Lythagon at his side. At the rear, Kollin released lightning bolts, the electricity arcing from monster to monster. It was a glorious fight.

Jace stood with Priella at the rear of the room, watching the slaughter and waiting for his chance.

"When this clears," he said, "head up to the tower via the lift shaft. Just follow the smoke."

"Thanks." She arched a brow. "I could not have figured that out myself."

He drew a throwing knife, the blade already blackened by goblin blood. "Well, sometimes one must state the obvious."

When monsters began to respond to the attack and form a modicum of resistance, he spotted the shaman behind them, near the fire. The magic user waved his hands over the flame, preparing to unleash some dark spell.

Jace burst into a run, darting through a gap between Brogan and Lythagon. As he sped past, he cocked and threw, the blade turning end over end and striking the shaman in the chest. The creature clutched at the hilt and staggered, red eyes bulging.

Stopping just in time, Jace dodged a broad swing by Adyn, then burst ahead again. Two goblins stood in the way, swords raised. Jace leapt high and kicked with both legs, striking each goblin in the chest, sending them crashing to their backs. He twisted as he fell to land on his hands and knees, hurriedly rising, spinning, and racing past the stunned monsters.

～

Narine saw Jace rushing toward her, right through her illusion. She dismissed her magic, the demon suddenly disappearing.

Jace leapt onto the dais, eyes filled with concern. "Are you all right?"

Tears blurred her vision. "I am now."

He smiled and drew his dagger. "I'll have you free in a moment."

The battle behind him continued…if it could be called a battle. Without a shaman to control them, the terrified goblins put up little resistance.

He cut one of her wrists free, then the other, Narine wincing from the pain in her arm as she tried to wake her numb fingers. By the time he cut the rope around her chest, the battle was over, the room falling silent, floor littered with corpses. Narine took a deep breath as Jace pulled the last of the ropes away. He leaned in and touched the side of her head. She flinched in pain, his fingers coming away covered in sparkling blood.

"Your head looks horrendous, as does the gash along your arm."

The others neared the dais, some covered in blood, foreheads damp, panting. Only Adyn appeared unaffected.

Priella stepped onto the dais. "It is time *I* helped *you*, Narine. It is the least I can do before I face my destiny."

She placed a palm on Narine's head, her skin glowing with the pale blue magic of Pallan. The flow of energy caused Narine to gasp, a chill wracking her body. Skin regrew on her arm, the pain in her head fading, the weariness she had felt replaced by hunger.

Priella stepped back, the magic still glowing around her body. "And now for the final throne."

She floated into the air and followed the black smoke up into the lift shaft.

Within a bubble of solidified air, Priella floated up the smoke-filled tower. The tower itself was square in shape, intermittent windows offering brief glimpses of the desolate city. As she neared the top, she focused on the opening, unsure of what to expect, hopeful the wyverns would not notice her until the gem was altered by her magic. The bubble, Priella inside it, rose through the opening, the wizardess prepared should anything be waiting.

She opened the bottom of the bubble, her feet stepping onto the stone floor behind a ten-foot-tall dais, a crystal throne sitting upon it, the back facing her. The dais had stairs on three sides, mimicking the pyramid-shaped roof above and palace below. Four thick, stone block columns supported the roof, the sides open to the sky where wyverns circled. One was near enough that she could hear the deep thumps of its wings with each flap, the creature's attention toward the city below. Priella remained still until it sailed past, then she turned toward the stairs.

As she rounded the corner, she froze, a gasp slipping out.

A wyvern waited in front of the dais, wings folded in like a cocoon. Even so, it stood twice the height of a man, its serpentine tail twenty feet long. The monster's yellow, slitted eyes opened wider, wings spreading to reveal short, clawed arms attached to them. The monster opened its maw and released a shriek that shook the floor beneath her feet.

Still holding on to her magic, Priella thrust her arms toward the beast, releasing the bubble surrounding her. It struck the monster, making it stumble backward. She formed another construct, threads of magic encircling the monster's torso, the other end winding around one of the pillars. The wyvern lunged, the chain of magic holding, the stone block in the pillar shifting, dust raining down from the ceiling. Hands covering her head, she cringed, fearing a collapse. Hastily, she discarded the magic tied to the monster and crafted a heat construct, a cone of flames billowing out, engulfing the beast. High-pitched shrieks of agony shook the tower, the wyvern rearing backward, tail thrashing toward her. She tried to leap but wasn't quick enough, the tail smashing into her shins, flipping her over. Her shoulder struck the floor and she tumbled through the lift opening.

Quickly crafting a cushion of air, she caught herself, her magic instantly healing her. Angry, she rose back above the floor and over the dais.

The wyvern was severely burned, scales blackened, holes in its wings. Priella struck it with a blast of air and sent it off the edge. She shifted her position and lowered herself to the top of the dais, casting a globe of light over her shoulder to better see.

The recess in the back of the throne was occupied by an orange garnet in the shape of an octahedron. She extended threads of magic into the opening, wedging them between the gem and the crystal until the garnet popped out into her palm. Visualizing the augmentation construct, eight panels formed and bent together to become a sphere, which she centered around the gem. Her magic flowed into it, the garnet glowing brightly, the orange shifting to pale blue until it became an aquamarine.

High-pitched cries echoed. She turned to find a wyvern landing behind her, three others converging. Quickly, she flung a ball of electricity at the first. It reared back with a shriek as another landed to her left and one to her right. Having little choice, she jammed the gem back into the throne, the pale blue glow of Pallan spreading. A ring of fire came to life at the rim of the tower, burning the creatures near it. She sat on the throne and called upon her god, embracing the magic in the gem until she and it were one. The tower burst into flames, blotting out all else, as prayers across the world flowed into her.

She heard squeals of pain, the wyverns caught in the fire and consumed by its glory. Soon, all sound was lost to the rapture of Devotion, the magic filling her beyond comprehension. Time and the world grew distant, irrelevant. Her magic swelled, flesh burning, heart racing, unable to breathe. Her skin cracked, sparkling, magic-charged blood leaking from it, only to heal again. Immense pain came from her chest as her heart burst, then from her eyes when they burned. Again and again, she thrashed between agony and ecstasy, the magic destroying her body and healing it in a repeating cycle. It was all too much, the raw power roaring through her threatening to destroy her sanity.

Desperate and near the edge of complete madness, she carved off a safe, divided corner of her mind and hid within, the shell protecting her hardened by a lifetime of guilt, regret, and self-loathing. Inside that corner, she huddled and waited for the storm to pass.

26

CRUSHED

The battlefront was chaos, an island of soldiers amidst a sea of darkspawn. The bulwark had been destroyed, the ships along shore burning, sunk, or vaporized. As the darkspawn army poured past the human resistance, Rindle and the others upon the city wall grew more anxious.

Five hundred feet down the wall, a clutch of wizards stood upon a tower, each taking turns launching attacks as wyverns dove in. Lightning and fire-balls arced from the wizards, some hitting their marks and sending wyverns crashing down inside and outside the city walls. One wyvern made it through the defenses, the creature landing upon the tower and biting the head off a wizard. Cries came from the other wizards, some running, others fighting back with magic. The creature burst into flames, shrieking as it thrashed, taking out three more wizards before it fell from the tower, landed on a rooftop, and set a building ablaze.

At shouts from the other direction, Rindle turned to find the darkspawn rushing the city walls. His gaze shifted farther out, searching for surviving soldiers, but they were far to the south, cut off from the city.

Odama barked, "This is it! We are the last line of defense!" He strode along the wall. "We must keep the darkspawn out or the city will fall!" The man glanced over his shoulder. "What are you waiting for, thief?"

Squad leaders called for archers to loose, a steady twang of bows ringing out as Rindle rushed past them to catch up to Odama.

~

Smoke filled the air, carrying the stench of burnt bodies. Hundreds of goblins burned at the base of the wall, thousands more standing beyond the flames, hooting and waving their weapons. Those with bows loosed, arrows sailing over the wall and into the city. Now and then, an unlucky archer took a goblin arrow in the head or neck while taking aim, but the ratio of kills was ten to one in their favor. Even so, the darkspawn outnumbered the humans so greatly, the damage to the horde was insignificant.

Shaman fireballs repeatedly sailed through the sky to strike the city or the walls, setting structures and people ablaze. One dropped toward where Rindle stood. He feared it might strike close, but it sailed past the wall to land in a square filled with soldiers. Armored men on fire flailed and screamed in horror, leaving Rindle trapped somewhere between relief at the fireball missing him and fear of the nightmares that would haunt him should he survive.

Still, the gates held.

A deep roar echoed in the night, the sound terrifying and unfamiliar to Rindle. He peered into the darkness toward where it had come from and saw movement. The ground rumbled once, then again. A shape appeared from the darkness, impossibly tall and horrific. Its gray-blue skin was covered in warts, black hair long and greasy, facial features oversized. The monster stood half the height of the wall, its giant feet crushing anything in its path.

"A rock troll," Odama said.

"You've seen one of these things before?" Rindle asked.

"No. But I have heard stories. None of them good." Odama began shouting orders, calling for ballistae to get ready.

The giant troll stomped through the horde of darkspawn, crushing any unfortunate to remain in its path. The goblins hooted while holding fists and weapons in the air as the troll ran toward the eastern gate. Thumps echoed in the night as ballistae loosed bolts the size of spears. One plunged into the troll's left shoulder, another burying in its abdomen. Neither stopped the monster.

The behemoth smashed into the gate, the impact shaking the wall hard enough to cause soldiers upon it to stumble. Rindle fell to his stomach, preventing himself from rolling off. Two nearby archers were not so lucky, their screams fading as they plummeted.

As he regained his feet, another strike shook the wall, causing him to stagger. He leaned between two merlons and peered toward the gate. The troll smashed its fists against it and the surrounding wall repeatedly, each strike shaking the battlements. Archers loosed upon the giant, arrows covering it until it resembled a pin cushion. Still, the monster roared and attacked.

"We need help." Odama turned to Rindle. "See if any wizards still live. Maybe they can kill this thing."

Rindle spun and ran off in search of the wizards. They had split into two groups, one upon a tower south of the gate and another on a tower midway between the eastern gate and the harbor gate. The latter group had been destroyed by wyverns, but he hoped the prior remained intact.

He raced past hundreds of archers as a bolt of lightning arced from the tower ahead, giving him hope. Another appeared, narrowly missing a diving wyvern. As the creature neared the tower, a dark shape leapt off to fall the last thirty feet. Rindle slowed and watched the demon land amid a dozen wizards. The human magic users attacked, striking the towering demon with lightning, fire, ice, whatever they could. The demon burned, parts of it falling off only to rapidly reform, frozen limbs thawing, fire smoldering. It was an awesome display of magic, the kind that had kept Rindle away from such things for most of his life. When it settled, the demon raised its head to the heavens and laughed. The sound, even from fifty feet away, chilled Rindle.

The demon then shot forward, picked up two wizards by the necks, and smashed their heads together, blood and brain matter spraying out. Purple light enveloped both, and their bodies faded away.

The other wizards made to bolt, but the demon was ready. With a taloned hand, it grabbed the nearest wizard, picked him up, and flung him into the others. They fell in a pile, two sailing over the edge and to the city streets below. The demon attacked those remaining, its dark magic consuming them in a flash. Laughing, it leapt off the wall and faded from sight, undoubtedly going after the wizards who had fallen off.

During the skirmish, Rindle had not moved for fear of the creature noticing him. From what he had seen, the demon was impossible to kill, and he had no desire to be consumed.

Even after it had gone, he remained in place, worried he had wet himself again.

The troll's pounding had ceased, leaving him wondering if the thing had finally died or if it had broken through the gate. In fact, the whole area had grown quiet, the fighting distant from where he stood. He heard hooting and squawking nearby, but when he looked around, he saw nothing. It happened again, this time even closer and from outside the city.

When Rindle leaned between two merlons, he almost yelped in surprise.

Right below him was a pyramid of goblins standing upon each other's shoulders. A shaman stood among those at the bottom, waving its arms and barking orders, while darkspawn climbed the backs of their brethren, armed and just a few feet from the top of the wall.

He drew his rapier and got ready. When a goblin head appeared above the wall, he thrust, skewering it through the eye. The creature shrieked and fell back, disappearing from view. Another appeared. He thrust, the tip of his blade taking it in the throat. Like the first, it pulled back and fell from view. Again and again, Rindle killed any monster that came within reach.

The gateway opened, the Balmor Tower of Devotion visible. Priella and Kollin stepped through and stopped abruptly.

The night sky over the city was orange, screams and the sounds of battle echoing in the distance. Just steps from where they had appeared, Vanda and four hulking Balmorian soldiers waited, along with a man wearing black and orange leather armor and having the dark skin of Kyranni.

The sorcerer approached the gateway and held up his palm, stopping anyone else from coming through. "Remain where you stand!" he commanded before turning to Priella. "The city is under attack." He glanced up as the dark shape of a wyvern sped overhead. "You must embrace your destiny and face H'Deesengar. Only a woman can become the ultimate wizard lord. Only a woman has the mental fortitude for what is required. If you defeat the demon lord, the darkspawn will crumble, for it is his influence that drives them."

Vanda gestured, and the soldiers, each with a heavy pack and a trio of waterskins draped over their shoulders, jumped through the gateway. "This is where the rest of us depart."

"Why?"

"When the demon lord is defeated, the Dark Lord will awaken. We must be there to face him, or all the rest is meaningless."

Priella frowned and glanced at Kollin. "What if I fail?"

Vanda put a hand on her shoulder. "I pray you will not."

The sorcerer stepped through the portal, leaving the couple behind. The portal snapped shut, the Arboretum falling quiet. Priella hesitated, unsure of what to do. An explosion near the eastern gate rocked the city, breaking her from the spell.

"I must go face him."

Kollin took her in his arms and stared into her eyes. "Take me to the wall. I can help save lives." He leaned in and kissed her, his soft, warm lips and firm embrace causing her pulse to race.

When he pulled away, she used her magic and lifted herself into the air.

"I know this is selfish," Priella said from fifteen feet above him, "but I refuse to place you in harm's way. If I survive, I could not bear carrying on without you."

She turned and sailed over the palace, toward the outer wall.

Rhoa stared at the sky through the window, amber clouds rising from fires in the city, the dark shapes of wyverns speeding past. Movement appeared in the Arboretum, drawing her attention to the plaza.

"I see Vanda down there," Rawk said.

The sorcerer stopped in the plaza with five soldiers behind him, each armored and carrying a heavy pack. A shimmer appeared in the air, two people emerging.

"Priella and Kollin have returned," Rhoa exclaimed. "Let's go see if we can help them."

Dragon talon still in her grip, she spun and rushed out of the room, Rawk close behind. They raced downstairs and outside. Not slowing, Rhoa followed the shadowy path through the trees and emerged into the plaza just as Priella floated into the sky.

Kollin turned toward them. "What are you two doing here?"

She looked around. "Where are Vanda and the others?"

He walked toward them. "Gone. Off to join your companions." His eyes softened, voice lowering to a hush. "They intend to face Urvadan."

Rawk gasped.

"But what of the demon lord and the darkspawn attacking the city?" Rhoa asked.

"Priella holds the power of all eight thrones. With it, she intends to face the demon herself. As for the darkspawn… We can only pray she can end the battle."

Rhoa lifted the talon and frowned in frustration. "There must be something we can do."

Kollin nodded. "I intend to hold the palace should the darkspawn break through. Perhaps you can do the same."

"Where to?" she asked.

"The battlements on the roof." Not waiting, Kollin ran off, Rhoa and Rawk chasing after him.

Adyn still held her swords, warily watching the darkspawn corpses in the throne room. Even if none still lived, she secretly feared should she relax, some dark magic might bring them back to life. The memory of the wraith was still fresh in her mind.

Vanda and a group of soldiers came through the gateway before it closed, all eyes going to the mysterious sorcerer.

"What's with the guards?" Adyn asked.

Vanda pointed at a bearded soldier dressed in Balmorian armor. "Sergeant Numell and his men are here to carry our gear." He gestured toward the man with dark skin. "Thendu will be our guide. He is Kyranni and served in the Murguard. They know this is a suicide mission but thought it better than dying in the fracas outside Balmor."

"Sometimes a soldier's job is to die," Numell said. "In this battle, that job will fall to most of us. We thought it might be nice to see something new before it happens."

Brogan smirked, then turned to Vanda. "I heard you mention the Dark Lord when speaking to Priella."

He nodded. "We must journey to the city of Murvaran and confront Urvadan. If we do not, the world will perish."

Jace rubbed his chin. "Astra said we would have to travel to Murvaran before this was finished, but how are we to confront a god?"

Vanda smiled. "Astra is a wise man. Like most wise men, he shared only the information you required, nothing more."

The sorcerer turned to Narine. "When you journeyed to Balmor, you traveled to Prianza?"

She nodded. "Yes, but the city was destroyed, devoid of life."

"We must travel northeast, into The Fractured Lands. Prianza is the nearest city. If you can take us there, it will save time."

Narine nodded and frowned in thought, eyes narrowed for a long moment before she crafted a gateway. Swords in hand, Adyn leapt through and surveyed the area. She stood near the shoreline outside the fallen city's walls, empty docks waiting nearby, the silence nearly as thick as the humid jungle air. As with their prior visit, the odor of decaying flesh lingered.

The others followed, then Vanda led them along the river. When they reached the northeast end of the city, they came to a dock with a large, flat barge. The middle of the craft had a canvas roof supported by a series of posts, benches beneath it with enough seating for two dozen.

After climbing on board, the solders dumped their gear in the gap between the seats. The others followed, many taking seats, but Adyn stood and watched in curiosity as Vanda untied the ropes from the dock. The four guards picked up long poles and pushed the craft into the slow-moving river.

"Rest while you can," Vanda said. "We will rotate in the strongest of you to push, so Numell and his men can rest. When it is light enough, Narine can, once again, begin crafting gateways." He peered up at the full moon. "With the moon as a marker, we will travel through The Fractured Lands and into the Murlands. The city of Murvaran, the home of the Dark Lord, lies directly beneath the source of his power."

While the others settled in, Adyn stood alone at the rear of the craft and stared at the horizon. Somewhere far away, a battle raged. She looked up at the moon, recalling it from her vision in the Temple of Sol. Within a tower beneath its light, she would make a decision upon which the future of the world teetered. She only hoped to make the right one.

27

CONSUMED

Unrivaled power coursed through Priella's veins, her magic becoming an intrinsic extension of herself, no longer requiring her to cast constructs, the spells executing with a mere thought. She hovered hundreds of feet above the city, soldiers on the walls below her fighting for their lives. A countless swarm of darkspawn filled the fields to the east, fires dotting the outer lines, fireballs rising from them at regular intervals. Not only was shaman magic the key to controlling the darkspawn, it also appeared to be causing the most damage. So Priella attacked, channeling her magic and drawing upon its might.

In rapid succession, broad beams of foulfire blasted from her outstretched arms and toward the shaman fires. The pale blue beams struck, vaporizing anything they touched. Some missed, but most did not, snuffing out fires and any nearby goblins, leaving massive craters as a reminder of the raw power on display. In mere moments, half of the bonfires were gone, along with anything nearby.

A cone of dark purple light enveloped her body, undefinable pain erupting from every inch of her being. She would have surely been incinerated had Pallan's magic not healed her even as the malevolent force tried to consume her, body and soul. She withdrew the magic lifting her and began to fall, gravity taking her out of the path of the attack.

She spun as she fell, the pain gone, her concentration returning. Above her, a wyvern hovered, a black creature sitting on its back, yellow eyes filled with hatred.

I have found the demon lord.

Still rotating as she fell, the city came into view, the rooftops racing toward her. Calling upon the wind, a gust struck, driving her forward and up. She twisted with it to find the wyvern and demon chasing her. A cone of purple light came from the demon. Priella dodged by lifting herself higher. Countering, she released a bolt of lightning, striking the demon as the wyvern flew past. The electricity fizzled. As the wyvern banked, she tried another approach.

Drawing upon the surrounding air, she blasted it toward the enemy. It struck with the force of a hurricane, driving the wyvern backward. It spun, losing control as the gale sent it toward the harbor. The demon lost its grip and plummeted toward the city. It smashed into a rooftop, shattering clay tiles and disappearing into the house, leaving a hole ten feet in diameter. The wyvern, losing altitude as it tried to right itself, crashed into the wall near the harbor gate and fell to the street, unmoving, neck twisted.

Priella hovered in place hundreds of feet above the city, staring at the hole in the roof, wondering if the demon could be killed so easily.

A flash of black came from the opening as the demon burst upward, straight toward her. She tried to spin away, but it closed the distance too quickly, the demon's talons digging into her arm. It jerked her upward and tore with the other hand, talons ripping through the flesh on her back. Her mouth opened in a silent scream, the pain overwhelming, but her flesh immediately healed itself, even while the demon's talons remained in her arm and back. They reached the top of the arc and began to fall.

A wyvern flew beneath them, the demon dragging her with as it landed between the monster's wings.

His stomach in knots, Rawk raced onto the battlements along the palace roof, trailing Rhoa and Kollin. In a splash of flames, a fireball landed on a house across the square, the noise causing him to flinch. A throng of people filled the square, screams and cries rising from citizens who had thought the city was shelter from the assault. Smoke rose into the air, wyverns circling above.

He slowed when spotting a fight hundreds of feet above, Priella grappling with the demon as they fell toward the city. The pair landed on a hovering wyvern, and it soon became clear she was in trouble.

"Priella!" Kollin cried out. Thrusting his hands up, a thread of magic lashed out and wrapped around the wyvern's neck. He wrapped the other end around the Tower of Devotion in the center of the palace grounds. The magic thread grew taut, the wyvern stopping with a lurch, its tail whipping around. It shrieked and flapped its wings, pulling against its leash, trying to break free.

Standing on a rooftop six stories up, Rawk was far from the comfort of the ground where his magic was best suited. However, the battlements were made of stone blocks, and stone could not ignore his wishes.

He bent and dug out a massive chunk of rock, forming it into a ball bigger than his head and weighing as much as Rhoa.

"If I throw this, can you boost it with your magic?"

Teeth clenched, Kollin nodded. "Do it."

Rawk wound back with both arms and threw, his stout body flinging the rock into the air. With a wave of his hands, Kollin sent it higher, straight toward the tethered wyvern. The boulder hit the creature in the wing, knocking it sideways. It twisted and began to spiral downward, the demon and Priella falling with it.

Another wyvern swept in and caught them, as the first crashed into the Arboretum hedge maze. As the new creature rose into the air, Priella and the demon on its back, Kollin cried out in frustration.

Suddenly, a green dragon, four times the size of the wyvern, flew in and slammed into the trio, the dragon's talons tearing through the wyvern's wings like tissue, sending the two riders tumbling off. Other dragons appeared in the sky, some launching cones of flame to set wyverns on fire, others crashing into them with such force, the smaller creatures smashed into the city wall or fell to the building below.

Rhoa raised the dragon talon into the air and whooped. "It worked!"

But they all watched in horror as Priella and the demon slammed into the plaza below.

"No!" Kollin screamed.

~

Pain encompassed all thought, but Priella swam through it until she resurfaced. She opened her eyes to a pool of sparkling blood. Her own. She sat upright with a groan, her body still healing itself. The stone tiles beneath her crackled as the blood turned them to red, glowing crystal. Her dress was torn, body covered in sparkling crimson, but she lived. As she rose to her knees, she saw the demon standing before her, its lower teeth, sharp and lethal, jutting up over its upper lip. Its eyes, although slitted and yellow, revealed an intelligence she found daunting, giving the impression it had witnessed entire ages come and go.

"Your magic is strong, human." The demon lord grinned. "I will enjoy consuming your soul."

As it raised its hands, prepared to release some dark, twisted spell, she struck, launching a torrent of foulfire, a spell so destructive, few other than a wizard lord could execute it. The monster's flesh sizzled as the beam of pale blue light consumed it, burning it away to nothing. When she released the spell, only the head and slice of the demon's body remained intact. Yet it did not die.

In moments, the demon reconstructed, its body and limbs filling in. H'Deesengar laughed. "Puny human. Not even foulfire can hurt me. I am invincible."

Still on her knees, Priella wondered how she could defeat such a monster. Vanda's words rolled through her head. *"Only a woman can become the ultimate wizard lord. Only a woman has the mental fortitude for what is required."* She had never put much thought into those words before, but it suddenly became clear.

Diving forward, she thrust her hand out and grasped the side of the demon's leg, attacking its mind.

Once she had ascended to the throne, dominating humans, even wizards and wizard lords, had been a simple task, especially when boosted by physical contact. In contrast, the demon lord's mind was foreign and corrupt, twisted and terrifying. Rather than bend to her will or even try to resist, it attacked with raw fury, attempting to consume her mind.

She drew upon her magic and fought back. Crafting a shield in her mind, she walled off the monster and gathered her will, at the same time collecting as much magic as she could hold. It stormed inside her, skin cracking, eyes burning, heart bursting, all quickly repairing itself. She then released her shield and struck. Not to dominate, but to destroy. With every ounce of magic she could muster, Priella enveloped H'Deesengar's mind and compressed it tighter and tighter.

The demon screamed so loudly, the ground shook and Priella's ears burst, fluid running down her jawbone. Raw, negative energy flashed, burning her flesh away, but she did not…could not stop her assault. Wavering at the edge of death, her body healing itself again and again, she pressed against the demon's mind, seeking to crush it. As her magic began to wane and she feared she might fail, the pressure against her ceased. The demon's mind collapsed to nothing, its body imploding with a thunderous boom.

Priella collapsed to the ground, the flesh on her arm torn and shredded as darkness crashed in.

Exhausted, Rindle stabbed another goblin, the creature falling off the living scaffold of darkspawn. He had killed so many that he'd lost track, the blade of his rapier slick with dark blood.

A monster appeared two merlons down, another from the merlon beyond it. He rushed over to engage, his rapier killing the first, Rindle hastily jumping back to avoid an attack from the other. As he backed away, the monster stalked toward him, ready to fight. By then, three more poured through adjacent gaps to land on the wall. Tired and outnumbered, with more monsters climbing onto the wall, he turned and ran. The goblins hooted in excitement and gave chase.

For hundreds of feet, he ran, following the gentle curve of the wall, the towers above the east gate coming into view. Odama and his men were engaged with another group of darkspawn, soldiers and goblins falling off the wall. A hundred feet before reaching the skirmish, he came across two ballistae, still loaded, the massive bolts tied to a log resting upon the top of the wall. He had no idea how the weapons had not yet been fired, but he said a silent prayer and reacted.

He grabbed the first ballista, cut the rope with his blade, and spun the weapon toward the chasing mob, twenty feet away and closing fast. There were a dozen of them, weapons held in the air, red eyes filled with bloodlust. Aiming at the lead monster, he pulled the trigger. The four-foot-long bolt launched with a thud, the recoil causing him to stumble. The missile struck and blasted the monster back a dozen strides, the bolt ripping through five others behind the first, toppling the rest off the wall.

Turning, he spotted Odama and his men trapped a hundred feet down the wall, a mob of twenty-some darkspawn in front of them, their backs facing Rindle. He ran to the other ballista and turned it toward them, not bothering to cut the rope this time. He took aim and loosed. The bolt plunged into the goblins, the rope snapping taut. Rindle ducked just as the log launched over his head. Like a whip, it spun and crashed into the rear of the monsters, leaving shrieks and flailing bodies in its wake, monsters crashing into each other with many flying off the wall.

Standing upright, his heart still racing, he turned and saw another group of darkspawn coming from the south. *They keep climbing up the pyramid of bodies.* So exhausted he could barely lift his blade, Rindle began to weep. *This is the end. I am doomed. We are all doomed.*

A light flashed from the heart of the city, a thunderous boom echoing across the sky. Like an ocean wave, a thump of energy passed by him, the flash of light fading into the distance.

The goblins on the wall stopped and began to shriek. From the battlefield below, more screams emerged, the horde of remaining monsters running toward the darkness. The ones on the wall turned and fled, as well.

"She did it," he muttered. "Priella killed the demon lord."

He fell to a sitting position, back to a merlon, his bloody blade resting across his legs, tears cascading down his cheeks. He wept for all the destruction, for those who had died, for Garvin, but mostly, he wept for the fact that he, somehow, still lived.

Moments passed before approaching footsteps drew his attention. He lifted his head to find Odama a few feet away, the man's face bloody, arm hanging limply.

"Your timing was good, thief." The man cradled his arm, wincing. "Although the log you launched at us broke my arm."

"What?"

Odama grinned. "Still, you killed two dozen goblins with that shot, so I can accept my injury as collateral damage."

He nodded toward the gate towers. "Come on. Let's get a drink. After tonight, I wish to pass out and skip the nightmares I suspect are waiting."

Rhoa burst through the door into the Arboretum, Kollin and Rawk only a step behind. The three of them raced out to the plaza, slowing when they saw the devastation.

Priella lay on her stomach, her dress shredded, hair gone, skin cracked and blistered. The area surrounding her was charred and eaten away to create a bowl three feet deep. The exception was an island of glowing, crimson crystal in the center, pulsing as if alive.

Kollin sped past Rhoa. "Priella!"

He scrambled down into the crater to kneel by her side, lifting his arm to ward himself against the pulsing crystal, as he would when too near to a fire. When he rolled her over, Rhoa gasped.

Priella's eyes were blackened sockets.

"No," Kollin sobbed, cradling Priella's head in his lap. "Don't leave me. You promised, Priella. We were to be together."

Rhoa felt the pain of Kollin's loss but could find no words of comfort. She gazed up at the sky, dragons attacking the last of the wyverns, but the demon was nowhere to be seen. She wondered if it had been defeated or if they were doomed. Her gaze returned to the sobbing Kollin and the woman in his arms.

Priella then gasped. Kollin sucked in a breath as her eyelids reformed to cover the blackened sockets. The flesh on her arms sealed, burns smoothing, pale skin replacing the ruddy scars. Red hair sprouted from her head.

Her eyes blinked open to focus on Kollin. He smiled, tears dripping from his cheeks and onto hers.

"I thought I lost you," he whispered.

"I was ready to die, had given myself over to it. Then I heard your voice and realized I wished to live. My magic was all but expelled. Just enough remained to heal myself."

He bent and kissed her, the moment bringing tears to Rhoa's eyes. She glanced at Rawk, who had turned away, embarrassed.

She put her hand on his shoulder. "Are you all right?"

"Yes." Rawk swallowed. "I... It is difficult to concentrate. The gemsong of the crystal is so compelling, it is hard to think."

Kollin helped Priella stand, the couple climbing out of the crater and walking toward Rhoa and Rawk. Her destroyed dress covered nothing of her upper body and little below the waist. When Rawk glanced toward them, he quickly turned away and began kneading his thick hands. Rhoa smiled at his embarrassment.

"Perhaps you should find something so the queen can cover up?" she suggested.

"Allow me." Kollin loosened his sash. He shrugged off his robes, exposing his long, lean frame covered in only his smallclothes and boots. "Wear this, Priella." He slid the robes over her shoulders and pulled them together at the front.

It was Rhoa's turn to feel embarrassed, her cheeks flushing, but she refused to turn away, instead focusing on Priella, who gave Kollin a small smile.

The thumping of wings arose. Rhoa turned toward the sound as a massive green dragon landed in the plaza. It bent its iridescent, purple head toward her.

Kollin pushed Priella behind him and gathered his magic, prepared to fight.

Rhoa leapt in front of him before he could loose a spell. "No!" She held up the dragon talon. "This dragon is a friend. She and the others came to help us fight, not harm us." She looked over her shoulder. "Isn't that right, Zyordican?"

The female dragon dipped its head. "The human child is correct. Darkspawn are a blight to this world, a product of foul magic. While we have no love for humans, we outright despise the wyverns and other creatures created by the demon lord."

Kollin gaped at the dragon. "It can talk."

Rhoa smiled. "You are quite observant." She turned to the dragon. "Where did the others come from? I thought you were the last."

"Did you forget about my egg already?"

Turning her gaze to the horizon where dragons battled the last of the wyverns, Rhoa's mouth dropped open. "They all came from that *one* egg?"

"Dragon magic is unique in nature. When it hatched, thirteen young emerged."

The dragon turned to Priella. "I sensed the battle you fought against H'Deesengar, but I can no longer feel the demon lord."

Priella nodded. "I believe it is dead...or at least no longer of this world."

"If true, every being alive is in your debt. The demon lord should have never left the Netherplane. Its negative magic was a poison to our world, destined to destroy everything. Urvadan must pay for his betrayal, for he brought us to the brink of doom."

"My companions...friends are on the way to face Urvadan. I believe they intend to kill him," Rhoa said.

Zyordican stepped closer, the dragon's massive head lowering until level with Rhoa's. "They will fail."

"What? Why?"

"Because you are not with them. Only one immune to Urvadan's magic can face him and survive."

28

SUCCUMBING

W hen Rawk first encountered the dragon within the elven city of Silvaurum, he had been so worried about Rhoa, he paid little attention to the dragon itself. This time, he had no such worry. He ogled the majesty of the giant beast, which was the size of a small ship. While he had once heard Salvon call wyverns cousins to dragons, anyone who had been close to both would disagree. Other than scales, wings, claws, and teeth, the two had little in common. To call them the same was to say a finch was the same as an eagle, or a squirrel the same as a moarbear. Wyverns were fierce and frightening, but were little more than twisted, mindless monsters. Dragons, on the other hand, were creatures of beauty and grace, in addition to power, intelligence, and daunting size. More than anything, Zyordican's presence exuded magic. Somehow, the dragon's magic tempered the gemsong of the red crystal, allowing Rawk to focus.

He replied to the dragon's statement. "But Rhoa could not travel with them. They used gateways to reach Murvaran quickly, and her immunity to magic makes it impossible."

"Then," the dragon said, "she must travel via another means. Urvadan must be defeated. The time is ripe, for the balance of magic has shifted and he no longer holds the demon lord in the Temple of Tenebris."

Rhoa bit her lip, concern evident on her face. "How... How could I possibly face a god and win?"

Zyordican's eyes glazed over, the dragon staring into space. "Urvadan's weakness is his own magic. A weapon forged of the essence of his power could harm him..."

"What does that mean?" Priella furrowed her brows. "And where would we even get such a weapon? We don't know anything about Urvadan's magic."

The dragon turned to her and tilted its head. "Are you not a wizard lord?"

"I... I am."

"Then the magic of Urvadan flows through you. Wizard magic was Urvadan's gift to the world. The magic of wizard lords includes the god's own essence, as well."

Rawk turned and stared across the plaza, toward the crimson-hued crystal. When he looked at it, the gemsong returned with a vengeance, calling him with the promise of ecstasy. He had seen the same crystal twice – once with Taladain's death, then after Thurvin was killed by the stone spear Rawk wielded.

"Their blood...," he said aloud. "Wizard lord blood creates the crystal. It is made of the Dark Lord's magic."

Without waiting for a reply, Rawk knew what must be done.

He crossed the plaza, walking dangerously close to the dragon but sensing he had little to fear. His attention was fixed on the crystal, the gemsong luring him forward. Stepping down into the charred pit where the demon lord once stood, he drew close to the crystal and extended his hand. Intense heat radiated from it. It burned his palm, but he ignored it, the gemsong demanding he obey. The first touch was agony to his body and pleasure to his soul, despite his melting flesh. His other hand touched it, the pain excruciating, the crystal pulsing. He closed his eyes and embraced his magic, the rapture taking him deeper and deeper until he was lost.

"Rawk!" Rhoa called out, but the dwarf ignored her.

When he touched the crystal, Rawk screamed, his hand beginning to burn. Rather than pull away, his other hand thrust into it. He screamed again.

She ran to the edge of the pit. "Rawk! Stop!"

His eyes opened, only the whites visible, eyeballs rolled up, jaw dropped as he moaned. The crystal crackled and sparked, his hands covered in burns, flames licking up his arms, but he did not stop. Sweat poured down his bald scalp, his moans turning to sobs, but he still did not release it.

"*Rawk!*" Rhoa cried, horrified. "Please, stop!"

She ran into the pit and grabbed him by the shoulder, pulling with all her might. It had no effect. Wrapping her arms around his chest, she pulled. She might as well try to topple the tower looming above her. When she stepped back, his entire body burst into flames, the heat forcing her backward and out of the pit.

Sitting on the rim, Rhoa cried, tears rolling down her cheeks. "Rawk!" She looked over her shoulder, pleading to the dragon. "Please. You must do something to stop him."

With sadness in Zyordican's eyes, the dragon said, "I am sorry, child. It is too late. This is his gift to give, and to deny him now would make his sacrifice meaningless."

Through a blur of tears, she turned back toward her friend, his body covered in flames, yet still shaping the crystal. He collapsed to his knees but kept working, the crystal crackling with energy. Finally, he fell backward and lay still, his body burning, skin scorched, bubbled, and melted. It was the most dreadful thing Rhoa had ever seen.

The ground shook, giant, taloned feet appearing beside the edge of the pit, Zyordican standing over her. The dragon inhaled deeply and blew, a cone of fire shooting out and enveloping Rawk. It was so bright, Rhoa flung up her arm and turned away, but she felt no heat. As before, she was immune to such magic.

When the roar of the fire ceased, she lowered her arm to find her friend gone, nothing but gray ashes left in the outline of his stout form. A gust of wind swept through, the ashes dispersing on the breeze, leaving nothing but her memory of him and his final gift.

Wrapped in a shell of grief, Rhoa stared at the shimmering, crystal sword at the bottom of the pit, burning as red as the hatred rising inside her. She hated Taladain for killing her parents, hated the demon lord for the destruction it had caused. Most of all, she hated the gods for the games they played, the lives they ended for their own greed. Rawk had sacrificed himself so Urvadan could die. The least she could do was repay his sacrifice with one of her own.

Rhoa stepped down into the pit, bent, and gripped the hilt. The sword felt hard and cold in her grasp, but nothing happened. It did not crackle and burn her, nor did her clothes catch on fire. In fact, it felt like she held a sword of red glass rather than a weapon of power.

She turned toward Zyordican, hurriedly wiping her eyes. "I cannot travel to Murvaran by gateway. Will you take me there?"

The dragon dipped its head. "Yes, child. Climb on, and we will be off."

29

THROUGH THE FRACTURE

On his back with his coat as a pillow, Jace lay on a bench, Narine beside him, her head on his chest. He opened his eyes to find the soldiers poling the barge upriver, the dark jungle slipping past. It was still dark, the sky to the east glowing with the promise of dawn. He wondered how many sunrises remained. *How are we expected to face a god?* As usual, Vanda had circumvented the question when asked the evening prior.

No longer able to sleep, Jace slipped out from beneath Narine, placing his coat beneath her head as he gently laid it down. She did not need a blanket, not with the humid jungle weather. Even at night, the air had not cooled enough to matter. He did not look forward to the heat of mid-day.

The others were already awake, except Vanda. The sorcerer rested against the pile of packs in the middle of the barge, his hood covering his face. Jace circled the island of benches and stepped out from the awning above them.

Brogan turned toward him. "Ah. So you are finally awake."

"Finally? The sun's not even up yet."

Blythe sighed. "Neither Brogan nor I could sleep. We gave up about an hour ago and found Tygalas here, staring out toward the jungle."

The elf turned toward them. "This forest is…different. It speaks of rain and heat, lizards and large insects…and an evil to the east."

Jace snorted. "Of course. We are heading east." He then frowned. "You talk to the trees?"

Tygalas gave him a wistful smirk. "Not exactly. It is more of a...feeling. I get a sense of what they feel, of what they know."

"How do trees know anything?"

"They know their surroundings."

"I wonder what trees would talk about anyway." He lowered his voice, deep and booming. "My, this is wonderful dirt. You should come over and have a taste. What? Oh, yes. I forgot to tell you. A man relieved himself on that patch just this morning."

Hadnoddon and Lythagon burst out laughing, Brogan joining them. Even Adyn snickered, but both Tygalas and Blythe remained quiet, him appearing confused, her with a reproachful glare.

"Tygalas was sharing something special," she said. "Something humans do not understand. You could try to be more supportive." Resting a hand on the elf's shoulder, she added, "Unlike them, I understand, for I feel it, as well. It is...as if the jungle tells us it is dangerous, yet any danger it poses is irrelevant in the face of what lies to the northeast."

Brogan rubbed his goatee and stared toward the brightening sky. "I can tell you what lies to the northeast. Death."

"Ominous first words to hear on a day I was already dreading."

Jace turned at the voice, seeing Narine standing behind him. "Sorry if we woke you."

She shook her head. "I am rested well enough."

"Good," Vanda said from his position on the deck. He stood and lowered his hood. "As soon as you get a clear view, you must begin opening gateways." The sorcerer approached Thendu. "You are familiar with this river. How far are we from The Fractured Lands?"

The man frowned in thought. "We are likely fifteen miles upstream from Prianza, for the river has narrowed greatly. We should see the landing at any moment."

Brogan grunted. "I remember that landing. It's where fresh Murguard soldiers are dropped off."

Thendu nodded. "You are correct."

"Good," Vanda said. "Get us to the landing and we will eat. By the time we are finished, we should have sufficient light."

From the top of a rise two hundred feet above the river, Narine held the solar lens to her eye and peered through it. She spotted a distant hilltop capped by a rock formation, a brown patch amid the green of jungle. With the image in mind, she crafted a gateway, allowing them to cover ten miles in a matter of steps.

Odd, she thought as she released the portal. *Mere days ago, the ability to travel this way stirred a sense of wonder. Now it has become a thing of utility, no different than a ship or carriage...other than the time saved.*

From her new position, she peered across the top of the jungle canopy and spotted an oddity – a land formation unlike any other.

A sheer cliff wall, hundreds of feet tall and bracketed by a range of impossibly tall peaks, ran for miles to the north and south. The wall was marred by narrow, shadowy crevasses.

"The Fractured Lands." Brogan scowled while staring at the distant landmark. "When I left the Murguard all those years ago, I swore I would never return."

Blythe arched a brow. "What did I tell you about swearing?"

Jace, Adyn, and Hadnoddon chuckled, but Brogan's grimace remained in place.

Thendu nodded. "I can see it in your eyes, Brogan Reisner. You understand."

Rather than respond, Brogan asked, "Does anything of the Murguard remain?"

Vanda shook his head. "I do not believe so. The Murguard's collapse happened weeks ago, precipitating Kyranni's fall. Only Kelluon's magic prevented Anker from succumbing to the darkspawn sooner." The sorcerer stared into the distance. "As he discovered, a wizard lord might hold off an army, but a demon lord is another matter."

Narine lifted the solar lens and peered through it, seeing broken, man-made walls at the base of numerous openings in the cliffside. "Where do we go from here?"

"Seek chasm sixteen," Brogan said. "It is the widest and will enable us to travel faster."

She moved the lens until she spotted a chasm larger than the others. A clearing was visible just outside it, surrounded by stone buildings. Narine concentrated on the view, the aspects that made it unique. Picturing it firmly in her mind, she cast another gateway, the opening appearing before them. They passed through and found themselves in the shade of the cliffs, the morning sun still low in the east.

The area was quiet, the ground covered in dirt and rock, the jungle just beyond the buildings to either side. Many of the structures had collapsed, stone blocks shattered. Skeletons and rotting corpses in leather armor lay everywhere, many piled atop one another. Among them were the dark, twisted bodies of goblins. The smell was horrible, forcing Narine to cover her face.

"These soldiers deserve better than this," Brogan growled.

"What would you have us do?" Blythe asked. "We cannot bury them all, nor do we have time to build a pyre."

His scowl deepened. "I know." He shook his head. "I understand, but I don't have to like it."

"We need to keep moving," Vanda said as he headed toward the chasm.

Jace walked beside Narine, still covering her nose with one hand, gripping the solar lens in the other.

The chasm itself was a half-mile wide, jungle growing up the tan cliffsides. The wall spanning the gap had been destroyed, but small sections remained, standing fifty feet in height. With Vanda, Numell, and Thendu in the lead, they climbed a pile of rubble twenty feet high. At the top, they stopped and gazed into the chasm. What Narine saw made her gasp.

Thousands upon thousands of goblin corpses covered the ground from chasm wall to chasm wall, the bodies strewn about in piles. Among them lay four giant bodies with blue-gray skin, each the size of a house. Their faces were grotesque with overly large, bulbous noses, warts, and bulging eyes.

"What are they?" she asked.

"Rock trolls," Brogan said. "They are roughly as smart as a rock, but difficult to kill. My guess is that some did not die on this side of the wall. Once breached, the trolls likely climbed over and lay waste to the soldiers in camp."

"This place gives me the creeps," Blythe said.

Tygalas nodded. "The trees scream for us to turn around and leave this place."

Hadnoddon grunted. "I think the trees might be right this time."

"The view is clear, Narine," Vanda said. "Craft another gateway, and we will continue."

She tore her gaze from the nearest rock troll and peered through the lens. In the distance, she saw the chasm turn and found a spot below the wall where a large boulder waited. Once pictured, she crafted a gateway.

As they advanced deeper into The Fractured Lands, other chasms joined theirs, reminding Narine of river tributaries, with them on the main branch. Twice, they had come upon pools of water, one with a wicked stench, the water undrinkable, the other fed by a fresh spring. At the second, they drank deeply and refilled their waterskins before continuing.

When visibility was less than a mile, they walked rather than consume Narine's magic. Those stretches made her body weary, often having to climb since the ground seemed to be forever rising.

With the sun directly overhead, the humidity unbearable, they stopped beneath an overhang and ate lunch. The respite was welcome, allowing Narine to rest. She was covered in sweat and needed a wash, but such niceties were no longer available.

A chill drifted past, and Narine gasped, her hair standing on end. A guard farther back in the cavern screamed, stiffening, eyes bulging as he fell onto his side.

Brogan sprang to his feet. "It's a wraith! Get out!" He drew his sword and stepped out of the shadow, gazing into the dark recess.

Narine and the others scrambled out into the sunlight, Lythagon last. He did not make it. Eyes bulging, he collapsed and lay there, unmoving, skin pale, mouth open in a silent scream.

Everyone stared in horror. Their packs remained in those haunted shadows.

Sword in his grip, Brogan returned to the shade, stepping over the dead dwarf. Suddenly, he darted forward and lunged. A shadow swept past him. The man spun with a slash. The blade cut through the wraith, an ear-piercing wail emerging. The shadow dissolved, and Brogan lowered his sword. He frowned down at the dead soldier, a Balmorian named Graymor, his gaze then shifting to Lythagon's corpse.

"May the gods smile upon you, my friend," he said softly before raising his voice. "We must be wary of the shadows. Like other darkspawn, wraiths cannot abide the light."

Hadnoddon knelt beside Lythagon, lowering his head and closing his eyes. Tygalas approached and put a hand on the dwarf's shoulder, both sharing a silent moment for their lost companion.

From the middle of the chasm, Blythe pointed east. "What is that?"

Narine and the others walked over to stand beside her for a better view. The eastern horizon was covered by a dark cloud tinted red at the edges.

"Is it from a fire?" Adyn asked.

Jace snorted. "That would be one massive fire."

"It is not," Vanda said. "What you see is neither cloud nor smoke."

"What is it then?" Jace questioned.

The sorcerer pushed his hood back and stared northeast. "It is a blanket of evil, crafted by the Dark Lord himself. Sunlight is unable to penetrate it, leaving the Murlands forever in shadow. Beneath that umbrella live the dark-spawn." He turned toward them. "We must reach the Murlands before we lose light. It will be dangerous, but so will these chasms if we are caught in them after dark."

With the sunlight behind her, swords ready, Adyn stepped through the gateway and into darkness. It was not the blackness of night, but more akin to the dimmed light of a full eclipse. She continued forward until reaching the edge of a steep decline. Beneath a layer of thick, red-tinted clouds was a desolate valley, the ground covered in rocks and odd, twisted, leafless trees, despite it being late spring.

Dead, she thought. *Everything down there appears dead.*

The far end of the valley widened to a lowland, dark and foreboding. A red light shimmered in the distance, drawing Adyn's gaze. She had seen the image before in the vision she experienced in the Temple of Sol. Knowing what she must do, her stomach twisted.

The others came through the gateway and gathered around her, their footsteps on the dirt disturbing the silence.

"I have never heard of anyone coming this far before now," Brogan said. "None could do so without surviving one or more nights in the chasms."

"You may be the first humans to ever gaze upon these lands," Vanda said. "You may also be the last. Only time will tell."

Jace turned to the man. "That does not instill much confidence in our mission."

Vanda shrugged. "Nothing is assured. Killing a god is no simple feat."

"No simple feat? You say that like it has been tried before."

The old man closed his eyes and took a deep breath. "It has...long ago."

Adyn looked at her companions, their brows furrowed, eyes narrowed in thought, but nobody pressed the man further.

Vanda looked up at the clouds. "We have reached the Murlands and leave the sun behind us." He pointed toward the red light in the distance. "There, the Dark Lord awaits."

Narine lifted the metal tube to her eyes and peered through it. A moment later, she lowered it with a frown. "I can't see anything."

The sorcerer nodded. "With the sunlight shrouded, the enchantment will not work. However, I have another solution."

He squatted and produced a vial of dark liquid. After tracing in the sand, swirls and lines intersecting in a complex symbol, he dripped some blood onto it, then waved his hands while mumbling words in a language akin to Hassakani. The symbol began to glow, the sand swirling. Faster and faster it spun, like a tiny tornado. He rose to a standing position, hands spread over the swirling dust as it lifted off the ground. When he extended his arms toward the red light in the distance, the glowing dust storm followed. Through the eye of the cyclone, an image coalesced.

The ground was dark and rocky, a murky fog swirling. A plateau loomed ahead, occupied by a city with a massive tower in the center capped by what appeared to be huge claws. Crimson clouds hung over the city, a gap directly over the tower. Through the opening, a beam of moonlight shone down, feeding the magic of the god that lived there. Wyverns were visible in the moonlight, massive wings outstretched as the monsters circled above the city.

"Picture it, Narine," Vanda said. "Open one last gateway and bring us to the foot of Murvaran."

30

MURVARAN

Following a zig-zagging trail, Jace and his companions climbed the hillside to the city of Murvaran. A quarter of the way up, they came to a tunnel entrance, the interior dark and foreboding. Vanda told them the tunnel system was vast, a temple of darkness at the center. He warned them not to enter. Ever. Jace could think of nothing he would wish to avoid more than entering those warrens.

As they drew near the top of the rise, it grew brighter, their surroundings taking on a warm hue and giving Jace the sensation he had traveled to another planet – a barren place that died thousands of years ago. It felt odd to see nothing alive. Not a single plant, insect, or animal. While he worried what terrifying creature they might stumble across, he began to long for *some* sign of life, even if it were darkspawn.

No longer able to use Narine's magic to travel, Jace removed the amulet from his coat pocket and slid it over his head, tucking it beneath his tunic. Just having the cool metal against his flesh felt like he had donned armor. Not against swords, but certainly against magic.

It worked against shaman magic, but will it help me when facing a god?

Acknowledging the sheer insanity of their quest, his mind returned to the question he had asked himself often of late. *What am I doing here?*

One look at Narine answered the question, her gaze staring intently ahead, jaw set in determination. *How did I ever let a woman capture my heart?* He had once heard an old man say, *"When you fall in love, you lose your mind."* Jace had laughed it off at the time, thinking the old man was a kook. Now he knew better. *He* was the kook and, for some reason, enjoyed it.

They crested the rocky rise and gazed upon the city itself.

There was no outer wall, the buildings made of stone, the entire city circular in design. A flat ring a few hundred feet in depth surrounded it, paved with both light and dark stone blocks. The dark tiles were laid out in a repeating pattern of huge triangles. Within the city, the streets were straight, leading to the massive tower at the center, like spokes of a colossal wheel. It was quiet, no movement in sight.

Jace was the first to speak. "There is something familiar about the way this city is built."

Vanda pointed toward the flat ring to their left and right. "This pattern is an eight-pointed star, the tower positioned at the center. The entire city itself was crafted as a massive rune to gather prayers and feed them to the lord of the tower."

Frowning in thought, Jace gripped the Eye of Obscurance through his tunic. "It is designed similar to my amulet...and also to the pattern on the floors of both the Temple of Sol and the Temple of the Oracle."

Vanda smiled. "Very good, young thief. All three are used to focus power, as is the chamber Narine visited during her Trial at the University."

He waved them forward. "Come. This place appears vacated. I believe H'Deesengar took every darkspawn he commanded when he marched west."

Brogan pointed up. "What of the wyverns?"

Pausing, Vanda looked toward the sky. "Yes, they might pose a problem. However, I suspect they watch the top of the tower while something else waits below."

Jace frowned. "What are you not telling us?"

Vanda shrugged. "The Dark Lord is unlikely to leave himself completely unguarded, even while resting. The creatures that normally occupy the surrounding area might be elsewhere, but that does not mean he is alone."

With the sorcerer in the lead, Adyn, Tygalas, Hadnoddon, and Brogan on the flanks, the four remaining soldiers in the rear, they marched toward the nearest street.

The buildings were made of charcoal-colored stone, the streets laid with bricks of the same color. Cracks had formed along many walls, some collapsed, the rubble strewn across the street. A layer of dust covered everything, their passing leaving footprints easily traced. Arched bridges over the street connected the upper stories of the buildings, some cracked, others crumpled and leaving only stumps jutting up on both sides of the street. Every window had been shattered, doors removed, interiors dark and empty. Much like the surrounding, desolate land, it felt like the ghost of a city – a grave marker of a time long forgotten.

As they neared the center, the street widened and buildings grew larger. With entrances a flight above the street and columns atop the stairs, each structure had short towers capped by domes of tarnished copper, giving the impression they had once been majestic. Cracks, broken columns, missing windows, and a layer of dust now marred every structure.

They arrived at a sprawling, circular square paved by colored tiles in the pattern of a giant eye, the tower itself the iris. It was hundreds of feet across at the base and was the tallest structure Jace had ever seen.

"It must be a thousand feet tall," Brogan muttered.

"Mur Tower," Vanda said softly.

Jace turned to the man. "I don't suppose this Dark Lord is at the bottom?"

The sorcerer shook his head and pointed to the sky. "See that light?"

A shimmering, pale glow came from the top of the tower.

"Yes."

"It comes from Urvadan."

"I was afraid you would say that."

They crossed the square, the mosaic of the eye vaguely reminding Jace of the one in Shadowmar Castle. There, the tiles had been in the image of an eight-headed dragon, each head a different color. It had been an elaborate trap intended to set fire to anyone who tried to claim the treasure. Anxiety suddenly twisted in his stomach.

"Stop!"

Everyone paused, some in mid-step, some mere inches from the edge of the mosaic.

"What if this is a trap?" Jace pointed toward the lines of the eye.

"A trap?" Adyn asked.

"Yes. If the colored tiles trigger some sort of trap, they are simple to avoid for those who know better, likely to kill anyone who does not. It would be a good way to protect the tower from enemies."

Brogan snorted. "What nonsense is this?"

Jace gave him a level look. "Remember what I told you about the treasure room in Shadowmar? I would have been fried alive if I didn't think about such things."

The big man shrugged. "True…"

Hadnoddon rubbed his beard. "The thief has a point. Makers often use such tricks to create passive guardians against intruders."

Vanda nodded. "Good enough for me. Everyone, careful where you step. Make an effort to reach the entrance without touching any colored tiles."

They each leapt over the five-foot-wide outline of the eye and headed toward the center. Red tiles in jagged patterns trailed from the tower itself, giving the impression of a bloodshot eye. Jace wondered if the color of the tiles resulted in something far more sinister. With care, they walked between two such streaks and toward the tower entrance. There, a twenty-foot-tall black door waited, rounded metal bolts dotting the panels.

"It is as big as a city gate," Blythe noted.

"How does it open?" Brogan asked. "There is no knob."

"Allow me." Jace approached and held his palm close to it. The hair on his arms stood on end. He pulled back. "Don't touch the door."

He glanced up at the arch above it, the symbol of an eye at the top. He looked down at the ground, a streak of red tiles to each side of him, spaced six feet apart. Off to the side, he saw something that caught his eye. Hopping over two lines of red tiles, he walked past the door and knelt. A gouge had been worn into the stone. He looked up, the wall beside him appearing innocuous.

"Hadnoddon. Come here but avoid the red tiles."

The dwarf leapt over, his armor clanking.

"Could this be a doorway like those leading to Oren'Tahal?"

Placing his hand on the wall, Hadnoddon closed his eyes, fingers trailing across the surface. He then stopped and pushed, the brick sinking in, a click sounding, a section of the wall creaking open.

Grinning, Jace turned toward the others. "Let's go." He crept inside, unsure of what to expect.

From behind, he heard a cry. Spinning, he saw one of Numell's men on the ground, writhing, red sparks of magic skittering across his body. The man fell still, smoke rising from empty eye sockets.

Numell stepped close to the man, peering down while shaking his head. "May the gods watch over you, Kaleel."

"What happened to him?" Brogan blurted.

Vanda gestured toward the man's foot, still touching a patch of red tiles. "It appears Jace was correct. The tiles hold a deadly enchantment. I suggest we take care to avoid touching them."

Everyone turned toward Jace, who still stood in the open doorway. He gave them a nod, turned, and entered the tower.

His gaze was drawn to the center, where a column of crystal ran from the floor to the ceiling a hundred feet above. The crystal shimmered with light, illuminating the spacious interior. Along the outer wall stood statues three times the height of a man. A narrow beam of light gleamed from a glass disk mounted to an ornate brass pole, the other end of the beam shining a small circle on the nearest sculpture. The statue depicted a muscular man with leaves growing from his body. A massive emerald sat in the center of the chest, the beam of light just to the side of it.

Narine walked past Jace, straight toward the middle of the room. He followed, curious, as she stepped up to a rail some fifty feet from the glowing column. The rail stopped them from dropping into a room below filled with brass gears. At the top of the contraption was a horizontally placed gear a hundred feet in diameter, the pole with the glass disk mounted to it.

Narine leaned over the railing and extended her palm toward the crystal column, eyes filled with wonder. "It is raw magic. So powerful. I feel as though I can actually touch it."

Adyn stepped up beside Narine. "What do you mean?"

"I have always been told magic comes from our surroundings, but this… This *is* raw magic. This crystal column is filled with it. If I could just touch it, I—"

"Would be destroyed." Vanda shook his head. "With the objects on your hand and ankle, your power is impressive, Narine. Yet compared to the energy coursing through that crystal, you are but a candle to the sun."

Jace turned and crossed marble tiles that glittered with specs of gold, ducking beneath the beam of light to examine the next statue. It depicted a muscular, bearded man with lightning bolts on his skin and a blue sapphire in his chest.

"Farrow…," he said. "This is Farrow." He pointed toward the neighboring statue with the green jewel. "That must be Oren."

As he stared at the beam of light, a tick echoed from the gears, the beam of light shifting ever so slightly.

He frowned in thought. "The Darkening occurred in Tiamalyn two days ago, right?"

"Yes," Adyn agreed.

He pointed toward the circle of light on Oren's chest. "If this light moves just a little each day, it will point at Farrow when the Darkening reaches Fastella."

Narine gasped. "You're right. This…machine, this entire chamber, has something to do with the Darkening and the gods."

"But how?" Brogan asked.

Jace shook his head. "I don't know." He looked at Vanda. "What about you, sorcerer? You seem to know more than you let on."

Vanda's eyes narrowed. "I believe you are correct, but I would be remiss to guess at something so elaborate."

The room fell silent, Jace scowling at Vanda, who scowled right back. From the beginning, Jace had been irritated by the man's tendency to hold secrets until he was forced to reveal them.

He is likely annoyed by my curiosity, as well.

Adyn said, "Why are the statues spaced unevenly?"

Turning slowly, Jace surveyed the room. There was a massive gap between Pallan and Hassaka, which made sense, since Pallanar was the most southern wizardom and Hassakan the farthest north. Among the others, the gaps varied from a dozen strides to several dozen.

"The gaps between each are dependent on their relative distance from the equator." He walked along the railing, heading toward the far end of the ring. "This contraption likely turns at a steady pace, and the statues themselves are positioned so the light strikes the heart of each the same day the Darkening reaches the capital of that wizardom." As he passed the other statues – Gheald, Cora, Bal, Kyra, and Hassaka – he noticed something odd. A shadow flickered in the gap between Hassaka and Pallan, the shimmering light from the column unable to penetrate it. He approached the wall and stood right beside the shadow but still could not see anything. Finally, he gripped the talisman around his neck, took a deep breath, and stepped into it.

The darkness enveloped him as he heard Narine call out.

"Jace!"

The murk faded to reveal a lift five strides deep and twice the length. It was in a blind alcove and attached to a faintly glowing stone column.

"Jace!" Narine sounded panicked.

He turned but only saw darkness behind him. When he walked back through the shadow, the room reappeared again, Narine and Adyn rushing toward him.

"What happened?" Adyn asked.

He thumbed over his shoulder. "I found a way up."

She frowned, looking behind him. "All I see is a blank wall. The same one you just disappeared into."

"It must be some sort of illusion." He shook his head. "Odd, but I can't see through it. Instead, all I see is some sort of shadow."

Vanda walked over, the others at his side. "It must be the Dark Lord's magic. It is stronger than wizard magic, the Eye only partially affected by his illusion." He motioned toward Jace. "Lead the way."

With everyone gathered, Jace stepped back into the shadow and onto the lift. One by one, the others appeared, arms extended before them as if they were blind. Each blinked when they reached the lift, wide-eyed gazes surveying the surroundings.

"See if you can get it to work, Narine," Jace suggested.

She put her hand on the control panel and focused. A hum came from the lift as it began to rise toward the black opening high above.

31

MUR TOWER

T he soft glow from the Arc of Radiance fought against the encroaching
darkness as the lift entered the opening in the ceiling. Blythe held her
bow ready, the warm pulsing of it in her grip soothing her nerves. While they
had yet to encounter anything aggressive since entering the Murlands, everything about the place – from the desolation, to the malevolent clouds, to the
ghostly city of Murvaran – emanated a sense of foreboding. The image of
Kaleel's corpse in the plaza lingered as a reminder that anything could be
deadly

The lift passed through a tunnel and emerged into another sprawling
chamber. It stopped just above the floor, the hum ceasing, Narine removing
her hand from the panel.

Like the one below, this level was open with no interior walls, the same
column of shimmering light running through the core. Also similar to the
level below, statues stood along the outer walls. However, these were not of
men or gods, but of creatures. Some had wings, others tentacles, one had the
head of a dog and the body of a vulture. Blythe recognized one as a centaur –
the head and torso of a man, the lower body of a horse – and another as a
minotaur – a massive bull head atop the body of an impossibly tall human.
On each, the eyes drew her attention, for they were made of black onyx, a

stark contrast to the pale stone from which the rest of the sculpture was carved.

"Now what?" Brogan asked.

Vanda pointed to an opening across the chamber, the foot of a stairwell visible inside. "We begin our climb."

Thendu stepped off the lift and turned toward them. A hiss came from across the room, the eyes of the minotaur glowing as a beam of purple light shot out. It struck Thendu, his body convulsing, glowing for a moment, then dissolving. In a heartbeat, the man was gone, no trace of him or his gear remaining.

"What in the blazes?" Brogan exclaimed, taking a small step forward. "Where did he go?"

Vanda spread his arms to block Brogan from stepping off the lift. "That was negative magic. It comes from the netherworld." He looked at where Thendu had been standing. "He is dead, his soul captured, doomed to never be reborn."

Adyn shuddered. "That sounds awful. How do we proceed?"

The sorcerer frowned. "Netherworld magic is darkness itself. The only way to negate it is with the power of light."

"Easy," Jace said. "We make a bright light and we are safe, right?"

Vanda shook his head. "Not that kind of light. The light of goodness and strength." He turned toward Blythe. "Like the arrows of light from the Arc of Radiance."

"My bow?" Blythe tilted the bow in her hand and looked down at it. She had seen the arrows do the same to darkspawn as the netherworld magic did to Thendu. "What do you propose?"

"I propose we cross under your protection."

She stared at the old man, thinking. The statue made a hissing sound and the eyes came to life before anything else. Jaw set, she nodded to Vanda, lifted her bow, and stepped off the lift.

A hiss came from the minotaur, the eyes glowing. She took aim, an arrow of light appearing, and loosed. The streak of light sped across the chamber. Blythe leapt back onto the lift to see what would happen.

The arrow struck the statue in the face. A film of white formed over the minotaur's eyes, and sparks of light sizzled across the sculpture. The effect lasted for a few breaths, then faded. She cautiously stepped off again, the statue hissing and eyes aglow once more. Loosing, her arrow struck its face again. Caught in a stasis, no beam of light came from it. The sparks faded, the statue hissed, and she loosed again.

"All right." Blythe waved them forward. "Stay close."

She advanced as they all followed. Five steps later, a heavily tentacled creature hissed, its eight eyes glowing a dark purple. Blythe took aim and released an arrow, striking the creature in the middle of those eyes. They glossed over, sparks dancing from it, but nothing else happened.

They continued across the floor, Blythe responding as each statue awoke, her arrows of light working just long enough for them to pass the statues' gazes. After passing by all eight, they darted into the alcove with the stairwell.

Sword in hand, Brogan walked forward. "I'll take the lead since I can see in the dark. Hadnoddon should take the rear for the same reason. Blythe, come with me so the others can follow the glow of your bow."

The two of them began up the dark stairs, their companions trailing close behind.

Brogan held his sword ready as he reached the top of the stairs. Panting from exertion, he and the rest of the rag-tag squad gathered at the top, staring toward the open entrance to another chamber.

"This is it," he gasped. "The stairs end here."

"That was another ten flights," Jace said, blowing out a breath. "I think we are a third of the way to the top."

Brogan scowled at Jace, the thief's face dimly lit by the glow of Blythe's bow. "Don't remind me." He wiped his damp brow with the back of his hand. "I far prefer the lift than the climb."

"Can you see anything?" Adyn asked.

Brogan stopped at the arched doorway to peer left and right. A wall stood five strides before him, rounded to follow the outer curve of the tower. A corridor led in both directions with nothing to distinguish one from the other.

"Do we go left or right?"

Vanda shook his head. "I do not know. Many elements of the tower have changed."

"So..." Jace looked at him, eyes narrowed. "You *have* been here before."

"No." Vanda shook his head. "Of course not. I refer to the notes of the legendary explorer Baan Helix."

"Who?"

"Helix was an explorer from the early Second Age, around the time the wizardoms were formed. He was among the squad who defeated H'Deesengar. At the time, they thought the demon lord dead. They were wrong."

Jace shrugged. "Whatever they did kept the demon away for two thousand years, which is impressive, even if the thing eventually came back."

"Enough chit-chat," Brogan growled. "Unless someone has a serious objection, I say we go left."

He began in that direction, felt a deep chill wash over his body, and stopped. Two shadows, both tinted red in his enhanced vision, slid from the interior wall just ahead of him. Brogan reacted with a roar, blade flashing as it cut through both wraiths. Wails echoed in the corridor as the shades withered to nothing.

Jace cleared his throat. "I vote we go the other way."

Brogan spun and walked past them. "Fine. This way."

Narine crafted a globe of white light that floated above her hand, casting shadows ahead of Brogan.

"Keep your weapons ready," he said as he advanced down the curved corridor. "There might be more wraiths or other darksp–" He stopped when the air grew frigid.

Six shrieking wraiths burst from the interior wall, arms outstretched. Brogan lunged, his blade piercing the nearest. Blythe loosed arrows of light, striking three wraiths in rapid succession, the creatures dissolving, while Adyn dispatched the last two spirits with her blades, their death wails echoing as they faded.

A scream came from behind, the soldier at the rear collapsing to the floor, his skin pale. Hadnoddon swung over the man's corpse, the hammer striking a wraith, the phantom dissolving with a wail.

They continued forward, wraiths appearing in clusters, Brogan, Adyn, Hadnoddon, and Jace dispatching them with their metal weapons, Blythe with her arrows of light. By the time they reached the far end of the tower, Brogan was, once again, panting and covered in sweat.

"Well, fewer wraiths now haunt this tower," Jace said.

Hadnoddon grunted. "I'd say we killed forty. Maybe more."

"You forget, Maker," Vanda said. "Those creatures were already dead. You did them a favor by releasing their souls."

"Our numbers dwindle with each step we take," Numell uttered.

Vanda shook his head. "We cannot stop."

Brogan stepped into another shadowy stairwell and stared up for a moment, wishing he had another lift. He sighed. "Same as last time. Blythe and I are in the lead."

Her at his side, he took a deep breath and lifted his weary leg to the first step, knowing there were many more to follow.

They climbed flight after flight, passing numerous open doorways leading to dark corridors. Adyn imagined each filled with wraiths, the mere thought of the ghostly specters giving her the chills. Since donning the Band of Amalgamation, she had feared little. Wraiths were at the top of the list. Although she was made of metal, which was what killed the wraiths, she had no idea if her living flesh would have the same effect. She also had no desire to find out.

Nine stories later, the stairwell ended at a chamber with a single door, ten feet high and nearly as wide. An odd contraption occupied the middle of the chamber. It was twenty feet long, eight feet across, and eight feet tall. Mounted to a rail, it had windows all around and a single door on one side. Through the windows, Adyn saw four rows of seats, reminding her of the horizontal lift that ran over the streets of Cor Cordium.

What was the name of that thing?

Narine tilted her head, looking at the rail beneath the contraption. "This reminds me of the magnavessel the Enchanters use."

"That's it!" Adyn exclaimed. "I couldn't remember what it was called."

Jace chuckled. "It was an interesting invention. I wonder if this works the same way."

Following the rail to a closed door in the far wall, Brogan placed his hand against it. "I don't see any handles, levers, or triggers. How does this thing open?"

Jace patted the contraption in the middle of the room. "Maybe we get inside this magna-thingy and the door opens automatically."

Vanda nodded. "Very good, Jace. I believe you have the right of it."

Brogan frowned. "You want us to climb inside that thing?"

Adyn shrugged. "If it's like the one on Cor Cordium, it is a handy way to travel. Fast, too."

Hadnoddon asked, "But where will this one take us?"

"Unless you can find another way to get through this door, we don't have a choice," Jace replied.

The dwarf hefted his hammer. "How about I break the door down?"

"You could try." The thief smirked.

Grunting in reply, Hadnoddon stepped before the door, pulled the hammer back, and swung. The head struck with a tremendous boom, but the door appeared unaffected. He swung twice more, not making a dent or a crack.

A grimace on his face, Hadnoddon stared at the door. "Fine. Let's try the magnadoodle."

"Magna*vessel*," Narine corrected.

Jace laughed. "At least it wasn't me this time." He opened the door to the magnavessel. "Come on. Let's see if we can get this thing to work."

Two rows of seats were to each side of the door, all turned to face the middle where a panel with runes etched into it stood atop a post.

Jace sat in front of the panel, eyeing it closely. "This looks like the lift panel we saw downstairs. Perhaps Narine can make it work."

Adyn stepped aside. "Go on, Narine. Take a seat, then the rest of us will climb in."

Narine slipped inside and sat beside Jace, Adyn following to sit on her other side. Hadnoddon, Tygalas, and Vanda sat across from them, Brogan and Blythe took a rear seat, as did Numell. With everyone inside, Adyn pulled the door closed, latched it, and nodded to Narine. Hand on the panel, Narine's eyes narrowed in concentration, and the machine began to hum. A click sounded, the door in the wall lowering into the floor. Beyond it was an open chamber, the high ceiling blanketed in shadow, a crystal column rising in the center, aglow with magic. The vessel moved forward slowly.

Once inside, arched openings became visible, open to the outside. Beneath the dark red sky, hundreds of feet below, was the city.

"Why is this level open?" Jace wondered.

"I have no idea." Adyn shot a questioning look at Vanda. "Sorcerer?"

The man shook his head. "Nor do I."

At the pace of a trotting horse, the machine ran along the track positioned halfway between the crystal column and outer walls broken up by a number of arched openings. Other than the hum of the vehicle, it was quiet.

Suddenly, a shriek came from above, followed by another. A thump shook the vessel, Adyn gripping the seat in front of her.

"What was that?"

Another thud struck, rocking the vessel. Then something flew past and faded into the shadows.

"Did you see that?" Jace asked, frantically looking around.

"What was it?"

"I think it was a–" Two simultaneous thumps struck, one from each side. "Wyverns!"

A winged creature grasped each side, talons locked on the vessel, wings outstretched, sharp teeth flashing as they tried to bite through the glass.

"They are small," Narine said. "Far smaller than the others we have seen."

"Babies?" Jace guessed.

Vanda nodded. "Yes. They are young." He looked toward an arched opening slipping past. "Perhaps the creatures use this level as a nest."

Hadnoddon snorted. "You make it sound like they are merely birds."

Four more young wyverns appeared, one on the front of the vessel, one on the rear, two at the door, all squawking and attacking, eager to get at them. The space inside the vessel was too tight for Adyn to use her swords, so she drew her dagger and held it ready.

One of the wyverns landed on the rail, the vessel slamming into it and slowing suddenly, everybody inside lurching forward, the hum turning to a low buzz until the thing stopped.

"Why did you stop it?" Jace asked.

Narine shook her head. "I didn't. It... It isn't working."

Brogan put his forehead against the front window and peered down. "One of those things is pinned between us and the track."

More young wyverns appeared, some flying past, others attacking the vessel, the noise of them becoming louder and louder.

"We are trapped," Blythe cried. "Those things might be young, but each is bigger than any of us. And look at those teeth!"

Adyn turned to Narine and saw the fear in her eyes. Any sort of fight would result in injuries or worse, except for Adyn. With her metalized flesh, she was impervious to physical attacks. Resolved, she made her decision.

Gripping the door handle, she put her shoulder against it and shoved, dagger flashing as she jumped out. Her strike sliced through the wing of the creature on the door. It released a high-pitched wail and flapped off.

"Adyn!" Narine cried. "What are you doing?"

"Saving you." She slammed the door closed and jammed her dagger into the handle, locking them inside.

A young wyvern slammed into her, knocking her down. It bit down on her shoulder, sharp teeth scraping across her metal flesh, leaving shallow gouges. Adyn bent her knees, placed her feet against its chest, and thrust, launching the beast off her. It twisted in the air, flapped its wings, and looped around as she regained her feet. Crossing her arms over her chest, she drew her swords with a flourish. Talons extended, the wyvern attacked. Adyn slashed, spun away, and slashed again, the first strike lopping off a foot, the second tearing through a wing. The creature screamed and crashed to the floor.

Two more came at her from opposite sides. At the last moment, she fell to her hands and knees, the creatures crashing into each other and landing beside her. She rolled and thrust her blade into the chest of one, its slitted eyes bulging as it writhed. The other tried to take flight, but Adyn slashed through its wing and it fell. Another slash cut its throat.

She turned and rushed to the front of the vessel to find a dead wyvern pinned against the rail. Sheathing her swords, she gripped the thing by the neck and pulled. It did not budge. She put her foot against the rail and tugged harder, straining until it came free. Stumbling, she fell to her back-side, the young wyvern's corpse landing on the floor between her and the rail. A hum arose, and the vessel lurched into motion.

Adyn scrambled to her feet and ran to catch it. As she neared the rear, she leapt and grabbed the edge of the roof, placing her feet on a lip above the rail. Through the rear window, she saw her companions watching, expressions shifting from concern to relief.

A thunderous screech made her flinch. She turned as a full-sized wyvern struck, talons wrapping around her torso and pulling her off the cart.

~

"No!" Narine cried, removing her hand from the control panel as Adyn was yanked away.

The hum ceased, the vessel slowing to a halt.

"What are you doing?" Jace gripped her arm as she started to rise.

"We need to help her."

Vanda put his hand on her shoulder, pushing her back down onto the bench. "While you might be right, she chose to put herself in harm's way so you would not do the same. She freed us. If we were to leave the vehicle and die trying to save her, would that not make her gesture futile?"

The interior of the vessel fell quiet, Narine watching the retreating wyvern fly through an arch and out of the tower.

"He's right, Narine," Jace said gently. "We must continue. Adyn did what she needed to do, regardless of the risk. We must do the same."

Tears tracking down her cheeks, Narine turned back toward the panel, channeled her magic, and let it flow into the controls.

32

GUARDIANS

Walls of stone slid past as the lift rose toward the top of the tower. The mood among the group was somber, thoughts of those left behind mingling with worries of what lay ahead. Seven members had been lost over the course of the day, and Brogan worried others would follow. He placed a hand against Blythe's lower back. She gave him a sad smile. Narine stood beside her, eyes red and puffy, the pain of Adyn's death still raw.

Light came from above as the lift drew higher, the glow growing brighter and brighter. They emerged into open air, the moon looming directly overhead.

The roof of the tower was surrounded by a chest-high wall and four claw-shaped turrets, each rising another hundred feet above the rooftop. Giant statues of winged, human-like creatures stood at the base of each turret. Like the sculptures they had seen earlier, these stood three times the height of a man, bodies muscular and perfect. Half were male, the other half female. Notably, each had eyes made of crystal.

An eight-pointed star made of black tiles, hundreds of feet across, marked a floor. In the middle, stairs led to an octagon-shaped dais, a massive altar at the top. A naked man lay upon the altar, his flesh brighter than the moon above, a halo of light surrounding him. The sight was stunning, Brogan and his companions staring in shock, eyes wide and jaws gaping.

The being's presence was undeniable. Like the blowing of wind, heat of flames, wetness of water, and frigidness of ice, the force of this entity before them could not be ignored. Rather, Brogan found his mind fogged, impossible to think of anything else.

A wyvern sped over them, breaking the spell. It had a metal form in its grip, sword flashing. The tip thrust into the creature's leg and it shrieked. The talons opened, and Adyn fell, her body spinning as it plummeted. She struck the tower roof with a clatter, tumbling and sliding across the stone until she crashed into the base of a statue.

"Adyn!" Narine screamed and burst into a run.

Jace tried to grab her but missed as she sped across the roof.

Vanda shouted, "Don't cross the star!" But he was too late.

Narine's slippered feet crossed the black outline. A hum arose from the statues as they came to life, white stone turning to pale flesh, wings pure white, eyes glowing with moonlight.

"Look out!" Brogan yelled as one of the giant beings leapt forward and smashed down with its fist, narrowly missing Narine as she ran past.

Reacting, Brogan leapt off the lift and ran toward the winged statue, unsure if his sword would even hurt it.

Narine flinched when the statue's massive fist smashed down just behind her. She raced past as quickly as she could, focused on Adyn's still form. The statue standing over Adyn bent to grab her. Narine reacted, using her magic to quickly form a shield over her friend. The creature's hands struck the invisible barrier, bouncing off. It lifted its fist and pounded against the shield in frustration. When it raised both fists in preparation for a mighty strike, Narine crafted a thin wedge of solidified air and drove it beneath the giant, sweeping its feet to the side. The winged creature lost its balance and fell with a massive thud.

She reached Adyn, who was face down, and rolled her over. "Adyn! Please be alive!"

Liquid metal eyes opened, Adyn moaning.

A shadow fell over them as the giant rose to its feet.

Focused on Narine and Adyn, Jace raced past Brogan as the big warrior swung at the lower leg of one giant. The statue Narine had toppled sat up and swept a massive hand toward them, striking an invisible shield, the force of it knocking Narine backward. She landed on her back and slid across the floor. Desperate, Jace drew his dagger and threw.

The blade struck the towering giant in the neck and bounced off, falling to the roof with a clatter. The creature turned toward him, crystal eyes glowing brightly. It reached out and grabbed Adyn by the leg, flinging her toward Jace. Her metallic body speeding toward him, he leapt, her skidding just underneath. He landed on his hands, tucked into a roll, and rose to his feet a few strides in front of the giant statue. In rapid succession, he threw the blades strapped to his wrists, aiming for its glowing eyes. They both landed true, the giant's head snapping back, the crystal turning dark, statue stiffening, flesh turning white as it morphed back to stone.

He spun around as the giant Brogan fought backhanded the big man and sent him flying to land five strides away.

"The eyes! Aim for the eyes!" Jace shouted.

After Brogan and Jace ran in one direction, a statue from the other side spread its wings and took flight, straight toward them. Blythe raised her bow and loosed, an arrow of light striking the creature's wing. It twisted and crashed down, sliding across the rooftop. Hadnoddon stormed past, hammer raised, and smashed it into one of the statue's giant legs. Rather than shatter like stone, the weapon bounced off, but the creature did not cry out. Instead, it sat up and swung at Hadnoddon, the massive hand striking the armored dwarf and knocking him across the rooftop.

"The eyes!" Jace shouted from across the roof. "Aim for the eyes!"

Tygalas leapt in, raced up the body of the giant, and jammed the butt of his staff into its eye. The giant's head snapped back, the light in the eye going dark. It swiped a hand at the elf, missing when Tygalas flipped over and thrust again. When his staff struck the creature's other eye, it stiffened and began to quake. He leapt off, hit the roof, and rolled forward to his feet. The glow faded from the giant, its flesh and wings taking on a milky appearance as it turned back to stone.

Blythe turned and saw Brogan sprawled out on his stomach, one of the towering statues stomping toward him. She raised her bow and loosed, striking the creature in the arm. When it looked toward her, she released again, an arrow clattering off its face, causing it to flinch. The next struck an eye socket, the crystal going dark. It turned away from her and lifted a massive fist over Brogan, prepared to crush him.

Pain seared across Brogan's side with each breath. His head pounded to the beat of his heart, feeling like it might explode. He rolled over with a groan, eyes blinking open to see a towering shape above him, one eye dark, an arrow through it, the other shimmering with light. The statue raised a fist and slammed it downward. Brogan rolled to the side, directly over his fallen sword. The fist struck the floor beside him, cracking the stone in a spray of shards. He grabbed the blade as the thing prepared itself for another blow.

The words Jace had shouted ran though his mind. *"The eyes! Aim for the eyes!"*

The giant fist drove toward him as he sat up, thrusting the sword into the crystal eye, the blow careening off his back. Pain shot through his body when his spine shattered. He fell sideways in a heap, the statue doing the same.

Narine sat up and blinked at her surroundings. Three of the giant creatures lay on the roof, turned back to stone. Adyn, Brogan, and Hadnoddon were down, as well. Jace ran up to Narine and knelt beside her.

"Are you all right?" He took her hand and helped her to her feet.

"Yes…" Her eyes widened in alarm. "Look out!"

She tackled him, driving him to the floor just before the last giant flew past. It struck the roof beside her in a thunderous crash, rolling until it was on its hands and knees.

Tygalas leapt past her, planted his staff on the floor, and launched himself into the air. Twisting as he rotated, he drove the staff into a crystal eye, the force of the strike snapping the giant's head to the side. He landed and rolled out of the way as Hadnoddon rushed in, eyes filled with rage. The dwarf swung his mighty hammer over his head, arms extended. The head of the hammer struck the giant's other eye, the face turning to stone and cracking down the side before it exploded, a chunk of marble striking Hadnoddon in the head and knocking him to the floor, his forehead bloody, eyes closed. He did not move.

The night quieted, the only sounds coming from the breeze and heavy breathing of the tired combatants.

Narine looked down at Jace, still pinned beneath her.

He grinned. "I always did have a thing for aggressive women. You should jump me like this more often."

She hugged him briefly before climbing off and standing.

From beyond a fallen statue, they heard Blythe call out, "Narine! Brogan is hurt. Come quickly!"

Narine circled the statue and saw Blythe kneeling over him. The man looked like he was folded over, upper body resting on his legs. She rushed over and fell to her knees, embracing her magic. Through a construct of repair, she delved into him. His heart beat weakly, breaths ragged. His spine was shattered, ribs crushed. If not for his armor, he would already be dead. The spinal cord appeared intact, but she knew it would require a delicate hand.

Jace knelt at her side. "What can I do?"

She turned to him and Blythe. "I will try to repair his spine first. Once I tell you, lift him by the shoulders and lay him on his back."

Without waiting for a reply, she dove in with magic, willing the man's body to heal itself, spine slowly realigning, bones mending. The pain was too much, causing his heart to seize, breathing to stop.

"Now!"

Jace lifting one shoulder, Blythe the other, they sat Brogan upright, then laid him on his back. Narine repaired his broken ribs and knitted the man's internal injuries. She then altered the construct, holding it ready.

"Release him."

The moment Blythe and Jace pulled their hands away, Narine released the spell, a bolt of lightning striking his armor, his body jerking as his muscles spasmed. She delved again, finding no heartbeat. Calling upon another lightning spell, she shocked him with two rapid pulses. Again, his body jumped with each. He suddenly gasped for air, his eyelids flicking open.

Narine sat back with a sigh as Blythe leaned in to place a hand on his forehead, tears rolling down her cheeks.

"Thank you," she whispered.

Narine gave a quick nod. "I must see about Adyn and Hadnoddon."

She stood, turned, and froze.

An overwhelming presence weighed upon her, mind fogging, body stuck in stasis. Her gaze was fixed upon the dais, the figure rising from the altar. He stood twenty feet tall, body sculpted perfection, face so beautiful Narine began to weep. Skin glowing, as if he were made of the moon itself, the god slowly descended the stairs and stared at Vanda, the sorcerer in black appearing puny before this being of power.

His voice reverberating across the rooftop, Urvadan said, "Hello, brother."

Vanda's visage altered, his beard growing longer, skin lightening, nose lengthening, wrinkles deepening, black robes shifting to a tattered cloak made of multi-colored patches.

One clear thought emerged from the haze in Narine's head. *Salvon…*

33

BROTHERS

J ace stood immobile, as did the others. Yet he was able to flex his fingers and wiggle his toes, informing him that the spell holding them in place did not affect him in the same manner. *It must be the amulet.* However, the presence of the god made his head fuzzy, as if he had downed three cups of swoon.

Urvadan's form was a blur, like two beings occupying the same space. One stood three times the height of a man and glowed like moonlight. The other stood no more than six feet tall with golden hair and blue eyes, appearing only slightly older than Jace himself. The image of the two fluctuated and distorted as Urvadan moved. Watching it made him nauseous, so he focused on Vanda, who had been Salvon all along, revealing a piece of the puzzle that had been nagging Jace from the beginning.

"I have come for you, Urvadan," Salvon said.

Urvadan laughed. "Come, now Vandasal. After all this time, you use my name while hiding yours behind the likes of Solomon Vanda, Lord Astra, and Salvon the Great?"

Jace gasped. *Astra, as well?*

Salvon…Vandasal arched a bushy brow. "You were aware of all three? I had hoped H'Deesengar's sleep spell would have been more effective." He shook his head. "No matter. The die is cast. It will end one way or another."

Urvadan's gaze swept across Jace and his companions. "So, is this your squad of would-be saviors? I see a child of the forest and a son of stone, but the others are human. You continue to turn my own people against me."

"You turned against them long ago."

"Oh, please. You have spread those ridiculous tales for centuries, labeling me as the *Dark Lord*. You blame the world's troubles upon me out of spite. I won. You lost. It is as simple as that."

Vandasal's expression darkened. "You went too far, *brother*." The last word was filled with disdain. "Your quest for power destroyed the balance and broke the world."

Urvadan waved the comment off. "The world was repaired and remains well enough. As for the balance, it was you who held the upper hand prior to my victory. You made no such complaints while I wilted in shadow and you basked in the light."

Vandasal shook his head. "We will never agree. I have come to accept it."

"Have you also come to accept that I have won?" Urvadan lifted his hands to the heavens. "The moon forever feeds my power while yours suffers. You cannot defeat me, and neither can any of your heroes, even the one who wears the Eye."

For the first time, Vandasal appeared flustered. He turned to Jace with a furrowed brow, then looked back at Urvadan. "You know of the amulet?"

He laughed. "Creating such an object was cunning. While it helped you defeat my wizard lords, none of them ever approached my might. Not even the one who defeated H'Deesengar."

The god extended a hand toward Jace and light shot out, enveloping him. He cried out in pain, his body convulsing as he collapsed, his veins feeling like they were on fire. The glow faded, leaving Jace curled up and gasping for air.

"See." Urvadan smiled. "My power is unequaled, my being immortal, my mind omniscient. The amulet is merely an item of enchantment and no match for the power of a god."

Vandasal scowled. "If you knew of the amulet, did you sense our approach?"

"I knew you would come someday. Thus, I crafted the challenges you crossed to reach the top of the tower." His gaze went to the nearest statue, lying on its side, eyes hollow and blackened. "Although your actions now force me to recreate new guardians."

"Guardians?" Vandasal snorted. "I find it an ironic term when they were undoubtedly created in the likeness of your own heralds…which you betrayed."

Urvadan shook his head. "I regret having to take such measures, but Al'Ucindar left me little choice. I needed H'Deesengar's power to feed the spell, and the god of the Netherplane would accept nothing less in trade. Without the demon lord, I never could have captured the moon."

"Without it, you never could have defeated me."

"True." Urvadan nodded. "But without your interference, the demon lord would have never escaped his prison."

Vandasal smirked. "That puzzle was the most difficult to solve. I admit, it was brilliant to use the crystal thrones and the power derived from Devotion to imprison the demon. If those thrones fell vacant, the demon would feed upon the world. Yet the only way to stop your own harvesting of prayer was to eliminate the wizard lords. Giving the world to H'Deesengar was unacceptable, so I sought a means to stop him.

"It took me centuries to understand how the crystal thrones operated, the gems being the key." He stroked his beard, brow arched. "When I discovered that you altered the blood of those you raised, attuning the metal in it to match the color of the gem in the throne, I also realized those thrones were nothing but tools to gather prayers." Vandasal chuckled. "Luckily, the greed of mankind is a flame easily stoked.

"Once I had created a human with the mental fortitude to wield the power of all Eight Wizardoms, I initiated my plan. Thrones toppled to pave the way for her to claim the power as her own. With her magic a counter to that of a demon lord, I sent her against H'Deesengar. It was a gamble, but if eight stones could imprison him, a wizard lord wielding the power of all Eight Wizardoms might prove sufficient to end him. Turns out, I was correct."

Urvadan shrugged. "You did me a favor in that regard. The demon lord and his darkspawn minions needed to be addressed at some point." He looked toward the sky, winged creatures soaring above. "Of them all, wyverns have proven most useful as guardians, the ogres being the best workers." He grimaced. "The goblins are a nasty, useless lot, and the rock trolls only know how to destroy. With the darkspawn gone, there is one less thing for you to use as lies against me."

Vandasal pointed a finger at him. "You speak as if you are above using deceit. What of your young gods? You used those false idols to control your own people."

"Sometimes controlling others is the best way to protect them. You do the same with your false prophecies, steering the Order and the Seers in whichever direction best suits your agenda." Urvadan tilted his head in consideration. "I am surprised you did not try harder to denounce the new gods. It might have been an easier path in reducing my strength."

Vandasal tugged on his beard. "I considered it, then decided it was best to use them for my own benefit. Only within the Order of Sol did I actively go after your false gods." He stroked his beard again. "I also admit, the device you created at the base of Mur Tower was ingenious – timing the waking of each god with the local Darkening."

Urvadan scowled. "Your flattery will not help you, brother. I am afraid this is where your scheme ends, for I have grown tired of this conversation."

"Wait!" Vandasal held up his hands. "I have one last thing to share. Something you never considered."

"Go on."

Grasping his hands behind his back, he began to pace. "For over two thousand years, I have roamed this world as a shell of my former self, my thoughts consumed by how I might reclaim my past glory. I then arrived at an epiphany. It was a pointless pursuit. Too much time had passed, the balance now beyond repair. When I accepted my fate, the true answer became obvious. With the use of sorcery–"

"Which is filthy and perverted."

Vandasal stopped and glared at the other god. "Oh, come now. You helped Barsequa create wizardry. I needed something to combat it, for my reduced powers were far too limited to be of use."

Urvadan screwed up his face. "Did it have to be blood?"

"You know quite well why blood is the key."

"Disgusting practice."

"Which is why you instructed the clergy from every wizardom to forbid it."

He nodded. "True."

"Be that as it may, sorcery has its uses. With it, I was able to control a pregnancy and a birth, creating a child unique to the world. Unlike any other living being, this child was immune to all wizardry."

Urvadan jerked back, eyes widening in shock. "The blank spots in your recent activities… They weren't caused by you directly, but were actions taken by this…*abomination*?!"

Vandasal grinned. "Yes, but she might take exception to being called an abomination."

"She?" Urvadan smiled. "So, it is a woman I must seek and destroy." His gaze swept the rooftop again. "I do not see her here. Has she failed to make the journey?"

"I am afraid so. We traveled using gateways. With her immunity to magic, she could not join us."

Urvadan laughed, deep and reverberating. "You went through such lengths…killing off the wizard lords, defeating H'Deesengar, traveling to Murvaran, scaling Mur Tower…only to fail because you did not bring the one being who might defeat me?" He laughed again, the sound shaking the battlements. "How pathetic."

With a malevolent grin, Urvadan said, "Now, you will all die."

34

KRAGMOR

C hasms, deep and dark, slipped past as Zyordican sped toward the red glow on the horizon. Legs draped over the dragon's thick neck, Rhoa held tightly to the crests along the spine. The pack on her back was empty, save for a waterskin and the sword of crystal she had jammed through it. Even with only the hilt visible over her right shoulder and the sharp tip resting on her left hip, the red, pulsing glow from the sword was a distraction. She had chosen to name it *Kragmor* in honor of Rawk and Algoron. The two dwarven stone-shapers had given their lives to save the world. It was the least she could do in return.

She glanced back toward the other dragons, thirteen aligned in an arrow-shaped pattern as she had seen birds do so often. When she asked, Zyordican explained that the trailing dragons benefitted from the updraft created by the one ahead of it. Rather than dwell on the explanation, she allowed herself to marvel at the fact she rode at the head of a dragon army. None of the young were more than half the size of Zyordican, six the green of female dragons, seven the orange of males. Yet she had seen how quickly the dragons defeated the wyverns, despite being outnumbered three to one. Anyone who survived the battle of Balmor would surely recall the sight with a sense of awe.

When she turned forward, the chasms were behind them and only dark, desolate land lay between her and Murvaran. Beneath red skies and a gleaming moonbeam, the dark city surrounded a tower reaching into the sky like the clawed limb of a giant beast, giving Rhoa the impression it could grab the moon itself should it ever draw near enough. As the distance closed, she noticed dark shapes circling the tower.

Wyverns.

"Will they try to stop us?" she shouted over the wind noise.

"Surely," the dragon replied matter-of-factly. "And they will fail."

Zyordican released a roar, echoed by the thirteen younger dragons. They picked up speed, the tower rushing toward them. Dozens of wyverns burst from dark recesses near the top of the tower, joining those already in the sky. The dragons headed straight for them.

Just as they reached the vanguard, Zyordican released a mighty blast of fire, setting three wyverns ablaze, before banking. The dragon's talons tore through the wings of another as she lifted high above the tower. Rhoa glanced back as the younger dragons smashed into the wyverns. The reptilian creatures tangled in mid-air with a flurry of dagger-like teeth and razor-sharp talons.

Zyordican banked again and dipped toward the tower, lit by the moon directly overhead. On the roof, Rhoa saw her companions, some lying prone, others standing still, all staring toward a yellow-haired man wearing archaic clothing.

"Remain hidden behind my head and say nothing until it is time," Zyordican said.

Without waiting for Rhoa to reply, the dragon arched its wings, hovered, and fluttered down to land upon the dais in the center of the rooftop, the man watching the entire time. Carefully peering around the dragon's neck, still staying out of sight, Rhoa noticed a familiar form standing near the man. *Salvon?* She could not fathom how the old storyteller had ended up in Murvaran. Beyond him, she saw Narine, Brogan, Blythe, and Tygalas standing, Adyn, Jace, and Hadnoddon lying prone. Among them, giant statues lay on the rooftop, eyes blackened.

The dragon growled, "We have come for you, Urvadan."

"I am surprised you lived so long without your mate, Zyordican," he replied.

An orange dragon sped overhead, chasing a wyvern with a bloodied tail.

Urvadan nodded. "I see you had a new clutch. You must have been pregnant when Gyradon died."

"I was. His young and I survive to see him avenged. H'Deesengar is no more. It is time for you to join him."

He laughed. "Your magic cannot harm me, Zyordican, just as mine cannot harm you."

"True. Which is why I chose to help your brother rid the world of your taint."

Urvadan spun around to look at Salvon. "Is this true, Vandasal? You would side with a dragon to seek your revenge?"

Salvon is Vandasal? Rhoa's shock was short-lived as the tapestry of the man's lies suddenly made sense.

Vandasal nodded. "The choice was simple, for you cannot be allowed to continue as you have for the past two millennia. Zyordican was quite receptive to my invitation once I explained how you betrayed Gyradon."

Urvadan pressed his lips together. "I did not betray him. The dragon chose to fight H'Deesengar but could not survive the aftereffects of the demon's magic."

"Yet if not for your machinations, Gyradon would be alive today. Bringing a demon lord into our world was a crime against creation. For this, I sentence you to death, just as you did when you convinced Gyradon to join the others and go after H'Deesengar."

Zyordican growled, "I also sentence you to death, Urvadan."

Urvadan looked from one to the other, face twisted in a grimace. "You may not approve of my methods, but there is nothing you can do about it. I am all-powerful and immortal. Your magic cannot harm me."

The dragon twisted its neck, revealing Rhoa. "No. But she can."

Urvadan's eyes grew wide. "It is true. I cannot sense her." He extended his hand toward Rhoa, light shooting from it only to fizzle when it reached her. He glanced toward Vandasal. "I thought your story was a ruse." He shook his head. "No matter. I may not be able to harm her, but there are other means."

He spread his arms. The four giant, winged statues on the rooftop came to life, eyes glowing as they stood and lumbered toward the dragon. One had only a single eye, the side of its face missing. The four statues stretched their wings and flew straight toward Rhoa and Zyordican. At the last possible moment, the dragon took flight, lifting off with such speed, Rhoa nearly tumbled from her perch. Two statues collided into one another and fell to the dais, the other two banking and rising to follow.

Zyordican released a mighty roar and burst beyond the tower roof, the statues following closely. Just before one reached them, an orange dragon smashed into it, mighty jaws clamping down on a wing, tearing it. The dragon released it, and the winged creature plummeted, the intact wing flapping uselessly as it spiraled toward the city a thousand feet below.

When the other winged statue grabbed hold of Zyordican's tail, the dragon banked sharply, straight toward the tower, the assailant holding on tightly. At the last moment, Zyordican banked again, flinging its tail and the statue into the tower wall with a mighty crash. The giant let go, eyes dark as it fell.

The other two statues appeared above them in a dive. Before they reached Rhoa and her mount, four dragons struck, smashing into the winged creatures, biting, tearing the enemies apart.

Zyordican tilted and sailed into the sky, glancing at Rhoa. "Get ready!"

The dragon sailed over the roof's outer wall and slid to a landing. Rhoa spun and ran down the dragon's back, leaping off to land on the rooftop in a crouch. Zyordican took flight again and disappeared beyond the lip of the tower. Rhoa tore off her pack, pulled Kragmor free, and turned toward Urvadan, the blade glowing with a red hue.

He stared at the crystal sword, eyes unreadable. "So, you have discovered my weakness."

"It was not so difficult," Vandasal said. "You used my own magic against me all those years ago, revealing the key to your own demise."

"I'll not go so easily."

Urvadan extended his hand toward Narine. Her body flew to him, and he gripped her throat. "Drop the sword, or I will kill your friend."

Rhoa stared into Narine's wide eyes, unsure of what to do.

The Dark Lord's back facing Adyn, his massive, glowing hand gripped Narine's neck, his focus on Rhoa and the dragon. At the foot of the dais, Jace rose and crept behind Urvadan. The others remained locked in place, bound beneath the will of the god. Despite her pain, Adyn willed herself to crawl, claiming the sword lying nearby and gripping it as she stood. As she had seen in her vision, she had reached the moment of decision. The guide in her vision stated she would need to choose between saving the world or her best friend. She chose neither.

Adyn pulled the sword back and threw. The blade spun end over end, narrowly missing Urvadan before plunging into Rhoa's stomach. Her eyes bulged, mouth gaping. To Adyn, the pain she experienced in her own heart felt like she had done it to herself. Rhoa dropped to her knees, the crystal sword falling from her grip and sliding across the rooftop as she collapsed onto her side. Her companions released a collective gasp.

The crystal sword, the only instrument that could harm the Dark Lord, lay near the unconscious dwarf, pulsing, as Rhoa whimpered in pain.

Urvadan laughed and tossed Narine to the floor. "So much for your assassin, brother."

Hadnoddon suddenly opened his eyes and grabbed the crystal sword as he leapt to his feet, ready to attack. Instantly, his body burst into flames. The dwarf screamed and collapsed in a blinding inferno, the sword hitting the rooftop with a clatter. Hadnoddon continued to burn, unmoving.

Chuckling, Urvadan rubbed his palms together while standing over Rhoa. "You crafted a weapon so powerful nobody can touch it lest they be destroyed. Nobody other than this girl. This...*abomination*." He spat the last word and nudged her with a foot, Rhoa moaning, Adyn's blade jutting from her stomach. Urvadan lifted his gaze to Adyn. "Well done, my metal guardian. You have just earned yourself a place of honor in my kingdom."

Adyn glared at him in defiance. *I am sorry, Rhoa. I could not allow you to do it, especially if it would cost Narine her life, as well.* She gave Jace a small nod, drew the other sword at her hip, and turned it upright. "Free will shall decide our fate. With my free will, I choose to not accept your offer."

Opening her mouth, Adyn slid the blade in and drove it into her brain. Debilitating pain sliced through her head, the world going dark as she collapsed.

~

With careful, silent steps, Jace advanced toward Urvadan. The pressure of the Dark Lord's presence had eased, allowing him to think more clearly. However, the god still had the odd appearance of a towering illusion of light draped over a handsome but otherwise unremarkable man. He suspected one was an illusion and one was real but was unsure which was which.

When Hadnoddon burst into flames, the crystal sword falling to land between the Dark Lord and Rhoa, Jace froze in shock. *What if the amulet won't protect me?* He recalled the pain when Urvadan had attacked him, despite the protection of the amulet. *I must try. If I don't…* One glance at Narine solidified his resolve.

He hurried to circle around Urvadan as the god turned toward Adyn. The Dark Lord addressed her, Adyn's eyes meeting Jace's for a moment, giving him a slight nod. *She is planning a distraction, buying me time.* He never could have guessed how she would do it.

Adyn drove the blade into the roof of her own mouth, staggered, and toppled to the stone tiles. Her liquid mercury eyes dimmed to black as she fell still, charcoal metal body turning back to human flesh

"No!" Narine cried out.

Hurrying, Jace reached Rhoa and knelt. She was still alive, but her breathing was ragged, a foot of steel sticking out of her back, her hand holding the hilt. *You can do nothing for her*, he told himself. Instead, he reached for the crystal weapon. When he gripped the hilt, it burned, and he nearly pulled back. Forcing himself, he clenched his other hand around the first and lifted the blade, red sparks dancing around his hands and up his forearms. The intense pain caused his eyes to water and breath to catch.

His back facing Jace, Urvadan walked up to Adyn and nudged her with his foot. "What a shame."

Jace rushed forward, hands burning, arms shaking from the pain. Three strides away, his toe struck a broken stone, tripping him. He stumbled forward as the Dark Lord spun with a sword of light extended, the blade passing just over Jace's head. With a desperate, upward lunge as he fell, Jace thrust the crystal blade into the abdomen of the smaller version of the god, the tip driving up and into his ribcage.

Jace landed on his shoulder, the impact driving the wind from his lungs, his scorched, blistered hands tucked against his chest. Above him, Urvadan stared at the crystal sword in shock, the illusion fading, the man beneath it stumbling backward until he fell onto the dais steps. There he lay, the pulsing, crystal sword sticking up from him like a grave marker.

Sadness in his eyes, Vandasal walked up to Urvadan. "This is the end, brother. Even gods are not immortal...not when they were never meant to be."

"But...if I die...you die, as well."

Vandasal nodded resolutely. "I am ready."

Urvadan closed his eyes for a long moment. "I can feel...Mother."

"As can I. She will take us soon."

"What...then?" Urvadan choked out.

"I cannot say for sure, but I suspect we will be together."

Vandasal turned, his gaze landing on Rhoa, then shifting to Brogan, Blythe, Tygalas, Narine, and finally Jace. "You have done well. Go. Now. Before it is too late."

Jace rose to his knees, damaged hands still clutched to his chest as he stood and looked around. The dragons were gone. Hadnoddon, Numell, and Adyn were dead. Rhoa was alive, but not for long.

"What about Rhoa?" Blythe asked. "Can you save her?"

Vandasal walked over to the diminutive acrobat and knelt. "This will hurt, brave one."

He quickly drew the blade from her stomach. She gasped, eyes bulging. His other hand went to her wound as he closed his eyes. A glow like the heat of the sun arose and quickly faded. He removed his hand, but the wound remained.

Rising, Vandasal turned to Narine. "Heal her."

She shook her head. "But...I cannot. My magic will not affect her."

"It will now. I have replaced the metal missing from her blood. Heal her and begone."

Narine knelt beside Rhoa, put her hand on the wound, and closed her eyes. Rhoa gasped again, then her breathing came easier. She opened her eyes, and Narine hugged her, tears running down her cheeks.

Narine stood and turned to Jace. "Let me heal you."

He jerked away. "I can wait. Salvon...Vandasal said we must leave. Make a gateway before it's too late."

His concern evident, Narine turned and crafted a gateway, revealing the light of sunset shining upon the Tower of Devotion in the heart of Balmor

Palace. Blythe helped Rhoa to her feet, Brogan following them through the gateway. Tygalas gave Jace a nod and joined the others.

Jace turned to Narine, holding out his damaged hands, red, raw, and blistered. "I can't remove the amulet myself."

He dipped his head. She pulled it off and jammed it into his coat pocket.

Narine turned back to Adyn, tears streaming down her face. She faltered as she walked to her friend's side and pulled the blade from her mouth, tossing it aside. Kneeling, hand to Adyn's cheek, Narine whispered, "You were my best friend. I will never forget you."

Jace crouched at her side for a moment, arm around her shoulders, then cleared his throat. "We had better go."

He helped her rise, gaze catching on the gold band around Adyn's arm. Bending, he gripped the band and pulled. It came free and sprang back into a coil.

Leading her toward the gateway, Jace cast one last glance toward the two fallen gods.

Urvadan's face was pale, the pulsing sword still in his stomach. Vandasal sat beside him, holding his brother's hand.

The man Jace had known as Salvon, as Vanda, as Astra gave a final nod, his expression one of peace. "Do not worry, Jerrell. All is as it should be. Soon, it will be as it should have been from the beginning."

Blood dripped down from Urvadan's wound, a single drop striking the tower rooftop. The stone turned a bright, glistening red, a massive crackle resounding as the stain spread in all directions.

Alarmed, Jace wrapped an arm around Narine's waist, hefted her over his shoulder, and leapt through the gateway.

"What are you doing?" she cried as he set her down.

He pointed toward the gateway, everything in sight already a sparkling, red crystal. "That burns. Badly." He held his hands out as evidence. "I thought it best to be away."

She nodded. "Good thinking."

Through the gateway, a brilliant, white light descended upon the two gods, enveloping them, the brightness forcing Jace to turn away. When he looked back, the gateway and the view of Mur Tower were gone.

35

AFTERMATH

Narine stirred, eyes blinking open to morning light filtering through the curtains. She rolled over to find the other side of the bed empty, covers thrown back. Jace sat at the foot of the bed, his back to her. He wore black breeches and nothing else. Rising to her knees, she crawled to him, slid her hands down his bare chest from behind, and kissed his neck.

"Mmm," he moaned softly. "I'm glad you are awake."

She whispered into his ear, "Did you have something in mind?"

Rather than respond as she expected, he sighed. "I wish…"

Brow furrowed, she leaned forward, one hand on the foot of the bed, so she could better see him. "What's wrong?"

"Nothing. Well…not really. I was just thinking about last night. About the things Urvadan and Salvon…Vandasal said."

"I still cannot believe he was a god in disguise all this time."

He looked at her. "*Multiple* disguises. Salvon, Vanda, Astra… He used us, manipulated us into doing what he wanted. Perhaps that wasn't even the end of it."

She slid her hand to his arm, gaze going to his wrists. Odd scars, appearing like thin lines of lightning, remained from the crystal sword burns. Despite Narine's efforts, she could not heal those. *I am just thankful his hands remain nimble.* Most of Jace's skills came from those hands. Skills Narine appreciated greatly.

"Are you upset about being manipulated into killing a god?"

"You say that as if it were inconsequential. I worry that our actions were only to satisfy Vandasal's desire for revenge." Jace looked at her. "Urvadan was not just a god. He was *every* god. You heard what was said. Gheald, Farrow, Pallan, and the others were all illusions cast by Urvadan so he could harvest prayers from across all Eight Wizardoms. If there are no gods remaining, what of us?"

Narine had not considered the gravity of what they had done. She began to contemplate what would happen to society. *What will the future hold without gods? Do the people need gods to worship? Or was it Urvadan that needed the people for their prayers?* The depth of the concept made her head hurt.

Finally, she said, "I think it best if the truth remains a secret. If everyone learned that Urvadan was behind the gods all along, it could lead to disaster."

He nodded. "I agree. But what of the wizard lords? It will be impossible to hide the fact the fires no longer burn...and will never burn again."

"We will forge a new path, with or without wizard lords."

"I know, but it doesn't make me feel any better since we...*I* caused this situation."

She wrapped her arms around him and kissed his cheek. "You merely did what you had to do, Jace. If you weren't wearing the amulet as protection... We saw what happened to Hadnoddon. Anyone else would have been destroyed. Only you or Rhoa could have done it."

He sighed again. "I suppose."

Her thoughts turned to Adyn. To witness her best friend kill herself... Once they returned to the palace, Narine's grief had led to an evening of tears, Jace holding her as she cried.

"I miss her so badly."

He touched her face. "I miss her, as well."

Narine wiped her eyes and sniffed.

"She was a warrior at heart, Narine," Jace continued. "But she was also your friend, your protector. She did what was needed to save you."

She nodded. "I know."

Hand to her cheek, he kissed her. "Sometimes heroes die to save others. It is what makes them heroes and is the way of the world."

She closed her eyes for a beat, took a deep breath, then opened them again, giving him a small, grateful smile. "Let's get dressed. We are to meet with the others soon." She stepped off the bed and smoothed her shift, his gaze following the motion with a leer.

He reached out, gripped her hips, and pulled her close. "There is something we must do first."

Smiling, she held his face, bent, and kissed him, giving herself to the moment.

When Narine and Jace entered the dining room, the others were already eating. Priella sat at the head of the table, Kollin to one side, Brogan to the other. Blythe and Tygalas sat beside Brogan, Rhoa across from them. Odama – shoulder bandaged, arm in a sling – sat beside Rhoa. Two chairs remained empty. Narine took the one at the foot of the table, Jace the one between her and Tygalas.

"Sorry we are late," Narine said.

"Nonsense." Priella smiled. "This is an informal gathering. Simply a chance to eat and share stories."

"What did we miss?" Jace asked.

Priella motioned toward Odama. "The captain was just informing me of the state of the city. The fires are all doused, but over thirty buildings were destroyed. In addition, we cannot open the east gate because of the damage incurred during the battle. Twenty-some ships lie at the bottom of the bay. A number of ships and the men aboard them are missing, apparently consumed by the demon's magic. Fewer than three thousand troops remain in the area, and Balmor is depleted of male wizards." She glanced toward Odama. "Does that summarize it?"

The man nodded. "Yes, Your Majesty."

Priella shook her head. "No. This is not my wizardom. I merely stepped in and did what was necessary to stop the invasion. Pallanar is my home and is where I shall return." She smiled at Kollin, taking his hand. "Here, I am known simply as Priella."

Odama frowned. "But who will lead us? Will there be a new wizard lord?"

"I do not know." Priella pointed toward the window, the Tower of Devotion in the heart of the palace visible through it. "The flame of Pallan no longer burns in the tower. I cannot even get the lift to work."

Narine glanced at Jace, who nodded. She then turned back to the table. "There will be no more wizard lords."

"*What?*" Odama exclaimed.

"The gods you have known, including Oren, are no more. The Dark Lord...Urvadan destroyed them." It was an easier story to share than the truth. If the populace learned they had been duped for centuries, it would only lead to trouble.

"By the gods, no."

"In the end, we destroyed Urvadan. What remains...is humanity." She looked at Tygalas. "And the Cultivators." Turning toward Rhoa, she added, "And the Makers. These three peoples must forge a new future together. We have been the pawns of gods for too long. It is time we believe in ourselves."

The table fell silent for a moment, then Odama asked, "If we have no wizard lord, who will lead Balmoria?"

Priella smirked. "You defended the city well enough. Perhaps it is time for a king to rule rather than a wizard."

Odama blinked. "Me?"

Brogan grunted. "Why not? The military and the Black Wasps already report to you. You also have access to Jakarci's spies. With the wizards in the city dead, I doubt anyone else would challenge such a declaration."

The man rubbed his jaw, grimacing. "A change in power, particularly in a time of chaos, is likely to lead to problems. Any hiccups would leave openings for the ambitious to take advantage. The other military leaders have been wiped out. Perhaps it would be expeditious for me to step in. However, I have other concerns."

"Such as?" Priella asked.

He put a finger to his lips and pointed toward the walls.

Spies, Narine thought. She embraced her magic and formed a construct she had not used for years. A shield surrounded the people at the table, invisible to the naked eye.

"You may speak," she said, her voice sounding eerily dead, lacking any of the usual echo in the room. "Nobody outside of the ward will hear us."

Odama nodded. "Thank you. Our spy network has long been held in check by Jakarci's power. Without the threat of a wizard lord to keep Halzedd honest, I fear subterfuge and betrayal likely. The man would bend to anyone whispering of wealth or power."

"Halzedd?" Narine asked.

"He runs the spy network."

"Do you have someone you trust? Perhaps another spy you could raise to his position?"

The man's eyes narrowed. "I don't. Anyone within the network would be suspect. However, I know of someone I might trust."

Rindle stood in the receiving hall, waiting. He had been woken from a dead sleep and escorted from the inn to the palace. No explanation had been given, and he worried he had done something wrong. He peered into a mirror on the wall, his reflection showing disheveled, dark hair, eyes bleary. His mustache had grown to touch his upper lip, cheeks covered in scruff, clothing more appropriate for a tavern than a palace. *I look a mess.* Still, he had survived, both the battle and the cleanup afterward. Most were not so lucky. Thoughts of Garvin resurfaced. He missed his steady presence, but thought his behavior since returning to Balmor would have made the man proud.

The door opened, a guard waving him inside.

Rindle strode into the throne room, the interior shaped like a cube, the ceiling four stories above. Windows covered the upper portion of the far wall. Through them, the Tower of Devotion loomed, fire dormant. It had been burning the day after the battle. *Has Priella died?* The question was answered when he spotted her standing beside Odama at the front of the room. Drawing a breath of courage, he strode down the aisle.

The seats were vacant, save for the front row, a yellow carpet running down the aisle. He followed it to the dais at the front where a single throne sat empty. Before it stood Odama and Queen Priella, both watching as he advanced. His armpits grew damp, sweat running down his back. He had survived the worst, facing an army of darkspawn and a demon that would forever haunt his nightmares, yet he was nervous in the quiet throne room.

When Rindle came to a stop, Odama nodded. "Master Rindle. I am glad you arrived." He gestured toward the people seated in the front row. "Queen Priella and company, I would like you to meet Master Rindle. His heroics played a major role in our victory against the darkspawn horde. Of course, the monsters broke and fled once Priella dispatched the demon lord, but if not for this man and others like him, the city would have been overrun prior to that occurrence."

Rindle glanced over his shoulder and saw a stunning blonde seated behind him, bright blue eyes and luscious curves stirring his blood. The man beside her put his arm over her shoulders and smirked.

"Jerrell?" Rindle asked, aghast, forgetting himself. "What are you doing here?"

The rival thief shrugged. "Nothing special. Just discussing the future of the wizardoms with Queen Priella and King Odama. It seemed appropriate after killing a god and saving the world. Again."

Rindle's brow furrowed, lips turning down into a frown. "What?"

The pretty blonde jabbed Jerrell in the ribs, eliciting a grunt. "Stop showing off, Jace. Be nice."

"I'm just having a bit of fun, Narine."

Rindle suddenly recognized her. *Princess Narine? How is Jerrell with a woman like her? Will his luck never end?*

The princess' tone carried a warning. "Stop, or you won't be having fun later."

Jerrell rolled his eyes and sighed. "Fine." He stood and walked up to Rindle, hand extended. "I want to congratulate you."

Rindle eyed the outstretched hand with suspicion. "For what?"

Jerrell grinned. "Because you finally stopped worrying about me and forged your own path. To see you this far from Fastella and acting as a hero... I am proud. You have earned what is coming."

When Rindle grasped his hand, the shorter thief pulled him close and hugged him. In a soft voice, he whispered into Rindle's ear, "I always told you not to compete against me. We were never rivals, regardless of what you believed. Now that you finally found yourself, be the man you want to be."

Stunned, Rindle said nothing as Jerrell released him and returned to his seat beside the princess.

He shook his head to clear it and turned back to Odama. "Did he say king?"

"It appears I am destined for a crown." Odama grinned. "Things are changing in the world. With change comes opportunity. I have need of men such as yourself...if you are so inclined."

Rindle nodded numbly. "Nothing of my prior life remains, so consider me interested."

Odama put a hand on Rindle's shoulder. "Commander Garvin did well and had as important a role in our survival as anyone. You should be proud of your friend."

"I am."

"Good. Now, let us discuss your new role as head of Balmorian intelligence."

36

REMEMBRANCE

B eneath the light of the afternoon sun, Brogan stood in the plaza beside the Balmor Tower of Devotion. It was a quiet, somber moment, he and his companions surrounding a shallow pit. An island of pulsing, red crystal occupied the middle of the pit, an angry heat coming from it as a warning to anyone who came too close. Seeing the crystal stirred memories of Hadnoddon's death.

Rhoa climbed down into the pit and set a single, purple flower on the blackened ground before climbing back out. Her face was blotchy, eyes red from crying. The sight broke Brogan's heart. While he had never felt close to Rawk, the dwarf had been his companion for half a year and had certainly become an important part of Rhoa's life.

Blythe, who stood beside him, slipped her arm around Rhoa, the smaller woman leaning against her as she sobbed. Feeling like he was intruding on a private moment, he turned away, his gaze sweeping the group. Most had tears in their eyes, even Jace, who uncharacteristically had refrained from making some inappropriate comment.

Rhoa wiped her eyes and cleared her throat. "We gather here today to remember our lost companions. Not only Rawk, but his uncle, Algoron, the Guardians from Kelmar, including Hadnoddon, Lythagon, and Filk, as well as Adyn Darro, whose bravery saved the rest of us." She then smirked, touching her stomach. "Even if she nearly killed me in the process."

Everyone chuckled, the comment breaking the melancholy mood.

Blythe continued. "I will forever remember the bravery and valor of our lost friends. We, and all those who survived, are here today because of their sacrifices." She turned to Brogan, nudging him.

"Yeah," he muttered. "I will miss them."

Jace snorted. "Is that all you have to say?"

He glared toward the thief. "What else should I say?"

"Don't ask me. This is your sentiment, not mine."

Brogan lifted his fist. "I'll give you a sentiment, you little–"

Blythe grabbed him by the wrist. "Brogan..."

Hearing the tone of warning, he fell silent.

"Fine," Jace said. "I'll go next." He took a deep breath. "Hadnoddon was a grumpy pain in the arse–"

"Jace!" Narine exclaimed.

"Let me finish." He looked down into the pit. "He was also a courageous, loyal, steady friend. Rawk was quiet and reserved, sometimes odd, but always honest. His heart was bigger than his body. The other dwarfs I did not know well, but they did the right thing when the time came." He sighed. "As for Adyn..." Visibly swallowing, he rubbed his eyes. "She was the sister I never had. I have never met anyone braver. She saved me more than once and, more importantly, kept Narine alive through some of the scariest moments of my life." He peered toward the sky. "I will miss you dearly, my friend."

Brogan rubbed tears from his eyes. "Damn you, thief. I don't like to cry."

"Then don't attend funerals, you big lunkhead."

The comment stirred another round of laughter.

Priella and Kollin appeared at the edge of the plaza, drawing their attention.

The Queen of Pallanar shook her head. "Sorry if we are intruding. We are ready to depart when you are."

"We are nearly finished." Blythe turned back toward the pit. "Narine?"

Eyes red, cheeks splotchy, Narine looked a wreck. She shook her head. "I have nothing to add."

Tygalas cleared his throat. "I will miss you, honored friends. Your courage saved us all. May your spirits soar in the afterlife."

With that, everyone fell silent.

After a few breaths, Brogan clapped his hands. "All right. Let us be off. It's time to drink to the memory of our companions."

Blythe turned to Rhoa. "Are you sure you don't want to come with us?"

The smaller woman shook her head. "No. After everything that has happened, it is time to find my family and figure out my life. They were camped outside of Balmor before the battle, so I will seek them out. I pray they are safe."

"Very well." Blythe hugged her. "I love you like a sister, Rhoa. You will always have a place in my heart."

Rhoa stepped back, wiping tears away as she nodded. "Take care of yourself…" She pointed toward Brogan, "and this big lummox."

Blythe gave him a sidelong glance. "He does have a tendency to get himself into trouble, but I will try."

Jace patted Brogan on the shoulder, drawing his attention. "I am sure you will miss my charm and humor, but you will have to get by somehow." He grinned. "After all, you made it through seven years between our adventures."

Brogan snorted. "You are a cheat and a liar, but I cannot think of another thief I would rather call my friend."

The grin on Jace's face grew wider. "Same here, but I'll have to swap in *big idiot* for cheat and liar."

In spite of himself, Brogan chuckled, hugging Jace, thumping him on the back hard enough to make him cough.

The goodbyes continued for a while longer, Priella and Kollin waiting patiently. Then Narine walked over to the wizardess.

"Are you sure you recall the construct?" she asked.

Priella nodded. "Well enough."

"Just remember, it is a taxing one."

"And I no longer possess the magic of a wizard lord."

Narine hugged her. "You are stronger than you think." She backed away. "You defeated a demon, which was made possible because of your will and determination, not your strength in magic."

Priella smiled. "Thank you."

Narine turned to Kollin. "Be well. I wish you the best. I always have."

"Thank you, Narine," he replied. "Have a wonderful life."

"Oh, this goodbye is not forever." Narine grinned. "The future is full of possibilities. I suspect we will see each other again."

"Come on." Priella turned and extended her hand, a gateway opening before her.

The doorway was only five feet tall, barely four feet in diameter, forcing Brogan to duck through. Blythe and Tygalas followed, Kollin and Priella coming last. A cool ocean breeze struck. It felt clean and refreshing after the heat of Balmoria. They stood upon a hillside, a familiar city stretching out below, a quiet bay beyond. Brogan then turned to gaze up at the battlements and structure looming over them, guards in gleaming armor standing outside the gate.

Slipping his arm around Blythe's shoulders, he said, "Illustan Palace. It is good to be home."

"Yes." Priella flashed him a smile. "It is."

The gateway snapped closed, Rhoa's friends fading from view. She turned toward Jace and Narine, the only others remaining. "I suppose I had best be going. I have a life to rediscover."

Narine hugged her. "Find happiness, Rhoa." Pulling back and placing her hands on Rhoa's shoulders, Narine looked her in the eye. "I promise. It is out there if you are willing to accept it."

Rhoa gave her a thankful smile. "Thank you. I hope you two are happy, as well."

Wrapping her arm around his, Narine pulled Jace close. "As long as we are together, we should be fine."

Jace smirked. "I can live with that." He stepped closer to Rhoa, the smile sliding off his face as he rested a hand on her shoulder. "You and I have not always seen eye to eye, but we share something unique. We have been used as pawns for most of our lives...right from the beginning."

Rhoa frowned. "Do you speak of Salvon and what happened to my parents?"

He shook his head. "No. Even before that." Taking a deep breath, he continued. "Your parents were members of a secret sect known as the Order of Sol. They were part of an experiment. It led to them giving birth to a unique baby girl, one whom magic could not affect. Salvon…Vandasal was behind it the entire time."

She blinked in shock. "But my parents were Hassakani and–"

"The Order is located in Northeast Hassakan. After your birth, your parents fled with you and hid in Fastella, likely in the hopes of giving you a normal life." Jace shook his head. "Vandasal would not have it, arranging for them to be selected in the lottery. I'm sorry I played a part in their deaths, albeit unknowingly."

Rhoa's stomach churned. "My entire life has been a lie."

"No!" he said vehemently. "It was beyond your control. Merely a victim of a god's machinations. Vandasal is gone, as is your immunity to magic, any tethers he had to you now severed."

He took her hands in his. "When we first met, you were driven by a thirst for revenge. Whether sated or not, Taladain is dead, as is every other wizard lord. More importantly, with the gods gone, the Immolation of Darkening can come to an end. No other families must endure the tragedy you experienced. Put it all behind you and look to the future. For the first time, your life is your own, Rhoa. Find happiness and live it well. I believe it would be the best way to honor your parents and the friends lost along the way."

Tears ran down Rhoa's cheeks, emotions roiling in her chest. Everything she had endured…the pain, the hatred, the deaths…had been a result of a god's grand scheme. For years, she had wondered if something were wrong with her, if her parents' deaths had been her fault. To discover she was manipulated from the start, even before her own birth, was a revelation. With Salvon gone, she was free. It felt like a heavy burden had been removed, allowing her to walk upright for the first time.

Rhoa burst forward and squeezed her arms around him, her head resting against his shoulder. "Thank you, Jace. Thank you for telling me the truth."

When she stepped back, she wiped her eyes dry, him staring at her in surprise.

"I had to tell you…"

"Now that I know, my entire life suddenly makes sense."

"Yeah." He ran his hands through his hair. "I'm just glad you aren't angry."

She laughed. "Why would I be angry?"

"Because I've kept this secret for a while. Salvon made me promise not to tell you until he was gone."

Arching a brow, she said, "So you *can* keep a promise."

His face clouded over. "Of course I can."

"I'm just teasing," she laughed.

He grinned. "You got me."

"I'm not as innocent as I once was."

"No. I suppose not."

He glanced down at the blades strapped to his thighs. "Are you sure you want me to take these?"

"Yes. It's not as if I could use them anymore anyway."

"You could…if you had the amulet."

Narine laughed. "Oh please. You are addicted to that thing, and you know it."

Jace grinned. "I'm more addicted to you."

Rhoa rolled her eyes, groaning. "That's it. I am leaving before you guys do something to make me blush." They laughed as she backed away. "Be well. Perhaps we will meet again one day."

"If you happen by Marquithe, pay us a visit," Jace said.

Rhoa's brow furrowed. "Marquithe? You aren't returning to Fastella?"

He glanced at Narine. "Oh, we will go there, as well, but you'll find us in Marquithe."

"All right." Rhoa smiled. "I'll try to find you next time I visit the city."

Narine crafted a gateway, the circular opening shimmering in mid-air. They saw a sunlit chamber, a servant across the room making the bed. The woman looked up, eyes going wide as she stared at the gateway. Jace and Narine stepped through, him saying something completely inappropriate to the maid just before the gateway closed. Rhoa laughed, turned, and headed down the path to the nearest door.

Nobody said a word as she strolled through the palace. Not one person expected anything from her, not even to answer a question.

She walked out the front entrance, crossed the drawbridge over the moat, and entered the square, people busy packing tents and loading wagons. It had been among the areas the people from the Bazaar had sought shelter from the battle. Her gaze swept the crowd as she crossed the square and entered the main street leading to the harbor, seeing no familiar faces. Again, nobody paid her any attention.

Outside the city, ships loaded with people who had fled started return- ing. Families huddled on deck, parents' expressions filled with determina- tion, children laughing and smiling. Dockworkers scurried about, busily unloading ships, others repairing damage done during the battle. It was a heartwarming sight to see the resilience of humanity, leaving her wondering how much time would pass before evidence of the battle was erased.

She followed the docks heading east, toward the main battlefield. Fires burned in the distance, smoke rising from piles of corpses, mostly dark- spawn. If not dealt with, those bodies would create pestilence that could be as deadly as the battle itself.

The gravel where the Bazaar had once stood was stained red, some areas blackened and scorched. Other spots were freshly raked, dozens of workers churning up the earth to bury the tainted soil. In areas where they had finished, new tents were being assembled, workers stringing massive, white sheets across the poles.

Once beyond the activity in the Bazaar, she spotted garishly painted wagons arranged in a circle amid the scorched earth. Her heart soared and stomach swirled, caught between excitement and anxiety. The excitement won over, urging her into a run.

When she neared the wagons, she slowed. Stanlin stood off to one side, calling out orders as the crew secured lines to one of the tall, thick poles used to hold up the performance tent. It was blackened in areas, yet appeared intact. Other poles lay nearby, each in a similar state. Caught in a trance, Rhoa walked toward the people she had known for most of her life.

"Rhoa!"

Turning, she saw Rhett emerge from the wagons, a shovel in his hand. He tossed it aside and ran toward her. He had a smudge of dirt on his cheek, his hair disheveled, his white vest stained and sweaty. She could not recall seeing anything more beautiful.

"I am so glad you are all right," he said. "I was so worried. I–"

She grabbed his face and rose to her toes, kissing him. He stiffened for a moment, then his lips moved with hers, and she allowed herself to feel all the things she had buried. She poured all the pent-up emotion built upon the trials she had endured, the friends she had lost, and the sacrifices she had made into the kiss.

When she pulled back, both of them breathless, she stared into his kind eyes. He opened his mouth to speak, but she put her finger to his lips.

"No. Don't say a word. Just listen."

Rhett's brow furrowed, but he nodded.

"I do not claim to know what the future holds, nor if I can be who you believe me to be. However, I am ready to forget the past and hope to try for something more. I have been alone all my life, even when surrounded by people who cared. It was not your fault, nor Sareen's, nor Juliam's, nor anyone else's. I was alone because I refused to allow myself to be happy, as if living as a martyr was the best way to honor my parents." She shook her head. "I now realize they sacrificed so much to give me a normal life, and I threw their sacrifice aside by chasing any opportunity to right a wrong. That is just another form of sacrifice. Me putting everyone else above my own needs. It is time to do what makes *me* happy."

Gaze intense, he swallowed. "What does that mean for me?"

She bit her lip and clasped her hands behind his head. "You get the first shot at being something that makes me happy. It might also involve you joining me for a bit of exploring in Ghealdor."

"Exploring?"

"Rumor has it a lost dwarven city hides somewhere in those mountains. I want you to help me find it."

He grinned. "I accept those terms."

Their lips met again, Rhoa's pulse racing, the troubles of the world fading away.

37

NEW AGE

J ace lay on the bed, Narine in his arms, him staring down at her. Unfortunately, they were both clothed. It was not the time for such adventures... At least that was her response when he suggested it. He glanced toward the snoring maid, still passed out on the floor.

"Since we have a moment," Narine said, "wasn't there something else you wanted to tell me?"

He turned back to her. "Yes. It was another secret I promised not to reveal until Salvon was gone."

"You mean, Vandasal."

"Honestly, I have a hard time calling him that."

"Fair enough. What is it?"

He took a deep breath, recalling the conversation from the vision, visitation...whatever it was. He still was not sure. Everything else the man had told him had come to pass, so he no longer had reason for his doubts, other than a desire not to believe. Still, it took effort for the words to pass his lips, so he told it as Salvon would, his voice taking on the quality of a person reciting a tale from the distant past.

"Rhoa's unique birth was not the only thing he manipulated. It turns out, he also performed sorcery of a unique sort in exchange for a young woman's soul. This woman told Salvon she resented her life as a whore and wished a better future for her son. Willing to give anything, she promised him her soul should her son have a charmed future – a future of fame and glory. She gave herself, blood and all, in exchange for a special kind of curse...a good curse."

"Like a blessing?"

"I guess. Anyway, this blessing was cast upon her son, gifting him with an innate ability to twist odds in his favor."

Narine's eyes narrowed. "She had Salvon use sorcery to make him lucky?"

"Well, that was the story he told me." He ran his hand through his hair, still unable to fully come to grips with the tale. "The woman died a few months later, for the spell had taken from her what it gave to the boy. Although young and strong, she succumbed to a rare pestilence. The worst part, it left her child homeless, forcing him to survive on the streets of Fastella. With no other family, he turned to thievery, a profession perfectly suited to such a blessing."

She gasped. "It was *you*."

He nodded.

"And you were the one to kill Urvadan. Do you think–"

"Vandasal planned it all along? That he simply used Rawk to carve the crystal sword and Rhoa to bring it to me? That Adyn's role was to act as a distraction and Hadnoddon's death to give the Dark Lord a false sense of security?" He shook his head. "It's all just so...elaborate. If true, the perfection to which it all came together... It seems unfathomable."

She cupped his cheek. "He was a god. What do we know of gods?"

"Indeed."

Noise came from the stairwell outside the room, footsteps ascending. Jace slipped off the bed and put his ear to the door, listening as the steps rose to the story above. From the sound, it was at least two, perhaps three people. He glanced back at Narine and waved for her to follow.

"What about the maid?" she asked.

He gripped the knob. "You only put her to sleep, right?"

"Yeah."

"Let her wake up in due time then."

"But won't she get in trouble for sleeping when she is supposed to be working?"

He rolled his eyes. "You can't feel guilty about every little thing, Narine.

Sometimes small misdeeds are necessary in order to get the bigger, more important ones accomplished."

"Now you sound like Adyn."

"Smart woman. I always liked her." He opened the door and stepped into the corridor. "Come on."

After casting one last glance toward the sleeping maid, she followed, taking his hand as he led her down the corridor and to the stairwell. They walked up the stairs, to the palace's uppermost level. At the top, he peered around the corner and pulled back, recalling the image.

Two members of the Hounds stood outside a door at the corridor midpoint. Both wore helmets, armor, and purple capes, swords at their hips.

He glanced at Narine and held up two fingers. Her brow furrowed for a breath before she grinned. "I have an idea," she whispered. "Put your hands behind your back as if shackled. Keep them beneath your cloak just in case."

"All right."

Her hands twisted. He felt the tickle of magic, the hair on his arms rising as she cast the illusion. Yet, since he wore the Eye, he saw no other evidence. After a moment, she nodded, gripped him by the upper arm, and pulled him around the corner. Jace stumbled and followed, the guards turning toward them as Narine marched down the hallway.

"Who are you, and who is this man?" one asked.

In a gruff voice, Narine said, "My name is Kandrick. I am a recent transfer from Starmuth. My partner and I were on patrol near the Willola Estate when we heard screams."

Jace knew the name. *Everyone* in town knew the name. Not because the wizard and wizardess were exceptional with magic, but because she was among the most beautiful women in the city, something she flaunted often.

"This miscreant is the famous thief, Jerrell Landish. He had the poor luck of getting caught while peering through Wizardess Willola's washroom window while she was in the tub, naked as the day she was born. The woman cast a spell and struck him. He fell into the courtyard and was promptly apprehended."

The guards chuckled, one replying, "I thought Landish was the most cunning man in the world. What's he doing peeping on a bathing wizardess?"

Narine shrugged. "Doesn't surprise me, really. I had heard he was twisted and depraved, as likely to steal the smallclothes right off you as to steal your purse."

Jace rolled his eyes.

The other guard laughed. "Yeah. I've heard that story, as well. In fact, I heard he once stole the smallclothes off every person in The Mangy Dog without anyone knowing. They say he did it on a simple bet after some old man said it couldn't be done. The thief reportedly kept them all as trophies, too."

"Stains and all I bet!" Narine added.

All three laughed while Jace grimaced. *That story has been twisted in more ways than a flag in a storm.*

When the laughter calmed, Narine continued. "Anyway, I am to bring him to High Wizard Cordelia. Apparently, she has a past with him and wants to deal with the thief herself."

Both guards nodded, one saying, "We heard about the bounty."

Jace's ears perked at that. *Bounty?*

"Five gold pieces is a lot for one person to spend," the other said. "Any way you can include us?"

Narine's brow furrowed, and Jace wondered what, exactly, the other two men saw when they looked at her. He dismissed the curiosity. *I'd rather look upon the real her than an illusion of some ugly guard.*

She leaned toward the guards and whispered, "Since you have been friendly and all, I'll cut you in with five silver each. Just don't tell anyone."

The two men grinned at one another. "Kandrick, you said?"

"That's right."

"Hold a moment."

The guard knocked on the door, a gruff voice coming from inside. "What is it?"

"We have a guard named Kandrick out here, claims to have arrested Jerrell Landish."

The door opened to reveal a hulking man with a heavy brow, his dark eyes falling on Jace.

"Hello, Herrod," Jace said. "I hear Cordelia misses me."

The big man grunted and stepped back. "Bring him in."

Narine shoved Jace into the room, the door closing behind him with a thud. Herrod stalked off to the neighboring room, his deep voice coming through the doorway as he spoke. Moments later, he returned with a petite, middle-aged blonde wearing a black and purple dress.

Cordelia smiled. "Jerrell Landish. You have returned. Again. This time, you do not have a company of guards and wizards to protect you."

"I am disappointed, Cordelia," Jace replied.

The high wizard arched a brow. "In what?"

"Your bounty. I am worth far more than five gold."

She smiled. "I am aware. However, most others are not."

He pulled his hands from behind his back and worked his shoulders, revealing he wore no shackles. "I am glad the charade is over. You can dismiss your illusion, Narine. It's time to talk business."

Herrod jerked with a start when Narine dismissed her magic.

Cordelia, on the other hand, merely arched a brow. "Princess Narine."

"Hello, Cordelia. Do not worry. I have no interest in claiming the throne."

Tilting her head, the woman asked, "So you came here to see me?"

Jace sat on the sofa and leaned back, legs crossed. "We have a proposal."

"Do tell." She sat across from him.

"Since we last saw you, we have saved the world...more than once. However, things have changed. Wizard lords are a thing of the past. Rather than one's strength in magic, it will be cunning, guile, and connections that make it possible to ascend to a throne and remain in power."

Cordelia leaned forward with apparent interest. "Go on."

Jace grinned, knowing he had her.

The new dress fit snugly, but Narine did not care. A year earlier, she couldn't have fit into it if she had slathered herself in butter first. *I earned this new figure*, she thought. *Best to flaunt it while I can.* She glanced at Jace, who walked at her side, and caught him leering. For that, alone, the tight fit was worth the discomfort.

They walked up to the gates of Marquithe Palace where eight armored guards waited, each wearing a dark blue cape. Narine was not surprised to find the men focused on her, eyes on her chest rather than her face. Two guards moved to intercept them.

"Halt," one said.

Another, a tall man with a wolfish grin, said, "How can I help you?"

Narine grinned back. "You can move aside for your new queen."

"Queen of my bedroom?"

She reached up and touched his cheek while crafting a construct. The man's eyes rolled back as he collapsed under her sleep spell, landing with a loud thump, a deep snore following. The others jerked in alarm and drew weapons.

"Oh please," she said, nonchalantly using threads of magic to snatch the swords from their hands and send them skittering across the square. "Anyone who raises a hand toward either of us dies."

Wide-eyed, the guards backed away, opening the path.

"Follow us at a distance. All of you. We need witnesses for what is about to occur." Narine, in her most regal posture, walked through the gate with Jace at her side.

They crossed a plaza, passing evenly spaced statues made of black stone. At the top of the stairs to the palace entrance, they paused before a pair of guards.

"You two, follow us." Not waiting for a reply, she and Jace entered the receiving hall.

A few dozen people stood inside, including guards, merchants, farmers, clerks, and magistrates.

Narine stopped and used her magic to boost her voice. "Behold. The world has come to a crossroads, a time of change before you. Gone are the days of wizard lords, Devotion, and leaders who rule by fear alone. A new age is upon us – an age of kings and queens. Justice and equal opportunity for all await. I invite you to witness firsthand the change in power."

The silence palpable, their footsteps sounded in time with one another as they crossed the open hall, toward the throne room. A pair of guards stood outside the doors, one bald with a hooked mustache and a barrel chest, the other tall with broad shoulders.

"The high wizard is busy," one guard said.

"High wizard?" Narine arched a brow. "I think not."

The men looked at each other. "With Lord Thurvin away–"

"Lord Thurvin is dead," Jace interrupted.

"Regardless, no flame burns in the tower, so High Wizard Palkan Forca has taken over until tomorrow's Darkening."

Jace grinned at Narine. "Forca is a blowhard. This will be easy."

The taller guard stepped toward Jace, looming over him. "Forca is a hero, returned from conquering Ghealdor."

Jace glared up at the man. "Forca is a weasel who ignored orders to join the army in Balmoria. *We* saved the world while he hid here, pretending to rule."

The guard swung, but Jace was faster, dodging below the fist while driving his own into the man's exposed groin. The guard bent forward, and Jace smacked the hilt of his knife into the base of the guard's neck. The man slammed to the tile floor, face first, bloodying his nose. When the other guard moved to grab Jace, Narine struck, her spell driving him through the doors to land fifteen feet into the throne room.

Jace grinned at her, extending his arm. "Shall we?"

She took it, stepped over the unconscious guard, and walked through the doorway, her increasing entourage whispering to each other as they trailed behind. Upon entering the room, Narine recalled the fight with Malvorian.

It feels like things have come full circle.

At the far end of the room, a tall, thin man sat upon a wooden throne with dark blue, velvet cushions. Before the dais, a trio of wizards stood, dressed in variations of blue and black robes, all staring in her direction.

Forca stood from the throne. "What is the meaning of this intrusion?" He grimaced. "And how dare you hold your magic in the presence of the high wizard?"

Not replying, Narine and Jace continued toward the four men, closing the distance as the tension mounted. When he was two strides away, Jace burst forward and leapt, kicking both feet into the chest of the tallest wizard. The blow knocked the surprised man backward to fall upon the dais, landing at Forca's feet. Jace then drew the blades strapped to his legs, the spiked tips crackling with electricity. He held one to the throat of each of the two standing wizards and cast a grin toward Forca.

The high wizard growled, "How dare you attack your betters?" He waved to the guards who had followed Jace and Narine inside, standing at the fore of a gathering throng. "Arrest these two!"

Nobody moved.

"Careful, Forca," Jace said. "These two sycophants would be dead if that were my goal. What you do next will decide their fate, as well as your own."

He sneered. "Go on. Kill them. It will get you nowhere."

"As I suspected." Jace turned to the two wizards. "As you are aware, this man only cares about himself. If you leave now, we will let you live. The choice is yours."

The two men stepped back, both casting a glance toward Forca, who growled, "You two are pathetic. Go on. Run away with your tail between your legs."

Glancing at each other, they rushed out of the room.

The wizard Jace had attacked rose to his feet, a construct forming around his hand just before he lashed out. A cone of fire enveloped Jace, Narine shying away from the heat as she used her spell and prepared for Forca. The fire faded to reveal an unharmed Jace grinning.

"You missed."

Like lightning, Jace burst forward and jammed the fulgur blade into the tall wizard's chest. Eyes bulging, the man's jaw dropped, and he fell to his knees. Jace pulled the blade free and stepped back.

"Nothing personal, but I cannot have anyone believing they can betray my queen."

The wizard fell over, dead, Forca staring down at him in shock.

He lifted his astonished gaze to Jace. "You should be dead. The fire... How did you survive it?"

Jace grinned as he sheathed the fulgur blades. "I am Jerrell Landish. I am full of all sorts of surprises."

Magic ready, Narine stepped forward, glaring at the wizard. "I am Narine Killarius, daughter of Taladain Killarius. I am here to claim the throne of Farrowen. Abdicate now and you live. Resist and you die."

Scowling, Forca glared at Narine, holding his magic ready. The throne room fell silent for a long, tension-filled moment.

Finally, he sat down with a sigh. "Fine. If you want the throne, you can have it." He stood quickly. "Over my dead body."

The man thrust his hands toward Narine, a bolt of lightning arcing out. It passed through the illusion, the man's eyes widening. Releasing the curtain of illusion hiding her true self, she slapped her hand against Forca's head, using the spell Priella had taught her. With it, she attacked his mind, bending it to her will in an instant. Rather than kill him, she did something worse.

Forca began to shriek, loud, horrifying wails. Eyes bulging, he collapsed to the floor, writhing as he wet himself. She reduced the flow of terror, and his screams quieted. Curled up in a ball, the wizard whimpered like a child waking from a nightmare.

Narine waved to the guards across the room, their faces etched with fear. "Please, take him away and lock him up. Do not worry about his magic. He won't be able to perform at the moment."

Four of the men rushed forward, picked Forca off the floor, and carried him out of the room.

With a sigh, Narine sat upon the throne. In a loud voice, she said, "The Darkening is tomorrow, but there will be no sacrifice. Such a practice has already ended in Farrowen, Pallanar, Ghealdor, and Balmoria. Soon, the other wizardoms will follow, for we no longer bend our knees to false gods. Go and inform others that Narine Killarius is the new queen of Farrowen. I intend to rule with fairness and compassion, for the times of ruthless wizard lords are past."

Jace thrust his fist into the air. "Long live Queen Narine!"

The crowd at the back of the room repeated the statement, chanting it louder and louder. Narine sat back with a smile. She would hold a formal coronation ceremony in a week, making her position official. Once the story circulated of how she took the throne from a known wizard with such ease, she would have little or no resistance.

I will protect my people above everything else. That was where her father had failed during his reign of terror.

When Jace stepped up onto the dais and stood beside the throne, she took his hand and gave him a smile. "Have you ever considered being a prince?"

"A prince?"

"Yes. Once we are married."

He frowned. "Why not a king?"

She rolled her eyes. "Do you really wish to rule a kingdom?"

Shrugging, he replied, "Not really. I have other plans."

"Yes, I know." She smiled. "Now, about this wedding…"

38

HORIZONS

Jezeron climbed the secret stairwell in the back of the Marquithe Bureau of Trading. Built in a narrow cavity between two walls, the stairs were steep and just wide enough for one person at a time. He scaled them in complete darkness, as he did each morning prior to his first meeting of the day. For years, Jezeron had longed for the position of The Whispering Man, but the one who held it before him was also a wizard, leaving him reluctant to attempt a coup, not with Malvorian looming behind Thurvin. When Malvorian died, Thurvin claimed the throne, which opened the door for Jezeron. He only had to kill two other agents to secure his position. While Thurvin had never mentioned it, Jezeron suspected the wizard lord knew about the contest and what had happened to Pelliwick and Zern.

He reached the wall at the top and pressed a panel to release the latch for the secret door. Stepping through, he fumbled for the enchanted lantern on the table, activating it to illuminate a small, unoccupied room. He reached into his cloak, producing a packet of missives from across the Eight Wizardoms, all of which had arrived during the evening hours. He dropped the packet onto the desk and opened the door to the neighboring room, the lantern casting his own shadow as he stepped up to the other door to unlock it.

"Leave it locked."

He spun at the voice from behind him, the lantern light revealing a face he knew well.

"You! What are you doing here?"

The man smiled. "I have come to claim your position, Jezeron."

"You cannot have it." Jezeron slid his hand into his belt, gripping the coil secured there. "I have worked for years to attain my position."

"There is a new queen in the city."

"So I have heard. I also heard you arrived with her."

"The underbelly of Marquithe belongs to me, Jezeron, as does the network Thurvin created."

"Never!" Jezeron flung his hand out, the coil of the whip unwinding to strike the thief.

"Ouch," Jerrell said, lifting his wrist, the end of the whip wrapped around it. "That smarts."

His grin faltered. "How..."

Jerrell burst forward, a blade crackling with blue electricity driving into Jezeron's stomach. "Sorry, Jez. The whip's enchantment doesn't work on me. I guess your informants forgot to mention my immunity to magic."

The burn from the blade was intense, his body shaking violently until Jerrell pulled it out. When Jezeron tried to speak, his reply emerged as a strangled cough.

"Let me guess," Jerrell said. "You didn't believe the witnesses who said I survived wizard fire."

He had not, dismissing it as a mistake in the report. People often misperceived things during tense engagements.

"You...must...have...the...Eye."

Jerrell grinned. "I do." He lifted another knife, the pick-like metal crackling with electricity. "Otherwise, holding this would cause intense pain." He sighed. "I knew you would not capitulate, Jez. You were always too ambitious to bend. I cannot spend my life peering over my shoulder for fear of your attempt to reclaim what you have lost. Thus, I must end you. Nothing personal. I happen to love the queen, and the only way for me to ensure her protection is to control the less savory side of Farrowen."

Despite the situation and the fact Jezeron was at the losing end of it, he understood. He would have done the same thing.

Jerrell wound back. "This will be quick, Jez. Goodbye."

The blade came forward and plunged into Jezeron's forehead, the world going dark in an instant.

~

For the third time in the span of two seasons, Brogan found himself on a pier outside of Illustan, saying goodbye to Ariella. This time, Priella stood at the old queen's side, a silver and aquamarine crown nestled in her red hair. Kollin stood beside her, dressed in silvery robes that reminded Brogan of Priella's father, Raskor.

Ariella gripped Brogan's hand. "Again, thank you for returning my daughter."

He shook his head. "I told you, Ariella. I had nothing to do with it. She stands here as a savior to us all. It was her own strength that saw her through."

"Thank you, Brogan," Priella said.

"Still," Ariella insisted, "you said you would find and help her, and you did so."

Brogan glanced at Blythe, hoping she would take the cue. Instead, Priella saved him.

"Brogan, Blythe, are you sure you must leave? I have need of people I trust."

He shook his head. "Blythe and Tygalas..." He cast a glance toward the elf, who gazed over the bay. "They are both set on resurrecting relations between elves and humans. Apparently, it begins with us."

"Brogan is correct," Blythe said. "Our two peoples should help each other, particularly since the threat of wizard lords no longer exists. The elves have things to offer to us, and we to them. We must try."

Tygalas stepped forward and bowed. "I will be sure to send my mother your well-wishes, Queen Priella. Once she understands what you have sacrificed to save the world, she will be forced to acknowledge your sense of honor."

Priella smiled. "I hope to meet her someday."

"I hope so, as well."

Brogan glanced over his shoulder. The ship appeared loaded and ready to set sail. "Well, we had best be off. We don't want to keep the captain waiting."

Ariella hugged him, squeezing tightly. She whispered into his ear, "You have done an honor to Rictor. He and Raskor would be proud of you."

When she released him, he turned away, trying to keep the tears at bay. Rictor had been like a brother to him, Raskor a father. He could think of nothing he would rather hear from her. "Thank you," he choked out.

They each said goodbye to Priella and Kollin before turning and heading toward the waiting ship.

"It feels odd," he mumbled as they walked down the pier.

Blythe gave him a sidelong glance. "Leaving Illustan again?"

"No. Leaving with no intention of returning."

She stopped. "I told you before. You do not have to come."

He took her hands in his, her fingers long and elegant in his thick mitts. "And I told you before. My place is with you. I understand why you want to return to Silvacris. Where you go, I go." Glancing back toward the city, he said, "Besides, if I truly wish to leave the past behind, it is better to do it elsewhere. Too many memories, good and bad, linger in Illustan. They would haunt me as long as I remain."

She nodded. "All right." Pulling him by the hand, she led him down the pier, trailing after Tygalas. "Let's see what lies beyond the next horizon."

He grinned. "So long as we do it together."

From an arching bridge above the village of Sol, Chandan peered east. The sun had set, the horizon darkening. In the gloom was a distant red glow, pulsing and alive. He turned and crossed the bridge. Hands on the rail, he leaned over and peered down toward Order members, everyone assembled and wearing their golden-hued robes.

"It is as Lord Astra's vision foretold. A new heart beats to the east, marking the passing of the Dark Lord. Soon, a new god, the true god, will rise.

"We must watch for the signs and prepare, for when the heart in the east expands, it will bring chaos and destruction, the end of the world as we know it. Only if we are vigilant and keep the faith may our peoples survive. The fate of all rests in our hands."

With that, he fell silent. For so many years, the Order had been driven by a solitary goal. With the Dark Lord's demise, Chandan was certain a new god would come forth. It might take weeks, years, or decades, but the god would come. When that happened, the Order would need to act before all was lost.

FAREWELL

This is where my tale ends.

With my passing and that of my brother comes the end of an era, leading to a time of change, a time of recovery, a time of rebirth...if only I fully understood the cost when I chose to pursue such a fate. A single drop of blood was all it took to alter destiny and doom the world.

But that is a story for another time.

- Salvon the Great

NOTE FROM THE AUTHOR

Thus ends the **Fate of Wizardoms** saga. While *this* story is complete, I am not finished weaving tales from the world of Wizardoms. You can expect a sequel series titled **Fall of Wizardoms** in early 2021, with the first title releasing in January. The series will include your favorite characters along with a host of new heroes and villians.

To make sure you do not miss the release, join my author newsletter. As a gift for joining, you will receive Wizardoms companion novellas featuring Jace, Brogan, Narine, and even Despaldi.

If interested, proceed to www.JeffreyLKohanek.com.

Best Wishes,
Jeff

Follow me on:
Amazon
Bookbub

ALSO BY JEFFREY L. KOHANEK

Fate of Wizardoms

Book One: Eye of Obscurance

Book Two: Balance of Magic

Book Three: Temple of the Oracle

Book Four: Objects of Power

Book Five: Rise of a Wizard Queen

Book Six: A Contest of Gods

* * *

Warriors, Wizards, & Rogues (Fate of Wizardoms 0)

Fate of Wizardoms Boxed Set: Books 1-3

Runes of Issalia

The Buried Symbol: Runes of Issalia 1

The Emblem Throne: Runes of Issalia 2

An Empire in Runes: Runes of Issalia 3

Rogue Legacy: Runes of Issalia Prequel

* * *

Runes of Issalia Bonus Box

Wardens of Issalia

A Warden's Purpose: Wardens of Issalia 1

The Arcane Ward: Wardens of Issalia 2

An Imperial Gambit: Wardens of Issalia 3

A Kingdom Under Siege: Wardens of Issalia 4

ICON: A Wardens of Issalia Companion Tale

* * *

Wardens of Issalia Boxed Set

Printed in Great Britain
by Amazon